EDITED BY

JOHN F. CARR

Pequod Press

PARATIME WARS
A Pequod Press Anthology

First Edition

Printed in the United States of America
First Printing 2019

V 10 9 8 7 6 5 4 3 2 1

ISBN: 0-978-0-937912-76-8

Paratime Books by H. Beam Piper

Paratime
Lord Kalvan of Otherwhen
The Complete Paratime

Paratime Books by John F. Carr

Time Crime (with H. Beam Piper)
Paratime Trouble
Paratime Parasites (with H. Beam Piper)
Paratime Wars

Lord Kalvan Novels by John F. Carr

Great Kings' War (with Roland Green)
Kalvan Kingmaker
The Hos-Blethan Affair (with Wolfgang Diehr)
Siege of Tarr-Hostigos
The Fireseed Wars
Gunpowder God
Down Styphon!

ACKNOWLEDGEMENTS

Thanks to Alan Gutierrez who came up with the cover design and executed it so well. He also drew the fine maps.

Special thanks to Victoria Alexander for all her help editing the early drafts and her expertise as editor.

To the Paratime Study Group, Jim Landau, Jevon Kasich and Eric Fisher.

Finally, to H. Beam Piper, who never got the opportunity to finish the Paratime story….

ACKNOWLEDGMENTS

TABLE OF CONTENTS

KALVAN KINGMAKER

JOHN F. CARR

I

1966 A.D.

Paratime Police Chief Verkan Vall watched while the trees and scrub brush of Fourth Level flickered through the wavering silver sheen of the Ghaldron-Hesthor transposition-field, as the transtemporal conveyer carried him toward Fifth Level time-line on the Litzn Equivalent where former Chief Tortha Karf had his villa. The civilized Second and Third Levels were behind him now. Once in a while Verkan caught flickering glimpses of Fourth Level-buildings, airports, occasionally a raging battle. Fourth Level was the highest probability level of all the inhabited Paratime Levels. There the First Colony had come to complete disaster, in the past fifty thousand years, losing all knowledge of its origins. It was the most barbaric level, as well as the largest. Its cultures ranged from idol worshippers on Proto-Aryan to nuclear reactors and hydrogen bombs on Europo-American, Hispano-Columbian Subsector.

The conveyer was now entering the low-level probability Fifth Level, where nature, not man, was triumphant. The only humans—other than some sub-human apes—were Service and Industrial Sectors Proles and their First Level overseers who labored there to keep heavy and light industry off of First Level, Home Time Line. On Fifth Level only the mountains remained constant. Occasionally, a large beast could be made out, while several times large pools of water appeared and disappeared. There was always a bit of variability between time-lines, sometimes nothing more than trees growing in different spots, other times bodies of water flowing in otherwise deserts.

The Service Sector Proles were not indigenous to the Fifth Level, but were brought from time-lines of near savagery. The Paratime Transtemporal Code limited the colonization of Service Sector time-lines to natives below second-order barbarism. The Serv-Sec Proles were the ones who did most of the administration and record keeping for Home Time Line. The Proles who were dumped in the Fifth Level, Industrial Sectors, where the machines and robots of First Level were manufactured, were at the bottom rung of the Service Sector. Here also were the survivors of Paratime screw-ups, when policy or criminal mistakes had made it necessary to transplant entire tribes and sometimes nations to protect them from famine or hostile neighbors, or to protect the Paratime secret. No matter—it seemed—how diligently the undermanned and overworked Paratime Police worked, there were always new bodies to fill another industrial time-line on Fifth Level.

Few, on First Level, realized just how many of these uncountable time-lines had never seen man's imprint. Even after twelve thousand years of parasitism upon other Second, Third, and Fourth level time-lines, First Level Para-topographers—including the Paratime Police Survey Division—had described less than one tenth of one percent of all the 'known' time-lines. In actuality it was an impossible job; few Paratime theorists still believed they would ever completely map this near infinity of diverging time-lines.

In theory the transposition field was impenetrable; however, when two craft going in the opposite directions collided, other objects and life forms could and did pass through. It was why unscheduled trips like his were limited to the highest echelon of the Paratime Police. It was also Paratime policy to have a weapon drawn just in case the hitchhiker was dangerous, or a threat to the Paratime secret. Most human pickups were killed immediately and disposed of back at the conveyer-head. Only a few escaped, and even fewer flourished in their new 'homes.'

Fourth Level Aryan-Transpacific, where his friend Kalvan and his lovely wife, Rylla, ruled an unruly kingdom, was the exception. There Great King Kalvan, formerly Corporal Calvin Morrison of the Pennsylvania State Police, had accidentally boarded a conveyer in Europo-American, Hispano-Columbian as a Paratemporal hitchhiker, and was dumped off on Aryan-Transpacific, Styphon's House Subsector. Thrust into a ruder and deadlier culture, Kalvan not only survived, he prospered. In less than a year he'd married a princess, founded an empire, broken Styphon's House monopoly of gunpowder and more than held his own against the worst that band of priestly tyrants—who worshipped a gunpowder god named Styphon—could manifest, including the unholy Holy Host, the largest army ever assembled on that backward time-line.

Kalvan's intervention into local politics had created a new time-line. In many ways Kalvan's Time Line was unique. It was the first time in First Level history when Paratime observers had been present at the start of a new time-live and possible subsector, identified from the exact point of divarication. The Paratimers had been close before, the President John F. Kennedy assassination, only a few years earlier, had been the critical event in the formation of the Europo-American, Kennedy Subsector. The Kennedy assassination, while newsworthy, had not been considered a divarication event until months later. The Kalvan split had been discovered almost as it happened, since Verkan Vall himself had tracked down the Paratime conveyer that former Pennsylvania State Trooper Calvin Morrison had stumbled into and exited out onto Aryan-Transpacific.

Because of growing instability between the two competing nuclear-powered sovereignties, the Kennedy Subsector—where President Kennedy had survived his assassination attempt—was far too dangerous to risk intensive study and monitoring. Kalvan's Time Line, on the other hand, was backward enough there was little danger to outtimers. The Dhergabar University had sent out five Kalvan study teams to survey Kalvan Prime, as they called it, and a number of Kalvan 'control' time-lines.

True, there were some—mostly bleeding hearts and professors who'd never traveled outtime—who still believed it was Home Time Line's duty to colonize these barren time-lines, even here on Fifth Level. Or worse, that it was their duty to spread the 'benefits' of First Level civilization and Psycho-Hygiene.

Worlds without number, thought Verkan; only a politician or do-gooder would think they could be tamed in even ten thousand lifetimes.

Finally the conveyer came to rest outside a white marble villa. Solid mesh appeared overhead, out of the iridescence, and Verkan holstered his sigma-ray needler. He stepped out of the conveyer and saw two lovely prole girls, draped in white togas, tending flowers in the garden. *So much for ex-Chief Tortha Karf's solitude,* he thought!

Verkan watched with amusement as a small, brown, long-eared rodent scurried through the flowers causing the girls to squeal in assumed outrage. It appeared that Tortha was losing in his attempt to rid his hide-away, known in Fourth Level, Europo-American as Sicily, of its indigenous rabbit population. He caught the girls' coy glances in his direction, and was glad his wife, Dalla, wasn't along. A catfight would not be the proper introduction for the bad news he had to share with his former boss and the ex-Paratime Police Chief.

The commotion brought Tortha Karf to the doorway. "Verkan, from your message ball, I didn't expect you for several hours."

"We managed to home-in on the missing Paracop's beacon and were able to extricate him from the Fourth Level mess he'd fallen into. His mission was locating and then extracting French Impressionist paintings from a *Gauleiter's* mansion on a particularly nasty Fourth Level, Europo-American time-line. Unfortunately, someone had already removed the paintings and he was picked up by the *Gestapo,* a rather brutal quasi-police force."

"Must have been in the Hitler Belt or the Axis Subsector."

Verkan nodded.

"I remember that Subsector well," Tortha continued. "Its impact reverberated across the entire Fourth Level. Adolf Hitler's public works and culling of the regional populations on that subsector makes your Pennsylvania State Trooper's transtemporal interference look like a tempest in a teapot—to use a Europo-American Sector cliché! Remember when the Opposition Party claimed that Hitler was really a renegade Paracop?"

Verkan refused to be baited.

Tortha noticing his discomfort, added, "Come on in. I've been by myself too long. It seems I've forgotten all my manners."

Verkan gave a pointed look at the girls who were watching them closely.

Tortha gave an avuncular shrug of his shoulders in feigned ignorance, leading Verkan through the foyer and into the grand main room. The rich gold-veined white marble walls were covered with Cretan murals, while the floor was covered with Fourth Level, Etruscan-Zoroastrian rugs. There were several embroidered purple divans, decked with gold fringe, which appeared to be Alexandrian-Roman in origin.

"So this your 'little cottage?'" Verkan asked. "I don't remember it being so palatial on my previous visit."

Tortha smiled smugly. "I've made a few additions and changes. Compared to Paratime Headquarters, this place is tiny. And much quieter. So what brings you to paradise?"

To Verkan his ex-Chief looked a little twitchy. *Too much of a good thing?* Maybe paradise was better dreamed about than lived. He was sure Kalvan, in the midst of a war with three great kingdoms, might very well agree.

"It's the Wizard Traders."

"Wizard Traders. You mean slave traders, Verkan. We busted that outfit up just before I retired as Chief."

"You weren't so sure a year ago. True, we arrested the obvious ones;

those who were passing themselves off as wizards on backward Third and Fourth Level worlds, using their privileges to steal forbidden artifacts and buy and sell people to unscrupulous Home Time Liners. Plus, a couple of First Level dupes, who were manning their secret conveyer-heads. Now, we've uncovered evidence that they may be connected to the Opposition Party. Remember how you always told me 'follow the money trail.' I've been following your advice and we've found some evidence that much of it went into the Opposition Party coffers."

"But that doesn't make sense, Verkan. The Oppositionists run on a policy of non-interference and Prole equality. You're trying to tell me that blood money has been paying for Prole equality votes?"

"I think you've been on this big island for too long. Yes, I do. Don't you remember: the means justify the end. The lesser evil for the greater good!"

"Maybe I have been outtime too long. Could this be the break we've been looking for, Verkan? Get word of this out to our friends in the media and we can break their backs once and for all."

"Break is not the right word. The Opposition Party has been gaining adherents and I'm afraid they may well find a way to point the blame right back at the Department."

"How? We've never been linked to the Oppositionists—just the opposite."

"True, but it did happen on our watch. Didn't it?"

"Don't look at me like that, old son. It's not my watch anymore. I've got some lemons to harvest."

"What should I do about it?"

"What you have to do, according to your commission. You're the top Paracop. Find out who they are, who's supporting them; then root them out. Who's your goat?"

"Hadron Tharn."

"That fatuous prig. He's not smart enough to be behind stale bread much less the Wizard Traders."

"He's not behind them, but we've linked one of the Wizard Traders to his organization."

"It's too bad they used hypno-conditioning to commit suicide."

"We never got all the trigger words. Every one of the important Wizard Traders committed suicide, when one of the implanted suggestions froze the Vagus nerve—instant heart attack." Verkan shook his head. "No two of them shared the same trigger words either; it left the experts at Bureau of Psych-Hygiene in a state of paralysis. The rest of the Wizard Traders were just proles doing a job. I'm still getting bad press over the casualties."

"Not your fault, Verkan," Tortha said, shaking his head. "It does lend credence to the big conspiracy theory, though. That kind of deep conditioning doesn't come cheap. Anything more?"

"Yes, we've traced a new batch of Wizard Traders to Aryan-Transpacific."

Tortha's mouth dropped open. "Already!"

"Yes, they've gotten into bed with Styphon's House on every time-line they've entered. Trading the upperpriests weapons technology in exchange for young bodies and precious metals."

"Have they penetrated the Kalvan Time-Line?"

"No. Although we do have a suspected spy on one of the University study teams."

"Why don't you bring him in for questioning?"

"It's a she. And we don't have any evidence other than a relationship with Hadron Tharn. Besides, Tharn is too stupid to set up and run any decent spy ring. We suspect she's a red herring, as it's called on Fourth Level, Europo-American. Just as Tharn himself is just a cat's-paw to lead us astray."

"Good hunting. Every time I start to think back fondly of my time as Chief, you come along and remind me of why I retired."

"Tortha!" one of the girls called. "It's time for our swimming lessons. Will you be joining us?"

"Yes, of course. Must not neglect my guests. Please, excuse me Verkan, but I've got my duties here to contend with. Oh, do you have any presence on the study team."

"Verkan nodded. "One of our best agents."

II

The army Styphon's House had thrown at Hos-Hostigos had also let loose the great miracle of fireseed—the magic powder that made muskets and bombards such terrible weapons of destruction. Now anyone, even nonbelievers, could duplicate Styphon's Great Miracle or buy fireseed direct from King Kalvan. Now even those allies who still believed in Styphon's divinity were shaken in their faith by Kalvan's otherworldly ability to shake victory from almost certain defeat.

Grand Master Soton himself, ruler of a domain equal to that of any Great King's in the Sastragath border lands, was not pleased that the fanatics within Styphon's House had taken command of the Temple—aided and abetted by Supreme Priest Sesklos' growing senility. Yet, were it not for the Temple taking him in as an orphan thirty-some winters ago, he would now be a simple farmer or blacksmith in some isolated backwater village. For that and allowing him to raise himself so high—as Grand Master of the Order of Zarthani Knights and Archpriest of Styphon's House—the Temple had his undying loyalty.

Furthermore, there was no denying that Archpriest Roxthar and his followers had put new mettle into Styphon's Way On Earth. They had certainly given him an unlimited draft on the Temple's earthly resources; all of which, gold and arms especially, he was going to need if he was going to turn the broken Harphaxi Royal Army into any semblance of a military power.

Soton halted his party before the next steep grade and peered down onto Port Harphax, which appeared surprisingly busy for this late in the year. Galleys, hulks, and wide-bottomed carracks were scooting across the harbor below like water beetles. As he kneed the donkey into reluctant motion, Soton cursed the memory of Erasthames the Great, the legendary king who had conquered the Iroquois Alliance. Four hundred years ago it might have made sense to put Tarr-Harphax up at the top of these cliffs when the native Ruthani were an everyday threat; now it was a beastly nuisance.

It made feeding Harphax City and the castle a nightmare. Since the lower Harph flooded almost every spring, cutting off river transport, the city had to take in enough stores to last a long winter and spring as well. Food that arrived by sea had to be carted or packed up the Upper Road, at great expense in time and animals, or pulled up in great iron buckets by the rope tramway.

During a bad year such as this one, when fields had been trampled and burnt, most of Harphax City's food had to be imported by seagoing merchants. Thus the great number of boats crowding Harphax Port's limited docking facilities. Now there was less than a moon half before winter storms made sea passage impossible. Most of the captains were less than pleased at chancing the seas this late in the year and only generous gifts of Styphon's gold kept them at sea at all.

If all this weren't bad enough, the burnt fields and farms had brought tens of thousands of refugees into the already bursting-at-the-seams capital. Plus all the war casualties who were too crippled or maimed to work, yet had to be housed and fed. Already the strain of short rations and overcrowding were visible on the lean faces of the city's beggars. Only great need could force them to take their chances on the steep Upper Road and the occasional visitor's generosity.

At the top of the cliffs the city walls showed the abuse of more than a hundred years of neglect and civil complacency. Here and there teams of workmen were shoring up walls and replacing fallen stones, but—as far as Soton could see—it was clearly a case of too little, too late. He guessed that Kalvan's eight-pounder field guns would bring down most of these walls. As for the old castle itself, Tarr-Harphax, with proper siege guns Kalvan would have a dozen breaches in a moon quarter.

Soton shuddered to think of the slaughter Kalvan's veterans would make upon the shattered remnants of the Harphaxi Army. It was a good thing that acting Great King Lysandros, since his brother King Kaiphranos' death two moons ago, had taken his advice and appointed the mercenary Phidestros Captain-General of the Royal Army, rather than one of his cronies or aging mercenaries. Phidestros was young for such an appointment, but he had fought against Kalvan three times and lived to tell about it.

If anyone could turn this whipped rabble into a fighting force again, it was Phidestros. He had more ambition than an Archpriest of the Inner Circle of Styphon's House and as much gall as Kalvan himself. Even so, Phidestros would need Appalon's luck and Lyklos' cunning to forge this base metal into good fighting steel.

For all that, Phidestros was still a mercenary and owed his allegiance to the highest paymaster—gold before god. Therefore, he would have to make sure that the pupil did not come to best his master in the art of war.

The cobblestone and dirt streets of Harphax City were lined with makeshift tents and temporary housing. The stench alone was enough to bring tears even to the eyes of a seasoned soldier. Twice Soton had been forced to use his mace to beat off attempts by thieves to steal the trappings off his horse right under the noses of his guards. It took a full sandglass to navigate through the narrow city streets to Tarr-Harphax where Captain-General Phidestros had his headquarters.

Soton was pleased to note the severe appearance of Phidestros' audience room; the only adornments were a pair of crossed muskets, a well-used sword and a large deerskin map of Hos-Harphax, which included the new Great Kingdom of Hos-Hostigos outlined in red ink within its borders.

"Please take a seat, Grand Master."

"Thank you, Captain-General. My men will bring it in." This time he'd had his own seat brought with him from Balph and when he sat down on his elevated chair, he was eye-to-eye with Phidestros. The long-boned Captain-General looked thinner than he had last spring and the lines of his face were etched bolder and deeper. Soton sighed; at least, it showed that Phidestros had no illusions about the near impossible task set before him.

After Phidestros' aide had filled their wine goblets, Soton asked, "How does your command look these days?"

Phidestros frowned. "Not so good. The Harphaxi were not much of a fighting force before Kalvan ground them up. Now they're little better than a rabble."

"That bad?"

"Many of the units are at half strength—probably more due to desertions and the flux than Kalvan's lead. Some, like the Royal Lancers, were almost annihilated. That might have been a blessing, though. I would like to disband the entire unit if Lysandros would let me—or the nobles let him! The Lancers are more worried about gaining honor than winning battles, I fear."

"You might think that Kalvan's artillery would have taught them a thing or two."

"Those iron hats! No such luck. They see Kalvan's style of fighting as unjust and dishonorable. With the Succession Crisis, Prince Lysandros doesn't dare dismiss them. But, with Kalvan's help, I've reduced their number by almost half. I'm also turning them into more of a Household Guard than a line unit. I've also recruited about two thousand more mercenaries and brought the Royal Pistoleers back up to full strength. The Foot Guard is still seriously undermanned."

"How many troops could you muster if Kalvan were at the city walls tomorrow morning?"

"A little over four thousand Royal troops and another five thousand mercenaries. I am supposed to have about twelve thousand city militia, but they are next to worthless—even though I've made them spend at least one day a quarter-moon in training. Most of them would take off, as they did at Chothros Heights, at the first sound of cannon fire. At least I've managed to get them uniforms and guns that fire without exploding. You wouldn't believe the ordnance I had to replace—musket locks that were rusted shut, stocks half-rotted away and barrels fouled beyond belief."

'I believe it," Soton said. "Kaiphranos the Timid was more a tight-purse than a coward. I was aghast when his son asked to meet Kalvan on the field man to man; well, he paid for his impertinence. What you're telling me is that I'd better not depend upon the Harphaxi Royal Army for any duty more pressing than staying inside the City walls."

Phidestros looked crestfallen. "If Kalvan invades Hos-Harphax next spring, only the gods will be able to stop him from taking the entire

Kingdom, Tarr-Harphax included. The only bright news is that I don't believe Kalvan has any idea just *how* desperate our situation really is."

"I take it you have told no one else this."

"Only First Prince Lysandros and yourself, Grand Master. Kalvan has his intelligencers everywhere, even here in Harphax City. We almost caught a big one a moon ago. I've made a big show of parading the militia up and down the city streets in their new uniforms and arms. They look all right, but those whoresons couldn't be counted upon to stand before a good sneeze!"

"You've done well," Soton replied. "Now it is up to the gods and I believe they have done well by us. I have come up with a plan that will keep Kalvan busy all next year. And, with Galzar's Grace, it may even cost him his throne. "

"By the Wargod's Beard, tell me! What miracle is this?"

"I plan to let the nomads fight the war against Kalvan for us. The Mexicotal in their war against Xiphlon have driven the fierce southern pony warriors into the Sea of Grass, driving the nomads from their traditional hunting grounds into the Middle Kingdoms and over the Great River in their desire to find a safe haven. Only a few thousand have crossed the Great River thus far, but already the entire Lower Sastragath is aboil as new tribes move in and others use the disorder to settle old scores or build great clans. Three times this year the Order has had to fight battles against barbarians trying to move into Hos-Ktemnos and Hos-Bletha.

"Now things are beginning to settle down as the tribes search for shelter and forage for the coming winter. The Order has seen these migrations from the Plains many times before and events should come to a head next year. The nomads are caught between an anvil, the Middle Kingdoms, and the Ruthani hammer from the south. The only place they have to go is across the Great River and into the Sastragath. Next year will see ten times as many tribes fording the river, which will push all the tribes and clans of the Lower Sastragath either east into our forts, or north into the Upper Sastragath.

"Instead of fortifying the border and holding our forts, my plan is to move half our Lances into the Lower Sastragath and drive the nomads up the Pathagaros Valley into the Lydistros Valley and from there into Kalvan's backyard. With a nomad invasion threatening the Trygath and Kalvan's westernmost princedoms, he will be forced to go on the offensive and call back his troops on the Hostigos/ Harphaxi border."

"It is a brilliant plan, Grand Master. But surely things are not so bad that our only choice is to allow the barbarians to enter the Five Kingdoms through our own backdoor?"

"In words for your ears only, our situation *is* that desperate. If Kalvan invades Hos-Harphax, he will conquer it before the first moon of summer. With Hos-Harphax defeated, Great King Demistophon of Hos-Agrys will quickly sue for terms; especially after the beating he took with his army from Prince Ptosphes last summer. Great King Cleitharses of Hos- Ktemnos is still in shock over the losses his Sacred Squares took at the Battle of Phyrax; he won't go to battle again unless ordered to by the Innermost Circle. Hos-Bletha is too far away to be of any consequence and Great King Sopharar of Hos-Zygros is flirting with the League of Dralm. So, without the Great Kingdom of Hos- Harphax as an anchor, the war against Kalvan is doomed."

Phidestros massaged his temples as if he had the grandfather of all headaches. "Things wouldn't be so bad, Grand Master if I could hire more mercenaries. They are nowhere to be found. I know it is winter and that a lot of them died at Fyk, Tenabra, Chothros Heights, and Phyrax...but still?"

"In Balph I learned that Kalvan has been offering mercenaries bonuses and *year*-round pay for signing up in his Royal Army of Hos-Hostigos. That is where many of them have gone."

Phidestros groaned. "Why didn't I think of that?"

"The very idea of year-round pay for mercenaries hasn't been done in living memory," Soton replied. "So don't blame yourself. Besides, most of the available mercenaries have been hired by barons and princes for protection from the nomads," Soton replied. "In all of Hos-Ktemnos there are no sell-swords to be hired at any price; I understand that things are likewise in Hos-Agrys. Even if Kalvan defeats the nomads, he will do more than just give us breathing space."

"How so, Grand Master?"

"He will give us the greatest gift of all—time. Time for you to train the Harphaxi rabble. Empty the prisons and the gaols. Take the strongest and the toughest and forge them into an army."

"By what magic will I turn riffraff into real soldiers?"

"By the magic of Styphon's gold and your own will. I will go to Prince Lysandros and tell him that you will build an army twenty-thousand men strong. Styphon's House will supply the gold and victuals.'

"It could be done—the Royal Foot Guard can be my petty-captains. I can train them night and day until they drop. It doesn't take great marksmanship to make an arquebusier. It will take a lot of work—"

"Excellent, Captain-General, you are already thinking along the right lines. Kalvan will think twice about invading Hos-Harphax—*if* he defeats the nomads—and hears tell of a great army being assembled here."

Phidestros smiled for the first time. "I say a toast to Grand Master Soton and the *new* Royal Army of Hos-Harphax!"

Soton downed his goblet in a single gulp. When it was filled again, he made his own toast. "TO VICTORY! TO THE USURPER KALVAN'S DEATH! TO STYPHON'S HOUSE!"

III

Ranjar Sargos leaped out of the tree, flapped his wings, and caught an updraft which propelled him high into the sky. It was dawn and the sun was rising above the distant horizon, bathing the world in red flames. Looking down he saw a great herd of beasts flooding the Pathagaros Valley.

As he glided closer to the earth, he was able to discern the true nature of the teeming animals—only they weren't animals but thousands upon thousands of men—the two-legged beast. They were painted in war colors and carrying bows, spears, axes, and all the weapons of war.

He glided above their heads and they looked up at him. Suddenly they began to beat their weapons against their shields. It was as if he was the sign they had been waiting for and it came to him that it was his destiny to lead this sea of warriors.

At the other end of the valley there was a rumble like thunder; he flew closer to see another great clan of men wearing the metal skins of the dirtmen.

He shrieked a warning to his followers and raised his talons. The roar of war cries smashed against his ears like clubs—

"Ranjar, wake up! Wake up!"

Ranjar Sargos, Warlord of the Tymannes, removed his hands from his ears and slowly raised up on the cot he had been sleeping on. *Where am I?* The open door let in enough moonlight that he could see that he was inside the tribal longhouse where he had been sleeping during the clan gathering.

"What is it?" Ranjar asked.

"Ikkos has returned."

"Where are the others?" By the others, of course, he meant his eldest son, Bargoth, who against his private words had ridden off with the scouting party.

"I do not know, Chief. Only Ikkos has returned and he was on foot with many wounds."

Sargos brushed the sleep out of his eyes. Take me to him."

"Follow me."

Sargos, who still had enough wits about him to tuck his pistol into his belt, followed the sentry into the night. The tribe's longhouses and sweathuts filled most of the small upper valley and he could just make out another score of men gathered near the palisade's gateway. *If none of the sentries have stayed at their posts, there will be blood spilled this night!*

The Tymannes had come to this gathering, not as in the past to settle tribal boundaries or exchange furs before the coming cold, but to talk about the great movement of people that was taking place in the lowland valleys and along the Great River. Never in living memory had so many tribes and clans been uprooted from their traditional lands; already his tribe had been forced to defend their valley from invaders.

Interrogation of the prisoners had told them little, only that many tribes and bands were being forced to flee their homes by other tribes and the Black Knights. Sargos had never fought against the Black Knights, but he had heard stories of their war prowess from those who had and in old tales passed down by the clan fathers. Yet, in times past the Black Knights had not burned villages and slain whole tribes without provocation. So a gathering of all the Tymannes had been called at a time when men should be setting traps, hunting, and fishing.

I wonder if this has anything to do with my vision? Before he could mull this over, they had arrived at the circle of men surrounding Ikkos. A few held torches and he could see that Ikkos was bruised and shirtless. Several tribesmen were trying to question Ikkos all at the same time; Sargos stilled their voices with a clap of his hands.

"Where is Bargoth?"

Ikkos shook his head as if dazed. "I left him with all the others when we were ambushed. He may be behind me, I don't know. The last I saw him, he was shooting his bow and telling me to escape."

Sargos mentally steeled himself for the worst. Bargoth had never been one to turn away from a fight, no matter what the odds. He was big for eighteen winters and could run, chase and fight as well as any man in the tribe; yet, Sargos had often wondered if he had the cunning necessary to make a good chief or lead his people. Tomorrow, at first light, he would send out a party to find out what had happened and if anyone else in the scouting party had survived.

"Did you recognize the tribe that set the ambush?"

"No, Chief Sargos. But one of them wore the blue tattoos of the Great River tribes."

Ikkos began to shake with fatigue and cold. Someone passed him a blanket and he wrapped it around his shoulders.

"We will get little more out of him tonight," Sargos pronounced. "Let him rest so that he can talk to the Council tomorrow. The rest of you, get back to your posts before our foes walk in through the gate!"

The men trotted off as if stung by bees. When everyone had left, Sargos squatted down in the grass and clenched his hands over his chest until tears streamed out of his eyes.

The next morning all the chiefs of the Tymannes sat in the clan's Council Hut. Only Old Daron—who every winter survived his half-moon winter trail—had his son with him, a middle-aged man with too much belly and watery eyes. *Why, if the gods had to take a son, couldn't they have taken one such as this?* Sargos shook his head to help clear his thoughts, then he rose to make the opening prayers so the gods might bless the Folk in this year of trial.

When the rituals were complete, Sargos had Ikkos called into the hut.

"We traveled five days until we reached the banks of the Great River. Many times we had to hide from strange tribes and war parties. Many of the villages and camps we passed were burned out or deserted. At the camp of the Lyssos we discovered only the dead; the entire tribe had been massacred—even the women and children."

There was a collective shriek at this news. The Lyssos had long been allies of the Tymannes; all had lost friends in their unclean passing. To kill unarmed women and children was usually a sign of madness or great drunkenness.

"At the banks of the Great River we saw many grass people cross the ford on rafts so large they could hold the entire clan! We saw little fighting there, but the river was clogged with the bodies of the dead. Whether from some earlier battle, or one upstream, we never did learn.

"Downstream we came upon a great battle. The Black Knights were attacking a large village, ten times the size of our own camp. They burned the palisades and used great fire tubes to knock them down. When the walls collapsed they stormed the village, killing everyone who did not flee and burning everything left behind. We ran too, for fear they might attack us as well!

"Later we talked to some of the villagers who escaped and they told us the Knights were burning and destroying every village and camp in the Sastragath. They claimed the end of the world had come. They left us to flee north where they hope to join up with others of their people. After that we began our journey home when, three days later, we were ambushed by the grass people."

Hearing about the ambush brought the pain back again, but Sargos pushed it aside. Little new was told during the questioning so Sargos pondered over the death of his son and the vision he had been gifted with last night. *Was his son the god-price for leadership over all the clans, or was it all some jest of Lyklos, the Trickster?*

Before he could make sense of all this, his other son Larkander entered the hut. The boy's eyes were red and Sargos felt his stomach drop like a stone.

"Father, the last of the riders has returned. They brought Bargoth's body back with them. They say he died with honor, surrounded by dead foes. Why, Father, why?"

Before this son embarrassed them both, he ordered, "Sit down. The time has come for *you* to prepare for your place in the tribe."

Larkander stifled his emotions and sat down with all the dignity his fourteen winters could muster. Not for the first time, Sargos was proud of his young boy—no, man now. His voice had already broken and he was halfway through his last growth. The time had come for him to learn a man's duty and responsibility.

Sargos rose to speak. "Where there is one army of Black Knights, there are more. Either they or the grass people will soon come to drive us from our lands. We have two choices: we can stay and fight—and die, since our foes are in number like the summer grass. Or we can join the other tribes and clans and move up the Pathagaros Valley. How do you vote?"

There was little discussion. The clan leaders agreed to move north as their Warlord had suggested. The women and children would go into the hills with the warriors of Old Daron's tribe to protect them.

As they left the Clan Hut, Larkander moved close to his father and asked, "Father, may I come along with the rest of the warriors?"

Ranjar Sargos looked down at this youngest son— now his only son. *Was this to be the price of his visions? Both sons dead?* He shook his head.

"But Father, I can ride a horse and shoot a bow as good as any man in this camp."

Sargos knew this was no boast. "Larkander, you are my only son now. I need you safe."

"Will it be safe in the hills with the women and children? If it is my time, I can die anywhere. I am only a few moons from my manhood rites. It is time I learned how to lead our people; where better than at my father's side?"

Sargos clenched his fists until his palms bled. "If it is your wish, you can go. Tell your mother now."

Larkander let out a loud whoop and took off at a run. At another time it might have lightened Sargos' spirits, but at the moment all he could see in his mind were the hundreds of bodies drifting down the Great River. The gods were capricious: Sometimes they gave a man great gifts, but often they took even more in return.

IV

Chief Verkan sat at his horseshoe-shaped desk, watching the viewer replay the takeover of the Memphis conveyer-head on a minor Fourth Level, Nilo-Mesopotamian time-line in the Alexandrian-Roman sector. The Nile delta had been suffering from a famine due to a series of aqueducts built over a period of centuries that had finally reduced the flow of the major river to a trickle. Damning the Nile River was not unusual; it had been done on First Level and most Second Level sectors, even some of the more advanced Europo-American sectors had completed, or were finishing major dams. The result, of course—regardless of level—was always the same; too little silt and too little water, leaving the Nile valley an agricultural wasteland. Famine was not the surprise, the real question was: Why had the populace decided to attack the Consolidated Outtime Foodstuffs' conveyer-head?

The battle was fierce and the prole defenders were disadvantaged by having to employ local weapons. Despite using a motley collection of clubs, cutlery and agricultural implements, the populace extracted numerous casualties among the Paratime staff. A few of the attackers were armed with swords and spears, probably members of the local constabulary. The soldiers didn't arrive until the buildings had been looted and burned. Outtime Foodstuffs First Level employees had gotten out before the doors were blown apart by battering rams. Most of the outtimers had died, but five of them had gotten to the conveyer in time. Verkan made a note that he wanted copies of all the interrogations and would like to talk to at least one of the survivors. As he recalled, Outtime Foodstuffs had been peripherally involved in the Wizard Traders case. *Maybe there was a connection?*

Verkan looked up when he heard his secretary's voice announce, "Inspector, Skordran Kirv, to see you, Chief."

"Tell him to come in," he replied, wondering why one of his top men had arrived unannounced.

He motioned for Kirv to take a seat, as he shut off the viewer. "Kirv, I've got a question for you."

"Yes, Chief."

"Why would half the population of Memphis, Fourth Level Alexandrian-Roman, attack our local conveyer-head?"

Kirv replied, "Consolidated Outtime Foodstuffs runs the facility and there's a famine in all of Egypt."

"And what were they exporting?" Verkan asked.

"Hummingbird tongues, ibex steaks, crocodile livers, sir —there's a good market here for all of that right here in Dhergabar. Probably someone got careless and let some of the indigenes watch them bring foodstuffs into the building. People are starving in the streets—isn't that one of the sectors where they damned up the Nile, or some such nonsense?"

"Yes," Verkan said, enjoying the way Kirv had reached almost the identical conclusion he had after watching the clip. "It's almost always carelessness or stupidity that brings disaster to our outtime operations. Someday, someone is going to slip up and one of these more advanced Second Level, or even Fourth Level, time-lines and they are going to figure out that they're nurturing a colony of vampires at their breast and the big bill will finally come due."

The Paratime Secret: the one inviolate Home Time Line secret that had to be protected at any cost. Not only to preserve First Level society in all the luxury it had become accustomed to, but also because it wasn't right to let the poor outtime devils know that they were secretly being taken to the cleaners—as his friend Kalvan might have put it—by a secret race of parasites. But sometimes the parasites got careless and mistakes got made, and then it was up to the Paracops to clean up the resulting mess. This looked like it was going to be another one of those times. Sure, a few careers might be uprooted at Consolidated Outtime, but the real losers would be the families of the outtimers who'd died defending a place they neither built nor profited from.

Verkan shook his head. He'd have to think of a more appropriate punishment for those First Level incompetents; maybe a posting to that new Second Level Ashthor Rammis subsector, where the locals shaved all body hair, practiced ritual self-flagellation, were strict vegetarians and believed the highest state of being was to forego all pleasure. That might just be the place for these miscreants to cool their heels for a century or so.

"Good analysis," Verkan said. "I've got something pleasant in mind for those in charge, for a change."

"I don't like that look, Chief."

"How does a penal sentence to the Ashthor Rammis Subsector strike you?"

"Just rewards, comes to mind." Kirv shook his head. "But let me change the subject, for a moment. I have news you need to hear: Dalgroth Sorn is getting ready to announce his retirement at Year-End!"

Verkan bolted upright in his chair. "Dalgroth!" The Paratime Commissioner for Security was one of his and the Paratime Police's staunchest allies. Dalgroth Sorn was said to be older than time, but Verkan—preoccupied with events on Kalvan's Time Line—had not considered his retirement, certainly not so soon after former Paratime Chief Tortha Karf's. It appeared that all the men he'd looked upon as mentors and friends would be gone from active service by the end of the year. That left Verkan not only feeling alone, but also isolated and with more weight upon his shoulders than any man should have to bear.

Kirv added, "It wasn't unexpected. He is a half century older than Tortha and they are good friends."

"I know," Verkan said. "I should have anticipated this and had a candidate ready to step forward and take his place."

Skordran Kirv winced. "The Opposition Party has put forward Councilman Aldron Ralth as their candidate."

"Already!" Ralth was the Opposition leader who had replaced Salgath Trod—who was assassinated during the Wizard Trader blow-up. "He's a good figurehead and rebuilt Opposition after the Wizard debacle, but he's probably the worst person—other than Hadron Tharn—to head the Paratime Security Commission."

"Ralth's sycophants in the Executive Council are saying that it's time the Commissioner stood on his own two feet, rather than being a rubber stamp for the Paratime Police force. He's getting a lot of media attention. Everyone knows that Dalgroth is a big Paratime Police booster."

"True, but he was no rubber stamp. Dalgroth had a very clear agenda, which was to protect the Paratime Secret and keep the Force strong and independent of the Executive Council. I've gotten more than one bawling out from Dalgroth, when he didn't agree with my policies or actions."

"You'll never convince the media or Executive Council of that."

Verkan shook his head wearily. For not the first time, nor last time, he wondered how Tortha Karf had run the Force for over two hundred years. "Who do we know that has the right background to serve as Paratime Commissioner?"

Skordran Kirv looked nervous. "We do have one exemplary candidate, Chief."

"And who might that be?"

"Tortha Karf. He's got the best background, great contacts and would back us to the hilt."

Verkan shook his head no. "Tortha's not about to give up his retirement; besides his nomination—after what Ralth has been saying—would stink all the way to Mars. Is there any way we can talk Dalgroth into staying in office for a few more years?"

Kirv shrugged his shoulders. "Maybe you could have a talk with him, Chief. I don't know anyone else, other than our ex-Chief, he'd listen to."

"Fine," Verkan said, in resignation. He knew when he was beat. "Set up an appointment for later this afternoon. I'll have to worry about

Nilo-Mesopotamia tomorrow." *I'd better be able to convince Skordran not to retire; otherwise, this job of policing umpteen millions upon millions of time-lines is going to turn into a dead certain impossibility! If Aldron Ralth becomes Paratime Commissioner, it'll be time for me to retire—right to Kalvan's Time Line.*

V

Colonel Kronos nodded to his sovereign to signify that everyone was seated. Great King Kalvan banged his pistol on the table for silence. "Princes, lords and generals, we have very little time and a lot of items to cover. Please keep your questions to a minimum. General Baldour, would you bring us up-to-date on the nomad invasion?"

General Baldour was a former mercenary Grand Captain in the Army of Hos-Ktemnos and thus more familiar with the western territories and Middle Kingdoms than any of the Hostigi generals. He walked over to the deerskin map of the Middle Kingdoms and pointed to a spot just north of the Middle Kingdom city of Kythar (Louisville, Kentucky) with his sword point.

"Yesterday, I talked to a merchant just returned from Kyblos City; the word there is the northernmost horde is just outside Kythar Town. In years past, the nomads would have stopped there to sack Kythar Town, but not this year with Grand Master Soton's army less than five days behind.

"Soon they will have reached the Trygath. However, we must remember that this information was a moon-quarter old when it reached Kyblos City and it took another moon half to reach us here in Hostigos Town. We can expect the nomads to follow the trade routes along the Lydistros River so that by now they should be less than a moon-quarter from the Trygath border."

There was a collective sigh from around the plank table.

Queen Rylla asked, "Do you think the nomads might possibly move into Hos-Ktemnos or will they travel through the Trygath until they reach

Kyblos and then invade Hos-Hostigos?"

"I believe the nomads would be going right into Hos-Ktemnos, as these migrations have done in the past, were they not being chased by the Zarthani Knights. The plunder is much richer in the Great Kingdom of Hos-Ktemnos than western Hos-Hostigos. Yet, if they travel east they are going to run straight into Tarr-Lydra, where they'd be caught between Soton's army and the Knights' garrison in Tarr-Lydra—which would be suicidal.

"Prince Tythanes of Kyblos and Prince Kestophes of Ulthor are right to believe the nomads are going northeast and will soon be invading their realms; thus, they have a legitimate claim to their overlord's protection. There is no way to avoid supporting them without our Great King acquiring the name of a king who advances himself at his princes' expense."

"That was my own analysis," Kalvan said.

Chancellor Chartiphon rose to speak. "Then it looks like we are going to have to delay the invasion of Hos-Harphax until the nomad problem has been settled."

Which is exactly what the Styphoni want, thought Kalvan, cursing Soton and his progenitors in four languages. Did he dare split the army into two smaller forces as he had done with such disastrous results last spring?

"Harmakros, what do you think of splitting the army in two, sending one half after the nomads; the other to invade Hos-Harphax?"

"I don't believe it would be wise, Your Majesty. We have reports that the nomad hordes number anywhere from one hundred thousand to just under a million—and that depends upon whether you're talking about the advance horde or the main horde and all its divisions. Nor do we know the proportion of fighting men to women, children and old men. We do not have enough information to judge what we may be up against. If we don't take at least thirty thousand troops we may be overwhelmed by sheer weight of numbers. In a situation this fluid I don't believe we can risk fighting a two-front war."

"On the other hand," Prince Ptosphes added, "we can be certain that the Army of Hos-Harphax is going to stay inside its borders and not be on campaign unless we attack first. If we do that now we may find ourselves fighting the Harphaxi in the east, the Ktemnoi in the south, and the nomads everywhere else. As our Great King has told us repeatedly, the only thing worse than fighting a two-front war is fighting one on three or four fronts, which is exactly what we will have if we undertake the invasion of Hos-Harphax."

Kalvan sighed and decided that in future he was going to have to be more careful about throwing out military maxims in front of his General Staff. Although he had to admit that his own advice struck him as frightfully sound. Here he was not only caught on the horns of a dilemma, but on the prongs and antlers as well!

At times like this he sometimes wondered if his friends and family might have been better off had he never been dropped off here-and-now by that cross-time flying saucer. It was when he landed that things began to get complicated. Hostigos was at the center of Pennsylvania, but nothing like the one he had known as a Pennsylvania State Policeman.

Here-and-now was an alternate world where the Indo-Aryan invasions had not stopped in India, but continued east across China, then by ships along the Aleutians until they reached the Pacific Coast as far down as Baja California. Later waves of related peoples had settled the in the Great Plains and the Mississippi River valley. They had brought with them horses, cattle and iron. A new civilization, five or six centuries old, had settled in the Appalachians and along the Atlantic Coast.

The new civilization, which called itself the Five Kingdoms, was the most advanced; they alone had discovered the secret of gunpowder. A theocracy called Styphon's House had grown up around the gunpowder miracle, dispensing the sacred fireseed to allies and subject states. Over the centuries they had used their monopoly of gunpowder to maintain their political status quo and enrich the priesthood. They almost matched the ancient Aztec priesthood of his own world for sheer bloody-mindedness.

It was a late-medieval to early Renaissance culture, with gunpowder and good hand weapons, including a modified flintlock. When Corporal Calvin Morrison, forcibly retired from the Pennsylvania State Police, had landed in the small Princedom of Hostigos, he had found himself in the midst of a war between Hostigos and Styphon's House—which wanted to annex the Princedom for its sulfur springs. After helping rout an enemy raid, he was accidentally shot by Prince Ptosphes' daughter, Rylla. He'd spent his convalescence in Tarr-Hostigos as a guest of the Prince.

Then he had fallen in love with the lovely Rylla and decided to stay and help them in their fight against Styphon's House. First, he had shown them how to make their own gunpowder, not only freeing them from Styphon's House but involving them in a war to the death with the gunpowder theocracy. After that Kalvan had been like a man hanging onto a runaway horse. There had been battles against Styphon's allies—the Battle of Listra-Mouth against Prince Gormoth of Nostor and the Battle of Fyk against Sask—both of which Kalvan had won.

Kalvan's knowledge of military history and stupid generalship by Kalvan's opponents had helped. So had new field artillery, with trunnions and proper field carriages, able to outshoot anything else in this world. A superior grade of gunpowder had helped too. Soon Hostigos was a major power, whether it wanted to be or not. There was nothing else, really, but to proclaim it the Great Kingdom of Hos-Hostigos. And Kalvan had become Great King and Rylla his Great Queen.

Following his enthronement, there had been a year of war, with attacks coming from Hos-Ktemnos to the south, Hos-Harphax to the east, and Hos-Agrys to the north. Kalvan had won three Great Murthering Battles and only lost one—the ill-fated Battle of Tenabra, where Prince Ptosphes had been given a good licking by Grand Master Soton. But three out of four weren't bad odds anywhere, even here-and-now, so Kalvan still held his throne—for now.

Kalvan rose to his feet. "I agree with Harmakros and First Prince Ptosphes. We must abandon our plans for the invasion of Hos-Harphax and draw up new ones for the defense of Kyblos."

All the assembled Princes and generals nodded their accord. Prince Sarrask of Sask stood up and said, "Let's raise our voices for Great King Kalvan, who has brought us several seasons of good fighting and now promises us more!"

There was a collective cheer and a chorus of 'Down Styphon!'"

Sarrask added, "Aye, and when we've finished giving the barbarians a good arse-kickin', let's come back and finish the job we started last year in Hos-Harphax!"

There were more cheers and Sarrask sat back down.

"Thank you, for the vote of confidence. Now, let's get down and work out the details of how we're going to get to the Trygath and which soldiers we're going to take. First, General Hestophes is going to need reinforcements for his Army of Observation at Tarr-Lorca in Beshta. We don't want to give the Harphaxi any cute ideas while we're away. What's Hestophes' army look like right now, Captain-General Harmakros?"

"Hestophes has four regiments of Royal Horse and one of infantry, plus about another two thousand Beshtan cavalry."

"That's only five thousand men," Kalvan said. "Let's send him the Second Musketeers, and the King's Heavy Horse and the Heavy Cavalry—they won't be of much use where we're going." Since so many of his cavalrymen, even the former mercenaries, were titled or the younger sons of the nobility, Kalvan had been forced to create three regiments of old-style fully armored cavalry. He had thought them almost useless until they had proved their mettle against the Zarthani Knights at the Battle of Phyrax.

Their real value now lay in the east where they could help shore up his defenses against the Harphaxi. In the Trygath they would be a liability in the hilly and broken terrain, and when matched against the much lighter nomad cavalry. Even the Roman heavy catiphracti had had serious problems with the Parthians.

"That will give Hestophes about seven thousand seasoned troops. Prince Phrames, do you think you can spare any men?"

"Some, Your Majesty. I can send a thousand musketeers and pikemen. But no cavalry, since I need all I have in order to train my recruits. I don't have to tell Your Majesty the shape I found the Beshtan Army in."

Prince Sarrask made a loud hoot. "Half-dead, half-starved and half-armed! Old Balthar the Black was a choke- purse, he was."

No one bothered to mention that Kalvan had taken the cream of the captured mercenaries—forty acres and a mule for each recruit—into the

Royal Army, leaving only those free companions too infirm or too old to fight for Prince Phrames and the other princes. Still, all in all, Phrames had done wonders with the remnants of the old Army of Beshta and had managed to retake a border castle that had renounced fealty during the war with Beshta in the dead of winter.

"We'll leave Queen Rylla"—Kalvan ignored Rylla's grimace as she realized she wasn't going to be invited to the party—"four infantry regiments, including the Hostigos Rifles." That got a smile out of Rylla. "And a regiment of horse. The rest will form the nucleus of the Army of the Trygath."

"That will give us better than eleven thousand men for a start, not including the Royal Artillery," Harmakros said. "Are we going to take any of the field guns?"

"A light battery at most, four-and six-pounders," Kalvan answered. "The guns will only slow us down. We are going to be crossing countryside that's a nightmare—everything from ravines to swamps. Mobility is going to be all in this war against the nomads. If I can—and I'm going to try—I'll mount every infantryman in the Army of the Trygath. We'll be taking the entire Mobile Force, which will give us another five thousand men. "

"You're not leaving me with much of anything," Rylla complained.

"That's right. Because you're not going to need anything more than glorified garrison troops while I'm gone. I want you to stay right here at Tarr-Hostigos the entire time I'm gone. Unless Prince Lysandros is crazier than a rat in a shithouse drainpipe, he's going to be holding firm in Tarr-Harphax. Grand Master Soton is busy stirring up the Sastragath, while Great King Cleitharses of Hos-Ktemnos is back to counting scrolls in the Royal Library. You, my love, are staying here to keep everyone else honest. If it makes you feel better, I'll leave the Army of Hostigos and the Army of Sask here under the command of Prince Sarrask."

Sarrask rose to his feet sputtering, dropping half a cup of dark wine down his robes. "But Your Majesty, I'm not one to set watch over the Royal Nursery—Excuse me, Great Queen Rylla, no offense meant. But I'm a man of plain-spoken words."

Rylla was up and fumbling for her dagger as if she meant to beard Sarrask or cut off his tongue.

"Order, please!" Kalvan shouted. "Prince Sarrask, you are a valiant warrior and one of my best commanders. I would prefer to have you at my side fighting the nomads, but I need someone here I can trust to guard my home and household. I can think of no one better able to protect my throne in my absence." Actually Kalvan could think of half a dozen in a moment, but all of those he needed by his side and those he didn't, like Prince Ptosphes, would take it as a personal slight if he left them home.

Sarrask swelled up like a peacock on display and made a courtly bow. Rylla, who sat at Kalvan's right, turned so that no one else could see the horrible grimace she made at her husband.

"I will ask Prince Pheblon of Nostor to support the Army of the Trygath with three thousand of his troops, Prince Balthames of Sashta with another two thousand, three thousand from Nyklos, and I'm sure we can depend upon Ulthor and Kyblos for an additional eight to ten thousand men—since they will be defending their own lands and can call upon their lordly levies."

Harmakros grinned. "That should give us more than thirty thousand men for the Army of the Trygath. Enough teeth to grind the nomads' bones to dust." Everyone smiled at that thought and there was another chorus of "Down Styphon!" followed by an equally loud one of "Death to All Barbarians!"

Once the noise fell to a low roar, Kalvan said, "Harmakros and Chartiphon, I want you two to get together with General Baldour and decide which passage we take, the northern Nyklos Road or the Akyros Trail through Sask. Then I want you to go over possible foraging areas, ambush sites, bad stretches of road and where to set depots in case we have to make a hasty retreat. Also consider that we might want to link up with some of the more civilized kings and princes once we reach the Trygath. Duke Skranga and General Klestreus, I want you both to make a list of every Trygathi king, prince, baron and everything we know about them, from their fighting ability to whether they are pro- Styphoni or anti-Styphoni. I'd like it by tomorrow at the latest."

Duke Skranga nodded and smiled as if he'd just been thrown a tasty morsel. His other intelligence officer, General Klestreus, looked like a fish that had just been hooked.

"Now, one last thing before I let you all get back to work. The Pony Express route we've set up between Hostigos Town and the Army of Observation at Tarr-Lorca has given us a quarter-moon jump in our border communications. I'd like to run a similar route into Ulthor, and possibly Kyblos, so we can obtain adequate intelligence rather than having to depend upon itinerant peddlers and vagabonds. Colonel Kronos, I'd like for you to attend to that. Don't hesitate to pull as many of the experienced riders as you need off the Great King's Highway.

"That's it for now, gentlemen. This meeting is dismissed." Actually, Kalvan would have preferred a working semaphore system to the Pony Express, but he'd decided that building the Great King's Highway was more important.

He didn't have enough trained manpower to do both. By Father Dralm's Beard, he didn't have a tenth the trained manpower to do any of the things he wanted done, but give the new University of Hostigos a few years.... Then he would not only have good interior communications and roads, but he could start working on some more reliable vehicles, like a Butterworth stagecoach. Anything would be an improvement over the Conestoga-style wagons the Zarthani used for everything from overland transportation to mobile homes.

Note: After road is finished start stagecoach line. With leaf-springs, too!

VI

Thunder roared and shook the rooftree of Ranjar Sargos' temporary longhouse. For a few moments it drowned out the squeal of horses and the babble of more tongues than he had heard in all his days. Not since the time of his grandfather twice removed had such a great wave of humanity flooded over the Great River and spilled its way into the Sastragath. Like flotsam tossed by the Great River, Sargos and his tribe had been picked up and pushed into the Lydistros Valley.

Yet, like a flood which replenishes the land it destroys, there was good which came with this river of humanity. Since few of the chiefs knew these lands, they had been forced to rely upon the knowledge of those who did. Ranjar Sargos, having spent four years of his youth as a mercenary in the Trygath, knew more about this land than all but a few of the headmen in this great warband. This, along with Sargos' renown as a warrior, had placed him at the forefront of this human wave. Now only the constant pressure of the Black Knights gave the wave its form and kept it from dispersing into hundreds of separate warbands. Without cohesion, each tribe and clan would be destroyed piecemeal by the Trygathi iron men and their allies. The time had come for a great warlord to guide the horde and Ranjar Sargos knew that this was his destiny—for had not his own vision foretold of such triumphs?

Sargos took several deep breaths, held them, and waited for Thanor's banging on his sky anvil to cease. When the air was still, he spoke again to the assembled Plains headmen and Sastragathi chiefs. "The gods have allowed the Black Knights to take the field. They have allowed the demigod Kalvan of Hostigos to bring his army into the Trygath—"

"Demigod or demon, this Kalvan is no friend to the Trygathi, less so to the Black Knights," Chief Alfgar interrupted. "Let all three of them fight one another, I say. *This* is what the gods intend. Then let us pick the bones of the survivors!"

"Or Nestros and Kalvan swear brotherhood and pick *our* bones," Sargos replied, his voice growing in volume. He had never been even-tempered and knew it. He also knew that since the Tymannes had left their ancestral hunting grounds he had grown even sharper of tongue.

"By Galzar's Mace, this is as the gods will—" Chief Alfgar began.

A wordless muttering stopped him, as Headman Jardar Hyphos once more tried to form words with a jaw yet unhealed from the blow of a Knight's mace. His son leaned over and put his ear next to Hyphos' mouth for a time, then nodded.

"Father says he doubts the gods have willed it that we come so far only to fall to our pride as well as our enemies."

"You yapping puppy! Your father is a man. You are—"

"Silence," Sargos bellowed. He did not know what this would do, except perhaps make all the chiefs angry at him rather than at one another. That could be a gain, if he was able to do something with their attention.

"To be proud is the mark of a warrior, as all here are," he began. "To let everything yield to that pride is the mark of a fool. More than four hands' worth of tribes in this great warband have set aside their pride and sworn to follow me. The gods have not punished them. Why should you fare otherwise?"

"Witlings and women," Alfgar muttered just loud enough that Sargos alone could hear. Sargos decided for the moment to ignore him.

"How many of these tribes are fighting as they please?" Chief Rostino asked. Of all those present, he appeared to have the most Ruthani blood as well as the most dignity.

Sargos chose an equally dignified answer. "I am not a Great King, with a host of armed slaves to punish disobedient warriors as if they were children. I am chief over the Tymannes, and those who swear to follow me as Warlord do so by choice."

"Then it is my choice," Chief Alfgar said, "not to swear any oaths to Ranjar Sargos or any other sachem or chieftain. We of the Sea of Grass have considered each chief his own master since the Great Mountains rose from the earth. Maybe the dirt scrapers and log builders of the Sastragath are more accustomed to following at the heels of their masters like curs!" Alfgar slammed his fist against his bone vest, making a sound like that of a gunshot.

The hands of about half the chieftains in the longhouse streaked for their knives, the only weapons allowed inside during the parley.

Sargos signaled for attention. "This is not the time to hurl baseless insults nor fight among each other. There is great booty to be won and much glory to be gained in fighting our real enemies."

Most of the chiefs sat back down and nodded their agreement to this sage advice.

But Hyphos' son stood his ground. "You have not fought Kalvan, Alfgar. We have fought others like him and know that to win we must stand as one, like wolves not dogs."

"Nor have you," Alfgar replied, his face twisted into an angry leer. "What has Sargos given you, that you take his word about Kalvan?"

Hyphos' son would have drawn his knife if his father's arm had not been sounder than his jaw—a bronzed arm gripped the young man's wrist and twisted. He gasped and dropped his knife.

"See! How the Sastragathi lick their master's hand. When Sargos nods his head, the old rein in the young. This is not the way of the plains!"

Rage flowed into Sargos, lifting him like a giant's hands—or perhaps the hands of the gods. Certainly he had never felt their presence more strongly, even in the steamhouse of his manhood rites.

"Let us submit this matter to the judgment of the gods." Sargos drew from the hides of his chieftain's chair the sacred axe of the chiefs of the Tymannes. "With this ax and no other weapon I will fight Chief Alfgar, this day, in this place. He may use any weapon his honor allows."

"No!" Chief Ulldar exclaimed. Next to Sargos, Ulldar Zodan was the wisest man in the room in the new ways of warfare. Two of his sons had served Chief Harmakros in Kalvan's wars and told him much. They had also brought him a tooled and engraved horse pistol that was the envy of every chief in the longhouse. "The gods have taken away Alfgar's wits. What if they have taken away his honor as well?"

Several of Alfgar's fellow chiefs had to restrain him from trying to kill Ulldar with his bare hands. When the uproar had subsided, Alfgar had found his voice again. "I will fight with the hand spear against your axe, you godless son-of-a-bitch who weaned you on stinkcat piss!"

"Let it be done, then," Sargos commanded. His rage was already fading, and in its place were doubts that he was really in the hands of the gods after all. If he fell—and Alfgar promised to be a formidable foe—his son would do well to see the Tymannes' great longhouse again.

Why not be hopeful? he thought. If you win, it will prove the gods' favor, and your own prowess as well. Then all the chiefs and clan headmen assembled here will proclaim you Warlord, and those lesser chiefs who were not here will quickly follow. Cast the bones and let the fates see to where they fall. By Galzar's Mace and Thanor's Hammer!

Sargos led the chiefs and headmen out to the square in the middle of the chiefs' longhouses. The rain was still falling and what had already fallen made the square a sea of foul-smelling mud. Sargos judged this would be to his advantage: Alfgar could seldom have fought on foot, on a slope, in mud up to his ankles.

So it went for a half-score of passes. Sargos quickly realized he had but one advantage. Alfgar was so confident of his greater youth and strength that he was careless of what fighting in mud would do to them. If the time ever came when Alfgar could not dance away in time—

As if to warn Sargos against hopefulness, on the next exchange Alfgar drew first blood. It was barely more than a thorn prick and on Sargos' left arm, but it held an arrogant message:

"I can do this at will. The next time, who knows where my spear will land?"

Both men's friends were shouting threats and promises. If Alfgar won, there would be a permanent breach between the plains and Sastragath chiefs. At first blood, all fell silent and remained so.

Sargos said nothing at all. He had better uses for his breath.

In time the rain stopped. Both men now bled in a hand of places, though nowhere seriously. Sargos began to wonder if he would have breath for any use at all before long. Beyond any doubt Alfgar was spending his strength freely. But he'd had rather more to begin with. The mud, it seemed, might not be the gods' way of saving Ranjar Sargos.

Alfgar made a thrust that would have disemboweled him had he not jumped in time and slipped in the mud. Sargos had to use all his arts in war while he still had the strength and speed to use them.

Silently he prayed to the gods: Guard my Folk and my son. Send them wisdom and courage, if there is justice in you. But if you sent Kalvan to be as a wolf to the flocks, then you are not gods and my spirit will tell my son to worship something else!

"Pray for an honorable home for your spirit, old man," Alfgar said with a sneer. "It will soon need one."

Then he sprang forward so fast that if Sargos had not been prepared, both in mind and body, for the final grapple, he would have been doomed. As it was he had already begun to turn, presenting his left thigh when Alfgar closed.

Offered a target, Alfgar thrust hard with his spear, forgetting that his target was mostly bone. As the spear point grated on that bone, Sargos' long arms whirled. His left gripped the spear, jerking it from Alfgar's hand.

His right arm brought the ax down hard on Alfgar's knife hand, as it leaped toward Sargos' groin. For an instant the gods might have turned both men into stone. Then the knife splashed into the mud.

The spear whirled in Sargos' hand, then seemed to sprout a red bloom in Alfgar's belly. The knowledge of what had happened was just dawning in his eyes when Sargos' axe came down on his head.

"The gods have spoken!" Sargos cried. He hoped if more needed to be said, the gods would say it themselves. Neither Sargos' wits nor his wind seemed to be fit for the task, and as for his legs, he prayed they would not tumble him into the mud beside his foe.

Sargos Ranjar, son of Cedrak Ranjar, you are too old for this and so you will learn the next time you confuse the voice of the gods with the memories of your own youth.

Egthar and Pydox, chiefs of his own clan, ran forward to aid him. "Stop treating me as if this was my first wound! It's more like my tenth, and one of the least." In truth it would need some care, and he would be riding more than walking in the coming battles. But only the flesh hurt.

Meanwhile the crowd around him had grown and was beginning to chant, "Sargos! Sargos! Warlord Sargos!" He wasn't sure if his own men had begun the chant or if it was a spontaneous outburst; regardless, he knew how to grasp the moment and squeeze it with both hands. He stepped back and raised his arms.

Together, Headman Jardar Hyphos and his son stepped forward and lifted Alfgar's motionless body.

Behind them came Chief Rostino. He knelt before Sargos and pressed his forehead against Sargos' hands.

"The gods have truly spoken. What do they wish that we swear to you?"

Had it been a Sastragathi chieftain making this pronouncement rather than a plainsman, there might have been jeers and catcalls—as it was there was naught but silence.

"They ask little," Sargos said. He took several deep breaths and found that he could hope to speak instead of gasp. At least, I will ask little. The gods will not help a man who asks more than those who follow him are willing to give. "Little indeed," Sargos repeated. "Only that you follow me in war and peace, save when I ask for war against blood-brothers or peace with blood-enemies. And that you bind yourselves by this oath until I release you or death takes you."

"I swear—" Chief Rostino began, but Sargos stopped him. "Rise, I will have no brave warriors swearing anything to me on their knees. That is more pride than the gods allow."

There was a boisterous round of oath-taking as all the assembled chiefs who had not already done so swore their allegiance to Ranjar Sargos as Warlord.

After all the oaths had been given, Sargos said, "Let us take a visit to the bathhouse, and heat us some beer. Or there is wine should any of you wish it. "

Sargos could not tell what drew more enthusiasm, the gods' judgment, the baths or the prospect of a good drinking party.

VII

Verkan flew his aircar through the Old Town section of Dhergabar, where there were still ground-hugging buildings, a square mile of densely packed ground level residences and commercial facilities. There were even a few buildings which could trace their history back to First Level PP (Pre-Paratime), but most only went back four millennia to after the Religious Wars when most of the city outskirts had been leveled and afterwards had taken its present shape of tall anti-gravity towers and spires. Old Town was where the infirm, those who found it difficult to live in townhouses only reachable by aircar resided; the indigent—even the Bureau of Psych-Hygiene hadn't been able to root out all the bums from First Level society; out of work Proles—which included those studying for their First Level

Citizenship; and a small criminal element that not even the most determined Psych-Hygiene treatments and techniques could eradicate, nor the Metropolitan Police sweeps take captive.

Right in the middle of Dhergabar City was the Paratime Commission Building, a two hundred-story edifice, an entire city-block square in size and shielded with a next to impenetrable collapsed-nickel shield. Verkan parked his green aircar on Chief's reserved landing port and took the lift down to the hundred and eightieth floor to the office of the Paratime Commissioner for Security, where he was quickly ushered into Dalgroth Sorn's office.

"Chief Verkan, nice to see you," Dalgroth said, "please, take a seat."

Dalgroth Sorn was a tall, thin man with the air of a scholar, which was belied by both his piercing black eyes and his raspy voice; there were still a few older Paratime Police who could recall, when during his term as an Inspector, that voice could peel paint. Dalgroth was more formal than usual and Verkan wondered if it was because he was aware of the reason for this visit.

Verkan paused long enough to remove his pipe, load the barrel and light it. "This is not easy, Commissioner, but I believe it's of utmost importance—"

"Verkan, you get right to the point. It's one of the things I like about you. But this time, I know what you're here to ask. The answer is yes."

Verkan blew out a lungful of smoke. "Thank you, Commissioner—"

Commissioner Dalgroth held up his hand to stop him again. "I hate to keep interrupting you, Verkan, but I've got some things I need to tell you."

Verkan nodded this time.

"I'm going to keep my job as Commissioner, but not just because you need my help. But, because, there are some serious problems facing First Level society, and I think I can do a better job right here at the Paratime Commission than as head of the First Level Social Stability Project. That was the job I was going to take after I resigned as Commissioner of Paratime Security."

"I am very relieved by your decision. I believe I heard something about this Stability study on the evening news."

"What you heard, Verkan, from some newsie was just window dressing, as our friends on Europo-American call it. The real subject and purpose of this Project is not for public consumption."

Verkan braced himself. "I know I've been spending too much time on Kalvan's Time Line and outtime in general, but—"

"Don't apologize, Vall. I'm one of the few people who completely understand how demanding the Paratime Police Chief's job truly is. I doubt you know this, but once—thirty years before Tortha's reign—I was offered the position of Paratime Chief. Oh, yes. I turned it down flat; I saw what it did to the man they wanted me to replace. Remember, back then I was Chief Inspector. I have seen four Chiefs in my lifetime and Tortha was the only one who resigned without a physical or mental breakdown."

Verkan realized that he had never really known Dalgroth; he'd just been another useful ally who knew how to tell a good tale. Verkan was beginning to realize that even with five times the normal human lifespan, there was still not enough time to do everything that needed to be done—much less what he wanted to do.

"I think your sojourns to Aryan-Transpacific are a great way to get away from the pressures and demands of a job that is simply too much responsibility for one man. Unfortunately, it has come to my attention, and that of several other highly placed persons, including former Chief Tortha, that something is fundamentally wrong with our First Level culture. This is the reason behind the Social Stability Project."

"By fundamentally wrong, just what do you mean?"

"Vall, this time-line stinks! Maybe it's the accumulated sins and bad debt of ten thousand years of living off the labor and sweat of other human beings, but—whatever it is—it's beginning to manifest itself here on Home Time Line."

"I haven't noticed anything. Well, maybe crime is up a little."

"That's just one of the many symptoms. Did you know that First Level population has been dropping for the past four centuries?"

"No. It certainly isn't obvious, Commissioner. There appear to be just as many Citizens as ever."

"True, but only because of the increase in Prole citizenship—even as hard as the tests have become. The Prole problem is another part of this issue."

"I have noticed there is more actual Prole prejudice in Dhergabar than I recall growing up."

"You're right, the prejudice is growing worse. As Scholar Elltar has proposed, the Prole in our society has assumed a place quite similar to that of the Negro in the Europo-American, Hispano-Columbian Subsector, in the political entity still known as the United States, during the period they call the Reconstruction—after the War Between The States."

"The Civil War, I remember that well. I was there during the worst of it and I can see the parallels. The Civil War, in a lesser part, was about freeing the slaves. Separate, but not equal. The threat of slave rebellion."

"Exactly. As you've noticed in your Europo-American Quarantine proposal, this situation has been exacerbated with the passage of time. A number of observers believe there will be large scale race riots on Hispano-Columbian Subsector in the next few years. There are a number of parallels to what's happening here on First Level."

"The Proles aren't slaves or former slaves, but I do see similarities. Do you believe that this is a threat to First Level Security?"

"Not now, but it could be. Are you familiar with a man who calls himself The Leader?"

"No. Should I be?" Verkan re-lit his pipe.

"Not really. However, the man—and we don't know who he is—that calls himself The Leader is becoming more and more influential amongst the youth and the politically disenfranchised Citizens. Those who most feel threatened by the former Prole Citizens and by society as a whole. He's even encouraging his followers to wear a uniform of sorts, blue shirts and pants."

"That sounds similar to the fascist black shirts in Italy, and brown shirts of the old Nazi Party on Europo-American." Verkan shook his head in disgust.

"You're not the only one who has come to that conclusion. There are some frightening parallels."

"Commissioner, as long as I'm Chief, I will not tolerate the harassment and murder of Proles on First Level, such as the Nazis performed against ethnic minorities and religious groups that lived under their rule."

"I don't think it will come to genocide here. It's a completely different situation on First Level," the Commissioner said. "No one here wants to eliminate the Proles, just keep them down and not allow them to become Citizens."

"Well, the whole idea of allowing outtimers to become Citizens is fairly new. Less than a thousand years old."

"Yes," Dalgroth said, "that's when it was first brought to the Executive Council's attention that the population decrease was going to continue, no matter what laws were passed. To counter this, a program was set up to administer citizenship to the best and brightest of the outtimers. It's been one of the last millennium's few successes. But the Proles are not the real problem; the problem is here with the Home Time Line Citizens."

"How bad do you think this problem really is?" Verkan asked.

Dalgroth's brows furrowed heavily. "Bad. Bad enough that I believe it is the biggest problem facing the survival of the Home Time Line."

"More dangerous than the possibility of the Paratime Secret being uncovered?"

"Yes, because it threatens the very core of our society. The fact is, Verkan, our society is crumbling before our eyes. There's enough social and commercial momentum that it might last another millennium—but it is dissolving. That is why, for right now, I decided it is more important for me to stay on as Paratime Commissioner to help stabilize your stewardship as Paratime Police Chief, than it is to delve into First Level social problems. Because, if you fail as Chief, the results will be so catastrophic it will no longer matter what the problem was or is. The Paratime Police are First Level's most stable institution and if the force collapses because it's Chief has been forcibly removed, well—the fact is—this whole time-line will go up like a thermo-nuclear blast!"

For the first time in many years, Verkan Vall was so nonplussed he was actually speechless.

VIII

"Present—aaarrrmmmss!"

Forty bayoneted muskets snapped into position across forty Hostigi breastplates. A hundred sabers leaped to the vertical. Even in the watery spring sunlight, the reflection from all the steel made Kalvan blink.

The herald of Nestros, King of Rathon and self- proclaimed High King of the Trygath, rode forward. His mounted escort rode up on either side, fifty big men on beer-wagon-sized horses. By the customs of the Trygath, heralds went guarded until they were actually in the presence of the men they were sent to parlay with. Also by custom, the horsemen rode with their visors up and their swords held upright by the blades, as proof of peaceful intent.

Kalvan studied the guards as they rode up the slope toward him. They reminded him more than a little of the late—R.I.P.—Harphaxi Royal Lancers, swathed head to toe in armor about as useful as cheesecloth in keeping out a musket bullet or a chunk of case shot.

Except that this was the Trygath, a frontier area where in nine years out of ten the only fireseed available was what neighboring eastern princes were willing to sell illegally, risking both shortages and Styphon's Ban. Against other armored men-at-arms or lightly armored nomads, riding around looking like a blacksmith's version of a lobster made a certain amount of sense.

This had already begun to change, with the emerging trade of Hostigos fireseed for horses, ale, and furs. It was about to change even more, but not quickly or easily. Military technology was generally about as slow to change as priestly ritual. So for now, the Trygathi iron men had a few remaining days in the sun.

The herald signaled; the Rathoni guardsmen reined in, leaving him to mount the slope alone. At a nod from Captain-General Harmakros, Aspasthar rode out, his first sword reversed in his hand and the sun shining on his first suit of armor.

"Who has come to the host of the Great King Kalvan of Hos-Hostigos?"

Aspasthar's voice was high-pitched but steady.

"Baron Thestros of Rathon, herald and envoy of High King Nestros." The herald took another look at the Royal Page. "Does the Great King so lack men, that he has me greeted by a beardless boy?"

"Had he thought you saw wisdom in a beard, my lord, the Great King would have sent you a he-goat!" Aspasthar replied.

In the ensuing silence, Kalvan and Harmakros exchanged eloquent looks. Kalvan's said, If the boy's tongue has run away with him and we have a fight, he is going to get the flat of my saber across his arse.

Harmakros' reply was: Don't worry. The boy knows what he is doing.

The herald was the first to break the silence, with a roar of laughter. Seeing themselves given permission, the Rathoni Royal Guard also broke into laughter. Everyone hooted and guffawed, while Harmakros rode forward to clap his son on the shoulder so hard the boy nearly fell out of his saddle.

At last silence returned, except for the distant rumble of thunder. Baron Thestros wiped his face with a yellow-gloved hand.

"Well-spoken, lad. You do honor to your sire, your King, and your realm. But I think there must be a person of more rank than you in a host as large as this. Might I seek the honor of speech with he who holds the most rank among you? Captain-General Harmakros, I believe."

Harmakros nodded. "At your service. But I am not the highest among those present." He turned in the saddle. "Your Majesty?"

Kalvan urged his horse forward, letting his cloak flow back from his shoulders. The herald did a good imitation of a man whose eyes are about to pop from his head. Then he swung himself swiftly, if not gracefully, from the saddle and went down on one knee.

"Your Majesty! In the name of High King Nestros, greetings!"

"Surely you have more than greetings to bring, Baron Thestros, since you have four thousand cavalry at your summons. Your King has a name for wisdom, and would not send such a host with a message a beardless boy could bring."

The imitation of eye-popping was even better this time. Kalvan let it go on until he was sure the herald needed reassurance.

"No. I have no demonic arts, only good scouts. They saw your men two days ago and rode swiftly to bring word to me. I came up to the van, so that there might be no misunderstandings about why the men of Hos-Hostigos and its allies have come to the Trygath."

"I believe Your Majesty. But then, pray tell me what *is* the reason for such a host setting foot upon the domain of High King Nestros? He wishes peace with all who wish it with him, but those who wish peace seldom come with twenty thousand armed retainers!"

"Your scouts are not inferior to mine," Kalvan said with a grin. That was a remarkably accurate count of the Hostigi who'd crossed into the Trygath. Another ten to twelve thousand were strung out all the way across Kyblos, ready to either join the main body or cover its withdrawal. Kalvan had hoped for a larger levy from Kyblos, but many of the southern barons had not responded to Prince Kestophes' requests for men and probably wouldn't at anything less than sword point.

"I thank Your Majesty. But—forgive me for being inopportune, but I have only the cause of peace at heart. I ask once more, why are you in my King's realm?"

To call the Trygath King Nestros' realm was more than just an exaggeration, thought Kalvan, since Nestros' sovereignty was only recognized by four of the Trygath's nine legitimate kings and princes. Two of whom, in fact, Ragnar and Thul, were subjects of King Theovacar of Grefftscharr. Diplomacy, however, was the order of the day. "We do not come in search of peace."

Kalvan would have sworn he heard the thud of the baron's jaw hitting the ground. Quickly he added, "We have come to wage war on the nomads, enemies common to all of us."

The herald shook his head. "High King Nestros has taken counsel with his princes and kings, and he has devised ways of meeting the nomad host. It insults him to think that he must wait upon an Eastern realm for the defense of his own."

"I am sure the True Gods fight for your King and his princes and people, likewise. Yet is it not true that the nomad horde counts more fighting men than the Trygath and the Great Kingdom of Hos-Hostigos combined?" Three times, if the estimate of a hundred and fifty thousand on the way northeast was correct.

"It is also true," he added, "that during the last moon riders of the horde reached the Lower Saltless Sea, sowing death with every step their horses took. They did not return, but would it not have been better that they not even start?"

Kalvan wanted to meet the local magnate who'd caught the raiders on their way back from the shores of Lake Erie. King Crython of Ragnar had outthought as well as outfought the nomad raiders. By all reports that kind of ruler would make almost as good an ally as King Nestros. But it was King Nestros who controlled the back entrances to Hos-Hostigos, not King Crython.

"Indeed," the herald said. "No such raids will come again."

"Is this certain? Certainly they will cease after the valiant men-at-arms and footmen of King Nestros have broken the strength of the horde. But Nestros will do this only if he gathers all his strength under his own hand. Then who will be left to defend the lands of those who march against the horde, against raiders and outlaws? Or those nomads who break away from the main body?"

Kalvan had pitched his voice loud enough to be heard by the Royal Guardsmen. All of them would be nobles or sons of nobles; all must share the fear of what would happen to their lands at the hands of nomad outriders and bandits. None of them dared think of the consequences of a tribal victory over their king.

"Your Majesty, do you swear you can prevent this if King Nestros and you become friends and allies."

"We are not enemies even now, nor shall we be. What you mean is, if we become *allies.* I only say this: if we become allies, there will be thirty thousand Hostigi to strengthen your King's forces."

"And if there is no alliance, there will be thirty thousand fewer?"

"The host of the Great King of Hos-Hostigos will fight the horde wherever we find it. But is it not better that we fight it together? Sticks separated are easily broken. Tied into a bundle, they defy the strength of a giant."

"Your Majesty speaks eloquently. I think, perhaps, it would be wiser if you spoke thus to High King Nestros."

"Nothing would give me more pleasure, if I knew where to find your High King."

"Let Your Majesty ride to Rathon City; I believe he will find no obstacles in his path."

Rathon City was the here-and-now equivalent of Akron, Ohio. About fifty miles away—two days' easy riding.

"The High King will see me in Rathon City before the horde can wreak any more harm upon his vassals. Now, I see that the sky promises rain. Would you and your guard commander care to accept the hospitality of my tent, which I believe is closer than your own?"

The herald and his guard commander exchanged looks, then the herald nodded. "We are honored by Your Majesty's hospitality."

"Call it the first repayment of the hospitality we have received from Nestros' subjects." The herald frowned, and still looked puzzled as he led his guards off behind Aspasthar.

When the Trygathi commanders were safely on their way, Harmakros rode close to Kalvan. "Your Majesty, far be it for me to tell you how to guide the realm—"

"If you ever stop telling me, Harmakros, I'll find another Captain-General. Out with it. I don't want to get caught in the rain if I can help it. A fine spectacle for our allies, me leading a charge with sword in one hand and handkerchief in the other!"

Harmakros quickly ordered the First Royal Horse Guard into a wide circle, then put them in movement toward the tent. Riding practically boot to boot with Kalvan, he grinned.

"Your Majesty is as silver-tongued as any bard, but is this the time to be so truthful about what we want?"

"It is the best time. Any earlier would have given the Union of Styphon's Friends or the League of Dralm time to make noises. Not to mention letting the Zarthani Knights send scouts on to our line of march, and maybe more than scouts. Four thousand Trygathi could give us enough trouble. Think about four thousand Knights."

"I'd rather think about more pleasant things."

"Like that blonde at Mnebros Town?"

Harmakros flushed. "I didn't know Your Majesty noticed."

"Just because *I* slept alone doesn't mean I don't know the officers who didn't." They were silent for a moment, guiding their horses over a rough patch of ground.

"It's Mnebros Town that made me think the time was ripe to tell the truth," Kalvan continued. "Those people were so Dralm-damned *glad* to see us, it was almost pathetic. We could have had anything we asked for, not just wine, women, and banquets. They were *scared* of that horde!"

"What the Styphon!" Harmakros exclaimed. "A horde that size scares *me!* But our lands are farther than they're likely to reach. Around here, nobody knows if they'll have a roof over their heads and all their family alive come winter. Nestros will do his best, but if that isn't good enough…"

"If that isn't good enough, the princes and barons will start looking around for someone whose best might be good enough. Which might not be so good for us."

"Exactly, Harmakros." The gray sky was overhead now, and to the northwest was turning black. The royal pavilion was in sight ahead, and the herald's party was just turning into it.

"The Trygathi nobles here," Kalvan continued, "have always had more independence than the ones in the east, at least since fireseed came along. Things aren't as settled here and a good castle gives you more bargaining power when the only way to take it is by starving it out. Nestros will be down to Prince of Rathon if he lets too many of his nobles' lands be overrun.

"An alliance with us is really a gift from the gods, which Nestros will see unless he is a greater fool than I can believe. An alliance with us would allow him to send home, to defend their homes, all the second-line troops he probably can't feed anyway. We will put our men into line with his, and he'll have twice as big an army as he would otherwise. And a better one to boot! Nestros will keep the loyalty of his barons, defeat the horde and have his title recognized all at once. How could any man—?"

At the word "resist," the skies split apart in a thunderclap that made the horses jump. As the thunder rumbled into silence, the hiss of rain took its place. A few drops spattered across Kalvan's hands, a few more across his face, then the deluge struck.

He reined his horse to a walk and sneezed as drops found their way up his nose. So much for Royal dignity.

IX

Hadron Tharn heard the portal alarm go off and looked over at the privacy screen, seeing the face of his older sister, Dalla. He tapped the release code and the door opened.

"Long time no see, Sis."

Dalla winced. She was still playing mama—a job their birth mother had rejected. They had been close during their youth, until she met the future supercop, Verkan Vall. Actually, he rather admired Verkan's single-mindedness and lack of squeamishness. Verkan's, problem was that he still retained too many of the ideals of the old nobility that he'd been born into. Whereas, he had cast off all those old-fashioned ideas when a visit to Europo-American had introduced him to the works of Friedrich Nietzsche.

"I haven't seen you in a half-year, where have you been?"

None of your business, he wanted to shout, but Big Sis still had her uses. Without her influence, the super Paracop might be taking a closer look at this wanderings and financial dealings. That would not do, at least, now while events were still percolating. "I've been overseeing some my outtime business affairs."

"I understand from cousin Falro that you've been making quite a stir in First Level financial affairs."

Falro was in banking and it was useful to know that he still owed his loyalty to Dalla, who he'd unsuccessfully tried to romance—after her breakup with Verkan. "It keeps me occupied. And, as you know Dalla, the only things our parents left to us were Paratime Exchange Units." That was a sore spot and he knew it, and smacked it whenever Big Sister wanted to play mama. The truth was their mother had left the family for outtime adventure and it had been no great loss to anyone but Dalla. He'd been too young to even remember her. He saw her once or twice every twenty years and oohed and aahed while she treated him like another older sister.

"So what really brings you here, Dalla? I've been a good boy; no more visits to Fourth Level, Europo-America Axis Subsector." He'd been fortunate to make his first visits there, while a student at Dhergabar University, secretly ferreting out future business as an agent with Outtime Foodstuffs before the Big War in Europo-America, when the entire Axis Subsector had been declared off-limits to all First Level commercial and travel bureaus. He still had his contacts, but no one knew of them but Warntha, his personal bodyguard, the only person in the universe he completely trusted.

Dalla blushed fetchingly. She was as beautiful without make-up as most women were with it. She could have been a film star on any Europo-American time-line. If she weren't so useful, he might have been tempted himself. She was so good at protecting him, protecting him from everyone and everything—but himself. It was good to know that she still felt guilty about telling Verkan about his little Axis excursions; fortunately, she hadn't known the half of it.

He decided it was time to punish her some more. "Have you told my esteemed brother-in-law about the Hadron family secret?"

She gasped. "No! No one outside of the family knows about that."

"Supercop hasn't even made a guess. I'm disappointed; maybe he's more smitten with my elder sister then I surmised. Isn't it ironic that your husband's toy policeman—Kalvern, isn't it—drops off rather conveniently on the same time-line created by our esteemed great, great, uncountable great grandfather? Don't they still have some devil god named after the old fossil—rather like the family name? Must be the family curse."

Dalla nodded listlessly.

Hadron laughed. "Good old Arnall. It wasn't enough to violate the Paratime Code, but he had to create his own time-line by scaring away the natives! Now, it's Kalvan—that's the name—who's getting all the attention. The first Paratime time-line observed from the moment of divarication—ha! Maybe it's time we set the record straight. Told them about how 'ol' Hadron Arnall' arrived on a Europo-America time-line a couple of thousand years ago and played god to one of the tribes. How he used to ride around in a big aircar taking the prettiest young girls with him and how he killed and tortured any of the tribesmen who 'objected.' Of course, he never brought the girls back—alive. He made such an impression on the primitives that they actually changed their migratory pattern and created a whole new Subsector—Aryan-Transpacific, if I remember. They even remember him as some sort of an underworld god. Now, that story would get good old Kalvan off the home screens, but I doubt it would enhance the family name."

"Now, that's enough, Tharn. That's not the least bit amusing!"

"I forgot what a prig you turned into when you were around me. Does supercop get to see this side of you, too?"

"Shut up about him!"

"I see the family temper has bred true."

For the first time since the Big Fight, he saw tears in her eyes. He wondered what nerve ending he'd struck. Maybe supercop didn't want to breed—now there was a frightening thought—little Verkans running around with toy needlers. If Verkan wanted to keep the family unit small, they were both in agreement; maybe there was common ground between them.

"Why do you strike out at the only people who love you?"

Oh no, he thought, Big Mama's coming. Time to change the conversation again. "So you still haven't told supercop the family secret. I bet he already knows."

"What do you mean? That file was purged from the records thousands of years ago."

"And you believe that! Oh no, I guarantee you that in some secret data file in the Paratime Police supercomputer there's a flagged file with our shameful family secret. Probably only accessible by the Chief. Maybe the reason supercop hasn't brought it up is: he's waiting for you to tell him. Maybe he does love you, after all!"

"Of course he does. You don't mean that really? There can't be any such file."

"Oh, yes I do, Big Sis. True, it cost the family a few million units to keep the story away from the newsies, but I didn't think you were gullible enough to think the Parafanatics buried it as well."

There were worry lines creasing Dalla's forehead and he wondered if anyone cared that much about what he thought. Probably not. Big Sis included.

"Enough of your verbal sparring, Tharn. I came here to warn you that the Paratime Police know all about your little spy."

For a second he was worried, but little was not a description that would describe his real agent in any manner. "She of the big mammaries. Yes, I admit she's working for me. One of my subordinate's had a daughter who needed a job; I sponsored her for the Kalvan Study Team. I still have friends at the University, even if they couldn't stop my expulsion. After my Axis studies on their Great Man, I did receive a *lot* of moral support from some of my fellow academics for what the Paracops did to my fledgling academic career."

"You still don't see the danger in what you did?"

"I wasn't telling the natives about the Paratime Secret, if that's what you mean, just soaking up some local flavor and finishing my studies on Great Men in history. A little firsthand research never hurt anyone; not that most of the University professors would agree—it's too much like work. What I want to know is, why do they always proscribe the 'interesting' subsectors and time-lines? And, how, in Zirppa's Foodtube, was I to do original research on Great Men without any subjects! And, trust me Big Sister, the *Führer* is one of the greatest men of any Paratime Level or time-line!"

"There are great men all over Fourth Level; the one you picked may have been a catalyst, but by no other definition could he be called great—especially in regards to height, or any other adjective."

"You're wrong there, Sis, but we could argue over these minor philosophical difference for days. What brought you here this time?"

"I wanted to warn you to be careful. Your tame little spy could get you in serious trouble if she's caught tampering on Kalvan Prime. Verkan and I both like Kalvan and I won't be able to stop him again if he catches you involved in some outtime contamination."

"I'll keep that in mind, Big Sis. Now I know the end line of sisterly devotion. I have no intention of contaminating supercop's toy soldier's field of play. And, as much as I do admire the priestly scoundrels in charge of Styphon's House, I really have no interest in the outcome of their little war. I do like to keep an eye out for any slip in the old family secret. After all, the Zarthani do have written records and who knows what oral history some priestly scribe might have heard around the campfire and saved for posterity."

"You don't think?"

"I really don't, Sis. But anything is possible and it's best to have a 'friend' on hand to help contain the damage, so to speak."

Dalla blanched.

"Sorry to upset your placid existence, but someone has to protect the family name." It was hard to keep from laughing at that lie. His sister was too preoccupied to notice his change of expression; it was amazing how love could screw up your life.

"Oh, at the risk of upsetting you further, I just thought I'd let you know that word of new Kalvan time-lines have reached the University and some of the scholars are quite upset. They propose the novel hypothesis that every time another Kalvan appears on a new time-line: well, the risk of exposing the Paratime Secret grows more real. Some are even asking why Kalvan's not been dispatched for the good of Home Time Line and all that other patriotic self-serving nonsense. Of all people, they're asking why the Paratime Police aren't doing their job. Your husband might want to consider the ramifications."

Dalla's face, if possible, grew even whiter. He enjoyed that even if he didn't give a fig over the Paratime Secret being exposed. *How could some barbarian from Europo-America teach a bunch of savages enough to uncover a technological marvel that had taken three geniuses in three different fields to concoct and had been the life's blood of First Level for ten thousand years?* The probabilities were so low they weren't worth thinking about.

"I'm sorry, Tharn, I don't feel well. I've got to go."

"That's fine, Sis. Be sure and give my best to supercop." For a moment he was bothered by the thought that almost all their meetings ended this way, with Dalla either in tears or feeling sick—sometimes both. Maybe there was something to the family curse. After all, even father had succumbed in his third century and was now a permanent resident of some Psych-Hygiene house of horrors. No, madness was the escape route of lesser men—not an overman such as himself. Not with all that he had left to accomplish.

X

None of the forts and towns Kalvan had encountered in the Trygath had prepared Kalvan for the sight of Rathon City. Unlike the wooden stockades surrounding most Trygathi towns, Rathon City was encircled by immense stone walls—about the size of the Great Wall of China—which dwarfed the out-buildings and storehouses that had sprung up at their base. Not even the great Eastern capitals had such massive stone bulwarks, but then they were not subject to periodic invasions and large-scale migrations.

The Great Gate was large too, wide enough that four of the Zarthani Conestoga-style wagons could pass abreast. Most of the inner city's two- and three-story buildings were of the usual beam and plaster construction. At the center of the city were a score of large public buildings constructed of stone, half of which appeared to have been constructed during the past decade.

Kalvan guesstimated the population at about seventy-five thousand; smaller than a comparable Eastern Kingdom capital, but very impressive for a so-called "barbarian" kingdom. Most of the people he saw in the streets wore homespun trousers and shirts, although there was a goodly number of hunters and trappers in furs and buckskins. The men, with a few exceptions, wore full beards, rather than the trimmed beards and goatees worn in the Eastern Kingdoms.

Kalvan suspected that being in Rathon City was like visiting one of the Eastern capitals three hundred years ago.

At the center of the city was a great plaza, covering about two city blocks. Surrounded by a great garden stood Nestros' palace, a magnificent building that made Kalvan's own "palace" (actually Prince Ptosphes' summer palace) look like a poor relation's summer home. When this Great Murthering War with Styphon's House was over, Kalvan was going to have to build himself a palace more suitable to his rank—maybe something dong the lines of Louis XIV's Palace of Versailles—or he would have problems maintaining the respect of despots like Nestros.

Half a dozen richly dressed ambassadors came to meet the Hostigi party at the garden gates. Kalvan noticed that all of Nestros' retainers had their beards cut and trimmed in the Eastern fashion. To either side of the road leading to Nestros' palace stood the King's Guard, all over six foot, with finely engraved ceremonial halberds and black armor trimmed in gold.

Inside the palace presence chamber, Nestros himself looked every inch the warrior King, from his bright, inquisitive eyes to his big calloused hands. He had the ruddy complexion of an outdoorsman with a face that was dignified if not handsome. He and Kalvan locked eyes and neither turned away until Nestros spoke first:

"Welcome, Great King Kalvan, to our humble abode. Can I offer you some refreshments? Ale or winter wine, perhaps?"

"Winter wine would be nice," Kalvan responded. It took at least two goblets to complete the usual diplomatic niceties. Before starting on his third, Kalvan said, "As I told your herald, we come in peace. I would like to aid you in your war against the nomads."

"If this be true, then fine. Yet, I have to wonder what brings a distant king, like yourself, to our land. Truly, throughout all our history, we have found that the Eastern Kingdoms care little about our wars and struggles. Why should this suddenly change now?"

"There are great changes afoot during these perilous times."

"Change may be new to you in the Eastern Kingdoms, but here it is constant like the seasons."

"Not in all things. Since when have the Zarthani Knights driven nomads into your lands, instead of chasing them back across the Great River?"

Nestros' forehead furrowed as he tried to puzzle out an answer. "Are you trying to say that the Knights are using the nomads as a cat's-paw against Hos-Hostigos?"

Kalvan was impressed with Nestros' instinctive grasp of *Realpolitik.* "Yes, that is exactly what Grand Master Soton hopes to accomplish. And since your lands are in the middle they are going to take the brunt of the bloodletting."

There was a harsh noise as Nestros ground his teeth. "The Grand Master may well think we are but tools to be used, but we have prepared ourselves well for this invasion. I need neither his Knights nor your help to keep my lands."

"How do you plan to keep the nomads away? They are now less than two days' ride from Rathon City itself."

"We are well provisioned here and our great walls will keep out ten times their number. All farms and gardens within a day's march of the city will be burned to the ground. All villagers and peasants will come to the City. There are royal storehouses in every large town in Rathon, Mybranos, Cyros, and Kythax. We shall feed our own while the nomads starve like wolves in the midst of winter famine. When they have grown hungry and weak, my men-at-arms will feed the earth with their blood and till the soil with their bones."

"That may be a good plan for normal times, but not now. You have never fought a horde as large as this one. I doubt there is a town or city in all Rathon, except for this City, which can hold back the nomad flood. But, say that you are right, and the walls of your towns and cities keep the nomads at bay. What then? In their anger they will poison your wells, burn your villages and sow your fields with salt in retribution. What will your people have to return to then? And what will your nobles have to say about a High King who saves lives by hiding behind walls so his subjects can starve once the wolves have fled?"

Nestros' face turned bright red and for a moment Kalvan feared he had gone too far.

"Aargh! As bad as they taste, there is truth in your words. The nomads are as numerous as the great herds of bison on the Sea of Grass whose numbers stretch from horizon to horizon. It is enough to make one believe in the old legends. What help can you offer?"

"My plan is simple. We join both our armies and drive the nomads back south as the Knights have driven them north. Let the nomads find *our* steel even less to their liking than that of the Zarthani Knights."

Nestros' eyes brightened at the idea of a direct attack. "Will we have enough swords even united to drive such a great horde?"

Not if we were facing the Huns or Mongols of Otherwhen, thought Kalvan. But these nomads had fewer horse archers and fought more in the manner of Caesar's Gauls or Hadrian s Britons. *And they lack a great khan like Attila or Genghis Khan.*

"In a way their great number is to our advantage, King Nestros. With so many warriors they are pressed to fight like heavy infantry, yet wear little armor and make massed targets for our muskets and arquebuses. Also, they have many leaders instead of one chief."

Nestros shook his head. "No longer, King Kalvan. We have just learned that the nomads have elected a Warlord, a Sastragathi chief named Ranjar Sargos. He is a former Cyrosi mercenary and knows our way of warfare."

"He may know Trygathi strategy, but I doubt he's ever faced a regiment of musketeers. Also, as a new leader his hold will be uncertain; we must exploit it by moving quickly. How soon can you muster your troops?"

"Most of my army is within a day's ride of Rathon City where there are enough victuals to feed them. However, before we clasp palms on this alliance, I have a request I'd like to make."

Suddenly Kalvan feared for his good sword and his richly-chased breastplate. In another incarnation, Nestros must have been a horsetrader like Duke Skranga. "What can I do for you?"

"I would like to change my title to Great King and claim my lands a Great Kingdom, as you have done in Hos-Hostigos. Will you recognize my claim?"

This looks too easy! There's a catch in here somewhere. If he recognized Nestros as Great King of the Trygath, it might legitimize him in the eyes of his own people, but it wouldn't mean twiddle-dee to the other

Five Great Kings—none of whom had yet recognized Kalvan as Great King. Furthermore, Nestros claimed sovereignty over several princedoms that were within Grefftscharri borders. Kalvan didn't need to start another war in the west with King Theovacar just because he needed to placate Nestros now.

However, if Kalvan worked this right he could bind Nestros to Hos-Hostigos and possibly bring him into the war against Styphon's House.

"King Nestros, I will recognize you as Great King of all those princedoms and kingdoms who agree to be a part of your new Great Kingdom and who are not already under the sovereignty of King Theovacar."

From the furrowed brow on Nestros' face Kalvan knew he had safely navigated one minefield, but if he estimated Nestros correctly this would not be the last, nor the most dangerous.

"I welcome Your Majesty's support of the new Great Kingdom of Hos-Rathon. I only pray you will be equally swift in helping us to modernize our army."

This request was going to be easy to fill since Kalvan still had half the ordnance of Hos-Harphax at his disposal after last year's war—much of it dropped without even being fired. Not that he would ever let Nestros know that.

"Great King Nestros, when our armies have defeated the nomads, I will have two thousand arquebuses and five hundred muskets delivered to Hos-Rathon to finalize the alliance between our two Kingdoms. I will also send five tons of Hostigos fireseed and will train two score of apprentices in its manufacturing and curing at our new University."

This must have struck Nestros as more than satisfactory as he jumped out of his throne to give Kalvan a bear-hug that all but crushed Kalvan's ribcage.

"Truly, Great King Kalvan, you are as generous as you are wise and a master of the art of war. But enough of this, we will have plenty of time to share ale and wine when the nomads have been vanquished. Now we must plan our campaign. I have ten thousand troops billeted in and around Rathon City and two times ten thousand within a two days' ride. And another ten thousand within a five days' ride."

"Excellent," Kalvan replied. "Send riders out to gather all those within a two days' march. Meanwhile, we can gather provisions and prepare our troops for the battle ahead."

King Nestros rubbed his big hands together. "You speak my language, Great King Kalvan. The time has come to teach the nomads that it is safer in Regwarn, the Caverns of the Dead, than it is here in the Trygath!"

XI

Dalla walked into the smoky bar at Constellation House, looking for Tortha Karf's comforting presence. She was still wrung out from her visit with her brother, Tharn. She paused to take out a cigarette and three different men approached her to light it. She smiled graciously and used her own lighter. Verkan would have been proud.

"Over here, Dalla." She heard Tortha's familiar and comforting gravelly voice.

She sat down at the booth and asked the robot bartender for a bourbon and coke. Unlike most First Level citizens, Dalla preferred the unobtrusive mechanical servants to the status enhancing proles that many of her contemporaries preferred. Possibly, it was because her adopted sister, Zinganna, was a former prole, but she liked to think it was that she had more respect for outtime people than to use them as personal servants, no matter what the cachet.

Tortha was wearing breeches and a well-filled civilian tunic; his hair was streaked with gray and thinning in front. He was too practical and too much a stick-in-the-mud to have a hair treatment. He reminded Dalla of a big old cross bear, with a soft heart. She offered him a cigarette and was surprised to note that instead of a lighter he used one of the peculiar Kalvan Time-Line back-acting flint tinderboxes to light it. She wondered if it was significant, deciding he probably missed palling around with Verkan and the other boys.

"Thanks, Tortha, for coming to see me on such short notice. I know you just arrived from Fifth Level, but Verkan's so busy and I really need—"

"It's all right, Dalla. You can stop blathering. I take it you've just come back from another visit with your lovely younger brother."

"How did you know?"

"Hadron Tharn is the only person I know, besides your husband, who can break through your impenetrable good humor. And, since I've stopped my meddling, you and Verkan have been happier than I can ever remember."

"That wasn't all your fault, Tortha. I could have turned down some of those assignments. In those days I was younger and didn't realize how rare it was to meet a man of Verkan's caliber. I do now and I don't ever intend to forget it, or chance losing him again."

"Good. I don't have to tell you that I agree with you wholeheartedly. Now, tell me, what's the problem with Honorable Hadron Tharn?"

"I don't know—he's nastier than ever. I've overlooked his tantrums and mean behavior for years. He was always jealous of Verkan, you know. Before Verkan, he was such a sweet boy."

"Whoa. Now, wait a minute, Dalla. Is this the same Hadron Tharn, I knew? The one who burned your house down? And that was years before you met Vall."

"Yeah, well, maybe I exaggerated a bit. But, his personality took a real nose dive after Verkan came into the picture."

"Dalla, that might be because Verkan was the first man you really fell in love with."

"True," Dalla said, trying not to blush.

"I think Hadron's problems are deeper than mere sibling jealousy. Yes, I know you both were left to fend for yourselves, after your mother went outtime. Your father was always too busy to spend any time at home. He bedeviled the Department as Chief of the Opposition Party. It may sound horrible, but I was neither surprised or disappointed when the Bureau of Psych-Hygiene decided to put him in 'protective' custody."

Dalla felt her eyes begin to well again.

"Sorry, Dalla, damn this tongue of mine. I didn't mean to stick a soft spot."

"It's not father I'm feeling bad about; it's Tharn. Today, I finally saw him for the spoiled, mean, horrible little man that he's become. He's not a boy anymore, flirting with danger and oddball cults. He's a devious and—sadly—unprincipled grown-up, who I really don't know at all. If anything, I think he's—"

"You don't have to say it. I know all about your family."

"I know," Dalla said sadly, "Insanity runs right through it."

"Yes, and no." Tortha replied.

"What do you mean?"

"It always begins in the early thirties after the first longevity treatments. The longevity serum may well be the trigger."

"How do you know?"

Tortha looked very uncomfortable. "After your first companionate marriage with Verkan went sour, I decided to do a deep background check when I learned you two were getting back together. I also learned that the Psych-Hygiene people told this very thing to your brother and he disregarded it. It happened while he was at the University just before he got involved with those awful Axis people and got expelled for going outtime without a proper Paratime Permit. He knew that subsector was proscribed—"

"You don't have to defend yourself to me, Tortha. It was Tharn's decision to spend time with those terrible Nazis. It wasn't your fault he got caught! He still looks up to them, you know; that's one of the reasons I believe he's insane himself. There, I've finally said it—admitted it to myself. He's mad as a loon and it scares me."

"That's not all that scares you, is it?"

"Tortha, you can see right through me! This is a burden I've never told to anyone, not even Vall. Promise you won't ever tell anyone."

"I promise, Dalla, you have my word."

"Good. There's no better bond. I'm worried about my own children becoming like Tharn or my father or his grandfather, well—you get the picture. I love children, but I'm afraid to have any of my own. Look at the horrible choice I have to offer: be sane and die young, or live long and go crazy!"

Tortha shook his head. "That's not what I was expecting. I thought you might be worried about yourself."

"No. The family curse only strikes the males in our family; probably one reason why they marry so badly."

"That I didn't know. You could always adopt or there are ways to guarantee birth sex."

"Sure, and give my daughters the same terrible choice I'm faced with! I won't do it."

"You could adopt, or get a surrogate mother, or clones of you and Verkan. Today on Home Time Line there are lots of choices."

"Yes, I know. But I want children from me—like Rylla and Kalvan are having. Still, the clone idea isn't terrible. It would be nice to have a little Verkan around, one *I* could house train."

Tortha laughed. "Good luck. You can see how successful I was with the original."

Dalla laughed, too, feeling as though a terrible weight had moved from her shoulders. It was almost like having a father, talking with Tortha. "If you've made a study of the Hadron family, I guess you know the family secret too."

Tortha nodded, not saying a word.

"Does Verkan?"

Tortha shrugged. "I've never brought it up. I always believed if anyone should tell it, it would have to be you."

"Thank you, you old bear!"

Tortha actually blushed when she reached over and kissed him on the cheek.

"Should I tell him, Tortha?"

"That's for you to decide. It won't change his feelings for you that I know. Or I'm a complete romantic idiot."

Dalla laughed. "I will, I promise. But not now; poor Verkan, already has more problems than any three people I know; well, except for Kalvan and Rylla—and poor Ptosphes, of course. He still blames himself for the defeat at Tenabra."

"Not his fault; he was up against Styphon's varsity—and he's no Kalvan. But, my advice to you, young lady, is, don't wait too long. Secrets are burdens and no one understands that better than myself."

Rylla nodded. Tortha had spent almost half of his life protecting the Paratime Secret, and many times from the very people he was trying to protect. Now, her man held the same untenable position.

To change the subject, she asked, "What are you doing here so far away from you farm on Fifth Level Litzn-equivalent?"

Tortha shook his big head. "Too much of the same old, same old."

Dalla smiled mischievously, "That's not what I heard from Verkan. He told me about your nieces and their swimming lessons!"

Tortha blushed right down to his hair follicles. "Dralm damn-it! That blabbermouth!"

"Don't blame Verkan, I weaseled it out of him. Why did you really come?"

"Oh, you want the real reason as opposed to the one fit for a broadcast story. The truth is Dalla; I'm bored out of my skull. I'm tired of trapping rabbits and gophers. I'm tired of grapes and silly young girls. I'm tired of myself, I don't wear well; just ask any of my six former wives! I've spent the last two hundred years of my life doing important work and I'm still too young for the scrap heap. Paratime Commissioner—harrumph! It was a rubber stamp job in my day, and even more so with Vall. I came back here to help Verkan, if I can, or just help myself, if I can't."

"I understand. And, really, Tortha, Verkan needs all the help he can get. I've never seen him so 'involved' with an outtimer as he is with Kalvan—not that I blame him, I adore Kalvan and Rylla is already my best friend. Now he's fretting because he's stuck dealing with this Europo-America shutdown project of his! I've been going to all these meetings and I can tell you it's going nowhere. Can you pump him some sunlight on the issue, Chief."

"Ex-Chief—really, Rylla," Tortha said, trying to hide a big grin.

"Sure, but you'll always be Chief to me. Anyway, Europo-America has become the public 'Sector.' It's been that way since Outtime Novelties brought back jazz and flappers. You know how these outtime fads and crazes run; everyone was Indo-Turanian crazy when I was a girl. I still remember practicing yoga, wearing a turban and those tantric exercises, although those still come in handy with Vall."

Tortha turned pink again.

She smacked him on the shoulder, playfully. “You've been with those nieces of yours for too long, Tortha. Anyway, it's gotten worse ever since rock and racket became popular. Remember when every nightclub had to have their own ‘Elvis?’”

“What a headache for the Paracops! They were hi-jacking them from every subsector where that crazy noise was still undiscovered. For a while we had to guard that dumb hillbilly truck driver on a thousand time-lines. I'm still surprised we never designated a Presley Subsector!”

“Verkan's really never paid it any attention, because he doesn't hear or see what he doesn't like. I can't get through to my husband, because he's a snob—and I mean that lovingly—he just doesn't realize that everyone on Home Time Line doesn't have his class or taste. Well, it's worse now, since the Beatles. Not the insects, it's another noisy Europo-American singing combo. They're even noisier and louder than Elvis, if that's possible. And then there are the flat screen films and film stars—Marilyn Monroe, Clark Gable, Humphrey Bogart, and now James Dean—and art deco and all sorts of nonsense. Europo-America is—to paraphrase one of their aphorisms—the “cat's pajamas” and if Verkan doesn't quit this silly crusade of his he's going to derail his job and possibly the Paratime Police along with him.”

“Wow! Dalla,” Tortha replied, “you've just given me a needler shot of reality. Maybe we have the wrong Chief! I'm even worse than Verkan when it comes to these fads. And I never had any children, except you two—by proxy, of course—to teach me any different. I'll try to talk him into stalling this shutdown for a few decades until all this Europo-America sheep-dip becomes old hat. It will; I've seen half a dozen of these crazes just since I've been Chief. Meanwhile, you stay on top of these committees and study groups.”

“Good. I need something to keep me occupied while Verkan's glued to his Chief's chair. But what about you? What are you going to do?”

“Dalla, I don't know. Hang around the office, I guess, until Vall throws me out.”

“Well, I know two other people who need some help. And you would definitely be an asset to them.”

"Really. Who?"

"Rylla and Kalvan."

"I'm an ex-Paratimer. I can't deal in contamination—"

"Oh, stop being so huffy, Tortha. Hear me out. Sometimes you remind me so much of Verkan. The two of you! Anyway, you could give them moral support and be a Dutch uncle. I'm sure Verkan could come up with a suitable disguise. And don't tell me you're not interested—I see that smile."

"Dalla, that might very good idea. I'm curious myself to meet this Kalvan and his lady that I've heard so much about. And, with this Styphon's House Crusade, it sure won't be boring!"

"Tortha, you've just said a mouthful!" They both laughed.

XII

Great King Kalvan dismounted at the top of Gyrax Hill. While his dignity might require meeting King Nestros on horseback, his horse required a rest. The retreat of the Hostigi royal party from the left flank had been more speedy than dignified, over rough, muddy ground. A few of the Royal Horse Guard were still fishing themselves out from under bushes and rounding up their horses.

From the hilltop, Kalvan had his first good view of the battle in more than an hour. The nomad horde was large, maybe seventy-five to a hundred thousand warriors, a flood of men as hard for Ranjar Sargos to direct as for Kalvan to stop. Not much had changed, and that little for the better. The enemy's right and center, under Sargos, still overlapped the allied left. They had even advanced all the way to the redoubt on the banks of the Lydistros, then stopped among the caltrops and pitfalls, under the fire of the four-pounders Kalvan could spare for fixed defenses.

As far as Kalvan was concerned, Sargos could take his men halfway to the border.

On the allied right, masses of horsemen, light infantry (the only kind the horde had), and an occasional chariot surged back and forth. Each chief was giving his own orders to his followers and taking none from anyone else, including Sargos. They were the less dangerous but more numerous part of the enemy army, fifty thousand against Sargos' forty thousand, give or take a few boys.

They faced mostly Nestros' Trygathi, eight or nine thousand heavy horse, with twice that number of supporting infantry, spearmen, gallow-glasses, and missile troops: crossbowmen, archers, and some arquebusiers. They were stiffened by three Ulthori pike regiments, two regiments of Royal Musketeers, a battalion of riflemen, and two four-pounders. Not that the Trygathi needed much stiffening; they were fighting with the knowledge that they had a chance of victory and that meanwhile their homes were safe. The alliance with Hostigos had let Nestros leave a third of his army home to make raiders a poor insurance risk. The twenty-five thousand he had on the field were his best.

"Alkides," Kalvan called downhill. "Is the Flying Battery ready to move?"

"With Galzar's favor, yes," the smoke-blackened artillery general replied. "I wish the guns really did have wings. This cursed mud's going to butcher the horses!"

"Not half as fast as the guns will butcher Sargos' warriors," Kalvan called back. The gun crews cheered their Great King's words. There were only eight guns for the Flying Battery; three were in emplacements and one had been lost in a swamp on the Nyklos Trail. As much as he wished for another battery or two, with maybe some six-or eight- pounders, the Flying Battery was a far cry from the half-a-dozen catapults the enemy was using.

Kalvan walked over to General Alkides and asked quietly, "How is Great Captain Mylissos doing?" Nestros' chief of artillery had started the day a bit peevish over the council of war. It had been agreed that his ancient bombards would remain with the reserves, and not try to advance with the major attacks. Kalvan could even sympathize with him; after all, it was the first time in memory Mylissos actually had enough fireseed to fire his massive hooped-iron pipes more than once or twice without exhausting his magazines.

"A sight happier than he was, now that he's got targets and fireseed to burn on them. I think he shifted a couple of those twenty-pounders without orders, but I'm not complaining. A twenty-pounder loaded with rocks and old nails isn't something I would care to face!"

Kalvan would have said more, mostly to Aspasthar. The boy was fighting his first battle away from his father, riding with Alkides as one of his messengers. But the boy looked as if he would take the encouragement as an insult, and by Dralm, there were Nestros and his guards in their red and white colors coming up the other side of the hill!

By abandoning royal dignity and running back to his horse, Kalvan was mounted by the time Nestros reined in and hailed him.

"Greetings, friend and ally! We are smiting the horde as if the gods themselves fought for us!"

"So we are. Maybe, too hard. Corpses can't fight the Zarthani Knights. Thank somebody for Ranjar Sargos. He made the horde more dangerous, but if we had to take the surrender of every petty chief one at a time we'd be here until winter!"

A Hostigi messenger rode up and saluted both kings. "The lookouts in the Willow Spirit Grove report that Warlord Sargos is advancing on them."

"Tell them to wait as long as they can, and imitate a strong force meanwhile," Nestros said. "Then they can withdraw. Meanwhile, Sargos will be drawn forward. Perhaps we can meet him hand-to-hand!"

Kalvan and Captain-General Harmakros exchanged amused looks. Nestros was no fool; he was learning such Kalvan-style tricks as feints and deceptions almost hourly. He was also an old-style Trygathi warrior, whose highest ambition had to be meeting the opposing leader hand-to-hand and defeating him.

"As the gods will it," Harmakros said. Kalvan decided to let his Captain-General speak, even if protocol said he should be talking king-to-king. Even four-star generals needed something to take their minds off their sons' winning their spurs—or their shrouds.

"The gods willed that Sargos should be a tool," Nestros said cheerfully. "They also willed that Kalvan should come and bring his fireseed and strength to join ours. I think they will give us this one more small favor."

Kalvan doubted the accuracy of Nestros' description of his opponent. The Warlord had pulled his chariots back the moment he realized the ground was too muddy to let them get up speed. He still had his in reserve, while the other chiefs had mostly lost chariots, riders and teams together.

"Let the gods will that all our men hold their fire until they have a clear target, and that be an enemy," Kalvan said. "We have more fireseed than any army ever seen in the Trygath, but not enough to waste!"

"My men are not children," Nestros said with offended dignity.

"Then let the heralds sound for the advance," Kalvan said. Both kings looked at Harmakros; he signaled the trumpeter. The trumpet screeched, triggering the launching of two signal rockets.

When the green rockets rose into the sky over Gyrax Hill, six thousand reserve cavalry would be launched at the heart of Sargos' army.

Sargos flung a light lance high into the willow branches. A scream rewarded him; an enemy lookout toppled from his perch and lay writhing until an archer dispatched him with a knife.

The heavy thud of many horses on the move reached the Warlord over the noise of his warriors clearing the willow grove of enemies. Sargos jerked his horse around and drew his last lance from its leather bucket next to his right stirrup. His tribal guards followed suit, and the whole band streamed at a canter around the left side of the grove.

Ah, would that 1 had men to be my eyes and ears on parts of the field I cannot reach myself! Such is Kalvan's way, or so the prisoners have told us. Yet how could they reach me, in the midst of my foes, to bear their messages? To remain in the rear merely so that 1 may know more—that is a coward's way and no warrior would follow me.

A contrary voice in Sargos' mind muttered: Kalvan leads that way, as often as not, and who says that those who follow him are not warriors? Enough of yours are with the spirits after meeting them!

Clear of the willows, Sargos reined in and stared in disbelief. Down the hill in the enemy's center moved two mighty bands of armored horsemen, like vast steel-scaled serpents. At the head of each band floated banners, the red and white colors of King Nestros and the red and blue of King Kalvan.

So Kalvan will take his chance of joining the spirits today? Well and good. Warlord Ranjar Sargos stood tall in his stirrups. "Meet them at that hedge. Cydrak and Trancyles, ride like the wind and bring all the warriors Chiefs Hyphos and Ruflos can spare!"

The two were young men on fresh horses; they vanished in a spray of clods. Sargos drew his sword and adjusted his throat guard, his one piece of armor that was metal all through and through instead of metal over leather.

The sword hummed over his head as he whirled it. The day was too overcast for sunlight to shine on it, but those close by saw it and heard it humming. Their shouts told others what was happening, and the war cries rose until they seemed a solid wall across the front of the advancing foe.

Then Sargos lowered his sword and spurred his horse toward the hedge.

Only one of the green rockets flew high enough to be seen. That was enough. The cheers from both armies drowned out the trumpeters and captains like a hurricane drowning out a mouse's squeak.

Nestros was pointing frantically downhill. "There! Behind that hedge. Sargos forms his battle line. We must reach it before he brings up reinforcements."

Nestros couldn't have been in more of a hurry if he'd read Napoleon's maxim, "Ask me for anything but time." Once again he was doing the tactically sound things, out of a desire to cross swords with an enemy chief.

So be it, Kalvan thought.

No, wait a minute. If Nestros gets too far ahead of you, the Trygathi will say their Great King was braver than the Great King of Hos-Hostigos.

"Harmakros!" What would have been a shout under other circumstances was about as audible as a whisper.

The Captain-General reined in beside Kalvan. "Yes, Your Majesty?"

"You stay back here with the mobile command post. I have to charge with Nestros."

"That ass—" began Harmakros, who apparently thought better of using his trooper's vocabulary about an allied King, then mock-saluted. "As Your Majesty wishes."

Kalvan started to count off guards to ride with him, then saw Nestros and his heavies digging in their own spurs. This time Kalvan had to restrain his curses. Instead he signaled his own banner bearer and dug in his spurs.

The banner bearer took the reins in his teeth and drew his sword. Bearing the Great King's banner had been a much safer job than fighting in the front ranks—at least until today!

Sargos jumped his horse over a ditch and turned it, meanwhile drawing his last lance. To retreat was cowardly more often than not, but to stand with the men he had would not even slow the enemy. Like the Great River flooding over its banks, the enemy horse flowed on as if only the gods could stop them.

Archers were running up, but the range was still long. Against armored men they would waste most of their arrows. Against the enemy's horses, perhaps—

"Look, my chief!" Chief Ruflos was pointing. He had just arrived with a hundred and fifty men not six deep breaths ago. "My chief, the kings offer themselves to the gods!"

It was true. The two royal banners were forging steadily toward the head of the enemy horsemen. Under those banners, Sargos could now see tight bands of splendidly-armored men.

"They offer themselves to us!" Sargos snapped. He tried to quiet his own doubts. Have the kings had an omen, that the gods will give victory if they offer themselves as a sacrifice?

"Then let us take what is offered," Chief Ruflos said. He also sounded as if he wished to quiet inward fears.

Sargos patted his horse's neck and looked about him. The warriors he'd summoned were streaming toward him from all sides. Not all would be with him before he had to face the Kings, but the rest would follow to fling themselves upon the foe.

"Hoaa! Tonight we offer two Kings' heads, to the gods of our land and the spirits of our dead!"

The advance of the two Kings was turning into a race. Nestros reached the hedge first. Kalvan swerved without slowing, nearly colliding with his banner bearer. The trooper's sword pricked Kalvan's horse, who protested by nearly bucking his rider into a ditch.

By the time Kalvan had sorted himself out, Nestros was crossing swords with everyone in reach on the far side of the hedge. Nestros had won the race but not by enough to dishonor his ally. In fact, his ally was going to have a busy time in about two minutes, keeping this from being Nestros' first and last battle as Great-King-Elect. On both right and left, warriors were streaming toward the battle of the kings.

"Stands the standard of Great King Kalvan!" the banner bearer shouted. He thrust the butt end of the staff into the muddy ground and drew a pistol. The banner bearer pistoled the first warrior to come within lance-range, but the nomad stayed in the saddle. Kalvan shot him with his last loaded horse pistol, then drew his own sword and cut a second opponent across the face, a third in the arm.

After that Kalvan lost count of his opponents and all track of what he was doing to them. Somewhere in the next five minutes he managed one coherent thought that was not concerned with his own survival.

If I was fighting well-armored opponents, I'd be dead by now.

About five minutes after that, it struck him that armor might not make all that much difference. These nomads were damned hard to kill, like the Moro *juramentados* he had heard an Old Army veteran describe.

Come on, Alkides! Are you the Flying Battery or the Flighty Battery?

A moment later, Alkides' octet of four-pounders signaled their arrival with a blast of case shot that tore into the ranks of friends and foe with awful impartiality. A chunk of lead snapped the banner staff; the banner bearer dove to keep it from hitting the ground and sprawled with his nose digging up the mud. He held the banner clear of the ground, though.

Kalvan leaned down to pick up the banner, then found his horse sagging to one side. As the horse toppled, Kalvan leaped clear, the weight of his armor driving him to his knees. The horse fell on his side, blew blood from his nostrils, and died.

Kalvan waved his sword at the enemy and cursed Alkides' gunners, both emotionally satisfying if not very useful. At least the litter of dead men and horses around him included many more enemies than friends.

Let's hope to Galzar we didn't wing Nestros!

More cavalry were riding up, a second troops of Nestros' Bodyguard. Their captain reined in, shouting a request for orders.

'Look to your King!" Kalvan shouted back. "He's beyond the hedge. If you get no orders from him, advance cautiously five hundred paces."

"As Your Majesty commands, the captain called. "Will you be here?"

"Here or in Hadron's Realm!" was Kalvan's parting shot. The bodyguards cheered as their captain maneuvered his horse through the hedge.

Kalvan mentally crossed his fingers, hoping he had not sent away men he would need for his own protection. But no live enemies were within pistol shot that he could see, and Alkides' guns were now firing steadily. That meant Harmakros and the reserves had to be closer than any organized enemies.

He was safe enough, from his enemies. He wished he could say the same about Rylla's tongue.

When my lovely wife hears that I raced a Trygathi king into the enemy lines, the first thing she'll do is laugh herself silly. The second will be to remind me never to complain about her leading from in front again as long as I live!

XIII

Ranjar Sargos awoke with the sense that a blacksmith was driving a chisel into the side of his head. He stifled a groan and tried to reach to cradle the pain.

It was then Sargos discovered his hands were bound.

Outrage gave him a voice he would not have found otherwise. "Is this honor—to treat a warrior like a rebellious slave?"

At least that was what he had intended to say. From the blank looks on the faces around him, he suspected he had croaked like a frog.

A face Sargos remembered thrust itself forward, and the others gave way to either side. It was the last face he had seen before what appeared to be a thunderbolt crashed into the side of his head and flung him from his saddle.

"Ranjar Sargos! Who has bound you?"

"No one, Your Grace," a gray-bearded man said.

"Captain-General Mylissos, he did not bind his own hands!" snarled the man, who must be King Nestros. Nestros drew a fine, if somewhat mud-specked, dagger from his riding boots, knelt, and cut Sargos' bonds with his own hands.

"I trust your honor as I would my own or Great King Kalvan's," Nestros said. "You led your men most valiantly to the end, but the gods' favor was not with you. Yet if you are willing, you may win more in defeat than you could have gained by victory."

It seemed to Sargos that King Nestros was talking in riddles. Beyond him a tall man in fine armor stood, smoking a pipe and nodding slowly.

"Kalvan?" Sargos asked, pointing.

Nestros nodded.

So they have both come to gloat. No, that is not true. Nestros was truly angry with those who dishonored me.

"I have fallen, and doubtless those around me," Sargos said. "That does not mean victory for you or defeat for me."

"Your men from here to the redoubt are trapped against the Lydistros River," Nestros said. "The rest are fleeing. We are pursuing them, as wolves pursue rabbits. If you will sit down with us and discuss peace, we shall call off our pursuers and spare your trapped men. Otherwise, the Sastragath and the Sea of Grass alike will be lands of widows and orphans."

If he lies, he does so well. If he is telling the truth...but 1 must see for myself.

Sargos tried to rise. He not only failed, but would have fallen if Nestros and Kalvan both had not aided him.

To take healing from one's enemies is a sign of submission. Yet, if submitting will save those who swore to follow me...? Sargos knew from his days as a mercenary and as Warlord of the Great Horde that most casualties came not in battle, but in the headlong flight that followed defeat. Already too many of his people had died between the grindstones of the Black Knights and the two kings.

"Can you summon a healer and a horse? If I see with my own eyes what you have told me, then we shall talk."

The two kings nodded as if their heads were on a single neck.

The next morning Kalvan stepped out of the royal tent and nearly stumbled over Aspasthar. The boy woke up with a squeak of panic.

"Your Majesty!"

"Aspasthar, sleeping on watch is still a serious offense. Even after doing so well in your first battle."

"Your Majesty, I beg forgiveness. But my father came by and said he would watch in my place. He—"

A rumbling snore interrupted the page.

Kalvan looked into the shadows on the other side of the tent door and saw Captain-General Harmakros curled up under a blanket, even more soundly asleep than his son. Making sure that the armed sentries were all in place, Kalvan ducked back into his tent, burrowed into his piled baggage, and came out with a jug of Ermut's Best.

He raised his hand to quiet the panic-stricken boy. "I see your father. All is well."

By the time he came out of the tent, both his unofficial "sentries" were rubbing their eyes and yawning.

Harmakros did a double-take upon seeing his Great King. "Your Majesty, it is not the boy's fault. I relieved him of his duty, then fell asleep myself—"

"Don't berate yourself, Harmakros. There are other sentries, some of whom actually have slept within the past moon quarter. Think no more of it. I feel like celebrating, but I didn't want to drink alone."

"What about our friend and ally, Great King Nestros?" Harmakros asked.

"Please," Kalvan said. "Remember when I said it was all over but the shouting? I didn't know what I was saying. A discreet whisper for both

Nestros and Sargos is what you would use for drilling a whole regiment! I'd be as deaf as a gunner if we had any more private sessions. But, Dralm be blessed, that was the last one!"

"Then we have an alliance?"

"Signed, sealed and about to be delivered to Grand Master Soton. Sargos is no fool. The Zarthani Knights are the hereditary enemies of the Sastragathi. He'll fight them rather than anyone else if he has half a chance of victory. We are giving him much more than that."

"And the rest of the nomads?"

"Those sworn to Warlord Ranjar Sargos will follow us. The rest have half a moon to either join us or leave the Great Kingdom of Hos-Rathon. Nestros would like to make it a quarter moon, but he will swallow this."

"I imagine most men would swallow a lot more, to be a Great King."

"Likely enough," Kalvan replied. *Being a Great King must be the dream of everyone who doesn't know what a headache it is!*

Not to mention aches in other places. Kalvan couldn't recall having been out of the saddle for more than twenty minutes at a time from dawn until dusk. He could recall the fields three-deep in dead men and horses, and worse, those who weren't yet dead. He didn't want to recall them, but they had glued themselves to his memory.

Kalvan uncorked the jug and passed it to Harmakros. As the brandy gurgled, Kalvan added, "Even with what we have in hand now, we'll be leading a hundred thousand men south. That should be a real headache for our friend Soton—and no aspirin for it either!"

"Aspirin?"

"An alchemy potion from my homeland. Good for the headaches we'll surely have if we finish this jug."

"I'll gladly take the burden on myself, Your—"

"Hand that jug over, Harmakros, if you don't want to be charged with treason!"

XIV

Hadron Tharn knocked at the door, the peep-hole opened and a gravely voice asked, "The password?"

"Death to all Paratime Police."

The voice answered with a booming laugh. "That's a good one boss. Your 'friend' is already waiting in the privacy booth, like you requested."

Hadron, followed by Warntha Swarn, his personal bodyguard, entered the Blind Pig—one of a chain of speakeasies he owned—patterned on illegal bars on a Europo-American Subsector that had once attempted the 'apparently' noble, but futile, attempt to prohibit the consumption of alcoholic beverages. The effort had barely lasted two decades, glorified a group of sub-moronic gangsters and opened up the Sector to serious penetration by a number of First Level outtime firms.

The loud racket of some new outtime music called rock and roll washed over him. He grimaced, but noted in satisfaction that almost a quarter of the gyrating young people were wearing blue shirts and trousers. He could imagine their surprise if only they knew that the man 'they knew' as The Leader was present! He felt a wave of pleasure, knowing that they were at his beck and call should the need arise—although with Warntha at his back it was most unlikely.

Hadron motioned for Warntha to wait, while he tapped in his private access code on the privacy booth's terminal. The door opened to show a frightened, middle-aged man in a wig and some dark make-up on. A passable, but pathetic disguise.

"Tharn, are you crazy!" the man known as Landon Toldar, Vice President of the Opposition Party, shouted, as soon as the door closed. "If the Metropolitan Police ever found us together—"

"Shut your yap!" Hadron shouted, he liked to use the appropriate slang of whatever milieu he was in. It showed his uncanny ability to adapt to any period or background that he deigned to enter.

Not used to disrespect of any kind, Landon Toldar did just as he was told, Hadron noted to himself. He was not surprised; most First Level citizens were used to giving orders, not taking them and were easily intimidated. Especially those like Landon who were stay-at-homes and had never worked outtime.

In a loud whisper, as though they might be overheard—which was a laugh, Toldar continued. "Tharn, this is dangerous meeting in this part of town in a 'joint' that you own."

Tharn choked back a laugh at Landon's pathetic attempt to fit in. "This is just what the Metros expect from the eccentric Hadron Tharn. You should know, Landon, isn't that why you and the Party used me to head the 'Wizard Traders,' as my brother-in-law so colorfully described *our* Organization? Not to mention any pull that I might have with the Paratime Police is through my sister. Now, there's a laugh!"

Hadron could tell from the sweat beading on Landon's forehead that he had hit a nerve. He wasn't surprised; he'd spent most of his life cultivating his harmless, slightly mad image. If only they knew what really went on behind his masks— Well, someday they would. He had found his true calling almost two decades ago on a major off-shoot of Fourth Level Europo America, the Hitler Belt. There he met, using his disguise as the son of a wealthy South American German expatriate industrialist, Reinhardt Heydrich, one of the major architects behind the Third Reich. Heydrich had recognized a fellow soul mate and introduced him to the real minds behind Adolf Hitler—Goebbels, Himmler, Eichmann and others. That day, despite Landon's misconception, was the birth day of the Organization and his own incarnation as The Leader. He, too, knew his role: to bring order out of chaos and to rid Home Time Line of its own parasitic and outtime vermin—the proles.

Misinterpreting Hadron's silence as intimidation, Landon's voice grew more confident. "We told you to shut down the Organization, after the Paratime Police scoop. We can't afford to have any involvement with them; it would disgrace—if not destroy—the Party."

"Party be damned!" Tharn answered. He enjoyed the shocked expression on Landon's face; it secretly amused him the many ways others saw him. Only a chosen few—like Warntha—recognized and saw the real leader behind the facade.

"I did not create the Organization to fill the Party's coffers, despite you and your friends' misconceptions. Truth be known, ninety percent of the profits went into my own pockets; I've got wealth secreted away beyond your wildest imaginings."

"Why? How!" Landon looked like a man caught in the middle of Post-traumatic Paratemporal Shift Syndrome, as the Bureau of Psych-Hygiene would call it. "That money was for the Party so that we could finally evict Management from power and control the Executive Council and bring truly enlightened government to the First Level."

"Please spare me your Party cant, I've heard enough of it over the past decade! It's time you and your cohorts learned a few hard realities. "First of all, the Wizard Traders are still in business—"

"What! Are you trying to destroy us all? The Paratime Cops are onto the Organization; they've already captured several key figures. Half the Council members who disappeared or discorporated were Opposition Party members. What if they find a way around the narco-hypnotic blocks? Chief Verkan is no fool!"

At the mention of his hated brother-in-law, Tharn felt his blood beginning to boil. He took several deep breaths. *Focus on the moment,* he told himself. "That's not your concern." He neglected to tell Landon that he had come up with a much better method of dealing with Wizard Trader penetration or capture. All Organization members were now given a narco-hypnotic-command that stopped their hearts when facing imminent capture or detainment. Doctor Vermor claimed it paralyzed the Vagus nerve, which controlled the heart, or some such thing. All he knew was the demonstrations worked perfectly; dead men did not talk. "There will be no leaks from the Organization, I guarantee that."

Landon didn't look convinced.

"However, I'm not so sure I can count on the Opposition Party."

"We know how to keep our mouths shut, even if the Metros should come to suspect us. Men in our position do not get interrogated."

Tharn laughed! "Then you don't know my brother-in-law! In fact, as much as I hate to admit it, Verkan does possess some admirable characteristics, when compared to weaklings such as yourselves."

Once again Landon's jaw had dropped; it was getting to be a habit, Tharn thought. Maybe after all this was over he could find useful employment on some post-apocalypse Second Level world as a flycatcher! "As I was saying, the Wizard Traders are still in business. We still need more units, not only to fund your corrupt friends but to help finance The Leader."

"The Leader—you know how he is? He's doing more to destabilize the youth of our city than Verkan Vall himself, and this King Kalvan the media have chosen to make a hero out of!"

Hadron put on his mask, although he felt like screaming: *Who do you think The Leader is, you spineless jellyfish?* Instead, he said, "The Leader is but one more piece of the coalition to unseat Management Party and restore the Home Time Line to proper authority."

The familiar words seemed to calm Landon's fears as the color returned to his face. "Tharn, your rashness endangers all of us. However, the Party could use additional funds in the upcoming Dhergabar municipal elections. And, if as you say, the Organization is still in operation, we could use a 'donation' of half a million units."

It never ceased to amaze him how quickly political types could restore their equilibrium once they were on the familiar grounds of elections and Paratime Exchange Units. "It can be arranged. However, I didn't call you here just to arrange for a campaign donation. It's time to put some political and public pressure on Chief Verkan. Kalvan Prime is splitting into new time-lines. Verkan is endangering the Paratime Secret by protecting his friend King Kalvan—"

"That won't work, Tharn. The public is in love with this Great King Kalvan—he can do no wrong, at least, for now. If his ratings ever slip, then we may have some leverage. Right now every public station is broadcasting the latest Kalvan nonsense."

"Then hit Verkan from another angle. Log how much time he's personally spending on Kalvan Prime and show malfeasance of duty. I don't know; I can't do your job for you. YOU PEOPLE ARE THE OPPOSITION PARTY—" Hadron didn't realize how loud he was screaming until Landon put his hands over his ears.

"Do something, or you'll never see another unit from me—for this election or any other. And don't even think of threatening me, I'll take the whole Party down with me."

Hadron was pleased at how his remarks affected the Party hack; he was cringing with each word, as though he were wielding a nerve whip. He could see that his true self, The Leader, was at last beginning to emerge. The Opposition Party would not take him for granted again.

XV

"How many men does Kalvan now lead?" Grand Master Soton asked. He knew his voice was as high-pitched as the squeak of a new-hatched quail chick. He did not care. The number he thought he heard could not be what Knight Commander Aristocles had actually said.

"More than a hundred thousand men," Aristocles repeated. He sounded like a messenger bringing news so bad that he hardly cared if he was punished for bringing it.

Any gods worthy of their name would know that the news was bad. There was no fault in Aristocles for being unmanned by it. *Forgive me, old friend.*

"A hundred thousand," Soton repeated meditatively. "Is that the grand sum, or only those bound by oath to one of the three supreme leaders?"

"The second, Grand Master. The number of those who will march against us without being oath-bound is not small. It may exceed twenty-five thousand."

"That is very nearly all the rest of the great horde," Soton said. "Also, if the subjects of"—he could not shape his tongue to say Nestros' presumptuous new title —"the Pretender Nestros need not fear the nomads, all their garrisons will march south. Everyone will wish to be in at the death of the Zarthani Knights."

"Then they shall be disappointed, Grand Master. The audience may gather, but the players in the pageant are going to slip out the back door."

"Leaving all their tavern bills unpaid, of course. Are you thinking as I am?"

"What else makes any sense? We face odds of perhaps five to one. Two of those five are civilized soldiers under captains not to be despised, with more guns than have been seen west of the Pyromanes since fireseed was sent by Styphon! Half our strength are light troops or half-trained, or both."

This bald statement of the truth made it neither less nor more endurable. In the end, that did not matter, if one was the Grand Master and sworn to bear any burden in the name of the Order. Soton mentally ran over his mental army table of organization: fifteen Lances, comprised of nine thousand Order Brethren and two thousand auxiliaries; seven thousand levy, mostly Sastragathi mounted archers and lancers; and three to four thousand unreliable nomad light cavalry—who in a pinch might change sides or run off the field.

To stand and fight the great horde would be suicide. Yet it still seemed to Soton that his own death by Kalvan's hand would be easier to face than the orders he knew he would have to give before this campaign was done. Nor could he hope to find peace by seeking that or any other death.

To do that would be to cast the Order into the hands of Archpriest Roxthar, who in the name of Styphon would surely finish the work of destruction Kalvan had begun.

"We must be across the Lydistros within five days. Organize messengers and escorts to ride with word to Tarr-Ceros. The bridge of boats is to be ready within three days, or I personally will decorate the battlements of Tarr-Ceros with the heads of those who have delayed it."

"At once, Grand Master," Knight Commander Aristocles said. No one hearing him could have imagined this was one friend carrying out the wishes of another. "Ho, Heron! Summon Knight Commander Cyblon to the Grand Master's tent—at once!"

When he had heard the order repeated by his messenger, Aristocles turned back to Soton, hand on his sword hilt. Soton wondered if the tales of wizardry in Aristocles' sword had any truth to them. Certainly the sword was the better part of two centuries old. By grasping it in times of trouble, Aristocles appeared to soothe himself and sharpen his wits. Also, he had never suffered a sword wound on the battlefield. A half-score of weapons had left scars, but never a sword....

"Grand Master, what about sending some of our boats up the Lydistros to strike at Kalvan's barges?"

"With the river running as it must, after this rain? They would never be able to reach Kalvan's fleet and return in time."

Aristocles wished shameful and wasting diseases upon those who had sent the rains, finishing with some choice comments on the uselessness of Styphon's Archpriests and priests in general.

Soton shook his head. "Guard your tongue, for even I cannot save you from Archpriest Roxthar."

"Roxthar—" Aristocles began, in the same tone he would have used to speak of a pile of dung on his tent floor. Then he took a deep breath. "Roxthar serves Styphon with holy zeal. Doubtless he has done all that mortal men could do even with Styphon's favor. "Yet, I could still wish the rains had not come."

"The gods give with one hand, and take away with the other," Soton replied, glad for the opportunity to change the subject from priestly politics to other less dangerous topics—like war. "The wet ground and flooding will slow pursuit.

"Also, we know the Lydistros River. Kalvan does not. It will take much luck and more boats than he is likely to have just to cross the river. While he is trying to cross, *then* we can attack his fleet."

Conversation died for a while as the messengers rode up to receive their orders. Soton's servants took the opportunity to light the lamps in the tent, sweep the latest coat of dried mud from the floor and ask the Grand Master what he wished for dinner.

"Kalvan's heart," Soton said sharply. "If you cannot produce that, whatever is ready to hand."

The servants departed; Aristocles poured the last wine from a jug into the two least dirty cups in the tent.

"Another message, I think," Soton said after the first swallow. "To the Commander of Tarr-Ceros, to prepare it in all respects for a siege."

"Holding our whole host?"

"Hardly," Soton replied. "We will send to Tarr-Ceros as many as

Knight Commander Democles believes he can house and feed for a moon or two. The rest will fall back on Tarr-Lydra and Tarr-Tyros.

"Then we can pray that Kalvan will cross the Lydistros. Once his men have dug themselves into the hills around Tarr-Ceros, they will be like bears tethered in a pit. We will be the dogs, free to move where we will and strike when we think wise. Oh, the bear will take a lot to kill, but we will have him in the end."

It was an improbable vision, unless Kalvan lost his wits, but for a moment it warmed Soton more than the wine. Then he sobered:

"We must keep well ahead of Kalvan. That means lightening ourselves as much as possible. All the artillery, all the spare armor, all the horse bardings—"

"That makes Kalvan a free gift, Soton."

"But a lesser gift than the whole Order! Besides, the gold of Balph can buy blacksmiths to make new armor, saddlers to fit our horses, iron and bronze to recast the cannon. It cannot buy good men. If we save the men, nothing else matters. Nothing!"

Aristocles' eyes over the rim of his wine cup made all the answer Soton needed. He lifted his own cup and drank again.

XVI

Summer heat had come as the united host moved south toward the Lydistros River. The rain had not stopped completely, but it had diminished. So had the depth of the streams and the mud. While saddling up that morning, Kalvan had received a message from General Alkides, who had ridden ahead to the banks of the Lydistros (what Kalvan had once known as the Ohio) to meet the boats coming downriver from Kyblos.

"The high water has left no shallows and few rapids. It has also left less dry ground than one could wish. However, we may thank the gods for this, too. Prisoners say that the Zarthani Knights have withdrawn most of their river galleys and other vessels to Tarr-Ceros."

Thank the gods indeed. Counting bottoms, the Zarthani Knights had the second-largest navy here-and-now. Few of their ships could navigate beyond the mouths of the Great River, but they didn't need to. The rivers of the Sastragath, the Dellos (Tennessee) and Ellystros (Alabama) systems were their domain.

Harmakros was less grateful for what he saw as dubious favors. "His Grand Craftiness Soton may just be planning to lure us across the river. Then he can strike with us bogged down before the great fortress of Tarr-Ceros with the river at our backs."

"We'll play that one by ear when we reach the Lydistros,' Kalvan said. "Meanwhile, I won't have to answer to the Ulthori and Kyblosi for wrecked boats and drowned subjects."

"Your Majesty, with all due respect," Captain-General Harmakros said, "I suggest we decide beforehand. Right now the Sastragathi see us as a gift from the gods. We give them hope of final vengeance on their ancient foes. If we don't cross the Lydistros and besiege Tarr-Ceros, the alliance may wash away down the river with the downed trees and dead pigs."

"We shall see," Kalvan remembered replying. Now he wished he'd delayed his mounting-up to question Harmakros more closely. He should have remembered that Harmakros had commanded Sastragathi irregulars in the original Army of Observation, during the Year of the Wolf. The Captain-General knew more about handling them than his Great King, who was so damned tired he forgot to listen to advice even when he had it ready to hand.

Now sheet lightning played along the darkening sparks of light from the mountain of armor and equipment left by the fleeing Knights. There was enough here to equip an army, and that fact hadn't escaped the nomad warriors. They were swarming over the pile like ants on a heap of sugar.

Shouts of anger joined the shouts of triumph. Kalvan recognized Trygathi accents. He signaled to Colonel Kronos, his aide-de-camp. "Take two troops of the Royal Horse Guard and find out what's happening down there!"

Kronos took sixty men, leaving the rest around Kalvan. The Great

King dismounted to spare his horse. If the united host didn't end its campaign with everybody walking and half of them barefoot (half of those who'd had shoes to begin with, that is), it would be Galzar's own miracle.

Harmakros and Aspasthar rode up as the shouts reached a climax, then faded. A messenger breasted the hill, flinging himself out of his saddle as he reached Kalvan.

"Your Majesty, the Sastragathi wish to claim all the Knights' gear, against your orders. They say they're under orders from Warlord Sargos, and you had promised them first choice."

"Dralm-damnit!" Kalvan growled. "First choice" was a fair offer to the unarmored, sometimes unclothed nomads. It wasn't the same as "everything," but try to tell that to a Sastragathi warrior! It was like telling a wolf to take only one bite.

Captain-General Harmakros was carefully avoiding looking at his Great King. Then he turned in the saddle, and Kalvan saw his I-told-you-so expression, quickly replaced by surprise. A moment later Kalvan knew he must be matching expressions with Harmakros.

The Warlord rode at the head of a gaggle of his guards and subchiefs. Maybe they thought they were keeping a precise formation, but Kalvan couldn't tell which was the main body and which were the stragglers—

"Great King Kalvan! Is this the way you keep your promise to the clans? Your men have laid hands on mine, to keep them from their due. A treasure lies down there! Will you have us put it to use, or have a blood-feud with the tribes and clans?"

"I might ask you the same question," Kalvan replied, more patiently than he felt. Not all of the impatience was with Sargos either. "If blood has been shed, it was without my orders or consent. And against my will. Those who shed the blood of tribesmen will be punished (*tough luck, Kronos, but you were sent to find out what the trouble was, not make it worse)* and a blood-price will be paid."

"Will blood money guard the backs of men from the Knights' swords?" someone cried in a high-pitched voice. Kalvan saw that Sargos' teenage son Larkander was riding with his father tonight.

"No," Kalvan answered, raising his voice to keep the argument from turning into a mob scene. There was too much steel and firepower to make this safe; one hothead could blow the alliance sky high.

"No," he repeated, when Kalvan saw the nomads were giving him at least half the attention a Great King deserved. "Yet not all the bare backs are tribesmen. Will not the men of the Trygath fight better against our common foe with armor and weapons from the pile down there?"

"We of the tribes have fought the Black Knights longer," someone said.

"This is well known. Yet if the Zarthani Knights are cast down from their castles and the land cleansed of Styphon's minions, who loses? If they survive to fight us again, who wins? Let us join together and fight as one band."

Kalvan rested his hand on the butt of his pistol. It was a presentation weapon from the Gunsmith's Guild, an unsuccessful effort to prove they could produce elegant weapons quickly. It was a weapon Kalvan carried only when he wasn't riding with the vanguard.

"Let us divide the loot into two piles, one for the clansmen and one for the Trygathi. Then let each chief judge those most in need and give them their pick." This would cost them more than a day's travel time, (he could almost hear Soton's chuckle), but if it would keep his so-called allies from each other's throats, it would be worth the delay.

"I will begin the first pile with this pistol of mine. Whoever carries it, Trygathi or clansmen, he will carry it with my blessing. So speaks—"

"He seeks our Warlord's life!" somebody shouted. Kalvan's hand completed the drawing of the pistol before his ears could signal his mind to stop the motion. Then the sky appeared to fall upon him, a sky consisting of armored bodies.

Two shots crashed overhead, followed by a scream, a babble of curses and war cries, and Harmakros roaring above everything, "Take the bastard alive!"

The weight lifted from Kalvan, enough to let him draw breath for cursing. There was an audible sigh of relief from his Horse Guard. He spat out mud and grass, then rose to his knees. A Sastragathi subchief was on his back, with Aspasthar kneeling on one arm and several hefty

Sastragathi warriors holding other portions of the chief's anatomy—none too gently.

"What the Styphon—?"

Warlord Sargos answered. "This fool thought you sought my life. He drew a pistol. Your war leader's son seized his arm so that his shot went wide of you. It struck my son in the arm. Yet with his other hand he joined—Aspasthar—in dragging the fool from his saddle."

"There is more, Father," Larkander said. "Aspasthar shed blood too in the fight, and it mingled with mine."

"You are blood-brothers?" Both fathers seemed to speak at once, then looked at each other. Kalvan swallowed a laugh; he knew just enough about the Sastragathi to know that blood-brotherhood was a deadly serious business among them.

"It is an omen!" cried out one of the chiefs.

"This seems to be so," Larkander said. His voice was no longer high-pitched, but he was holding his arm against his side. His father's face was as white as if he'd seen a premonition of his own death.

Since nobody else seemed to have the wits to do so, it fell on Kalvan to call an Uncle Wolf to tend to the wound. The question of dividing the booty dropped from everyone's mind until both Larkander's arm and the subchief's were tightly bound.

"Question him rigorously," Sargos ordered. "It must be known, whether he was only a witling or a tool of Styphon's House."

Kalvan relaxed. If Sargos was ready to torture one of his own captains to help the alliance, the worst danger of the split was already past. *Note: Have to give Aspasthar something really impressive as a reward—consulting with his father and blood-brother first, of course.*

As the subchief was carried off, Sargos dismounted. He almost stumbled as he touched the ground. Kalvan realized that the Sastragathi Warlord had driven himself to the edge of exhaustion.

"I don't think our dignity will suffer if we sit down and share some wine." Kalvan wanted to wash the grit and grass out from between his teeth. Sargos looked ready to lie down and sleep for a week.

Well, the man is in his forties. He'd probably be just as happy if being

Warlord of the Sastragathi was a headquarters job, in a headquarters equipped with cool ale and warm women.

That brought to Kalvan's mind a picture of his own warm woman. He wondered what Rylla was doing. Her last letter had promised to take no drastic action against the Harphaxi unless provoked, but to patrol the borders heavily and keep the Army of Hostigos ready to move swiftly.

Knowing Rylla, Kalvan knew far too well how "border patrols" could be turned into scouts, and they into an invasion. From five hundred miles away, however, he couldn't do much but hope and consider learning how to pray.

XVII

From the grim look on Knight Commander Aristocles' face, Soton knew he was the bearer of more bad news. The Great Master's first thought was that it was too early in the morning to hear any more.

When he had heard Aristocles out, Soton realized there was no time of the day or night fit for the hearing of such a tale. Kalvan was driving his host on as though he truly had demons at his command to put them in fear. The vanguard was already past Xenos Town, two whole days before Soton had expected them.

"That means they will be up with us in their full strength before we reach Tryphlon."

Aristocles nodded. "Unless they can be delayed."

"By whom?"

The two men looked at each other. The both knew the answer. The rearmost four Lances would have to stand, fight, and most probably die to the last man—like the three Lances at the Battle of Chothros Heights.

"Who is senior Commander among of the rear?"

"Drakmos, of the Sixteenth Lance."

"May Kalvan's own demons flay him alive!"

Aristocles looked startled.

Soton knew that some of the agony he felt must have shown in his voice. "No, it's just that I am growing weary of sending friends to die."

"We could send another—"

"That would take time, which we do not have. His learning the land where he must stand would take more time. Besides, Drakmos would never abandon the Sixteenth." *You are doomed, old friend,* he thought. *All I can do is let you die with honor, as you have lived.*

Soton looked at Aristocles. The hard-bitten Knight Commander was a trusty right arm, a fine captain, and more often than not a wise counselor. Yet he had not been among the company of youths to whose ranks had come one day a peasant boy, small of stature but with an ambition to be a knight burning bright enough for six giants.

Some of the boys had bullied Soton in practice bouts, with wooden weapons or unarmed. Others had held back, out of pity for so small an opponent with such a large and clearly foredoomed ambition. Only Drakmos had done neither, giving Soton his best and taking Soton's best in return. Since Drakmos had been the best fighter among the youths, Soton learned more from the bouts with him than from all the others put together. It would not be too much to say that Soton's own prowess on the battlefield, which had saved his life a dozen times over, was in large measure Drakmos' gift.

And now Soton was repaying the gift of life with one of death. An honorable death, to be sure, but there was something to be said for an honorable life.

"Summon a messenger," Soton growled, to hide his urge to scream curses to Kalvan, the gods, and anyone else who had brought this about. Himself included, since it was his plan that Kalvan had turned so neatly and dropped upon his head! "Drakmos is to attack Kalvan's main body and keep on attacking until he has drawn that main body onto himself. We need not fear barbarians or light-cavalry scouts sent on ahead."

It hardly needed saying that the barbarians and scouts in advance of Kalvan's great host would cut off what little chance of retreat Drakmos and his Lances had. To balance the odds, Soton added, "We will leave a thousand of our Auxiliary light horses and all our Sastragathi irregulars."

The Sastragathi would probably all desert before Kalvan was within a day's ride, but the Auxiliaries would keep Drakmos from being stung to death by the light nomad cavalry. It was the least he could do.

"More orders," Soton snapped. "All the baggage, everything except a man's weapons and what he wears on his back, is to be left for Drakmos."

Aristocles' eyes were eloquent. Soton shrugged. "Drakmos will need what supplies we have left. For the rest of us, it is as true now as when I said it before. Styphon's gold can buy new armor, new tents, new fireseed, before the snow falls. If we lose the many more seasoned Knights, not all the gold of Balph will be able to rebuild the Order before Kalvan has crushed and cast down Styphon's House on Earth. If we do not think to the future, there will be none."

But there will be a large debt to pay, Kalvan Servant of Demons. A very large debt indeed.

XVIII

"Toss oars!"

The cry floated up from the boat on the muddy river to the hill where Kalvan stood gazing at Tarr-Ceros. The great fortress of the Order of the Zarthani Knights marched across nearly a mile of hills on the far side of the river. Some of those hills had clearly been flattened, others carved into the fortress's outworks. Kalvan counted three concentric layers of trenches and wooden palisades, each furnished with artillery positions and covered ways to let ammunition and reinforcements come up.

The stone walls only began beyond the trenches, rising like seats in a theater up the central hill to the massive keep in the middle. Two, maybe three, concentric circles of walls, each with its own moat and array of towers. Armor and guns glinted from the towers and the walls alike.

In the center the keep rose a good hundred feet above the highest tower. And were Kalvan's eyes playing tricks on him, or was the keep faced with something shiny? Marble? There were marble quarries up near the head of the Tennessee River in his own world; why not here? Certainly water transportation for the marble wouldn't have given the Knights any problem, not with their river fleet.

Marble was not the stone Kalvan would have chosen for a fortress. Under artillery fire, it would splinter and the splinters scatter like shell fragments.

But then, Tarr-Ceros had been built when the Zarthani Knights had no enemies who could bring artillery against their citadel. Until recently, neither the tribes nor the Trygathi had much to bring against Tarr-Ceros except numbers, archery, a few arquebuses and the odd wrought-iron four-pounder.

Kalvan signaled to the horse holders, who led Harmakros' mount and those of his aides down to the bank. So far the Tarr-Ceros garrison had paid their visitors less attention than cockroaches. If they changed their mind, some of the guns in the outer fortifications could certainly reach across the river.

Harmakros held his horse to a walk as he led his party up the muddy hillside, then reined in and saluted his Great King. The Captain-General's face was grimmer than ever, and far more than could be blamed on fatigue and the strain of a long campaign.

"Your Majesty, that floating barrier of spiked logs is no tale. There's no way through to the quay until the logs are removed."

"How long would that take?"

"With a few tarred barrels of fireseed and no enemy fire, an hour of any night. But they've got tarpots and what looks like bundles of arrows all laid out in the trenches right behind the quay. They could light up the engineers and pick them off like rats in a kitchen corner. Even if the barrier went, the trenches would be manned and ready for the landing party. "

"So going for the quay would be a waste, even as a feint?"

"The Knights would get a good laugh and we would get a bloody nose,' Harmakros said morosely.

He did not put into words what his tone added: *"And there is no need to send anyone up under the guns of the fortress to learn this. Once Your Majesty decides it has to be done, it becomes my duty. But if I don't have any more such duties for a while, it won't break my heart."*

"Harmakros, for at least the hundredth time—well done. If we find ourselves with a vacant Princedom, would you consider taking it?"

"Once Your Majesty doesn't need my services in the field, I won't say no. But I have a bad feeling that besieging Tar Ceros is going to take a long time. We've driven the badger into his lair."

Kalvan nodded. "The Grand Master spent several of his Lances to delay our progress so that he and most of his Knights could return to this fortress. Do we have any way of getting Soton out and taking his hide home?"

Again, tone spoke volumes, when Harmakros replied:

"Galzar Wolfhead might knock down those walls with his Mace, but nothing we have will even come close. As for a siege, unless you have figured a way to feed any army on air, forget it.

Harmakros was right. Kalvan had known as much the moment he'd laid eyes on Tarr-Ceros. It reminded him of one of the great Crusader castles in the Holy Land—but an aerial photo of a ruin didn't give the full picture. You had to see one of those stone monsters armed and garrisoned and intact, looming over you, ready to defy the worst you could do. And when that worst wasn't enough to do more than give the garrison a few sleepless weeks…what then?

There wasn't a gun in the Hostigi artillery stockpile that could both be moved here and make an impression on the walls. There wasn't enough food to keep a third of the allied host alive long enough to make the Knights tighten their belts. A simple attempt to storm the place would kill half the attackers and demoralize the rest.

Summon Soton to negotiate? That at least would waste only breath, not blood. Grand Master Soton knew the strength of his walls and the men who manned them. Probably less than half his garrison were seasoned fighters, but behind those walls children with croquet mallets could be deadly foes.

"Well, then, we can't do much at their front door," Kalvan said. "Let's wait until the scouts to the east and south return with their reports. If it's good cavalry country, maybe we can do something in his backyard."

That something was likely to be expensive in time, treasure, fireseed, horses and blood—but it had to be discussed. The rest of the allies had very little notion of what a hollow victory they had won. They only knew that they'd seen the Knights in retreat for the better part of a moon. The final battle against the four Lances of the rearguard had given them a taste for Knights' blood—they wanted more.

Kalvan remembered Napoleon's dictum about the advantages of making war against allies. Soton could wield his Knights as a single weapon, like his famous war hammer. Kalvan had to be chairman of a committee as much as a commander-in-chief.

One would think that the last battle would have made even a Sastragathi chief realize that the Knights' blood didn't come cheap. The four Lances and their support troops had numbered perhaps three to four thousand men at the outset; perhaps one hundred and fifty wounded prisoners survived. The allies lost more than eight thousand men, not counting the wounded, and that was with the advantage of artillery.

At least General Alkides had all the horse artillery ready to move. Where cavalry could go, the guns could follow. Something might be made of this—not much, but enough to keep the alliance from falling apart because the Sastragathi barbarians believed Great King of Hos-Hostigos had abandoned his allies!

Something else that might help, even more than artillery, at least right now—

"Harmakros, I forgot. Did we save any of that wine we picked up with the first batch of loot?"

"I had one of the barrels drawn off into flasks and loaded on pack mules under a trusted petty-captain.

"I reckoned we might have a use for it. Another job well done. I think we're going to call a Council of War. Just a small one, so I think one barrel should be enough to keep even Sargos happy." *At least until he finds out that he's still going to have the Knights on his borders, almost as strong as ever and out for vengeance.*

"Then there is *nothing* more we can do against those fatherless Knights?" Sargos glared at the men present in Kalvan's tent as if ready to challenge any king or captain present to personal combat.

Maybe he is. Kalvan began to think that breaking out the best wine hadn't been the best idea. Sargos had grown increasingly belligerent instead of mellow.

"Not *nothing*," Harmakros said, with the air of a man trying for the twentieth time to persuade a stubborn child to go to bed. But we can't knock down the walls of Tarr-Ceros or besiege it long enough to do any good. What else is there is what we need to ask."

Sargos emptied the last of a jug into his cup and looked into the ruddy depths. He seemed to find wisdom or at least a better-guarded tongue there.

"Nothing that will end the Knights for all time, I suppose. But is there anything else worth doing?"

"Yes," Great King Nestros said. Nestros wore a gold circled crown set with turquoise picked up from the Knights' baggage and hastily set into place by an armorer. "Anything that will keep the Knights quiet for a year or two will be almost as good. United, with no enemies at our backs, we're their match. We know it, they know it and none of us is going to forget it soon. Let us do something to make them remember it as long as possible."

Several faces around the tent wore, "Yes, but what?" expressions. It was time for the god-sent Great King Kalvan to take a hand. The rest had finally wrangled themselves into being ready to listen.

"Now a lot of what we can do depends on how long we can keep the boats and barges in range of Tarr-Ceros—"

"Oh, demons fly away with those boats and barges!" Sargos growled. "If they won't let us destroy the Knights, what good are they?"

"If we have half a moon, we can destroy the Knights' lands," Kalvan answered. "Alkides, do you think we have that much time?"

The grizzled artillery officer sucked on his pipe and released a small cloud of smoke. "Your Majesty, with guns mounted in the right places, I suspect we can keep off anything short of all the galleys at once. That's using mostly the Trygathi bombards, which wouldn't be much good in the field anyway."

Sargos looked ready to curse the boats and barges again, but Kalvan fixed him with a sharp look. "Warlord Sargos, those watercraft are like herds or chosen warriors to the Princes of Kyblos and Ulthor. Would any of your chieftains thank you if you lost all his horses or two score of his best warriors?"

Sargos appeared to ponder the question and came up with an answer that at least kept him quiet. Kalvan signaled to Harmakros, who handed him a map of the area around Tarr-Ceros. It was a rough map, but it was a historical document—the first here-and-now map ever drawn on paper. (There was also a second copy, on the more usual, not to say durable, deerskin.)

"The Knights have left a belt of forest around their fortress, between them and the lands that raise their food and horses. They've always relied on the forest to let their light-armed troops delay an enemy while the heavies moved in.

"Now suppose we throw two forces across the river. One infantry, with light artillery support. They'll hold the forest belt, keeping the Knights *in* instead of enemies *out.* I'll wager half the Treasury of Balph it will take even Soton a while to figure out what to do about that."

"Yes, yes!" Sargos cried. Eagerness crackled in his voice. "Our archers are without peer. Given time to hide themselves, they can hold the forest—"

"Boast about your archers when they've proved themselves!" Nestros snapped. "We of the Trygath are no children with our crossbows, as you yourself—"

"Hold!" Kalvan shouted. "There will be enough Knights to go around, I am sure. To the archer or crossbowman who kills the most, I will personally give ten Hostigos gold crowns and a weapon of his choice. Alkides, can you move your four-pounders in that kind of wooded country?"

"With a little help from Galzar and a lot of help from men who aren't afraid to drag a gun—"

The two allied rulers couldn't promise their help fast enough.

"The second force will be cavalry. It isn't intended to stand and fight. It's going to burn out every farm and village, run off every head of livestock, terrorize every peasant it can reach. If the Knights come out, they will have to fight their way through their own forest belt. If they stay in Tarr-Ceros, they will have to watch their peasants, crops and herds laid waste.

"They can get some supplies from upriver, but not all. It will be a lean winter and a lean couple of years for the Knights. Soton will gladly march the Knights out in their breechcloths with clubs if all else fails, but they won't be nearly so formidable."

The picture made the others in the tent smile. Harmakros produced another jug and began to pass it around. When the jug reached Sargos, he held it high in the air. "To the best ally a man could have in this lifetime—Great King Kalvan!"

XIX

"It's beginning to appear, Vall," Paratime Commissioner Tortha Karf said, "that you're more interested in playing Colonel Verkan of the Hos-Hostigos Mounted Rifles than you are in being Chief of the Paratime Police."

"That's hitting below the belt, Tortha," Verkan said, running his fingers through his blond beard. "I know I haven't been back on Home Time Line for more than a two ten-days, but it's imperative that I establish my cover in Greffa as Verkan the trader. If I don't, one of these days some Grefftscharrer merchant is going to arrive in Hostigos Town and someone's going to ask him about the merchant prince Verkan and he's going to go 'Verkan who?' Then, not only will two years hard work be plunged down the drain, but also the Paratime Secret itself will be endangered, along with Great King Kalvan and his family. You know how those Dhergabar University Professors would like to get their hands on a 'noble savage' like Kalvan and pick him apart in one of their Mentalist labs."

Tortha nodded his head in agreement.

The Paratime Secret was the keystone of First Level civilization. The only inflexible law concerning outtime activities was that the secret of

Paratemporal Transposition must be kept inviolate. Home Time Line was the ultimate parasite culture, secretly drawing off the resources and population of tens of thousands of other time-lines. A little here, a little there, but not enough to really hurt anyone. But unfortunately, maybe even tragically, that secret would be discovered on another time-line someday, just as Kalvan had brought an end to Styphon's House fireseed secret and monopoly by re-inventing gunpowder and then telling everyone about it—even his enemies! Which had made him many friends as well as the nemesis of Styphon's House.

When the Paratemporal Transposition secret—a thousand times more complex than the fireseed mystery—was broken; well, it wasn't too much to say that fate and welfare of ten billion Home Time Liners would depend upon the reflexes and ruthlessness of the Paratime Police.

"Verkan, it appears to me you've got a bad case of Outtime Identification Syndrome. As you yourself know, it happens to the best of Paratimers. But don't forget that for twelve millennia First Level civilization has depended on being able to secretly draw upon the resources of millions of alternate time-lines and we can't afford to let any one man—not even the Paratime Chief of Police!—put our way of life in jeopardy. One of these days you're going to have to make a choice between loyalty to a friend and your natural loyalty to the Home Time Line.

"If it ever comes to the point where King Kalvan or his subjects come between you and your job as Paratime Chief of Police, then I'll be the first to recommend the Paratime Commission that you be cashiered from your job." Tortha removed a cigarette from its pack and had to will his fingers to keep them from trembling as he lit up.

"Tortha, you know me better than that. You're the one who talked me into taking over as your replacement! My duty to the force comes first, before everything. Ask Dalla. Yes, I admire Kalvan; he's taken the tiny Princedom of Hostigos and turned it into a first class outfit. Without any real help from me, I might add. And, as much as I admire and like Kalvan, Rylla, Ptosphes, Harmakros, and the rest, I have no desire to go native and throw away three hundred years of longevity just to live a simpler, more honest way of life."

The wistful tone Tortha heard in Vall's voice indicated to him that on some deeper mental level Verkan might be quite willing to do just that, but Tortha couldn't see anything to be gained by picking at that particular scab. He'd just have to keep a closer eye on Verkan, try to help take some of the pressure off and then be ready to jump in whenever it appeared that the Chief's judgment was going awry.

"How is Dalla's work on the Fourth Level Europo-American Study Group going?"

Verkan laughed. "To listen to my wife talk you'd think she'd been shut up in the Innermost Circle at Balph and been forced to listen to one of Archpriest Roxthar's tirades for a year of ten-days! She's not sure what's worse, listening to the representatives from Tharmax Trading and Consolidated Outtime Foodstuffs pleas for open 'trade' lines, or the University cliques talk of the inevitability of outtime social interests conflicting with Home Time Line politics until First Level civilization embraces the benefits of post-industrial socialism, or some such garbage."

"Good, it's going just about as we expected. As long as they keep arguing semantics and ideology they'll never get down to what the Study Group is all about, a full embargo on Fourth Level, Europo-American. That will leave you and the Paratime Commission free to do what has to be done when the time comes. Although, I want to tell you that I hope it never comes. Without a Code Red situation, or all out nuclear slugfest, shutting down Europo-America may not be politically feasible—"

"What you too, Tortha? I get enough of that from Dalla."

"Well, maybe in this case, it might not hurt to listen. We get a lot of everyday products from that Sector, like the cigarettes I'm smoking."

"It would be inconvenient to relocate our sources of supply, but it could be done, Verkan answered. "I can't think of anything critical to First Level life or civilization, though."

"The Europo-America Sector has caught the public's fancy. They're behind the flat screen film craze and are the supplier of that hideous 'rock and roll' music that's been jamming the airwaves."

Verkan's eyebrows shot up. "The first time I heard that jangle of atonal sound waves, I thought I'd tuned into a cat fight."

"Verkan, just listen to yourself! You sound just like me: it must be that crazy horseshoe desk. Or the responsibility of protecting ten billion contrary timeliners who don't always know their own best interests."

Verkan shook his head. "I don't know how you kept going for so long."

"Maybe, just maybe, because I thought I was doing really important work."

"That doesn't sound like you, Tortha. Getting tired of that Fifth Level truck farm in Sicily already?"

"Actually, it's been so dull there this past year I've taken to watching Fifth Level Prole soap-operas."

Verkan shuddered in mock horror. "The only two things worse than prole soap-operas would be either attending an administrator's conference at Dhergabar University, or one of the Kalvan Study Team's argue-fests at the Royal Foundry in Hos-Hostigos."

Tortha laughed. "Actually, I wanted to talk to you about a cover story for a trip to Kalvan Prime."

"That's a wonderful idea. Kalvan and Rylla can use all the help they can get."

"Well, I'm not a military genius, or engineer—"

"I didn't mean that kind of help, Tortha. They need a good shoulder to lean on now, especially since Price Ptosphes took a mortal wound at Tenabra."

"I didn't know he was shot."

"Not that kind of wound—it's worse, he's stopped believing in himself. And that's the most terrible thing that can happen to a man like Ptosphes. There aren't a lot of people in Hostigos Kalvan can really talk with and you might be the best medicine he could get. I know how you've helped me over the years."

"Just my job, Vall." Tortha pulled a pack of Camels out of his pocket and reached for Verkan's tinderbox.

"We both know better. It wouldn't be wise to make you a Grefftscharrer merchant, too. Xiphlon's far enough away that no one in the Northern Kingdoms knows much about it, and it's in a bit of a bind. Another of those Aztec empires—the Zarthani call them the Mexicotal—that crops up on one Fourth Level, Europo-America time-line after another is trying to move their cannibalism racket into the Middle Kingdoms. Somebody's been selling them 'fireseed'—another local term for gunpowder—and last I checked they had some huge slave trains dragging these antiquated hundred and two hundred pound siege guns, old hooped iron bombards, to try and blast through the great walls. The Mexicotal are not familiar enough with gunpowder weapons to know that those stone balls will do about as much damage to the walls of Xiphlon as their ceremonial obsidian blades do on plate armor!

"Xiphlon is one of the most 'civilized' cities in the northern hemisphere. The city reminds me of Byzantium on Europo-America, Alexandria-Roman. Huge outworks and walls as thick as the Great Wall of China and almost as tall, made of quarry stone that must have been transported by river barges for a hundred years. Very sophisticated inhabitants, they've done it all, seen it all and know it all. The city has been besieged a dozen times; they're got fresh water cisterns and provisions enough for a ten-year siege. Right now Xiphlon's biggest problem is all the trade and portage business they're losing. I wouldn't be surprised that after the Mexicotal have picked up their pieces and gone home, the High King of Xiphlon doesn't try and hire Kalvan to take his army down to their capital and teach those heart-stabbing barbarians a thing or two about gunpowder diplomacy!"

Tortha blew a series of smoke rings. "Sounds like my kind of place. I'll make a covert visit there, first, so I can familiarize myself with the city layout and find a place to set up my cover story."

"Great idea. I'll get Kirv to send in a team to help you. After you leave, they'll stay behind and establish a deep cover. Fortunately, these Middle Kingdom merchants do more traveling than a Paratime Policeman."

Tortha smiled. "This sounds like fun. Do you know how long it's been since I went undercover outtime? No, don't even try to answer."

Verkan laughed for the first time in what felt to be a year.

XX

Grand Master Soton of the Order of Zarthani Knights sat in his private audience chamber at the heart of the great fortress of Tarr-Ceros and stared at the stone walls. Too many good men dead, he thought, and four more banners to hang in the Hall of Heroes. During his term as Grand Master he had now hung a total of seven banners, representing seven decommissioned Lances; more than any Grand Master in the past two hundred years. Those seven Lances also accounted for almost a quarter of the Order's strength.

Am I destroying the Order to salve my own pride?

No, damnit! I am trying to save the Temple, and part of the Temple is the Order of Zarthani Knights —my part. Kalvan means to destroy the Temple and to do this he must destroy me and the Order. Kalvan is the enemy and must be stopped at any cost!

A gentle knocking at the plank door took his mind off Kalvan and these all too familiar thoughts. "Come in."

Knight Commander Aristocles entered the chamber. "Good news, Soton. Kalvan and his allies are leaving—at last!"

"Ahhh. Finally. They must be growing short of rations. Either that, or they have run out of farms and barns to burn."

"True. There will be little produce left to harvest this fall, but we can bring in victuals by boat. The real cost has been time—there we have cost Kalvan dearly. Just as you planned. It is already the middle of summer and by the time Kalvan's tired army marches back to his not-so-grand kingdom, it will be too late in the year to mount a successful attack on Hos-Harphax, or any of our other allies."

Soton paused to strike a flame with his tinderbox and relight his pipe. Suddenly his mood seemed to lift with the fresh smoke rising from his pipe. "Yes, there will be no war this year in Hos-Harphax—our friends there owe us much. I hope they have used this gift of time wisely."

"They have," Aristocles answered. "A messenger from Balph just arrived. Lysandros has used Kalvan's attack on us to persuade the Harphaxi

Electors to crown him Great King of Hos-Harphax. Now Captain-General Phidestros will have the full might of a Great Kingdom behind his rebuilding of the Harphaxi Army."

"Good news on an auspicious day. I must go to Balph and take council with the Inner Circle. It is time to make further preparations for the *real* war against the Usurper Kalvan. I will need Styphon's Voice to help to convince Great King Cleitharses to mobilize the Ktemnoi Army for next spring. There are many things to be done and already the summer is half gone. Call my oath-brother, we have a trunk to pack. And a debt to settle with Kalvan—on a bill that is long overdue."

SEA OF GRASS

JOHN F. CARR

I

1967 A.D.

Verkan Vall gazed at the mass of info wafers, message balls and data cubes that covered his desk and sighed. He was cooped up with beeping computers and chirping data writers while outside it was a beautiful spring day. At times like this Verkan wondered why he'd allowed former Paratime Police Chief Tortha Karf to talk him into becoming his successor.

Being the best-trained man for the job did not make him the best man for the job, nor did it make that job any easier—especially when that job was being the final arbiter over a near-infinity of alternate worlds. They all had to be policed. Maybe it was too much job for one man—Tortha Karf had been saying that for years. But committees did not like to make decisions and when they did, too often they were compromises. So, until the Executive Council legalized cloning, it looked as if Verkan was stuck with the job.

Verkan had spent the winter shuttling back and forth between Home Time Line and Greffa, establishing his cover as Trader Verkan. It would not do to have Kalvan bumping into another Grefftscharrer who had never heard of Trader Verkan. The consequence was he had neglected his work here at Paratime Police headquarters and would have to spend the next two or three ten-days catching up. The squawk of his intercom interrupted his thoughts. He touched the com button with his toe and said, "What is it, Orthlan?"

"Inspector Ranthar Jard to see you, Chief. Code Red."

"Send him right in."

Ranthar Jard was a broad shouldered man with a quick step and bright gray eyes; if Dalla was his right hand, Ranthar was his left.

"Hate to bother you, Chief, but this could be important."

Verkan nodded for him to continue.

"We turned up some interesting irregularities on that list of Opposition heavy contributors you had me check out with the Metro Records Division. Our prime suspect is one Jorand Rarth—have you heard of him?"

"No. Who is he?"

"He's an outtime importer with possible connections to the Novilan Syndicate, mostly gambling and prole prostitution."

"Those two Wizard Trader suspects who allegedly committed suicide last year both had connections to the Novilan Syndicate."

Ranthar smiled, showing his well-formed teeth.

"This sounds like the link between the Wizard Traders and the syndicates we've been searching for," Verkan said. The Wizard Traders, who called themselves the Organization, had been a large band of First Level slavers posing as sorcerers. Unauthorized, they had gone outtime, using First Level technology as magic to take advantage of the ignorant and superstitious. The Organization had captured refugees from local wars and other disposable locals on isolated timelines as slaves to be sold for gold and fissionables on other time-lines. The Paratime Police had closed part of the operation down over a decade ago, but were still trying to penetrate the upper layers of the Wizard Trader Organization.

"Where is Jorand now?"

"That's the bad news, Chief. We've had his quarters under close surveillance for the past four hours. Less than fifteen minutes ago, we picked up the landing beam from his aircar. Before we could move in, he fled. We lost his aircar in the city lanes."

"I take it his locator was off?"

"Yes, first thing we checked. Nothing registered for his aircar on the traffic monitors, either."

Verkan sighed. "Where do you think he may have gone, Jard?"

"A syndicate hideout—for now, would be my guess, Chief. Then he'll hop aboard the first illegal outtime conveyer he can find. There's no place on Home Time Line to hide for more than a few days. I'll put out a warning on him to all the registered outtime firms."

Verkan moved his head in agreement. "I want an ID and picture of Jorand Rarth distributed to every Transtemporal terminal on the First Level. I also want his face on every news broadcast in this city by this evening. Arrange a pickup for all known associates. This is one fish I don't want to see slip away."

"Yes, sir."

"Rarth may be the key we've been searching for. So far we've been looking everywhere but in the right places."

"I've got a few suggestions. Take a couple of the Opposition Party big-wigs and put them under narco-hypnosis; we'll get some answers, all right."

"You may be right, but it's prohibited for the Department to question any elected Party official unless he's actually caught red-handed in a violation of the Municipal or Transtemporal Codes. Otherwise our hands are tied."

It was one of the many reasons Verkan preferred to spend his off time on Kalvan's Time Line; there you could cut through regulations with the nearest dirk or sword.

II

Archstratagos Zarphu, who had fought in thirty battles in as many years without giving in to fear, noticed a tremble in his legs as he entered the Lord Tyrant's audience chamber. Dyzar, the Tyrant of Antiphon, was truly one of the greatest rulers in Antiphon's history, but that was not enough to make him a great man in Zarphu's eyes. Neither was the sparse beard that grew upon Dyzar's cheeks.

Dyzar did not view other people as living, feeling beings like himself; instead they were pieces to be moved or removed from life's game board. His outbursts of temper were as notorious as his women's quarters, which were filled with young slave girls and other young ladies 'lost' on the city streets after catching Dyzar's eye.

These days there was more silver than bronze in Zarphu's hair, and despite the recent victory over the Army of Leuctramnos, Dyzar might have finally decided that it was time for a younger man to command the city's army; maybe one more malleable to his will. He was certain he had not done anything recently to make Dyzar doubt his loyalty and good service. Yet, since when had the Lord Tyrant ever needed proof of anything beyond his own whims and suspicions?

The two palace guards, both Eternals, wearing gilded chain mail and sporting red horsehair crests in their helmets, stood as if cast in metal. Zarphu wondered how they endured the constant inactivity; perhaps they were secretly amused by the parade of visitors into—and sometimes—out of Dyzar's chambers.

The door swung open and the Chamberlain bade him enter.

The Lord Tyrant Dyzar wore a rose and black velvet robe and his scruffy beard was intricately braided with gold wire. The Tyrant was reclining on a long red divan trimmed with gold mesh. He indicated that Zarphu was to sit on the other end of the divan.

After kneeling and touching the floor three times with his forehead, Zarphu rose. "Your Magnificence, I am your slave to command—"

"Arch-Strategos, we will dispense with the usual formalities for We have an urgent matter to discuss with you. Are you familiar with the former refugees from our lands who have settled beyond the Iron Trail?"

"No, Your Magnificence."

"Certainly you have heard the fables from the Time of Troubles about those who chose to flee to the lands beyond the Sea of Grass?"

"Yes, Your Magnificence. But I did not know there was truth behind those tales."

The Lord Tyrant nodded his head. "They are mentioned in the Lost Chronicles of Domitios. These I'm sure you have heard whispered words about."

Discourse with the Lord Tyrant was like sword fighting against a skilled blade master; any feigns or missteps could be instantly fatal. "Yes, Your Magnificence, I have heard about them although I did not believe they still existed."

The Lord Tyrant grinned. "The Chronicles are part of my secret library. Of course, any mention of what has passed between us in this chamber will cost you and your family dearly. Is that understood?"

Zarphu nodded.

"Good. As you know the Time of Troubles began with the Echini War against the Echanistra Confederation and lasted for almost a thousand years. Near the end of the war, Echanistra's fleet was nearly destroyed; so many of the northerners decided to flee their homelands. Invited by King Chaldorec of Grefftscharr, many of them followed the Iron Trail and beyond to new lands, where in the winter snow is as common as the sand on our beaches. There they conquered the Ruthani, as our ancestors did three thousand years ago, and took the land as their own.

"We know few details about their conquest, but in time five major kingdoms were established—each dominated by a great city-state, much like our own rule. For many years they have grown and prospered, all without tribute or tithes to the lords they fled. Now a new kingdom has formed and they have asked for our help. Maybe the time has arrived for us to us to re-establish our dominion over these our strayed children."

There was an intense inner light in the Lord Tyrant's eyes that worried Zarphu. The Tyrant Laertru, Dyzar's father, had built the greatest army in the history of Antiphon. His son had used this army to subdue and conquer his neighbors, a feat no one had accomplished since the Time of Troubles. Now the Lord Tyrant's power extended from Amcylyestros in the south to Tyrantor in the north. Apparently, not even the domination of the Great Cities was enough to appease Dyzar's appetite for power. Were the rumors the Lord Tyrant wanted to forge an empire from Great Sea to Great Sea actually true?

"We have been approached by agents of Styphon's House—the Temple of a powerful eastern god—with a request to hire part of our army. The terms are generous and we have accepted their offer. Now that we have wrested peace from Amcylyestros, and have so soundly defeated Leuctramnos that they too seek a settlement—all due to your brilliant generalship—we have an unparalleled opportunity to learn about the eastern lands and their peoples."

"Who is this Styphon, Your Magnificence?"

"Some false god of war they worship." Dyzar continued. "He cannot be a very good god or they would not need our help. According to the Styphon's House emissary, they are embroiled in a war with a demigod named Kalvan and desire our help to defeat him. Demigod indeed! I care not one whit for their petty struggles, but there can be much to gain by going to their aid. We need to know more about these barbarians if we are to exploit their troubles and turn them to our advantage."

"How much of our army do they wish to hire?"

"Four stratgi of horse and fourteen of foot, including two stratgi of plumbati."

"Your Magnificence, that is almost a quarter of our entire army. Can we afford the loss of so many valuable men?"

"Yes. With Leuctramnos suing for peace there is no other city-state left to oppose us but Sybariphon in the north, and they are still at war with Echanistra. We may never have a better opportunity to search out the easterners' weaknesses."

Zarphu felt weak in the knees, as if he had been ordered to run his army into the ocean to fight the waves. What madness was this? He would have to cross the Sea of Grass, fight the warriors of the Iron City and defeat the barbarian kingdoms, who—if stories were to believed—fought with fire and stones, shot by fire sticks farther and faster than the fleetest arrow.

"I need you to lead them, Arch-Stratego. Only you will be trusted with the true secret of our mission."

Yanked out of his reverie by this pronouncement, Zarphu knew chances were small he would ever return and see his beloved city again. Maybe, as his friends had warned, his own success on the battlefield had made him too dangerous to be left alive. Certainly an honorable death on the battlefield, no matter how far from home, was to be preferred to the assassin's dart.

"How long will we remain in the barbarians' employ?" Zarphu asked.

"Until next summer, or whenever this Kalvan—be he man or demigod—is dead."

Seeing the boy—for boy he still was, to Zarphu, for all his arrogance and lofty ambitions—seated there looking so completely alone, an upsurge of that wretched emotion called loyalty stirred in Zarphu's heart. Without thinking he knelt before his sovereign with the ridiculous gold-threaded scruffy beard, took his hand and placed it atop his head in the older gesture of fealty among the Ros-Zarthani and quietly said, "I will serve Your Magnificence, until I bear Kalvan's skull as a drinking cup or my shield is hung in Hadron's Hall."

"I knew my trust was well founded," Dyzar purred. "I want maps dawn of the entire journey, a list of all cities and fortifications you encounter, samples of all new armor and weapons, notes on how an army can be supplied on each part of the journey and any documents of military importance you can obtain. I will send scribes and mapmakers to aid you with these chores. In addition, I will entrust you with a bodyguard drawn from my Eternals; they will guard you with their lives."

The Eternals were the Lord Tyrant's own personal bodyguard, as well as his eyes and ears—and occasionally his assassins. Zarphu was being both honored and kept safe. Why couldn't he shake the feeling that he was caught in an invisible undertow?

"Do not worry about your affairs in the city, Zarphu." Dyzar paused to stroke his beard. "Should you not return to us within five winters, we will gift your heirs our weight in gold."

The Lord Tyrant was notoriously tightfisted; Zarphu couldn't help but wonder why the sudden benevolence. While a few of his friends had whispered their complaints about the Lord Tyrant's growing capriciousness, he had never in any way encouraged this kind of talk. He had also heard from one of his confidants that there were actual factions opposed to the Lord Tyrant's rule, so perhaps Dyzar had some justification for his worries about his own security and the loyalty of his stratgi.

His own loyalty was incorruptible. "I thank you for your generosity, Your Magnificence. I shall return before the passing of five winters so your generosity will not be wasted." Zarphu prostrated himself before the crown again and kissed the Lord Tyrant's feet. He then rose, pausing only as he was about to cross the threshold to ask one last question. "When do we leave?"

"In a moon-quarter, Arch-Stratego. We are having the fleet fitted and provisioned to take you and your command as far as Mythrene. There you will disembark, buy additional provisions and wagons, and take leave for Olythrio. The Styphoni have will have additional guides there to help you with your travels. Now we will give you leave to muster your men and prepare for the coming journey."

III

Jorand Rarth pushed his chair back, to ease his bulging belly, and listened with pleasure to the jingle and clang of the slot machines in the front room of the Corkscrew. The slots were a recent *import* from Fourth Level, Europo-American Sector and they were proving to be—as had so many other Europo-American imports—a great hit. He estimated the average take was up fifteen percent at all three of his Dhergabar clubs since their introduction. He was going to have to *import* more slot machines and send them to his other clubs outside the capital before one of the other Bosses got the same idea.

While the Bureau of Psychological Hygiene saw gambling and playing games of chance as evidence of an anti-social character, gambling itself was not strictly illegal. To a society that liked to see itself as free of pre-literate and pseudo-scientific superstition, games of chance were a social embarrassment—a continuing reminder of the irrationality of human nature. As such, Psych-Hygiene agents liked to keep records on those who frequented gambling dens.

In an ongoing attempt to protect customer anonymity, the gambling syndicates carefully guarded the location of their clubs, moved them around at irregular intervals and paid large sums of shush money to certain captains in the Dhergabar Metropolitan Police Department.

Jorand needed to talk to his contacts at Tharmax Trading right away about acquiring more slot machines. It didn't help that they were quasi-illegal on most Europo-American Subsectors, either. If Paratime Police Chief Verkan Vall hadn't been monitoring that Sector so vigilantly, Jorand would have solved his problem very simply. He would have run a big conveyer into one of the Fourth Level Bally slot machine factories, taken all the trained mechanics and setup men, blown a gas main under the old factory and then sent them across time to an uninhabited Fifth Level time-line where he would have set up his own slot machine business.

Making them was clearly not as easy as hijacking them, but then slot machines were not as easy to obtain outtime as Fourth Level jukeboxes or Second Level subliminal hormone exciters. Plus, by using slave labor, the syndicate could save a lot of units as well as create a dependable supply base—one not dependent upon outtime politics and Paratime Police's good will to operate. Wars and revolutions had a nasty way of mucking up supply and delivery, especially when they splashed over whole subsectors, containing millions times millions of timelines.

Jorand's door sensor beeped and Metropolitan Police Captain Sirgoth Zyarr entered the room. Jorand quickly rose to his feet. Sirgoth had never physically come into one of his clubs in more twenty years of 'working' together. He wondered if he were about to be raided. Raids were ritualized, with both sides warned long in advance so each could play out their part to perfection.

Something big was coming down. “What is it, Cap—”?

“No names.”

It suddenly hit him that Sirgoth was not wearing his regulation blues, but a gray street tunic and cape.

“One of my men flagged your name in a data pool we share with the Paratime Police. They’ve tagged you for pickup. Don’t know when or where, but if I were you I wouldn’t waste any time finding a hole to crawl into.”

“Why the warning?” Everyone knew about the age old antagonism between the Metropolitan Police and the Paratime Police; the Metros—along with almost everyone else—thought the Paracops acted like a second government—with more authority than the Metropolitan Police and the Executive Council combined. Maybe they needed their autonomy to guard the secret of Paratime Transposition, but that didn’t mean everyone else had to like it. Or that the Paratime Police had to be so self-righteous in carrying out their job.

“I’ll give you one reason. Then I’m getting out of here. As far as you are concerned, you’ve never heard of me and I’ve never heard of you. Make any attempt to re-establish contact with me, and I will see that you are terminated.”

Jorand gulped.

“Ever since Chief Verkan and his Paratime squads saved our butts on Year-End Day, by helping us put down the riots, we’ve been given orders to assist them in all on-going investigations and to share our data pool. It’s a new game under Chief Raldor and all the old rules are changing. If the Paratime Police get their hands on you, the first thing they’ll do is pump narco-hypnotics into your system until you squeal like a frightened little girl. Then you’re going to throw up everything you know. My name is going to appear in whatever mess you regurgitate. If I were smart, I would have wired your aircar and cleansed the whole operation in one blast. But there are problems with that approach, as well. So just be thankful that in the past you’ve always been on time with the slush, and that you haven’t splashed any dirt on me.”

With that said, Captain Sirgoth spun around and left the small room.

Jorand felt his heart pound like a trip-hammer. *I could have a heart attack right this moment, race to the nearest hospice and wake up with a new heart and a Paratime Policeman at my side.*

He willed his heart to slow down and quickly began to draw up a mental list of what he had to take with him and what he had to destroy.

IV

Jorand Rarth felt weight return as the wheels of the air-car struck the rooftop landing stage of Hadron Tharn's penthouse and shut down the pseudo-grav. His driver opened the rear door and asked, "What should I do with the car, boss?"

Jorand looked around as though expecting a blue Metro or green Paracop police car to materialize on the landing stage. Yesterday afternoon he had been forced to flee his own tower just minutes before a squad of Paratime Police raided the place. Now there was a warrant for his arrest and the cover he had so elaborately devised a century ago was gone.

"The police should be able to ID it before long so drop it off at a public tower and meet me at the Constellation House in two hours. We can steal a new aircar out of the parking lot if we need one."

The driver nodded and took off. Jorand stepped into the lifthead of Hadron Tharn's penthouse; he keyed in his password and pressed his thumb on the thumblock. The lift door rose behind him to cut off the view of Dhergabar City under a winter sky as bright and blue, and as coldly unsympathetic, as Paratime Police Chief Verkan Vall's eyes.

The lift door opened, letting Jorand out into the maroon-carpeted entry hall of Hadron Tharn's private quarters. A robot rolled forward to take Jorand's coat. Behind it rolled another robot, holding a tray with hot spiked simmer-root in a silver cup. Jorand took the cup, triggering the robot's vocal circuits.

"Citizen Hadron Tharn is waiting to see you in the lounge."

Jorand mumbled an automatic thank you in return which told more about his prole origins than he liked known, since Citizens never spoke to robots unless giving them a command. He had spent decades setting up his First Level Citizen identity and had lived it for close to a century. It appeared he'd gotten fat and lazy; he was going to need all his old skills and moxie to survive this fracas.

A century ago he had been the head of an underground gambling syndicate in Novilan City. While all First Level Citizens' children become Citizens, Proles had to qualify by passing an intelligence and general psych test. Proles could be adopted and made Citizens, but even so they must pass the tests. The problem was that few Proles received a First Level education.

Jorand had tried with tutors, but hadn't liked the hard work. Instead he had searched for a decade to find a compulsive gambler within the Bureau of Identification. It hadn't been easy because the Bureau of Psychological Hygiene made periodic sweeps of the Records Division to keep such fraud to a minimum.

When he had his mark hooked and gaffed, he arranged the 'disappearance' of a respectable Citizen and the substitution of Jorand's DNA record for the mark had been affected. No one had been the wiser for ninety-eight years—until yesterday.

Jorand didn't have the time, or the patience, to set up another set of false IDs, so he had no other choice but to go outtime. With his usual contacts under suspicion, he would have to use his influence in the Opposition Party, using the influence he had spent decades building with large donations and conscientious attendance at Hadron's boring political action group meetings.

He had also been a boss in the Organization, a criminal syndicate that had kidnapped outtime peoples and sold them at high profits on other time-lines. Since most of these outtimers had been victims of wars or famines, he had only too happy to arrange their sale to those who could make good use of their labors. After all, they gained their lives while he in exchange made a fair return.

As far as he was concerned, none of those outtimers would have to face anything Jorand hadn't gone through himself during his childhood on Fifth Level Industrial Sector, where his own father had sold him to a slum overlord for drug money. Jorand had been raised by a man who had bought him as a slave, then raised him to second-in-command of a large burglary syndicate.

Now as a member of the Organization's second level, Jorand knew just how 'involved' in the Organization many of the top politicos of the Opposition Party had become. Unfortunately, the Paratime Police had put his branch of the Organization out of business; his boss had been detained and never heard of again. There were rumors that he'd been killed while under Paratime Police interrogation. Recently, Jorand had heard new rumors that the Organization was back in business, but no one had contacted him, or he wouldn't be here trying to cash in on that information—regardless of Citizen Tharn's feelings on the subject.

Fortunately, as a member of Tharn's Opposition Action Team, he hadn't even had to twist Tharn's arm for a private audience. Jorand almost looked forward to the day when the Action Team discovered they had a prole among their membership. Despite all their egalitarian cant, he had heard enough prole jokes to know their true sympathies. It had been his private joke, one that kept him awake through their interminable meetings. Too bad he would not be there when they learned the truth about him.

Jorand gulped the last of his simmer root as he entered the Blue Lounge. He thought of ordering another, then decided to wait since he would need a clear head for today's meeting.

"Welcome, Citizen Jorand," Hadron Tharn said, stepping lightly toward him. "I trust you had a good journey." Unfortunately, the warm greeting didn't extend to Tharn's chilly eyes.

"Except for the stratospheric winds, yes. That's why I'm late."

"It hardly matters. Would you care for another drink?"

Jorand shook his head and sat down in his usual red-leather chair. The only other person in the room was Warntha Swarn, Tharn's bodyguard and who-knew-what-else. Warntha was in his usual stance, hands clasped behind his back and eyes roaming the room, and as usual guarding Hadron Tharn's back.

Citizen Tharn gave one of his famous grins, but the blue eyes were as icy as an arctic gale. "What can I do for you Citizen?"

Jorand didn't bother to return the smile. "I'm in trouble and I need your help."

"I'm sorry to hear that, Citizen, but why me?"

"Call it a return on a three million credit investment. I need to go outtime."

Warntha visibly tensed.

"The only reason I'm not having you thrown out of here," Tharn said, "is that you've been extremely helpful in the past. I don't know what your problem is, but I suggest you go elsewhere for its solution."

"My personal rooms have just been sealed by the Paratime Police and by now I'm sure to be high up on their most-wanted list."

"You have my sympathies, of course." Tharn held both hands out to express his helplessness. "However, my brother-in-law, Verkan Vall and I have an unspoken accord; he doesn't ask me for favors and I don't ask him for any."

"Citizen Tharn, let us get to the heart of the problem. I have been one of the heads of the Organization, or Wizard Traders as the Paracops call it, for about thirty years. Don't look so shocked; I can name a dozen prominent Opposition Party members who are equally involved."

Hadron Tharn nodded, his face expressionless.

"If the Paratime Police pick me up, the lid will be blown off what's left of the Organization and the Opposition Party. Frankly, it is in both our interests to see me disappear from Home Time Line." Jorand saw a stealthy look slip between Warntha and his master and added, "My driver has a message ball he's to take to Verkan Vall if I don't leave this tower according to schedule."

"Where do you get these ideas?"

"Because, like you, I've found that the simplest solution to most problems is often the most elegant—in this case, my disappearance. Therefore, I've taken certain precautions, just as you would have done."

Hadron Tharn leaned back in his chair, his forehead furrowed in what appeared to be concentrated thought. He remained frozen for some time until he sat up abruptly. "I don't have as much access to Paratemporal

Transposition as you seem to think, but we do have one operation where you might fit in."

During the height of the Wizard Traders operation, Jorand would have had his choice of thousands of time-lines to hide on, but now he was forced to take whatever crumb Tharn threw his way. Despite his reluctance to take grudging charity; it was a vast improvement over psycho-rehabilitation, a year of unremitting physical and mental agony, the ignominy of having his private thoughts probed and twisted by psychotherapists and finally the horror of emerging as someone who would not be Jorand Rarth.

"What is it?" he asked.

"You've heard of Kalvan's Time Line?"

"Who hasn't? We've talked it to death at the Action Team meetings. What about it?"

"Kalvan's Time Line has become Chief Verkan Vall's major political vulnerability, one the Opposition Party intends to exploit. One way we can force Verkan's hand is by making life difficult for his outtime friend, Great King Kalvan. If things get sticky enough for Kalvan, Verkan might commit a breach of the Paratime Code—and then we will have him."

Right, thought Jorand, *a scandal big enough to break Management Party's stranglehold on the Executive Council. Sweeping reforms inside the Paratime Police would help many of the commercial houses who felt constrained in their theft of outtime resources.* It was enough to make an honest thief wonder who the real crooks were.

"So where do I fit into all of this?"

Hadron Tharn leaned forward, locking eyes. "Rarth, I could use a trusted agent I can send to Kalvan's Time Line to oversee a very important operation. This last year has been a very good one for King Kalvan. He defeated probably the largest army in his time-line's history. Now he's built up his army to the point where only the most concerted effort will root him out of his so-called Great Kingdom of Hos-Hostigos.

"Fortunately for us, the opposition has some good leaders, Archpriest Roxthar, Prince Lysandros of Hos-Harphax, and Grand Master Soton of the Zarthani Knights. They are planning a major counter-attack but need help. Kalvan has either killed or recruited most of the available mercenaries in the Five Kingdoms and the national armies aren't that strong as of yet on this time-line.

"But the picture isn't all bad. On the west coast there are a number of city-states who have built up formidable armies after a millennium of constant warfare. Now, for the first time in centuries, they have a great leader in one of the city-states, Antiphon. A leader who has become strong enough to conquer most of the others. The problem is that he is unstable and unpredictable, more a Hitler than an Alexander. Like Hitler, this leader—Dyzar—suffered from an untreatable case of syphilis, which has left him with delusions of grandeur, a homicidal temper, and massive mood swings—"

Jorand stifled a grin as he realized that this description might equally cover Hadron Tharn himself, who on occasion had been known to scream and berate his cohorts for hours. "What do you mean, suffered?"

"A month ago my agents used a neuro-prophylactic on Dyzar and were able to stabilize his condition. Due to the primitive conditions, the advanced stage of the disease and the lack of a fully trained medico, they were not able to restore normal mental functions. In the end they were forced to use the rejuvenation treatment to insure he survived the treatment. Dyzar should live a long and painful life."

"You used rejuvenation formula on an outtimer! Next to the Paratime Secret that's the most heavily guarded invention we have. We could all be fried for this—"

Hadron Tharn smiled a most unpleasant smile. "That is why we need an agent of utmost discretion for this job. One who will not be particular about a lengthy and somewhat primitive assignment."

And someone very expendable, thought Jorand to himself. *And unable to return to First Level without Hadron's help.* Unfortunately, for him, there were no other choices. "What is it you want me to do?"

"First, we will put you under narco-hypnosis and give you a pseudo-memory overlay as a merchant from Hos-Zygros; it's as distant as you can go from Balph, Styphon House's administrative center. You will be one of the guides of the expedition, which is under the authority of Highpriest

Prythos. In your guise as a merchant who has traveled the Iron Trail repeatedly—under narco-hypnosis you will be implanted with all the necessary details—you will become an essential member of the contact team. The team, headed by Highpriest Prythos, is currently in the City-Sate of Mythrene awaiting the arrival of the Ros-Zarthani army. Your job will be to make sure that the Ros-Zarthani forces arrive intact at the Eastern Kingdoms where they will be prepared for their role in the war against King Kalvan."

"Why not," Jorand answered. It wasn't as if he had any place else to go.

V

The moment Jorand Rarth left, Hadron Tharn turned to Warntha and asked, "What do you think of that one? Can we trust him?"

"For about two heartbeats after the Paratime Police pick him up. I tossed a sticky locator on his tunic when he walked by. Do you want me to follow and dispose of him and his driver? I don't believe his story about any documents ready to go to the Paratime Police."

Tharn shook his head. "He was flying by the seat of his pants! Still, we need an expendable agent on Kalvan Prime—Prythos has been useful, but in his last communiqué he asked for more help. I think he's getting tired of traveling across the continent by horseback."

They both laughed.

Hadron Tharn continued. "We have to be very careful on Kalvan Prime; there are more Paracops there than at the Dhergabar Paratime Terminal. Verkan has been pressuring the Executive Council, to put a Paracop on every outtime conveyer. Not even Management will go for it, because there's thousands of firms with outtime licenses and they'd have to curtail business or increase the Paratime Police Department by several orders of magnitude! Unfortunately, some of our late friends in the Organization got sloppy and gave Verkan valuable ammunition. If Verkan catches an unauthorized conveyer on Kalvan Prime—all bets are off! Still, it's too good an opportunity to give that sanctimonious bastard a black eye. This Jorand is perfect; no one will miss him and he no longer has any ties to the Organization. When his job is done—"

Warntha smiled. "Do I get to pull his plug?"

"After he's no longer useful, but that won't be for some time. Prythos, though…hmm. The time has come to terminate Highpriest Prythos, but first put him under narco-hypnosis, do a complete memory lift for Jorand—then kill him and dispose of the body. No witnesses, no crime."

"Do you think anyone will notice, boss?"

"Highpriest Prythos has been gone for over a year from Balph and we selected him originally because he was a newcomer from Hos-Zygros that wouldn't be missed. His most memorable feature is his big gut, and Jorand's big belly almost matches his."

They both laughed.

Warntha Swarn placed his palm over the portal plate and the door to the warehouse slid open—poor security. Typical of a University project, he thought scornfully. Inside the room was a large silver-mesh dome about fifty feet in diameter, large enough to hold the two score of scholars and academics moving around the storeroom. Most of them were dressed in homespun wool, leather and buckskin garments appropriate to Kalvan's Time Line.

Warntha wore the full-length, hooded yellow robe of a Styphon's House highpriest. He couldn't help but notice how the academics quickly moved out of his path, as though the trappings of a Styphoni priest had a sinister aura. Upon reflection, the big man decided it wasn't much different than the usual way Citizens usually acted around him—just more pronounced.

As a counter-military specialist, Warntha had spent over a century on the Industrial Sector, Fifth Level worlds, where he had infiltrated and helped to neutralize Prole resistance groups. Warntha had liked this work and had been very good at it. Unfortunately, he had single-handedly killed the top two leaders of a Prole Independence Movement cell unaware that there had been another active agent in the cell. Command had judged him as 'over-zealous' and given him the choice of Psycho-Rehab or retirement at half-pay. He had taken the latter. If Hadron Tharn had not seen some value in his services, he would be living on Home Time Line at about the same economic level of the Proles he had once overseen.

In the farthest corner of the warehouse, all by himself, Warntha spotted Jorand Rarth, wearing a battered back-and-breast—that hid most of his potbelly—a large floppy black hat and leather trousers with a buckskin fringe. He approached Jorand from his blind side to gain the maximum advantage of surprise. Warntha hoped this fool proved as useful as Hadron Tharn anticipated. If not, Jorand's life would come to an abrupt and permanent end.

"By Dralm's white beard!" Jorand cried upon seeing Warntha in his Styphoni robes. He quickly reverted to First Level language when he recognized Warntha as Hadron Tharn's bodyguard. "What are you doing here?"

"Councilor Tharn decided I should accompany you on this mission as a highpriest of Styphon's House. We will be accompanying the Hos-Harphax Study Team, which will be dropped off at the new Harphax conveyer-head in Harphax City. We have a small aircar secreted inside one of the conveyers. From there, we'll take the aircar across the continent to the City-State of Mythrene, the seaport where we're meeting Arch-Stratego Zarphu and his army. I will be accompanying the expedition across the Sea of Grass."

"Won't the locals see our aircar as some king of omen or premonition?"

Warntha laughed. "They won't see us without night goggles! We're traveling after dark; once we cross the Mother River it won't matter who sees us. They're all outies!"

"What'll we do with the aircar after we arrive?" Jorand asked.

"One of our agents has purchased a small warehouse where it will be stored in case we need to bug out in a hurry. It's getting more and more difficult to make unscheduled drops on Kalvan's Time Line. The Paratime Police are paying more attention to the University's use of Transtemporal conveyers. The University doesn't like it, and neither do we. But, it's the way things are now."

Jorand nodded wryly, as though he understood, but didn't like it much, either. Warntha suspected Jorand enjoyed his company about as much as he enjoyed spending time with the former Dhergabar crime boss.

"I've got some additional instructions for you as well. Instead of guiding the Arch-Stratego to the Hyklos River to where it meets the Great River, we're going to lead the Ros-Zarthani over the Old Iron Trail into Grefftscharr."

"But why?" Jorand asked. "It'll not only add at least a full moon to the trip, but it might draw us into a fight with the Grefftscharri. They're not going to look kindly at what they could easily perceive as a nomad invasion."

Maybe Jorand isn't a complete fool, after all, Warntha decided. "That's what the Councilor wants. The Ros-Zarthani haven't fought against gunpowder weapons before. It's important they have the opportunity to test their mettle before fighting Kalvan. If they break, then we abort the mission—"

The fat man turned pale. "Yeah, but where does that leave me? In Greffa as a prisoner of war or a galley slave on the Great Seas?"

"Then I guess it's important to see they don't break, Jorand—since it is only our necks at stake." Warntha wasn't the least bit worried, if things went wrong; either he'd get killed—in which case all his problems were over, or he'd find a 'job'—probably as a bodyguard, since they were always in fashion—in Greffa. "If the Ros-Zarthani show real mettle, maybe King Kalvan will have a big surprise next year."

"I guess it wouldn't help Chief Verkan's position in Greffa either," Jorand said, "if his patron, King Theovacar, loses a major battle to a bunch of barbarian spearchuckers. Nor would he be in a position, the following year, to help Kalvan with men and supplies."

"Very good. You're beginning to pick up the lay of the land. Just look at these kings as syndicate bosses and you'll get along just fine."

"When can I come home?" Jorand asked.

"After we get the army safely back across the Sea of Grass, or when it has ceased being an effective fighting force, our job is over. If they survive the fight with the Middle Kingdom forces, we'll lead the Ros-Zarthani to

Dorg where they will be Styphon's House's problem. Then we will make our way to Balph where you will assume Highpriest Prythos' identity—"

"How are you going to do that?" he asked.

Warntha quickly made a slicing motion across his throat with his index finger. Then continued:

"That should give our friends on First Level time to create a new cover and identity for you. Once the Ros-Zarthani are on the way back home you'll be able to return back to leading a civilized life on First Level."

Jorand appeared so pleased by this news that Warntha had to choke back a laugh. If the fat fool really believed that anyone on Home Time Line would go to that much expense and trouble for a drone like himself, then he deserved his fate. Jorand was nothing more than an over-weight, smarmy ex-Prole. Warntha stroked the hilt of the dirk hidden in his gold and leather girdle and repeated to himself, *Your time will come, my fat little friend. Yes, it will come—I promise you that.*

VI

Arch-Stratego Zarphu made room on the cluttered table for a freshly scraped deerskin parchment. He dipped his quill into the inkpot, making a notation that two hundred barrels of salt fish would be arriving from Hellos within the moon half. Zarphu knew that most soldiers considered provisioning and buying victuals scribes' work, but he knew that an army marched on its belly as well as on its feet, and woe to any Stratego who forgot that fact.

The sea journey from Antiphon to Mythrene had taken over a moon quarter, as the ships had been forced to go against the current and prevailing winds. Even with rowers it was a long, arduous trip and, praise to the weather god, they had only lost one ship to foul winds and none to pirates. Best of all, his stomach was once again his own and not leaping at every lurch of the ship.

Their greeting from the Lord Tyrant of Mythrene had been gracious, befitting an ally who came at the head of an army. The Lord Tyrant had offered him rooms at the palace, but Zarphu had refused. As long as he was in Mythrene, the local Tyrant's spies would be weighing their every move. Still there was no gain in making their job an easy one. Instead Zarphu had hired out the Black Thorn Tavern as his headquarters.

The army was garrisoned outside the city walls, although keeping them outside the city was a major headache. It would not be wise to have some of them mugged by cutpurses and the rest given the pox by local whores before they left the coast. In truth, Zarphu could hardly wait until they were on their way. He was going to have to wait for another moon—at the earliest—before his quartermasters could collect enough foodstuffs for the initial leg of their journey. He would have to place his faith in the stories the merchants told about great herds of bison and cattle moving across the Sea of Grass like schools of tuna and albacore. In case it was the stuff of legend, he intended to send several large pack trains out ahead of the army to set up depots, since there was no conceivable way they could take enough victuals along with them to cover the entire passage.

A hearty knock at the plank door told him his Eastern visitors had arrived. "Enter."

A big priest, with a shaved head and hard eyes, wearing a yellow robe—raiment of the god the barbarians called Styphon—was the first to enter. After him came several lesser priests in black robes. Next came the merchants, led by a portly man with a solid-metal breastplate chased with silver and gold that Zarphu would have traded his favorite horse for. The portly man had a wine merchant's smile pasted on his face. Zarphu wondered which, if any, of these foreigners he could trust.

The big highpriest, who he had met before and called himself Highpriest Prythos, was the first to speak. "My fellow priests, except for two, will return on your galleys to Antiphon as agreed by your Lord Tyrant. I will accompany your army to the Five Kingdoms as advisor and priest to those who need me."

Prythos spoke to him as if he were a lesser form of animal; the highpriest reminded him of Dyzar's Immortal Bodyguards. Zarphu didn't trust him the width of a lady's dagger. He would like to know more about this 'fireseed' that the priest had shown him the day before. Still, the priest had already crossed the Sea of Grass and, along with the portly merchant, had survived the journey, so he might prove helpful in their passage.

"Who will we be fighting when we reach the Five Kingdoms?" Zarphu asked.

"A usurper and blasphemer who goes by the name of Kalvan. I have been sent to aid you in bringing your army to join the Holy Host. You will have your part in what will be a great victory."

Zarphu could tell by his tone that the highpriest didn't think much of that part or his mission. Good, the priests of Styphon's House underestimated him. That would make his job easier. He was sure that once they arrived in the Five Kingdoms an opportunity would arise where he return this oafs' disdain. The Zarthani, as they now called themselves, might have better weapons, but he was certain they didn't have any better soldiers than his own—even this so-called Usurper Kalvan. If they did they wouldn't be riding the width of the continent for mercenaries.

One thing that he was certain of, not much good would come of an alliance with these priests of the false god Styphon. What he really wanted to know was why the other priests were returning to Antiphon. Just what kind of deal had the Styphon worshippers struck with Lord Tyrant Dyzar?

After he'd dismissed the foreigners, he had one of the merchants brought in. Garnoth was rapidly approaching old age, most of his teeth were gone and his hair and beard were braided with silver. But he dressed like a nobleman and the rings on his fingers were worth a small fortune; it was obvious that financial necessity was not his primary reason for joining the expedition. It was also known that he'd traveled the Iron Trail more times than any man alive.

"Trader Garnoth, I'm curious as to why you want to join our expedition." He rested his eyes on the trader's jewel encrusted fingers. "It's not as if you need the fee."

"This is true, Stratego," he answered, his words mushy because of missing teeth. "I lack little either in comfort or wealth, after fifty years of traveling the Iron Trail." He held up his right hand which only had two fingers and a thumb. "I lost those when a barbarian's spear clipped my hand; I was twenty-six winters old then. But we beat the Ruthani back, killing thirty of their bravest warriors. There was a challenge like that for every journey, although I never lost any more body parts."

He paused to make a wheezing sound that Zarphu took for laughter.

"It's a good thing, because we lost a lot of good men over the decades. My father was killed by a tomahawk blow to the head; my uncle was shot in the neck with an arrow. Fortunately, few of the Ruthani on the Sea of Grass have iron weapons; although more do now than when I was a youngster. The new breed of traders will make exchanges with anyone, if they can meet their price. We had ethics—" He paused to cough, an awful hacking sound that made Zarphu wonder if he'd even finish the journey.

"How do you think the barbarians will react to a force this large?" He was worried that the savages might believe they were an invasion force or guards for a rich caravan, since they were bringing three thousand wagons of victuals, supplies and weapons with them.

Garnoth repeated the wheezing sound that passed for laughter. When he ran out of air, he sputtered: "They'll run like the wind, Stratego. The tribes and clans rarely join forces, and even then only rarely to attack trade caravans. It takes them too long to band together, they have to have pow-wows and tribal get-togethers, before they can pick a war leader. They'll still be jawing about your Army three winters after you've departed. If they do attack, use your superior training and organization to grind them into the ground. Fear is the only thing barbarians respect!"

"You still haven't answered my question: Why do you want to join the expedition?"

The old trader grinned. "I'm dying of boredom, pleasant and enjoyable boredom, but dying just the same. I need to get away, to see and"—he paused to sniff the air—"smell the Sea of Grass one more time. And this appears to be the expedition of all expeditions!"

"You do understand, I do not know when, or even if, any or all of us, will return."

"Yes, Strategos, know. I also know that you are traveling to the lands beyond the Sea of Grass, places I've never seen. I would never forgive myself, if I missed such a grand opportunity."

He nodded, the old man made as much sense as anything else on this gods-forsaken expedition. He was fortunate to have the old trader; the younger merchants had refused the moment they learned that their destination was not Grefftscharr, but Hos-Ktemnos. Several traders had agreed to accompany the party as far as Greffa, where they planned to take their own wagon trains of goods. He was agreeable, since he might find their goods useful. Whether the merchants were allowed to depart would depend on the circumstances of their journey. Garnoth was the only one traveling to the lands of the Zarthani.

"There will certainly be new and strange sights, and as much adventure as any man can stand," he said.

Garnoth started wheezing again, while pounding his knees with joy. "The stories I'll be able to tell."

He didn't want to say it out loud, but Zarphu doubted the old man would survive the war against Kalvan the Usurper. Still, there were worse ways to die. He questioned the trader about his previous travels along the Iron Trail and made notes of the important things. Later he would have one of his scribes gather the old man and the other merchants to go over the old maps he'd brought from Antiphon. Together they should be able to provide a more accurate map than the one he already had. This Kalvan was said to positively dote on maps; it was a feature they both shared. After this expedition, he would have maps that would be the signposts for future armies.

VII

When he'd exhausted the trader's storehouse of information, Arch-Stratego Zarphu decided it was time to get to the meat of the matter. "What do you know of these priests of *Styphon*? They seem to be an untrustworthy lot in my estimation."

Garnoth the Trader nodded. "A nasty clutch of thieves masquerading as priests, Arch-Strategos. The Grefftscharrers don't trust them, and neither do I. There's not many of their heathen temples in Greffa, only one or two small ones. They do have several large banking houses. The

Styphoni priests over-charge for their fireseed, then sell the dregs to the Grefftscharrers. And only small amounts at that; they absolutely refuse—to sell their precious fireseed or their firetubes—to us! As if we were barbarians, ourselves, instead of the oldest civilization in the world. It's an abomination, Strategos!"

"I agree, but we were forced into an alliance with them by our Lord Tyrant."

The old trader made a sly grin. "By the *madman*. I've heard tales—are they true?"

They're worse than your feeble mind can conjure, old man, but he kept his thoughts to himself. "We have enough to worry about on this journey without fishing for more, trader."

"Aye, Your Excellency. However, beware of any deals you make with the House of Styphon. Their highpriests are not to be trusted."

VIII

After leaving Mythrene, the army made very good progress through the foothills, Zarphu considered, having covered almost a hundred marches in three days mostly in pouring rain. They made camp around a former stone way station for the Iron Trail; the old way stations were positioned a day's travel apart for a heavy loaded caravan. This station only had all four walls and none of the roof timbers had caved in, although the slate roof was long gone—probably scavenged by the locals. It showed signs of recent occupancy, but the scouts found no one in the vicinity except an abandoned lumber camp about twenty marches away; the land was heavily forested, mostly second-growth trees.

He made the way station the officer's bivouac. They erected a temporary roof and, after three days of riding in the rain, he welcomed the respite from the constant drizzle. The previous way stations had been reclaimed right down to their foundations. If their guide hadn't pointed the previous one out, he would have thought it was just another ruin. This station was far enough away from Mythrene to make hauling the stone too costly. Several centuries ago, it had been the Tyrant of Mythrene's responsibility to keep the stations manned and maintained; now, they were just a memory of the olden days.

From what his agents-inquisitory had been able to determine, less than four or five expeditions left Mythrene for the Iron Trail annually. Two-thirds returned each year, and those that did turned a good profit. Trade was mostly for copper, brass, glassware, furs, jewels and buffalo hides. Occasionally, one or another party would return with a firestick, usually rusted and useless, and less frequently some of the fireseed powder. He had promised the Lord Tyrant that he wouldn't return until he had both firestick makers and the secret of fireseed manufacture—even if he had to kidnap a highpriest of Styphon's House.

If he didn't return without them, it would cost his family their lives. Of course, he had to cross the Sea of Grass first and help the false priests win their war against the man they called a demon in human form.

He heard the noise of leather chafing metal and the sounds of boots on stone, indicating that the Zarthani merchant had been brought to the guard station.

"Strategos, sir."

"Yes, Baltrath."

"The Trader Jorand has arrived, sir."

"Good. Bring him in."

The portly merchant followed Sergeant Baltrath into his chamber, their footsteps echoing within the stone walls.

"Your Excellency, Captain-General Zarphu, I am delighted to meet you at last."

He doubted the veracity of those words; the merchant was sweating profusely and even his thick robe was stained around the armpits. The rain had ended half a candle ago and it was a cool evening.

"What can you tell me about the House of Styphon?"

"I try to avoid them whenever possible, Your Excellency," he said, with a sickly smile.

His tongue was heavily accented, but the words were similar to Ros-Zarthani. There was a falseness to the man that made Zarphu distrust him even though he was obviously doing his best to please him. However, in the merchant's favor, there was none of the false priests' arrogance or disdain in his manner.

"What about this fireseed? Where does it come from?"

"The priests make it from a formula given to them by their god, Styphon. The war between them and King Kalvan came about because he also knows the Fireseed Mystery."

"Does he…?"

"Yes, and Styphon's House says he has released it to the world; this has gained him the undying hatred of the Temple. They will do anything to bring Kalvan and his House down."

Maybe we hired out to the wrong party, he thought. Still, it appeared that half his worries were solved even before they crossed the Shield of God mountains. "Can you teach me how to make it?"

"No, I do not know the formula. There are princedoms in Hos-Hostigos and Hos-Harphax, where it is known. But not in Hos-Ktemnos, where even talking about it is worth your life."

That was unfortunate. He wasn't sure he believed the trader; on the other hand, he had no reason to lie. Maybe he was afraid of the priests.

"What about the firesticks?"

Jorand shook his head. "I'm not an artificer. I know you use an iron tube for the barrel and wood for a stock, but I wouldn't know how to make one of those tubes or flintlock gadgets."

"We have working models. Maybe if you had some encouragement…."

The merchant paled. "I'd have to do a lot of tinkering to get it right. Who knows how long it might take?"

Trader Jorand appeared to be all thumbs. It didn't appear that Zarphu was going to get out of this expedition that easily. *Too bad*, he thought, although, he might have had a tough time explaining to the Tyrant why he reneged on his contract, just to save the lives of a few soldiers. It wouldn't take long for their master artificers to produce the *calivers* and *arquebuses* in large quantities; the only thing holding them back had been the lack of fireseed. Once they got the formula from the Hostigi, then they would be able to make their own firetubes, too.

IX

Jorand looked down at the passes and mountains below and felt his breath grow short; the view was as magnificent as it had been the first time he'd come up the mountains, back when he was a forty-niner and working undercover. "The Rocky Mountains," that's what they were named on Europo-American, he recalled. The wilderness was as unspoiled as it had been over a hundred years ago, when he was passing himself off as a gold miner. At the time, he'd needed a quick source of money to pay off the last of his debts; purchasing illegal longevity treatments had cost a bundle.

True, gold was almost worthless on Home Time Line. There was enough cached in vaults and on the moon from uncountable expeditions to make it as common as iron. However, outtime it was still a very valuable commodity. With the gold he'd got from his mines, he'd built up quite a fortune in only a few years. It really helped when you knew where the good ore and rich veins of gold were before you left Home Time Line; all the unclassified data collected outtime was available to any Paratimer in the Master Resource Data Bank. Metals were useful, but of no great value.

The really valuable outtime resources were original artworks, jewelry, ancient artifacts, furs, incunabula, recordings of rare or new music, unknown fossils, secret knowledge and rites, new inventions, master paintings and, maybe the most valuable of all—beautiful women.

Jorand had specialized in providing gorgeous young girls, sold as mistresses or slaves or wives; he was indifferent to their fates. They were as lovely and as insubstantial—with their short lifetimes—as butterflies. In San Francisco during the Gold Rush, there had been plenty of gorgeous girls and women, many of them prostitutes or gold-diggers, most of them untraceable. He had secretly traded them on Home Time Line for Paratime Exchange Units and for influence. Those were the good old days....

Now, he was stuck in an even more primitive milieu on Aryan-Transpacific, dependent on a crazy man for a way home. He shook his head. He would have to make the best of it, but it wasn't easy. Everywhere he went, he felt Warntha's eyes on him. His impersonation of a Styphon's House highpriest was frightfully good. Even the real priests were afraid of him. Oddly, Warntha got along very well with the Ros-Zarthani soldiers; at least, the rank and file. He wondered what the Warntha's real mission was....

The trail leading down through the mountains was about the width of one of the primitive horse-drawn wagons, or as wide as the tracks on those railroads he'd rode when he crossed the great divide on his way from San Francisco to New York. He wondered what he'd do once the journey was finished. No one had told him anything; Tharn had told him to follow Warntha's lead, but he didn't trust the former mercenary. He suspected his life would end when the journey finished. He needed to prepare for that eventuality, which meant he needed currency, or what passed for it here on Kalvan's Time Line. And he needed a place to go....

X

Verkan was beginning to feel—and not for the first time—that his time on Kalvan's Time Line was more and more turning into a job rather than a hobby. The problems there followed him to Home Time Line, just like problems here followed him to Kalvan's Time Line. The mess on Alexandrian-Roman, Seleuco-Macedonian Subsector had been easy to clean up in comparison. One of the employees of Vendrax Luxury Imports had freelanced in local dives as a mind reader, using a miniature radio and a local confederate. The problems started when his confidence game began to bore him and he decided to return to First Level for help with his new con, becoming the God Alexander.

The would-be mind reader saw this as the opportunity of a lifetime, hypno-meched all the available data on Alexander the Great, had a cheap face sculpt. Unfortunately, he was recognized by the locals as Alexander as soon as he exited the Vendrax pottery factory. The locals went gaga and started a city-wide riot.

They overthrew their local tyrant and were threatening to restore the false-Alexander to Imperial greatness when the Paratime Police were notified of the problem by a supervisor at Vendrax who didn't buy his corpse switch.

Unfortunately, the local Paratime Police Inspector in charge of operations on that subsector was a drone waiting for his retirement and had botched a rescue job, killing several hundred locals and using enough technology for cries of witchcraft to be uttered in the streets. Verkan had been called in because the Inspector refused to leave and he had to personally fire him and those subordinates stupid enough to go along with his plan instead of notifying Paratime HQ.

By the time Verkan arrived, it was obvious the Paratimer was terrified at the havoc he'd caused and really only wanted to get out of town. However, he had his own bodyguard and several advisors who saw him as their ride to the top; they weren't going to allow anything to get in the way, including the false Alexander's desire to do a quick skip. Meanwhile, a major war was brewing and very little trade was happening at Vendrax Luxuries.

It had taken Verkan and his investigators three days to find out where they were keeping the false Alexander, on the top of a four-story warehouse in Alexandria. They came in at midnight on an airbus, dusted the place with sleep gas, landed on the roof, broke in and 'liberated' Alexander, who was now in the hands of the Bureau of Psych-Hygiene for a memory wipe and psycho-social adjustment.

Verkan had returned to his office to find Kostran absent-mindedly twirling his pipe, sitting across from Verkan's horseshoe desk. "You're supposed to be in Greffa representing the House of Verkan—what are you doing here?" Verkan asked, as he sat down.

"Chief, we've run across a real anomaly. Zinganna and I agreed that you needed to be brought up to speed on what's been happening in Greffa the last couple of days."

I haven't been gone that long, Verkan thought to himself. "What happened? A palace coup?"

"Nothing that bad. We've just verified local reports that a large army from the West Coast of the Northern Minor Land Mass is traveling north across the old Iron Trail. It will be arriving on Grefftscharrer territory in two or three days."

"What? Isn't that the home of the Ros-Zarthani—the supposedly decadent ancestors of the Zarthani populations on the East Coast? What are they doing on the old Iron Trail?"

Kostran shrugged. "Their army is too small to be an invasion force, but it's too big for anything but trouble—at least, that's how the Grefftscharrers see it. We believe they're from the city-state of Antiphon, but have been unable to verify this since we don't have any agents there. The Ros-Zarthani army has all of Greffa in an uproar."

"I don't doubt it. The Grefftscharrers usually expect their enemies to attack from the east or south, not from the west. What are they going to do about it?"

Kostran stopped twirling his pipe, loaded the barrel and lit up. "The Council of Merchants wanted King Theovacar to raise an army and send them packing. The Assembly of Lords was in agreement."

"That's a first. I can't remember the last time those two bodies agreed on the color of the sky! I take it that Theovacar wasn't too anxious to take on this invading army?"

"You're right, Chief. There's no gain for him no matter what he does. If Theovacar raises an army and defeats the barbarians, so what—they're just a bunch of hicks with spears. On the other hand, if he loses—Theovacar is in a mess of trouble and could lose his throne. Not that either the Council or Assembly of Lords would shed any tears. Neither body is happy about the way King Theovacar has been centralizing his authority in Grefftscharr."

"That's a given. So what did he do?"

"Theovacar told them that as long as the barbarian army did not commit an act of war he was not able to justify attacking them. However, if one of his barons or princes felt threatened, they were free to raise their own army. The Prince of Thagnor, who's been trying to slip out of Theovacar's leash for years, decided to raise an army of his own. Prince Varrack did a pretty good job; about six thousand levy, three thousand mercenary horse and the Army of Thagnor—another four thousand men."

Verkan nodded. "Good move, you've got to hand it to King Theovacar. Even if the Prince wins, he'll lose a lot of troops; if he doesn't win, he might not only lose face but his life as well. How did Varrack get his troops into Greffa without starting a civil war?"

"He's having them ferried over now. They'll be arriving in a few days. One might almost think Varrack had something to do with this invasion, if we didn't know better."

Verkan nodded. "You're right. I bet Theovacar isn't sleeping well these days. After all, it's Theovacar's job, not his nobles' place, to defend his kingdom from invasion, whether they can be classed as 'hicks with spears' or not."

"I think Theovacar's afraid that if he moves the Royal Army away from Greffa City, his enemies will attempt a coup—or start a civil war, while he's out of town. It's the same problem Great King Lysandros faces if he heads up the Harphaxi Royal Army and chases after Kalvan in Hos-Hostigos next spring. If Theovacar stays in Greffa while his troops march off, he's even more of a coup target."

Living in Greffa hadn't slowed Kostran's mental muscles; if anything it had quickened them. "So what's Theovacar's answer?"

"So far, he's not talking. There's lots of grumbling in the streets about Kings who don't honor their oaths and obligations—mostly from his petty barons, at this point. The commoners don't care since they feel safe behind the city walls. The merchants are too busy rubbing their hands together over all the profits they're making selling fireseed, food stocks and weapons to Varrack and his crowd. Meanwhile, Theovacar's most vocal opponents are playing soldier with Prince Varrack. Maybe he's hoping they'll get their heads handed to them on a platter!"

Verkan laughed. "I wouldn't put it past him. I'd like to see him work the Executive Council."

Kostran joined in the laughter.

After he'd stopped laughing, Verkan asked, "Kostran, what are Prince Varrack's chances?"

"It's hard to tell. We know very little about the West Coast city-states.

I've already picked two agents to infiltrate Mythrene City. They'll find out what's going on since that city is the drop-off point for Ros-Zarthani expeditions along the old Iron Trail.

"We have done some nighttime aerial surveillance and it appears that this Ros-Zarthani army is a first class operation by the way it's run, but they've never encountered firearms before—that's a big liability. On the other hand, the Greffans are over-confident and Prince Varrack's never been in a battle this size. I'd call it a tossup."

Verkan shook his head. "I hate to take sides, but I hope Varrack beats the iron pants off the Ros-Zarthani and sends them back to Antiphon where they belong. Kalvan's got enough problems without another army to worry about."

XI

Captain-General Phidestros watched as the two Knights, in blackened armor and white capes with Styphon's black sun-wheel emblazoned on the back, brought Grand Master Soton's chair in and then waited at attention while the Grand Master strutted in and took his seat. Phidestros was surprised to note how much Soton had aged; there were sharp lines around his eyes and mouth, and his beard had turned mostly gray. He wondered what had caused him the most pain, losing thousands of his beloved Knights on Phyrax Field or having to explain to the Inner Circle of Styphon's House his 'retreat' from Kalvan's army? Neither could have been easy, but knowing Soton as he did, he suspected the former.

"Grand Master Soton, can I offer you some winter wine?"

Soton excused one of his Knights, but the Sergeant stayed. "Yes, I could use a drink. I have spent far too many hours talking to nobles with more iron between their ears than in their spines." He sounded weary and a little hoarse.

"We could always meet tomorrow, Grand Master."

"No, I can only stay for a moon-quarter more, and then I have to return to Balph. We have a lot to discuss if the invasion of Hos-Hostigos is to be successful."

"Agreed. Mynoss, serve us some wine." After his servant had brought them all, including Sergeant Sarmoth, goblets of red winter wine, Phidestros made a toast. "To Styphon and the fall of the false Kingdom of Hos-Hostigos."

After a long swallow, Soton offered up another toast. "And to Great King Lysandros!"

"To Great King Lysandros."

"Unfortunately, that is about the only good news to come from the Sastragathi debacle."

"That is hardly true, Grand Master. You drove the barbarians into the Trygath, threatening western Hostigos, which prevented Kalvan from invading Hos-Harphax, something he could have done with ease this spring. Instead he spent the campaign season chasing you."

"I am glad to see *you* believe our sacrifice was not in vain."

"I don't just believe it, I know it, Grand Master. If you had not diverted Kalvan's attention to the west, Hos-Harphax would be no more—and Harphax a princedom of Hos-Hostigos! If you still believe, as you did last year, that Hos-Harphax is the anchor of the Five Kingdoms, then your sacrifice was well-made."

"I hope you are right," Soton said. "The entire campaign was a nightmare I'd just as soon forget...."

"We have made great progress here."

"Tell me about it."

"By Styphon's Grace and much of his gold, I have completely rebuilt the Army of Hos-Harphax; it now musters over eighteen thousand men: two thousand Royal Pistoleers, eight hundred of the King's Royal Lancers, four thousand Royal Foot Guard and four thousand Mobile Dragoons—mounted infantry much like Kalvan's Mobile Force, made up of the best of the City Militia—and a dozen mercenary regiments. I've recently hired another six thousand mercenaries, four thousand foot and two thousand horse; all have agreed to join the Royal Army—for a price. I've formed two mobile batteries of four six-pounders and six four-pounders each and one Royal Rifle Company with seventy-six riflemen.

"Excellent!—Captain-General. You have been busy. But how well trained are these troops?"

"Every third man in each company is a veteran, and we've been drilling them six days a moon-quarter since spring. They're not seasoned yet, but they are in good spirits. I'm paying them twice the usual salary and year round—"

"So that was how you convinced the mercenaries to join the Royal Army." Soton nodded thoughtfully. "Year round! I can hear Archpriest Drayton, the Temple's Treasurer, screaming all the way from Balph."

"No you won't. I'm not paying them all in gold. Half their salary is paid in iron coin, redeemable in gold *only* when Kalvan's army has been defeated."

"Brilliant." Soton shook his head as he took out a burl pipe with silver inlay. "By what spell do you convince soldiers to accept iron in place of gold?"

"All soldiers are gamblers and see nothing ahead but the piles of gold they will win when the Army of Hostigos has been vanquished. It has also given them a great incentive to work on their drills. Besides, many of the local merchants, ladies of the evening and gamblers accept the iron coins at a discount."

"If that is true, truly you have brought about Styphon's Own Miracle! Styphon be praised! If the local slatterns and sharpers are willing to take these iron rakmars in trade, then even the scum must believe that we will prevail. I wish the Archpriests of the Inner Circle shared their faith."

"They will, Grand Master. They will. The City Militia is now more than ten thousand strong, and are better armed and better drilled than in living memory. Every moon I have a thousand of them brought to Tarr-Anibra where they are drilled from first light to dark. They do much better away from Tarr-Harphax and the City walls. They will not run as they did at Chothros Heights."

"You have made great progress in the past year—even more than I expected. Yet, this shortage of mercenaries may yet prove our undoing. I had hoped you would have twelve to fifteen thousand Free Companions by this time, but far too many have died in this Ormaz-spawned war against the Usurper—or worse, have taken his colors. Archpriest Anaxthenes put before me an idea that may help solve our problem. Let me present it to you."

Soton explained how Styphon's House had merchants and agents-inquisitory who traveled as distant as the far off West Coat settlements of the Ros-Zarthani. One of these agents had been authorized by the Inner Circle to hire an entire army of Ros-Zarthani. Word had recently arrived in Balph that they were almost across the Sea of Grass.

"This is interesting news," Phidestros said, his face trying to hide his disappointment. He needed these western barbarians like he needed another regiment of royal lancers. "How do we know they will not break the first time Kalvan's guns fire?"

Soton shrugged. "They may be sounder troops than you suspect. The agent-inquisitory has informed Archpriest Anaxthenes that the Ros-Zarthani know neither kingdoms nor princedoms as we do. Each city acts as its own kingdom—yes, a chaotic system of rule that leads to much fighting. A highpriest was sent by Archpriest Roxthar to 'hire' an army from one of the larger cities to aid in our war against the Usurper Kalvan. The army will march from their home, across the Sea of Grass and through Grefftscharr."

"You mean some highpriest, who doesn't know a rake from a ramrod, has hired an unknown army and believes it will pass unmolested through the Sea of Grass? The Grefftscharri will pulverize it as grindstone mills wheat. Why not skirt Greffa all together, by taking the—"

"Fighting the Greffa Army is be their test, as I understand it. These troops have never faced fireseed, and it is well that they do so before they meet the Royal Army of Hos-Hostigos in the field. It will take Styphon's Own Miracle for them to arrive as an intact unit. Yet, this Highpriest Prythos believes that these Ros-Zarthani can more than hold their own against the nomads and Grefftscharrers. At least he has convinced Archpriest Anaxthenes and Roxthar that this is so."

"Anaxthenes may know all there is to be known about running temple services and pulling Supreme Priest Sesklos' strings, but he knows nothing of war."

"Don't underestimate Archpriest Anaxthenes. Any Archpriest who has survived for twenty winters in the Inner Circle has more understanding of command than you might think. There is even talk that he will become the next Voice of Styphon."

Suddenly all is clear, Phidestros thought. Lysandros might believe the gathering host was his army, but Styphon's House had a different opinion. "Since the Temple pays, we cannot lose. What weapons do they use?"

"They still fight in full armor and on destriers, much as our ancestors did and your Royal Lancers do now."

"Oh no, more iron hats! Kalvan's artillery will harvest them before they have time to set their lances."

"Not all of them. Many use bows or carry heavy throwing darts."

Phidestros shook his head. "Darts and bows! They will probably run when the first shot is fired."

"If half of what this Highpriest Prythos claims is true, they may surprise both you, me and—most importantly, Kalvan. At worst, they will serve as a screen for our own troops."

"For how long has Styphon's House purchased these *soldiers*?"

"Styphon's House has paid their city well; they are under contract to fight for two years, or until the Usurper Kalvan is dead, whichever happens first. Scoff if you must, but answer me this: where else do you intend to find more mercenaries to fight under our banners?"

Phidestros shook his head. "There are no more mercenaries to be bought in the Five Kingdoms, not for gold or glory. No, bring these iron hats, and we will find some use for them—if they ever arrive! If nothing else, they will give Kalvan's guns targets while my men do more serious work."

XII

A cloud of dust on the far horizon usually meant a herd of buffalo or cattle were moving across the Sea of Grass. Today Arch-Stratego Zarphu knew it was neither; it was the advancing Grefftscharrer Army. His scouts had already told him the disposition of the enemy army: six thousand infantry, mostly carrying long spears and firesticks, four thousand heavy cavalry and two thousand light auxiliaries, mostly Ruthani cavalry recruited from the grasslands. He told one of his orderlies to fetch the Highpriest.

Highpriest Warntha rode quickly to his side in a very soldierly and un-priestly manner that of which heartily approved. "I see the enemy is closing."

Zarphu ignored the snorts of disapproval from his senior officers; he knew the difference between priests and soldiers even if his officers didn't. "This is not an ideal place for a battle." He paused to indicate the flat lands on all sides. "Nor is it a good place for an ambush."

The Highpriest, who no longer wore his yellow robes, nodded. "If we can defeat the Grefftscharrer Army here, we can perform both a service to Styphon and a disservice to the Usurper Kalvan. The Kings of Grefftscharr only rule as long as they show enough strength to cow both their under-lords and the powerful merchants of Greffa. It has been rumored that arms have been shipped from Greffa to the false kingdom of Hostigos. A win here will be the first victory of next year's campaign!"

Zarphu was impressed with the priest's knowledge of things other than arcane rites and offerings of his trade and wondered if he had served in a military order before putting on his robes. He'd learned from the fat merchant that Styphon's House had two military arms of its own. Zarphu had tried to question Highpriest Warntha about his past but might have had better success with a stone, could any be found on this endless grassland.

Zarphu was not as convinced as the priest that his army—though greater in size—would be able to seize the battlefield. His knowledge of the enemy was negligible and his own army had no experience fighting against the firesticks. The Highpriest had demonstrated the noisy and smelly "muskets" and they had proved to be capricious. The fireseed had to be dry or they would not fire. However, the muskets were deadly when fired—if they hit their target. Unlike his archers, who could hit the eye socket of an approaching enemy from a hundred paces.

His soldiers were all experienced troops—fourteen maniples of a thousand men each, eight of horse and six of foot soldiers. Plus, two maniples of the Lord Tyrant's own Immortals—heavy armored cavalry who fought with spear and broadsword.

Zarphu turned to Stratego Lyphar and ordered, "The enemy is two marches away. When they are one march, have the foot archers and skirmishers run ahead and engage the enemy. They are not to hold, but fall back and draw the enemy in."

He turned to another general and ordered him to support Lyphar's foot with his light cavalry, mostly horse-archers and javelin throwers. Then he addressed Highpriest Warntha. "I would have taken the river route that my scouts recommended, but I also thought it might be best to test the mettle of the Eastern ironmen."

Warntha looked over in surprise, and even had the grace to blush. It was the first time Zarphu had read any emotion on the priest's face. If these priestly troops of Styphon's were not soldiers at arms, they were soldiers of the heart.

"You must remember, Highpriest, our records go back almost two thousand winters. We have traversed these lands and trails more times than there are nomads upon the Sea of Grass. While it is true that trade between us and the Middle Kingdoms has dwindled to a trickle, there are still among us those who trade along the old routes. Several of these are among our scouts. I am as anxious as you are to see how well my men hold up against the firesticks. However, I suspect you will be the more surprised."

It was also true that Zarphu sounded more confident about his troops than he felt. His people had heard stories about these fire weapons for centuries, and had obtained more than a few over the years of trading.

However, as long as the fireseed was scarce, they were more curiosities than real weapons. One of the traders had told him that the fireseed mystery was no longer a secret. If this were true, he would take back more than gold from these distant lands. With the firesticks, the Lord Tyrant would be able to complete his conquest of the city-states and expand his reach into the Sea of Grass and maybe even farther.

The light foot soldiers began to run forward and the heavy infantry, with full body shields and long spears, went into a double time. The massed heavy cavalry followed to exploit any breaks in the enemy lines. If all went well, the archers and javelin throwers would sting the enemy army, bringing forth the more impetuous cavalry and foot. Then the skirmishers would retreat behind the shield wall and the slaughter would commence; at least, that was how it was done in the homelands. Nothing was certain against an unknown enemy—except uncertainty.

XIII

Prince Varrack, purple plumes jutting out from the back of his burgonet, pointed to the growing mass of men, the sun sparkling off their armor, in the distance. "There are the Ros-Zarthani barbarians. We shall ride over them as the buffalo trample the Ruthani tent cities!"

"Your Lordship, I suggest we move to the rear just in case a stray spear comes our way," one of the Barons suggested. "Let the professional soldiers do their work."

"There will be few casualties today, my friend." Prince Varrack said, slapping the Baron on the back with his gauntleted hand. The nobleman, who wore no more armor than a silvered breastplate over his red and black velvet doublet, staggered forward, almost falling off his mount. When he had regained his poise, he gave Varrack a pained expression. "My back hurts!"

Varrack had to choke back a laugh. Such weakness was all too typical of Greffa's decadent nobility. Many of them wore more perfume than his courtesans. *This will all change after the vile dog Theovacar is put in his place. I will return the Middle Kingdoms to their past glory, with Thagnor the king of cities, and it all begins today with my crushing defeat of these barbarians.*

Another noble, this one with a cultivated lisp, announced, "Please, let us stay at the front, Varrack, so we can watch these creatures die up-close!"

A young Count, with a wispy blond beard, cried, "This is so much better than one of Theovacar's Spectacles. One grows tired of pantomime sea battles and bear fights."

Captain-General Errock said with gritted teeth, "Your Lordship, my men need to prepare for battle. We will be hampered if we have to spend our time protecting your guests." The way he stepped on the last word left no doubt about his own feelings concerning the martial ability of Grefftscharrer nobles in general.

"We shall retire, Captain-General. It is your job to win this battle." Under his breath, Prince Varrack added, "And win me the glory I need to challenge Theovacar in his own city."

XIV

The battle opened almost like a scroll-written exercise out of Arch-Stratego Zarphu's library. It appeared the Grefftscharrer soldiers held his army in contempt, allowing their own front ranks to break as they attempted to chase down the annoying skirmishers. The archers and spearmen quickly pulled back behind the now stationary shield wall and—once the enemy was within bow range—began to fire at will. Several hundred disorganized enemy light cavalry ran into the shield wall; many of them were impaled on spears or shot out of their saddles by arrows. When an enemy fell, a skirmisher would rush from behind the shields and dispatch him with a quick sword thrust.

When enemy cavalry advanced to the shield wall, the surviving skirmishers and light cavalry moved to the wings. Meanwhile the enemy foot soldiers marched forward, setting their long spears and firesticks. The archers continued their steady stream of arrows, with gratifying results as the enemy was forced to close ranks and cease forward movement. Now the Grefftscharrer cavalry was forced to stand and take fire until their own infantry arrived. Meanwhile the archers and spearmen killed hundreds of Grefftscharrers, since only the front ranks of the Grefftscharrer cavalry wore full armor.

The enemy horse parted and a large body of firestick men and others carrying short bows with stocks moved forward. Suddenly, the firesticks crackled and sputtered, and a cloud of smoke with the stink of brimstone filled the air.

A noise like thunder hammered Zarphu's ears! For a moment he thought his horse would buck him off its back. Several of his officers were thrown, but most quickly remounted. For a few moments there were holes in the shield wall, and the entire line buckled, until the rear ranks moved up. Only a few men broke ranks and they were cut down by the swords of their comrades. It appeared to Zarphu that most of the firesticks' force was spent on the shields. The flight of arrows fired in answer inflicted many more casualties among the unprotected Grefftscharrer infantry, especially the firestick men who were not wearing steel chest plates.

The firestick men fired several times, but the shield wall held. The enemy's own lines took many more casualties from bow fire and javelins.

Out of the cloud of smoke a large body of enemy horse, mostly armored, rushed forward striking the shield wall. Again the wall held, while the spear points spitted horses that screamed and bucked off their riders. Skirmishers rushed forward with long knives to slash the throats of the fallen horsemen and their mounts. The stalled enemy cavalry milled in front of the shield wall, futilely hacking at it with their swords or firing short firesticks, until their commanders ordered a retreat. When their surviving cavalry were back behind their own lines, the firestick men fired off their firesticks in unison.

One of his chief officers dropped off his saddle, sprouting a red hole just above his left eye. Zarphu cursed and wondered how many more irreplaceable troops he would lose in this battle.

The infantry battle continued, with the bowmen's arrows inflicting three times as many casualties as the firesticks. The enemy infantry began to bunch-up even tighter and the slaughter mounted. The Grefftscharrer foot became bunched together so closely that the enemy cavalry were forced to fight along the wings, where they were sternly rebuffed by the Immortals. Zarphu decided it was time to order forth his own heavy horse.

The horns sounded, and the infantry pulled back into lines. The iron-scaled cavalry moved forward through the infantry, while the shield wall reformed behind them.

The three maniples of plumbati pushed forward until they were within range of the enemy, then took out their heavy darts, casting them into the massed infantry. The enemy infantry were momentarily paralyzed, then forced together so closely only a few of the firestick men could shoot their weapons. The archers ran forward again, supported by horse-archers and began firing point blank into the massed Grefftscharrer foot. The slaughter was horrific, causing many of the enemy's long spearmen casting their weapons aside and trying to break rank—only to find there was nowhere to go. The ground ran with streams of the enemy's blood.

The plumbati pulled out their swords and cut their way through the ranks. Suddenly the entire body of enemy foot broke ranks, trampling those who stood in their way. The heavy spearmen now moved forward, cutting and slicing those left behind by the forward movement of the heavy cavalry. The enemy cavalry, spurred by the sight of their own retreating foot, rode over and through their own ranks to reach the plumbati—and died by the score.

Zarphu nodded and another horn sounded. Both left and right wings of heavy cavalry moved out in a flanking pincers movement to surround the enemy army. He was sorely disappointed when the enemy horns suddenly rang out, and the Grefftscharrer horse turned and retreated, leaving behind several thousand foot soldiers. The enemy horse reformed ranks before the wings could close, but the plumbati struck them hard from the rear.

The Grefftscharrer infantry were completely surrounded and disordered; the battlefield was littered with their brightly colored corpses. The cavalry reformed to chase the enemy horse, which fled so hurriedly they left behind their wounded.

Seeing their own cavalry flee, the Grefftscharrer foot surrendered, putting their helmets upon their swords. The survivors numbered less than half of those who had joined the battle. Zarphu rubbed his hands—a nice ransom.

Highpriest Prythos, too, had a big smile. He nodded, saying, "I am impressed, Arch-Stratego." They both watched as the enemy horse, under withering fire, left in a massed but orderly retreat. "Are you going to ride them down?"

"We could grind them into the dust, but they are not cowards. We would take unnecessary losses. Also, another army lies in wait some forty marches away. There is no profit in goading them to attack. Better to let them hide behind their walls and lick their wounds, Highpriest. They will not forget us soon. We have other more important battles to win. And there will be no reinforcements."

"Wisely put," the Highpriest said. "I think many will be surprised by the Iron Men from across the Sea of Grass. None more so than the Usurper Kalvan!"

XV

"What happened to my army?" Prince Varrack cried when Captain-General Errock pulled up alongside, his horse breathing and snorting like a bellows.

The Captain-General's face was white and there was blood splattered across his breastplate. "A lot of good men died because we underestimated the enemy. It's the Trickster's own luck that the Ros-Zarthani didn't decide to chase us to the City walls."

"This is good fortune?" Varrack screamed, looking around at the rag-tag collection of horsemen that surrounded him, their finery soiled and their plumed helmets discarded. "We have lost a great battle, and you talk of luck!"

"We will be laughed out of the City," one of the Barons shouted.

Varrack punched the Baron in the face with his gauntlet, knocking him off his horse and onto the ground, where he was stretched out frozen as if he'd been poleaxed.

"You've killed him, Varrack!" the young Count cried. "This day has been a disaster for all of us."

Except Theovacar, thought Varrack, *who right this moment is laughing himself off his throne!* He ground his teeth until they squealed. *If we'd had King Theovacar's support, this defeat would never have happened. He withheld his soldiers to play us as fools! This disaster is his fault. Theovacar is in the pay of the Usurper Kalvan, as the priests of Styphon's House claim, otherwise he would have helped us take the field. Yes, this disaster is the result of Theovacar's treason! Wait until the City learns of it.*

XVI

Warntha Saln was sitting by the campfire drinking the piss-water the Ros-Zarthani called beer and discussing close-order tactics with an under officer of the Fourth Maniple when he felt the vibration from his locater alert. He quickly excused himself from the conversation, using the time-tested excuse of going to the latrine. Instead of heading straight to the trenches, Warntha swung around to the northwest where his locater indicated, through increasing vibrations, the homing signal was originating.

Warntha spotted the silver mesh of the twenty-foot Transtemporal conveyer in a small glade. He had been wondering when Hadron Tharn was going to send someone to pick him up. After their defeat of the Grefftscharrer army, the Ros-Zarthani army had followed the trail to Dorg where water transport was being arranged to ferry the army down river south of Wulfula to Tarr-Ceros, where they would winter. The Dorgi had refused transit rights to ship Zarphu and his men down the river until the defeat of the Grefftscharrer army. Now they couldn't get the Ros-Zarthani across the Great River fast enough.

Warntha wouldn't have minded staying with the Ros-Zarthani; the company was good—mostly fellow soldiers who had accepted him as one of their own despite his disguise as one of Styphon's highpriests. The possibilities for future fighting seemed endless, so he was content. He was especially looking forward to fighting against Kalvan and his Army of Hos-Hostigos.

On the other hand, things were never dull when Hadron Tharn was around. Warntha was surprised to find he actually missed his crazy boss.

The conveyer door opened to show Tharn with a welcoming smile, flanked by two guards in the black uniforms. "How was your exercise?"

Warntha took a seat inside the conveyer across from his boss and said, "It was a nice vacation. The Ros-Zarthani soldiers are good troops, even without gunpowder weapons. They'll give Kalvan fits, but not enough to be decisive."

Tharn's face blanked. "None of my plans are working. I'm hemmed in on every side by morons and incompetents! The Opposition Party has refused my latest donation! They claim that Chief Verkan's new policy of phased harvesting of the Europo-American Sector is workable and acceptable by all parties. So Verkan wins once again!"

Warntha was used to his bosses' sudden mood shifts, but this one took him by surprise. He wasn't exactly sure why his boss hated Paratime Chief Verkan Vall, but he suspected it had something to do with his sister Dalla. Or maybe the fact that he was the more powerful of the two. "What about Jorand? I didn't have time to make the memory transfer."

"Leave him here to rot. He can't do us any harm at this point; besides, living here is punishment enough."

Warntha nodded. "So what's the next move, boss?"

"We're on our way to Fifth Level Base One."

Warntha, as an ex-military specialist, had been originally recruited by Tharn's Organization to help train troops, mostly proles being trained for military action, at Base One and Two, on the Fifth Level, Industrial Service Sector. This had been going on for almost twenty years and Tharn had created quite the private little army. The proles he was using as shock troops believed that Hadron was a supporter of the Prole Liberation Movement. Warntha, knowing Tharn's prejudices regarding proles, seriously doubted that. He still didn't know Tharn's plans, but he knew that Tharn had no good purpose in mind for any of the proles, whom he regarded as little less than beasts of burden.

Warntha had just finished cleaning his kit when the overhead flickering ceased and the silver mesh began to solidify, signaling that they had arrived at Fifth Level, Base One. The conveyer came to rest in a small room. The two guards remained behind.

From there the two of them entered a gravlift and went to the surface where they boarded a rocket and traveled to a large island. This island was at the base of the largest southern continental mass, one that usually served the Home Time Line people as a recreation spot, meaning there was very little possibility of a Paratime Police conveyer dropping in unexpectedly.

Warntha, who was dressed for higher latitudes, felt himself began to sweat as they arrived at a large military compound. There were hundreds of bat-wing fighter craft in the base airport. It took a great portion of Tharn's assets to keep this place running, but he had six air-strike teams and fifteen divisions of infantry for his own personal army. To the best of Warntha's knowledge, it was a bigger force than First Level's own military which existed primarily to put down prole insurrections and revolts.

He followed Tharn into a large conference room with a large visiscreen dominating one wall. A dozen proles in military uniforms decorated with gold braid sat around a long trestle table.

They all rose to their feet as Tharn approached.

"Citizen Tharn, when can we mount our attack?"

"General, the time has not yet arrived. More work needs to be done on Home Time Line. I advise patience.

Warntha choked back a laugh. Having Tharn advise patience was like having someone advise a friend to take a vacation on Second Level Arzl Dykx, a subsector where the survivors of an ancient nuclear holocaust still killed each other for table scraps.

One of the generals, an older man with a gray beard, said, "Citizen, with your long life, you can afford to wait. I was a young man when I joined the PML—look at me now!"

The other proles nodded in agreement.

"If all goes as I have planned, you will all receive longevity treatments. You and your children will live a long life, indeed."

Tharn's promise appeared to settle them down and the generals went back to the business of plotting the overthrow of Fifth Level Home Force Headquarters.

As a veteran of the Home Force, Warntha knew the headquarters would have to be taken by surprise for this band of half-trained and inexperienced resistance fighters to overthrow their base. *What kind of surprise attack does Thran have planned? By definition, as a Hadron Tharn plan, it would be irregular, dangerous and with total disregard to casualties—one either side.* He almost felt sorry for the proles, to say nothing of Home Time Line....

XVII

Jorand carefully approached the big-eared soldier who'd been identified as one of the last to see Warntha. "Do you know where the big priest went?"

The soldier, who was still drunk, said, "Naw, last I saw, he was off to the privy pit." He pointed to a nearby copse of trees.

"When was that?"

"Last night. Ahhh, curse and blast it! My bleedin' head hurts." He reached down and rested his hand on his sword pommel. "Enough with the questions!"

Jorand turned away and went back to the camp. *It looks like I got left behind,* he decided. If he was going to be stuck here on Kalvan's Time Line, a backward place at best, he needed a better cover than that of trader. He went back to the wagon he shared with Warntha and quickly searched it. Most of Warntha's possessions, and there weren't many, were still there; however, the money chest had been pried open and all the gold and silver removed.

"How could I be so stupid!" he asked the universe, as he quickly pawed through the remaining possessions and blankets looking for the lost coins. Only a few coppers turned up. *Now I'm broke and stranded!*

Jorand needed a new cover ID and quickly, being a broke merchant, with no friends and contacts, was not going to get him anything but a very nasty and short future. He thought rapidly and decided that he needed to learn more about Styphon's House, which seemed to be the biggest and most successful racket on Aryan-Transpacific.

He went over the Highpriest Prythos' wagon, which was bigger and better outfitted than the one he and Warntha had shared. He knocked on the side and Prythos' head emerged from the canvas slit. "What do you want?" the priest demanded.

Jorand drew out his tobacco pouch. "I thought we'd share a smoke."

The priest nodded. "Come on in."

The inside was lit by a flickering oil lamp; there were two benches, covered in thick bearskin, to sit on. He filled his pipe and then passed his pouch to the highpriest. Not being much of a smoker, he had a lot of his original supply left. The way the priest grabbed his tobacco pouch made it clear that the heavy-set man had either run out of tobacco or was down to his last few flakes.

"I can't wait till we get back to civilization so I can get some quality leaf." The Highpriest paused to shake his head, as he filled his pipe. "This journey will be my last, by Styphon's Brass Balls! Too much heat, too much dust and too many barbarians. Plus, no respect from Zarphu and his commanders, either."

"This was an important trip, wasn't it?" Jorand asked.

Highpriest Prythos nodded, and visibly swelled. "I was given this assignment by Holy Investigator Roxthar himself. The Archpriest promised that if I made a good deal with the barbarians and brought back the soldiers he wanted, I would be well rewarded."

Jorand eyes widened and he nodded, as if highly impressed. He also noticed that Prythos, with his bald head and shaved faced, looked pretty much like any other bald and shaven heavy man with a pot belly—rather like himself, less hair. The yellow robe would hide any physical differences. A plan began to blossom.

Prythos continued, "He even suggested that I might be elevated to archpriest! With no payment, either. What about that?"

"Very impressive," Jorand said, stroking his goatee. He used his First Level memory to pick up on the highpriest's voice and syntax so that he could impersonate him later on. "I suppose, as a highpriest you have your own manor in Balph?"

The priest practically preened. "Yes, it's in the northern quadrant, outside the city gates. A very nice twenty-room mansion, but nothing compared to what I'll have once I'm elevated to the Inner Circle." He went on in great detail to talk about all the slaves and servants he would purchase and what he would do to several of his enemies once he was an archpriest.

"An Archpriest! I'm fortunate to have known you." Jorand continued to fawn over the highpriest and ask him detailed questions about the Styphon's House racket and his own background. It turned out Prythos was new to Balph and didn't have a lot of friends there.

Prythos pulled out a goatskin bag of wine. "How would you like some of this? It was a present from one of the barbarians. He gave me six of them; this is the last bag."

"Sure," Jorand replied. He spent the next two candles plying the high-priest with more wine, while drinking sparingly himself. When Prythos left to visit the latrine, he used that opportunity to drug the wine. After the priest passed out, he used his knife to slit his throat, then waited until dark to dispose of the body.

Jorand dragged the body to his own wagon and put the priest inside. Then he went back to get the oil lamp. He spread the remaining oil inside his wagon and lit it on fire before returning to the highpriest's vehicle. The wagon was completely engulfed in flames before anyone in the camp noticed and no one made an attempt to try and save the merchant supposedly inside.

The next morning, using his knife, he cut off his hair and beard, then shaved any remaining hair with the priest's straight razor. Since the old robe had been fouled when Prythos' died, Jorand put on the dead man's cleanest yellow robe. Then he went outside to view his former wagon.

No one questioned him and took it for granted that he was Highpriest Prythos.

"What do we do with the merchant's remains, Your Worship?" one of the unkempt muleskinners asked. He looked as though he wanted to poke through the wagon's blackened shell to see if there were any coins or other treasures the fire hadn't consumed. No one appeared the least bit concerned about the dead man inside.

"You have my permission. The merchant was an unbeliever and does not merit our rituals."

"Praise Styphon!" the greedy muleskinner proclaimed.

Nor did it hurt that the dead highpriest hadn't been close to anyone in the party. The common soldiers and wagoners were intimidated by his rank and association with Styphon's House, while their commanders regarded him as a necessary pest. Jorand imitated the priest's bluff and hearty manner with the guards, telling them that it was time they made their way to Dorg. If he was going to be stuck in this wasteland, he might as well be at the top of the heap.

THE ALEXANDER AFFAIR

JOHN F. CARR

I

1967 A.D.

Davran Thal was sitting at the console in front of the visiscreen as he tallied up the Parian marble statues and red-figure pottery he was about to send back to First Level. He looked up when he heard the whoosh of a door opening into the transposition depot chamber buried deep underneath the factory floor.

Coming out of the portal was his friend and fellow Paratimer, Halthar Varn. "Hello Varn, I expected you back two ten-days ago?"

Halthar shook his head. "I used up some more of my leave time. Bored and tired is what I am. I not only hate this boring time-line, but the people who sent us here!"

They both had five-year outtime contracts with Vendrax Luxury Imports to locate and ship luxury goods from the Fourth Level Alexandrian-Roman, Seleuco-Macedonian Subsector where the civilization was frozen at the pre-industrial stage and the most recent innovation was the horse collar. A stage where it had remained static for the past two thousand years. Progress was as foreign to this subsector as good hygiene. In truth, one became accustomed to the smell of unwashed humanity, but never to the sameness of each day and the dreary stone and mud-block buildings of Alexandria.

In this subsector Alexander the Great had lived long enough to conquer most of the known world. After he died without issue, Seleucia I Nicator became regent of Alexander's empire and eventually consolidated his power by assassination and military domination. Davran doubted old Seleucia Nicator would have found many changes in this time-line, other than its size, were he to be brought back to life. All Davran knew was that there hadn't been anything new or different since he'd arrived some three and a half years ago. Nor would there be when he left in another year and a half—if he could last that long.

"Believe it or not, I've come up with something to break the monotony of this hellhole," Davran declared.

"What?" Halthar asked, frowning. "You're not using Black Henbane again, are you? The last time you used that drug you went into convulsions. Even the priestesses of Apollo have to be careful when using it for their oracles."

Davran dismissed his friend's concerns with a wave of his hand. "I was experimenting with different dosages and additives. I believe I added too much nightshade. But, I don't take Henbane anymore—too dangerous. This is something new."

Halthar gave him the same kind of look his crèche mother used to give him when he returned disheveled and late at night from one of his outings in Old Town Dhergabar.

"No, this is completely different. I've been going to the *taverna*, the Bronze Bulls. I've set up microdots for recording on all the tables so I can overhear conversations."

"Sounds boring to me," Halthar responded.

"Maybe, but not always. But it's not gossip or scandals I'm looking for. I'm picking up background information which I can use later in my new game."

"Game? What are you taking about…? These locals are dangerous. Their man-god emperor has all the powers of a total despot. Insult or inflame the wrong person and the result is death. Remember, they still use scaphism, or the boats."

Davran remembered seeing such an execution: the prisoner was wrapped in rawhide and put between two narrow rowing boats, with holes for his face and limbs. Then he was forced to drink milk and honey until it ran out of his orifices. This attracted swarms of flies and other insects which would feast and lay eggs on the culprit's exposed parts. It often took days for the miscreant to die, all the while suffering horribly.

"No, I'm not stupid. I have no intention of ending up in the lion's pit, or suffering any of the other terrible punishments for capital offenders this dead-end time-line offers. This is just some light-hearted fun, and it's profitable!"

Halthar's ears perked up.

Davran smiled. "They pay up with gold and silver coins to win my favor. I do a little fortune telling, as well. I've been able to get a nice big apartment and buy two more slave girls."

Halthar frowned. "You and your handmaidens…. You know that the Paratime Code forbids slavery. The penalties are severe: you could be stuck on Home Time Line for the rest of your life; that is, if you don't get sent to Bureau of Psychological Rehabilitation for a mind wipe and reconditioning."

Davran laughed. "When was the last time you saw a Paracop at this outpost?"

"Well, never—but there's always a first time."

"That's your problem, Halthar. You never want to take any risks. You live in a tiny sublet that even a prole would disdain. Work with me and I'll see that you profit, too."

That night at the Bronze Bulls tavern, Davran ran his psychic act on a fat merchant and an older woman dressed in colorful silks with gold trim. He told the merchant that his wine caravan headed to Dalmatia would be most profitable, but since the bandit problem was growing he should double the amount of guards. The merchant was thankful and dropped a handful of silver coins before departing. The woman was worried about a faithless lover, and Davran told her that her paramour would never change. It was time for her to cut her younger lover loose. She wasn't as pleased as the merchant and only dropped a few coppers.

"Marks don't always want the truth," Halthar observed.

Davran smiled. "I'm always truthful. Once they realize my prediction was right, they come back for more—and their return visits are far more profitable."

"Yes, but this is a slow way to get rich. What you ought to do is present yourself as a demigod or king, like Alexander."

"That could be dangerous.... But you might be on to something."

II

Davran Thal had to wait three ten-days before he could make an unscheduled trip to Home Time Line to visit a face place for a cosmetic overhaul.

"What if a supervisor makes a surprise inspection?" Halthar had asked.

"When was the last time that happened, two years ago? Don't worry about it; if one does show up, you can tell them I had a medical emergency."

"What kind?"

"Tell him I fell and broke my nose and cheek bones. I needed cosmetic surgery."

Halthar nodded. "I guess that'll do."

After bandaging his face, Davran took the stairs down to the basement, where he used the thumblock to open the collapsed-nickel plated door to the conveyer terminal. Inside, he was met by the two company guards. They ran him through a full-body scanner to make sure he wasn't transporting any of the rare ceramic vases and dishes that were this time-line's only profitable export. After a quick peek, they didn't pay any attention to the box of gold and silver coins he was carrying. Their metal content was worth no more than lead, but they had a special appeal to coin collectors, especially those who specialized in Europo-American subsector coins.

He usually earned a few thousand units for those coins he brought back to Dhergabar, since he was careful to choose only select mint specimens.

Davran knew the right places to visit; proof that his childhood visits to Old Dhergabar had not been wasted. Unlike the rest of Dhergabar City, which was comprised of thousand-story towers and spires that reached up to the clouds, Old Town was a place of ground-hugging buildings, all of them millennia old, and the streets that squeezed between them. Many of the buildings housed drug bars, taverns, inns, stim-palaces and underground grottos where anything went, limited only by the customers' perverse imagination and the number of Paratime Exchange units they could raise. Ground cars from every time-line imaginable crowed the streets. Some were sleek as greyhounds, others old wrecks. He recognized a red 1955 Chevrolet Nomad from when he was working on Europo-American.

His first visit was to Rare Outtime Artifacts and Unusual Oddities where the owner purchased most of his mint coins. "Unlike most of these clowns, you know what a mint coin is," Harlon Zald noted. "Unfortunately, for you—and thanks to you—I'm overstocked on Seleuco-Macedonian coins. So don't bring anymore until you get posted to a new subsector. Now, if you could bring me in some of those coffin masks...."

Davran shook his head. "Sorry, Harlon, but they take death far too seriously on that subsector. The penalties for grave robbing are horrific!"

He left the store and looked for The Body Shop. It was no longer in its former emporium, now an empty building housing some empty-eyed stim-glass addicts and a few filthy prole runaways.

His next stop was a nearby bar which featured the latest Fourth Level Europo-American craze, some mop-topped musicians caterwauling away on electric instruments and a drum. He approached the bartender, asking for a highball while palming him a twenty-unit note.

"What happened to The Body Shop?" he asked loudly, trying to overpower the machine-like noises screeching from the bandstand.

"A Metro squad busted them two years ago. You must've been outtime?"

Davran nodded. "Do you know where they've relocated?"

He shrugged. "Haven't heard a word."

As a serious gambler, there were several places he went during his "off-work" visits to Dhergabar. He was well known at the Corkscrew, where he'd dropped a small fortune. If anyone knew where The Body Shop had gone, Jorand Rarth would know. He left the bar and made his way to the Corkscrew.

He was greeted at the front door by a familiar big man with a red scarf, sporting white skulls and crossbones, covering his head.

"I'd like to speak with Jorand Rarth," he said.

The man shook his head. "Jorand is outtime. And we don't know when—or if—he's coming back.

"Maybe, you can help me?" Davran asked.

"Are you in need of a little boost?" the big man asked.

As a good customer, Davran could call on an advance to tide him over. However, the payback rates were astronomical and he'd—so far—avoided that potential tar-pit. He shook his head. "No, Citizen, I'm looking for The Body Shop. It must have relocated and I thought if anyone in Old Town would know where, it would be Jorand."

"It's moved down on Azthal Street, but they don't call it The Body Shop anymore. Ask around back for the Transformer. Tell them Varlan sent you."

He thanked the crime boss, promising to return for some games of chance when his business was finished.

It took some digging but he found the Transformer down a lower level and beneath a bakery. The entrance looked derelict until you passed through the portal. The room was furnished in Second-Level Interworld Modern and probably cost more than he'd earned in the last fifty years. The receptionist was a young hairless woman with fine features; her head was egg-shaped and her eyes big and bright. She was alien-like in appearance.

She looked at him closely, squinting. "Who are you?"

"I'm Davran Thal. Varlan sent me."

"How can I best direct you," she asked.

"I need some cosmetic work done," he replied.

"How extensive?"

He showed her the Tri-D slab of Alexander the Great he'd downloaded from the Dhergabar Outtime Library. "I want to look like this."

"That'll require extensive reconstruction," she said. "It'll be expensive."

He smiled. "I've got means." In preparation he'd just taken out a loan for a new aircar, and had accumulated over fifty thousand units worth of jewelry and coins using his psychic con.

She smiled. "Let me call the Medico and tell him you're here."

III

Davran was under medical care for two ten-days before he was able to return to his time-line on the Seleuco-Macedonian Subsector, Alexander Belt, hitching a ride on a supply conveyer. During his return trip, Davran hypno-meched all the known data on Alexander the Great. When he arrived at the terminal, his friend Halthar didn't recognize him.

"Who are you?" he asked, as Davran exited the conveyer.

"It's me, Davran!" he exclaimed.

"Oh! You did it! I thought your face looked familiar."

"Yeah, it's on every drachma on this time-line."

Halthar looked embarrassed. "I'm sorry I ever came up with this idea. I never thought you'd go through with it."

Davran smiled. "This is my million-unit face. It's going to make both of us rich beyond our wildest dreams."

"If it doesn't get us killed," Halthar muttered.

They left the Vendrax collection depot to go outside to the main street, which was a riot of color and bustling activity: horse and mule-drawn carts, a few camels, as well as men in multi-colored tunics and the occasional barbarian or nomad wearing trousers and shirts. In the distance they could see Alexander's Pillar and the Great Lighthouse.

Suddenly a voice split the air: "By Jupiter and Mars, it's Alexander!"

"Back from the dead!" someone else shouted.

"It's the God Alexander come to help us!"

A tall man grabbed his tunic and tore it. "God, you must help me!" the man demanded.

Davran pushed him aside and tried to turn around.

"It's Alexander!" a dozen voices cried out.

A man with no hair and terrible sores covering his face cried out: "Please help me? I beseech you, Alexander. Remove this terrible curse!"

More people came running. Halthar forced his way forward through the growing crowd, with Davran in his wake.

They reached the factory door and pounded on it. No time to use their keys! Now, more people were shouting and screaming. Hands were grabbing at them. Suddenly, the door jerked open and they slipped inside. They slammed the door closed catching one of the worker's hands, slicing off his fingers.

Outside, people were banging on the door with fists and what sounded like clubs. "We've got to get out of here!" Davran cried.

Halthar said, "I know, but where can we go?"

The workers were beginning to panic.

Davran shook his head. "I don't know.... I didn't expect to be recognized so quickly!"

Suddenly, the banging against the door grew louder.

"They're using battering rams," one of the factory workers cried out.

Guards rushed into the entryway along with some of the local workers. "What's going on?" the chief guard asked.

"Another riot," someone said.

"But why here?" another guard shouted.

The chief guard pointed at Davran. "Who's that?"

"Hey, he looks like the guy on the drachmas."

The chief guard nodded. "Alexander, right?"

Davran nodded.

"What did you think you were doing?"

"I didn't expect all this, Monitor Salar," Davran cried.

IV

"We've got a riot downtown," the Company Supervisor said, as he put down the handset. He pointed to his chief trouble-shooter, Garlen Darl, and said, "Find out why?"

"Where?"

"Near the pottery warehouse."

Garlen Darl went downstairs and took out an antigravity lifter from the shed at the top of the building. The lifter was gold-plated and designed to look similar to the local's chariots in case they were spotted. It wasn't an ideal solution, but better than the alternative of flying over the city in an unidentified vehicle. Both would attract attention, but the golden chariot would fit into local legends about their gods.

It was mid-day and as he glided over the city of Alexandria he was drawing more attention than he'd hoped for. Citizens down below on the streets were motioning upward and shouting things he was unable to hear. He supposed his flight across the city would soon be seen as some sort of omen.

It was against the Paratime Code to use advanced technology devices openly on Fourth Level time-lines, but this was an emergency; he'd worry about the ramifications later. He was sure that losing Paratime lives to a citywide riot outweighed the transgression he was committing. The superstitious locals would view it as some sort of magic chariot, or something along those lines.

Surprisingly, the city was quiet until he approached the quadrant surrounding the warehouse. There the riot was in full swing, the locals were not only attacking the warehouse but the nearby buildings and merchant stalls. A few structures were already on fire and dense black smoke was beginning to rise, like black fingers poking up toward the clouds.

Some of the figures had taken large timbers and used them as battering rams to force open the warehouse door. Now they were smashing the inside walls. *What are they looking for?* He shook his head. *Damn Paratime Police regs*, he cursed. If they'd allowed them to use collapsed nickel on the doors, they would have withstood anything this time-line had to offer, including a brace of elephants.

The front of the warehouse was burning and dark smoke was billowing upward. This was turning into a catastrophe! They had ten company operatives in the building along with over a hundred local artisans. To say nothing of hundreds of valuable pots and statuary. And somehow it was all going to be Vendrax's fault.

Part of the crowd had noted his arrival and were pointing upward, shouting and crying out. He couldn't tell if they were curses or hosannas. He quickly thought of using sleep gas to quiet the crowd, but the sheer number of gathering citizens made that impractical. *I'd have to gas half the city!*

As he neared the warehouse Garlen realized that it was every man for himself. The crowd was tearing the whole place apart, some were making off with pottery and a few were even smashing statues. Others were running from the growing flames. It was a complete cock-up and he had no clue as to why.

Furthermore, since the Paratimers and factory workers were dressed like locals in robes and tunics, he had no way of picking them out of the crowd. The lower he flew the more the crowd roared; now most of them were pointing or shaking fists at his lifter. A few even tossed pots and what looked like spears his way!

Others were crying out: "Another god has arrived on a golden chariot!"

It was time to leave and come back more anonymously.

"What in Great Blaxthakka's Beard is going on?" his Supervisor demanded. "And where are our people?"

Garlen shrugged. "From the air, it looked like half the city was looting our warehouse. I couldn't get low enough to find out why. I'm going to have to go in on foot."

"Put on a better tunic, one with gold-trim, like something the lower-nobility might wear. Use a litter; they're faster," his Supervisor advised. "And take a big purse of drachmas—for bribes, in case you need them. Silver, not gold; you don't want to attract too much attention. Things are bad enough as it is."

"Yes, sir."

"Just how ugly is it?"

Garlen shook his head. "Real bad, boss. It looks like a total loss of inventory! The rioters were taking anything and everything that wasn't nailed or bolted down."

"How about the warehouse?"

"That, too. What wasn't on fire, the crowd was smashing to pieces."

The Supervisor cradled his head. "Oh, no... I wonder what set them off. Damn, I took this post because it supposed to be low-key. We'd better come up with a good answer for why the locals looted our warehouse, or the head office is going to be all over us."

Or the Paratime Police, Garlen surmised, but kept that thought to himself.

"What about our other buildings?" he asked.

"Oh! I hadn't thought of that," Garlen replied. "I'll talk to security and have them evacuated and see what they can do to secure the premises without violating the bloody Code."

"Good thinking. We need to get ahead of this disaster before it takes us all down with it!"

A journey that had taken fifteen minutes by air took over two hours by hand-drawn labor. Plus, Garlen always felt like a fool being carried anywhere in one of these litters. It took one man to clear the way and four bearers to keep the litter balanced and moving at any kind of speed. The local upper classes took them for granted, but he thought they'd do better using their own feet or riding horses if they were in a hurry.

There was still a small crowd hanging around the demolished warehouse, but no one seemed to know what the riot had been about. There was some talk about someone seeing the God Alexander, but he took that for more local hooey. He figured he'd learn more at one of the local taverns. He did know, after a quick tour of the abandoned property, that the warehouse was a total loss.

No one back at headquarters was going to be happy about that.

The nearest tavern was called the Great Heron. Inside the tavern was filled to overflowing, but his litter handler, a big man with rough hands, forced his way inside and cleared a nearby table. Garlen gave him a dirty look and offered to buy drinks for the men he'd just dispossessed. This made him instantly popular and he asked a man in a smoke blackened tunic: "What in Jupiter's name happened out there?"

With a fresh drink in his hand, the man was eager to talk. "Your Lordship, I have a clothes stall down the street from the foreign-owned pottery factory. A few hours after dawn, I heard a loud commotion down the street from my stall. People were shouting 'the God Alexander has come' and praising the gods for his deliverance." He shushed and looked around warily. "Not everyone is happy with the current Seleucus."

Garlen nodded in return. From what he had learned of the current ruler, Seleucus XXI Soter, was an in-bred moron with a taste for rubies and young girls from noble families—and not necessarily in that order. To finance his jewel collection, he periodically raised taxes and generally made the local citizens lives miserable. Having seen the ruler's bow-legged and hirsute sister/wife, he understood why he looked elsewhere for his evening entertainment. However, everyone would have been happier if he'd confined his wandering eye to the merchant or scribe classes, but no, he wanted only the best. Fortunately for the Pharaoh, the locals were frozen in a permanent state of cultural paralysis; otherwise, he would have lost his crown and head years ago.

The shopkeeper continued, "Some voices cried out the name Alexander, as if he had returned to life! Blasphemy! Blasphemy, I say."

Garlen nodded in response. On most time-lines, it was safest to be neutral on religious issues. Other patrons were beginning to listen in. He quickly ordered a round of drinks for the entire tavern, refocusing their attention as well as gaining their favor.

One of the other men at the merchant's small table looked around warily, then added, "But, my friend, you did not see him!"

"That is true," the shopkeeper replied.

Garlen noticed the soot marks on the man's face and hands. He asked, "Did you?"

He nodded up and down, an almost universal human gesture.

"Who did you see?"

Even the shopkeeper was listening intently.

"It was Alexander himself returned to life," the soot-faced man said. Who then paused to spit on his hands, then rub them together. "By Osiris and Isis, I swear this!"

The merchant paled. "Is this true, Amosis?"

He nodded again.

"What exactly did you see?" Garlen asked.

Amosis continued, "I was leaving my shop when I saw the reincarnated Alexander, walking along with one of the foreigners—a Persian I believe—from the pottery factory. I heard several voices call out: "Alexander the God has returned!" Then, I saw the two men turn and run back to the factory, followed by the crowd."

Aha! Galen thought to himself. *The plot thickens.* He wondered what strange plan had been cooked up by indolent fellow Paratimers in amongst the pots and statuary.

"It was as if one of the marble statues of Alexander had come to life!"

Everyone in the tavern was listening to Amosis' story now. They all waited breathlessly for him to continue.

"People in the street stared pushing and shouting so they could see, then rioting broke out."

"He speaks the truth!" someone called out. "I saw the riot with these two eyes."

"Everyone," continued Amosis, ignoring the interruption, "wanted to view the reincarnated Alexander. Me, too. Then he disappeared inside the factory and rumors of his presence spread like a runaway fire causing the multitude to grow, overflowing the street. Before long, the crowd turned violent—too many idlers, vagabonds and master-less men—and began to pound on the doors. I left, in fear of my own stall, when some of the more fervent started lighting fires and using timber rams upon the door.

"The entire block was soon engulfed in flames and I lost everything I own. I curse Alexander and the spell that brought him back to life!"

A patron grabbed Amosis and hit him in the face, screeching, "How dare you speak such blasphemy!"

Another man pulled a knife from his belt and stabbed Amosis in the back. Blood was squirting from the cut and he began to scream. All the patrons were up on their feet, except for a few too deep in their cups to rise. Fists and feet began to fly. The bartender and two bouncers came out from the bar and began to lay into the crowd with lead-weighted saps.

Garlen jumped into the fray, knocking down the knife wielder and two others with First Level hand-to-hand fighting and a quick kick. When the man with the knife started to get up, he kicked him hard in the throat and the man grabbed his neck choking and sputtering.

It took him a minute or two to fight his way out of the tavern, which was now drawing a crowd from the street. From past experience, Garlen knew an inflamed bar fight could quickly turn into a city-wide fracas, especially a city on edge like Alexandria. He pushed past the newcomers and made his way to the street.

His litter handler grabbed him by the shoulder, saying, "Let us leave, Your Lordship, before we get caught up in this madness!"

V

Garlen Darl finished up, "So, boss, it looks like someone from the pottery facility screwed up—big time! All I know for sure is half the city is rioting and the other half is waiting for it to spread. The Pharaoh's ordered his guards to clear the streets, and word is he's called for reinforcements. It'll be a city-wide bloodbath before it's over."

His supervisor groaned. "And you know whose fault it's going to be back at the home office?"

"Sure, who else—you? Not the numbskulls that caused this catastrophe!"

"Exactly. Varthan Nar managed to locate the faux Alexander. He's being held at the Great Amphitheater."

"Is there any way we can extract our man?"

The supervisor shook his head. "He's heavily guarded, I understand. Varthan is in tight with some of the Palace officials."

Garlen nodded. A few bribes to the right people could do wonders for one's status on most Fourth Level time-lines. It always helped an outtime operation to have someone affiliated with the local nabobs. And Varthan Nar was damn good at his job.

"The word around the Palace is that the Pharaoh is worried sick about the sudden appearance of this Alexander," Varthan continued. "He's not sure whether to welcome him or execute him. I believe he's afraid that if Alexander is a god he'll be punished; considering the job the Pharaoh's been doing here—I don't blame him. Even the priests are divided; some believe he's a real deity, others believe Alexander the Great has been reincarnated. A few radical priests are whipping the locals in a frenzy to have him released!"

Garlen shook his head wearily. This just kept getting worse.

"I'm going to have to call in the Paratime Police," his supervisor said angrily."

"You're right, but that's not going to go over well in Dhergabar."

His boss nodded. This fracas would probably cost him his job; Vendrax had no patience with supervisors who called in the Paratime Police to resolve company problems; too many Paratime Police complaints could cost them their outtime license. At best, it could cost them thousands of P. E. units in fines.

"I'll send Varthan to deal with the Paracops, but I don't know what the subsector commander will want to do."

Garlen shrugged. It could be a while before they heard back from the local Paracop inspector, especially at an outpost for a subsector this minor. He'd probably have to send word back to Fifth Level Police Terminal for reinforcements—maybe an Army Strike Team. This could get ugly. Shpeegar help them if they got Paratime Police Chief Verkan Vall involved....

Three hours later Garlen got another call from his boss. He quickly made his way through the boxes and cartons of goods that covered most of bottom floor of the facility. Inside, his supervisor's office, he asked, "Any word from Varthan Thal?"

"No, we heard from one of the factory supervisors. He's on his way in."

A few minutes later, a slightly overweight Paratimer wearing a smoke-blackened tunic came wheezing into the office. He had a black eye and an ugly bruise on his forehead.

"Sorry, boss. I got here as fast as I could," he wheezed.

Garlen identified him as under-supervisor Kaltar Lar.

"What happened?"

"Phew," Kaltar puffed. "I'm still…out of breath." He bent over and put his hands on his knees. When he got back up, he said, "I got knocked out trying to escape from the factory"—puff puff—"It may have saved my life, since I was thrown into an alleyway when it was set on fire. Puff puff—I had a hard time getting here…."

"What do you know about the false Alexander?" the supervisor asked.

Kaltar paused to draw in a deep breath. "I was there when Davran came back inside the factory with his friend, Halthar Varn." Puff puff—He was the spitting image of Alexander the Great! I heard he'd gone back to Home Time Line after a bad fall that injured his face—"

"Probably a ruse to get him to First Level," Garlen interrupted.

Kaltar nodded. "Probably. He and Halthar Varn were most likely in on it together; they're both thick as thieves." He paused to catch his breath. "Halthar's been running some sort of mind-reading scan with the locals—"

"Why wasn't I informed of this?" the supervisor demanded.

Kaltar reddened, then shrugged his shoulders. "It was just a way to make a few units and pass the time. Harmless, we all thought."

"Idiots," the supervisor mumbled under his breath.

Garlen sympathized with the factory workers, although he would have never admitted it out loud. This kind of outtime work—supervising local working class types and artisans in repetitive labor—was deadly boring and didn't pay much, either. It could have been done better by proles, but the Paracops didn't trust the proles and certainly didn't allow them access to the transtemporal conveyers—and for good reason. There'd been more than one prole uprising in First Level history. And no Paratime chief in his right mind wanted to be the man in charge when another revolt broke out.

"Anyway, sir, the two of them must have been up to something. But it didn't get very far...."

"They were playing with incinomite and didn't know it," the supervisor said. "This is why we have Paratime regulations."

Kaltar shrugged again. "Don't look at me like that, it wasn't my idea!"

"We know the locals captured the false Alexander, but what happened to his accomplice?"

Kaltar winced. "I saw Halthar's body inside the factory. It looked like someone had stabbed him repeatedly. Some of these outtimers are pretty fanatical about their religion!"

"And foreigners, like us, are always an easy target," Garlen added.

When Sector Regional Subchief Dalnar Dall arrived, they went over the story one more time. Subchief Dalnar was an older man, probably in his late fourth or early fifth century, who looked as if he'd rather be any place else but in the middle of this cock-up. His face turned into one big frown as he announced: "I have an entire Army Strike Team waiting to pacify the city. Now, where are they holding the guilty party?"

"From what little information we've been able to collect," the supervisor said, "we believe Davran Thal is inside the Amphitheater of Alexander."

"Has anyone tried to negotiate his release?" Dalnar asked.

Varthan Nar spoke up: "Yes, I talked with several palace officials. Unfortunately, the Pharaoh himself is involved. He's convinced himself that Alexander is real and was sent by the gods to replace him as ruler of the Ptolemaic Empire."

Subchief Dalnar shook his head in wonderment. "Why?"

Varthan sighed. "First, the Pharaoh is an overbred idiot. On top of that he's paranoid—probably with good reason. He's just smart enough to know that he's in way over his head as ruler of the Empire. He doesn't trust any of his advisors. Anyone who becomes popular with his subjects, he has executed in a most barbaric and painful manner. As a result, no one wants to make a move without his direct participation or upon his direct order. To add to this quagmire, he takes a long time to make even a minor decision. If this were any other subsector, the Pharaoh's own subjects or outsiders would have had him replaced long ago. However, this particular subsector is in an advanced state of stasis, best characterized as institutional paralysis.

"So, the injection of a new element—in this case the pseudo-Alexander—has everyone involved at the palace in crisis mode. No one is willing to make a move without a direct order from Seleucus the Twenty-first."

Another Paracop came rushing into the room. "Sir, we have a new problem."

Subchief Dalnar sighed. "What now?"

"The locals are attacking the Amphitheater and attempting to free the pseudo-Alexander. What are your orders, sir?"

"Let's take a look."

A technician, wearing a green tunic, sitting at the back of the room flicked on the wallscreen and scanned through several sites until he came upon one which displayed a close-up of the Amphitheater, as viewed from the overhead sky-eye. The large gates had already been knocked awry and the screen showed thousands of ant-sized rioters in and around the large building. Many of the rioters were carrying weapons and torches. Fires were burning out of control at several contiguous sites.

"Where are the guards and soldiers?" the Supervisor asked.

Varthan said, "It looks like they've pulled out. Maybe a palace coup?"

"Look!" someone else cried out. "Isn't that our Alexander?" He pointed to a spot just outside the amphitheater.

Garlen looked closer, as the tech blew up the image. There it was: an image of a tiny man being carried on a silver litter by six or so black litter bearers. He was surrounded by what appeared to be priests.

"Can you magnify that area any better?" asked Subchief Dalnar.

The tech shook his head. "We're at maximum magnification, sir."

They disappeared a few minutes later as the litter went into the palace.

"Where are they going?" the Subchief asked.

VI

Davran Thal rocked back and forth in his litter as his bearers made their way through the endless maze of corridors inside the Seleucus palace. Following behind was the Pontifex Maximus, wearing his ram horns, with a dozen fellow underpriests of Jupiter Ammon. After several days of confinement in the amphitheater, he was unsure if he was being freed or about to be sacrificed by the djedi. No one had told him anything; he might as well have been a statue instead of the living god.

What a stupid idea to come here as Alexander, Davran concluded. *I only wanted to have some fun, not create a revolution!* The entire city of Alexandria was involved now and he hoped that his fellow Paratimers could come up with some sort of rescue—even if it meant an eventual mind-scrub at the hands of BurPsyHygiene. He didn't know why the priests had taken him and what they would do with him; he suspected the worst.

Deep in the palace interior, they came to a halt before stairs leading to a large presence chamber. Inside Davran was allowed to step out of the litter and refresh himself with a flask of wine. The room itself was a large chamber with statues of the gods in the alcoves. Terracotta oil lamps mounted in sconces set in stone walls lit the chamber with shadowy, flickering light. One entire wall was covered by a painting showing the God Alexander attended by Anubis and other Egyptian Gods and, towering above all others, the Greek god Zeus.

Two priests led him up onto a dais where he was seated on a gilded Egyptian throne chair.

The Pontifex Maximus came before him, bowed deeply and intoned: "We apologize, Great Alexander, for the confusion attending your Return. Sadly, it was not prophesized and we Your Servants were not prepared."

He wisely nodded in return, not sure of what his expected response might be.

Four tall Nubian guards, with gold-platted halberds and dressed only in white loin cloths, came forth from outside the chamber. Sandwiched between them was the current Pharaoh, or at least, someone who looked like his statues, since Davran had never been in his presence. There was blood dripping from the ruler's mouth onto his white and gold robes and one eye was blackened.

"Why have you laid hands upon your ruler?" the Pharaoh demanded, his voice high-pitched and slurred.

The high priest took something out of his red robes that looked like a riding crop and struck the Pharaoh in the mouth. "Quiet, fool. You are in the presence of the Reincarnated Alexander!"

The ruler turned his dark eyes upon Davran and they suddenly widened. He started blubbering and sobbing.

"Yes," the Pontifex said. "Now you are the presence of *true* royalty. Many in this great city have prayed to the gods for Alexander's return; it appears their pleas have been answered."

Everyone turned toward Alexander waiting for him to speak. Deepening his voice, Davran spoke up, "For too long I have been aware of how badly my descendants have ruled my city. Yet of the many fools and charlatans ruling in my name, you, Seleucia XXI Nicator, have been the worst. I appealed to Jupiter, God of Gods, and he agreed that it was time for me to return to the land of the living. I am here to render judgement upon you!"

All the priests went to their knees and bowed their heads.

"Have this odious fraud taken before my people and have his head removed from his body," he ordered, not sure if his words would be followed.

A strangled scream came out of the Pharaoh's lips

The Pontifex Maximus rose up and struck him in the mouth again with his crop. "Your order shall be obeyed, Oh Great One, Lord of Lords and King of Kings."

Almost immediately the Pharaoh was dragged from the room, writhing and screeching, with the high priest and his attendants following closely behind. The two priests left behind brought Davran a goblet of wine as well as fresh fruit, dates and honey cakes on plates of gold. *This is more like it*, he decided.

The rioting in the amphitheater had now spread throughout Alexandria. Many of the buildings in the foreign-owned section of town were being looted and then torched. The fires were spreading and the supervisor was getting worried; they could hear the sounds of a growing crowd outside. Wringing his hands, the supervisor turned to Subchief Dalnar Dall. "What can you do to stop this? I, I mean, we can't afford to lose our headquarters."

The Subchief shook his head in disgust. "Civilians," he spat. "Go down below to the conveyer-head depot. You'll be safe there."

The supervisor nodded and made his way to the depot door at a fast trot. Most of his employees followed just as quickly.

Garlen Darl stayed behind with the Inspector and two of his Paratime Police officers.

"Why aren't you running after them?" Subchief Dalnar asked.

"If the rioters break-in, I'll leave. Otherwise, I want to keep an eye on the situation. There should be someone here representing Vendrax's interests."

"Do what you have to, but don't get into my way," Dalnar threatened. "I'm going to use this building as my staging area."

"For what?" Garlen asked.

"For the attack, of course. We're going to have to break into the palace and rescue that fool masquerading as Alexander."

"Why?"

The Subchief looked appalled. "This Davran Thal has violated numerous sections of the Paratime Code. He needs to be removed before he says something that will tip the locals off to the Paratime Secret."

Garlen shook his head. "This isn't Second Level Interworld Empire or Fourth Level Europo-American. Even if the local authorities did torture Davran and he blurted it out, the locals would never put it together. At best, they would believe his words were the babbling of a moron or lunatic. At worst, something to do with their cursed gods. These are superstitious and uneducated natives, not sophisticated city dwellers."

"That's a chance we cannot take," replied the Subchief. He took the hand-phone from his belt and got in touch with the orbiting Strike Team.

"Red Alert. The miscreant, in disguise as Alexander of Macedon, has been taken by the locals into the main palace. Break into the palace, locate the false Alexander and take him into custody."

May the fates save us from well-meaning fools, Garlen thought. This will really stir up a hornet's nest back on Home Time Line.

VII

Paratime Police Chief Verkan Vall was seated at his desk going over the Outtime Duty Rosters on his screen, when Inspector Ranthar Jard entered holding a folder with a red flag sticking out.

"What's up, Jard?" he asked.

"We've got a big dust-up on Alexandria-Roman, boss. It's what they call a snafu on Europo-American."

Verkan leaned back in his seat and took out one of his ivory Zarthani pipes, sculpted into a likeness of Galzar, their war god. He used an outtime Zippo lighter to fire it up. "I'm familiar with the term. Give me a quick summary."

"The problem is on Fourth Level Alexandrian-Roman, Seleuco-Macedonian Subsector."

Verkan nodded. "I'm familiar with it; a dismal and unchanging hellhole, one of the worst postings on Fourth Level. Another plague or rebellion?"

"No, this one's more personal. It appears that one of Vendrax Import employees got a little too ambitions. First, he free-lanced as a prophet, or seer, in a couple of the local bars and taverns. When the scam wasn't profitable enough, he decided to return to First Level and get a face sculpt, as Alexander the Great."

"Ouch!" Verkan replied.

"Yeah, it got ugly in a hurry. The locals saw him as either a deity or the reincarnated Alexander, who had returned to solve all their problems. At first, it was localized in Alexandria, some riots and buildings set on fire. Now word is spreading throughout the Polemic Empire that Alexander the Great has returned and people are inflamed. All of Macedonia is up in arms; they want Alexander returned to his rightful home. Some of the bigger towns are rebelling and the Caucasus' nomads are rising up."

"How did it get out of hand so quickly?"

"You can blame that on Subchief Dalnar Dall."

Verkan cringed. "That old time-waster. I thought he'd retired years ago. Oh yeah, didn't former Chief Tortha exile him to Alexandrian-Roman to keep him from causing any more trouble?"

"Yup," Ranthar replied. "That was like putting out a fire without bothering to smother all the hot spots. The old fool decided the best course was to liberate Alexander from the local priests and return him to Dhergabar for a mind-wipe at BurPsyHygiene. First, he used an Army Strike Team to break into the Pharaoh's palace and liberate him. This set off a firestorm of protests as well as cries of witchcraft and demonic attack. On top of that, this Alexander look-alike was missing!"

"What a mess," Verkan said. "Does anyone know where the imposter is?"

Ranthar shook his head. "The only person onsite who hasn't lost his head is Garlen Darth, a local trouble-shooter for Vendrax. He's been trying to institute a city-wide search but hasn't gotten any cooperation from Dalnar."

"Of course not, it might actually work." Verkan pointed to several piles of papers, video tabs, memory sticks and various report cubes. "I'm still trying to clear my desk of all the stuff that piled up while I was on Aryan-Transpacific. Think you can handle this by yourself, Jard?"

"Sure Chief, but I may have to bust a few heads."

"Do whatever it takes. Just keep it away from the news services."

Ranthar chuckled. "So far that hasn't been a problem. Not too many newsies will voluntarily take an assignment on Alexandrian-Roman!"

The first thing Inspector Ranthar Jard did, after arriving via transtemporal conveyer to Seleuco-Macedonian Subsector depot head and taking over the supervisor's office, was fire Subchief Dalnar Dall. Dalnar protested vehemently until Ranthar showed him the termination notice from Chief Verkan, bearing his official stamp.

"You mean I'm actually fired, Inspector?" he asked, his eyes widening in shock.

It was rare for the Paratime Police Department to fire senior officers, but in view of his Dalmar's mishandling of the Alexander Affair, the Chief had thought it was necessary. The Department couldn't afford anymore screw-ups by this incompetent hack, although Ranthar didn't put it quite so bluntly.

Old Dalmar, his shoulders slumped in defeat, left the Vendrax office without his needler, badge and epaulets.

Next on Ranthar's things-to-do-list was to question Garlen Darth, the Vendrax trouble-shooter. He'd already shooed the Vendrax supervisor out of his office; the man was clearly in over his head. All he wanted was for an end to the Alexander crisis, but had no idea of how to bring it about. Ranthar suspected that this fiasco would follow the supervisor to Home Time Line and cost him his outtime supervisory position—if not his job.

Garlen Darth came into the office, poised and ready for action.

Ranthar approved. "Since you're johnny-on-the-job, what do you suggest we do now?"

Garlen nodded. He didn't seem the least bit intimidated by having this hot potato tossed into his lap. "As I suggested to the last officer, Subchief Dalnar, I'm certain the priesthood is hiding our man somewhere inside the city. We've shut down the harbor and closed off all the roads leading out of town."

"Whose idea was that?" Ranthar asked

"Mine. Once I learned it was one of our employees who was responsible for the rioting, I immediately closed off all the city exits. I wanted to contain the crisis. Unfortunately, word has slipped out of the city and now there are uprisings throughout the Empire."

"As they say at the Academy, the only thing faster than the speed of light is a good rumor. I've sent word to Pol Term Fifth Level for reinforcements. We should have about five hundred operatives arriving dressed as *astynomia*, or local police, and ready to police the city. I want a list from you of all the places we should search first."

"I can do that."

Over the next three days the Paratime Police *astynomia* tore Alexandria apart with no results. None of the locals knew anything other than that the reincarnated Alexander had returned to punish Ptolemy XXI. Ranthar was growing increasingly frustrated when Garlen Darth came into his temporary office with a big smile on his face.

"I've found him, Inspector."

Ranthar rubbed his hands together. "Where?"

"He's hiding in a waterfront warehouse, along with half the high priests in Alexandria."

"How did you pull that off?"

Garlen smirked. "I figured that the best way out of the Alexandria was by boat. So I hit a bunch of the dockside taverns and told the local captains—all who are incensed at being cooped up in the city—that I'd give anyone who brought me information on Alexander's whereabouts his weight in gold staters, if he was captured due to their information."

Ranthar nodded. Gold was one of the first items brought back in large amounts by the earliest Paratime exploiters. As a result, there was so much gold on Home Time Line that it was practically worthless, being used primarily for cheap jewelry and industrial fabrication. Gold was, however, quite useful for both trade and bribery throughout the various Paratime levels.

"The captain gave me the location of where our phony Alexander is hiding," he said, proceeding to give Ranthar all the details on the dockside warehouse. "The priests have been waiting for almost a ten-day for the hunt to die down so they can move Alexander to someplace safe—probably in Greece or Spain."

After checking the data against the detailed city map he pulled up on his visiscreen, Ranthar said, "Good job, Garlen. We'll pick him up tonight at roughly 0300, which should give us the least interference from outsiders. I'll post some men dressed as locals discretely around the warehouse so that Alexander doesn't slip out of our net."

"Inspector, if we want to contain the rumors that will follow Alexander's capture, I suggest we bring along an actor dressed as Anubis, the God of Death. That way the priests can claim that Alexander escaped from Hades. And that Anubis and his cohorts were sent to Alexandria to bring him back to the underworld."

"An excellent idea! I have just the man for the job." Garlen appeared to be the only competent man Ranthar had run into on this subsector, which gave him a good idea. "Garlen, after this case is wrapped up, would you be interested in joining the Department?"

Garlen stood back for a moment, then smiled. "Aren't I a little old for a Paratime Police recruit?"

Ranthar looked at him closely. "What is your age? I'd say seventy or eighty years old."

"Close, but more like ninety-three."

"Hell, you're still a kid. I'm twice your age. I can fast-track you through the Academy and guarantee you a place on my team."

"In that case, I'm your man."

VIII

Davran Thal was sleeping comfortably on the feather and down mattress provided for his comfort, when he heard the first explosion. He woke up with a start. Before the priests started fawning over him, he would have welcomed the Paratime Police coming to get him. Now, he wasn't so sure.

There was another loud explosion, causing an avalanche of wooden timbers and roofing material to fall, and suddenly everyone was awake. One high priest had been crushed and the rest were squawking like geese. There were some fifty to sixty soldiers inside the warehouse and they were forming up on the floor under harsh orders from their superiors.

Suddenly the interior of the warehouse lit-up as though it were daylight!

It must be the Paracops, he thought. *No one on this time-line has flash grenades.*

Some of the soldiers began to fire their muskets at distant figures which turned out to be a big mistake. The Paratimers shot back with heavy assault weapons and about half of the soldiers were killed or wounded in the initial barrage.

No, this kind of firepower means it's a Strike Team. How many men did they bring?

Davran started looking for a place to hide, but the priests surrounded him with their bodies.

Suddenly one of the priests cried out: "There's Anubis God of Death! We are doomed…."

Another priest screamed as a bullet blew through his torso.

The priests were now crying out and begging for deliverance. Within seconds all the priests were lying face-down on the floor and shouting for the remaining soldiers to do likewise. Figures dressed all in black and wearing beaked masks began stripping all the soldiers of their weapons. Others started tying up the priests. Finally, Anubis himself made an appearance.

"My priests, you have made a terrible blunder," said Anubis in a loud and deep voice that demanded reverence. "This shade escaped from the Underworld and we have come to bring him back."

The Pontius Maximus cried out: "We did not know, Lord. We beg your forgiveness."

"I will consider it. Now, leave us. I will take this shade back to where he belongs."

Trembling, Davran found himself in the grip of two big Paratimers."

"You really screwed up," one said in his ear, as he tied Davran's hands back in flexible restraints.

Ranthar Jard gave Chief Verkan a full account of the raid and subsequent capture of the renegade Paratimer. "The idiot actually thought he was going to get away with impersonating the most famous man on the subsector! What do they teach kids in school these days, anyway?"

Verkan sighed. "Clearly, not enough. You'd think that First Level companies would do their best to weed out the bunglers and criminal types before sending them outtime. It's probably just as well; if they did their job—what would we do?"

Ranthar laughed. "I'm sure we could find something. I did make one valuable find there."

"What was that?"

"I found a new Paratime Police recruit, Garlen Darth. Once he gets though the Academy, I'm going to add him to my special investigator team."

"I'm glad something worthwhile came out of this mess."

"What about our Alexander?" Ranthar asked. "What are we going to do with him?"

Verkan grinned. "He's not our problem anymore. I had him sent directly to BurPsyHygiene; he's their problem, now."

SIEGE AT TARR-HOSTIGOS

JOHN F. CARR & ROLAND GREEN

I

1967 A.D.

PARATIME POLICE CHIEF VERKAN VALL TRIED TO SORT HIS atypically jumbled thoughts as the transtemporal conveyer carried him toward Fourth Level Aryan-Transpacific, Kalvan Subsector. The civilized Second and Third Levels were behind him now. Once in a while he caught flickering glimpses of Fourth Level—buildings, airports, occasionally a raging battle.

Fourth Level was the highest probability of all of the inhabited Paratime Levels. There the human First Colony had come to complete disaster, in the past fifty thousand years losing all knowledge of its origins.

It was the most barbaric level, as well as the biggest. Its cultures ranged from idol worshippers to the technological sophistication and social backwardness of the Europo-American, Hispano- Columbian Subsector.

It was from one of these Europo-American lines that Corporal Calvin Morrison of the Pennsylvania State Police had accidentally traveled in a conveyor to Aryan-Transpacific, Styphon's House Subsector. Thrust into a ruder and deadlier culture, Calvin (or Kalvan, as the inhabitants of that time-line called him) not only survived, he prospered—until just a few days ago. In less than four years he'd married a princess, founded an empire, broken Styphon's House's monopoly of gunpowder, and more than held his own against the worst that band of priestly tyrants could do.

No more. Styphon's House had gone on the offensive and assembled their Styphon's Grand Host; at the Battle of Andros Field the Host—after numerous ten-days of fighting—broke and defeated the outnumbered army of Hos-Hostigos. Verkan had been there on an anonymous Beshtan ridgetop, fighting with his Hostigi Mounted Rifles until wave after wave of battle-crazed Harphaxi cavalry and infantry had broken their line. In the final push, he had taken a frightful chest wound, when an infantryman had fired a big-bore musket at close range. Unfortunately, the rest of the Army of Hos-Hostigos had fared almost as badly as his command; last he'd heard was that Kalvan and what remained of his Army were retreating to Hostigos Town and its nearby castle.

He was still officially recovering, although the Opposition Party members were still calling for his resignation in the Executive Council for abuse of power and violating the Paratime Code. Until the waters settled, Verkan had been tied to his desk on First Level by piles of routine business and some non-routine schemes by his political enemies. To put it mildly, his conscience was nagging him because he couldn't be there when his friend needed him most. He refused to think about what the Bureau of Psychological Hygiene would say, if they discovered that the top Paracop was suffering from Outtime Identification Syndrome. He'd already had enough headaches for one day.

The biggest of those headaches was the fate of the Dhergabar University Study Team which had been caught up in the Hostigi rout. Like all outtime researchers, they worked under Paratime Police protection.

That might not be enough, on the kind of Fourth Level time-line where civilians were likely to end as part of the body count when a victorious army swept through hostile territory. Too many members of the University Team were still unaccounted for; every casualty among them would be a gift to the Opposition Party.

Kalvan would have to fight his own battles for a while, against even longer odds than before. He'd need skill as well as luck to save his own life and Queen Rylla's, never mind refounding his empire.

Already the Grand Host's cavalry scouts had raided almost to the outskirts of Hostigos Town. Its main body could hardly be more than a day behind. Kalvan's father-in-law, Prince Ptosphes, might be able to hold Tarr-Hostigos for a few days. If the Grand Host had to stop and lay siege to the castle, Kalvan still might never rule a kingdom again. He and Rylla might at least escape westward, to sell the services of their army somewhere in the Middle Kingdoms, menaced by barbarians and now by the Mexicotal.

The conveyer dome shimmered into material existence. They had reached Kalvan's Subsector. Verkan checked his personal equipment and headed for the hatch. Somehow four Paracops reached it before him, all with drawn Fourth Level pistols and palmed First Level sigma-ray needlers.

"Sorry, Chief," one of them said. He didn't sound sorry. Verkan looked behind and sighed. The other eight men of his personal guard had closed tightly around him from the rear. Swaddled in bodyguards like a baby in cloth, Verkan stepped out into a large storeroom. The rest of the conveyer-load of Paracops followed, lugging equipment or pushing lifter pallets.

From the outside, the conveyer-head was disguised as one of four large storehouses attached to the Royal Foundry of Hos-Hostigos. The room before them held a desk, some First Level monitoring equipment, racks of muskets, two field-gun carriages, and hundreds of sacks of oats and corn.

No good to anybody except maybe the Grand Host was Verkan's thought as he strode across the room. Like the other Paracops, he held a flintlock pistol nearly two feet long, loaded and cocked. On his head he wore a high-combed morion helmet; his clothes were a sleeveless buff jack, dark blue breeches, a bright red sash, and thigh-high boots. Nobody from Kalvan's Subsector would have thought him anything but a Hostigi light cavalry officer.

As he'd expected, the storehouse was empty of anything except mice and rats. He opened the keyed magnetic lock, stepped back, let the four point men go first, then followed at their hand signals of "All clear."

The door was intact, as he had expected. Under local oak planking, it had a collapsed-nickel core. Nothing local could even dent that, not even a two-hundred-pound stone ball from a siege bombard.

Nothing else in sight had been as lucky. The main Foundry buildings had all burned; some had collapsed. Most of the outer buildings also showed battle scars, and bodies lay everywhere.

Smoke still rose from most of the buildings. That confirmed Verkan's guess that the attack had come only hours before. The half-dozen survivors of the University Team who'd reached First Level's Kalvan Subsector Depot had been incoherent with fright, except for Baltov Eldra, who was unconscious from a head wound.

"Too many tourists," a Paracop said.

Verkan nodded. The University had insisted on doing their own investigation of Kalvan's Time Line. Short of imposing quarantine, there'd been no way to stop them. For a moment Verkan wished himself back as Special Chief's Assistant, where he could do the sensible thing without having a dozen political potentates baying at his door.

The Paracops spread out, leapfrogging from building to building, covering one another until they'd reached the edge of the Foundry on all sides. Then they posted sentries, sent a miniature spyeye to hover a thousand feet up, and began the grisly task of recovering the bodies.

Verkan turned over the nearest civilian casualty with his sword. It was the Team's expert on pre-industrial sociology, Professor Lathor Karv. He had a gaping hole in his forehead and several stab wounds in his torso, but no signs of torture.

First good news all day.

No signs of torture meant that none of Archpriest Roxthar's "Holy" Investigators had ridden with the cavalry. Hypno-mech conditioning or not, it was asking a lot of anyone to resist the kind of torture the Investigators handed out. Not that they were as efficient as the Second Level priests of Shpeegar or some Europo-American secret police agencies, but they would improve with time and practice. The Grand Host's victory had bought them the time, and Roxthar's fanatical determination to find and extirpate heresy everywhere would guarantee the practice.

Of the fifty-odd bodies in the open, some were here-and-now Foundry workers, the proverbial innocent bystanders. About twenty were mercenaries of various persuasions or undercover Paracops, and the rest members of the University Team.

"Fiasco" is a mild term for this, was Verkan's first thought. Nobody is going to be happy about it.

"Chief!" the head guard called. He ran up and lowered his voice. "We've found Agent Skordran Kirv."

Nobody, starting with me.

Skordran Kirv's dead mouth was twisted into the parody of a smile, but it looked as if he'd fought as well as he'd lived. Five troopers in yellow Harphaxi sashes lay dead and bloody around him.

Verkan cursed out loud. There went an old friend and one of the few Paracops he could still trust absolutely.

The lifter teams started loading bodies for shipment back to First Level, while the rest began the house-to-house (or ruin-to-ruin) search. In spite of the danger from smoldering embers and falling beams, they turned up twelve more Paratimer bodies, three of them Paracops. Seven skeletons too badly burned for field identification made the last load before the conveyor headed back to First Level. Paratime Police Headquarters had a full medtech team on standby, for DNA identification.

Verkan spent most of the time before the conveyer's return wandering aimlessly among the ruins. Every Paracop on this team knew when to steer clear of the Chief; Verkan knew he was being guarded but so tactfully he couldn't complain.

One thought dominated Verkan's mind. He'd thought he had a crisis, with an alliance of Opposition Party chiefs and outtime traders after his scalp over closing Fourth Level Europo-American. He had a case—too many nuclear and chemical weapons in the hands of national governments. However, he and Dalla would live through it even if he couldn't persuade anyone else.

Kalvan and Rylla were running for their lives, which might not be very long if Ptosphes's garrison of the lame and the halt couldn't hold Tarr-Hostigos for at least a few days.

As the day wore on, Verkan began to hope that the Grand Host's scouts would reappear. It was out of the question to seek the main body and tear it apart with First Level weapons. A few hundred dead cavalry troopers, however, could be labeled "noncontaminating self-defense" in an Incident Report. Their demise would make the Grand Host only a little less strong but a lot more cautious.

Or it might make people genuinely believe that demons fought for Kalvan, and create enthusiastic support for Roxthar's fifty-times-cursed Investigation! That was the problem with contamination—you couldn't control how people would interpret your intervention. Good Paracops always remembered that.

Verkan Vall gritted his teeth and decided to be a good Paracop again. He hoped his present set of teeth would survive the experience—

"Vall?"

He started to glare at the interruption, then recognized Kostran Garth, his wife Dalla's brother-in-law, and another of that handful of good friends and reliable Paracops. The conveyor must have returned with the lab test results—although from the look on Kostran's face, he was not the bearer of good news.

"I'm sorry, if that helps any," Kostran said.

"Some. Better security would have helped more. Dralm-dammit, we could have had it!"

"By Xipph's mandibles, Chief, you did all you could!" He added several more curses from a particularly vile Second Level time-line where spiders and beetles were sacred fetishes. "They sabotaged everything you and Kirv tried to do."

"They paid for it, too. But keeping that from happening was ultimately the Chiefs responsibility. *My* responsibility." Verkan managed a wry grin. "Wasn't it Kalvan's own—'Great King Truman'—who said, 'The buck stops here'?"

The grin faded, but Verkan managed not to sigh. "All right. Who did we find?"

"Five locals, Gorath Tran, and Sankar Trav, the Team medic."

"That leaves Danar Sirna and Aranth Sain unaccounted for." The two Paracops' eyes met. If the two missing people were prisoners, they were probably on their way into the hands of the Investigation. Then they'd soon wish they had burned to death instead.

"Danar Sirna. Doctoral candidate in history?"

Kostran nodded. "Right. Tall woman, auburn hair. Great figure too."

"Let's wish her better luck in her next incarnation. The soldiers here-and-now have rough-and-ready notions about dealing with enemy civilian women. What about Aranth Sain?"

"He's ex-Strike Force, one of the few Team people with survival skills. He was their expert on pre-industrial military science." Kostran hesitated. "I wonder if he was forced to try putting some of his theories into practice?"

"You mean, take an unscheduled field sabbatical?"

"Exactly. His cover is an artillery officer from Hos-Agrys and you can bet he won't break it by accident. If he catches Phidestros' eye, he may even be safe from the Investigation!"

It rubbed Verkan the wrong way, to possibly owe anything to the man principally responsible for Kalvan's defeat. Still, if under the circumstances Aranth had succumbed to the temptation that most outtime workers felt every so often—Verkan could only wish him luck.

Now, to interrogate the surviving Team members thoroughly.

Verkan wasn't looking forward to the job, but maybe it would turn up some clues. He decided to start with Baltov Eldra, if she was ready; she had the reputation of both a cool head and a keen talent for observation.

II

The climb to the gun platform on top of the north tower of Tarr-Hostigos left Prince Ptosphes unpleasantly short of breath. Old age had been pursuing him for a long time. Now it had finally caught him. Under other circumstances he would have been angry at the prospect of not seeing his grandchildren grow up, but that matter had been taken care of four days ago at Ardros Field.

"Should we summon Uncle Wolf for you, my Prince?" the gun captain asked.

Ptosphes shook his head. "No. Just let me sit down and catch my wind."

He lowered himself on to an upended powder barrel and was about to light his pipe when he remembered what he was sitting on. The gunners and sentries, he noticed, had returned to their work as soon as they knew he needed no help.

Good men, and more than ever a pity that they had to stand here and face certain death even if most of them were like him, a bit long in the tooth. At least they were the last good men he'd be leading to their doom. No more battles like Tenabra, to haunt him during the long winter nights. Kalvan and Rylla wouldn't be so lucky, and Kalvan at least liked such work even less than Ptosphes. Kalvan would just have to endure Rylla's tongue on the subject, as Ptosphes had endured Demia's.

Ptosphes chuckled, as he thought of Rylla's mother for the first time in nearly a moon. Rylla had much of her mother in her, both the strengths and the tongue and temper. Ptosphes remembered Demia asking (at the top of her lungs) whether he hated war too much to hold even the little Princedom of Hostigos.

Well, she'd been right in a way. He would have lost even that to Gormoth of Nestor, for not wanting to fight the battles of Styphon's House, if the gods hadn't sent Kalvan. Why, then, had those same gods turned their faces away when he needed their help most? What had he or Kalvan done to earn their wrath?

Great Dralm, I ask nothing for myself. Let your wrath fall on me, and spare Kalvan, Rylla, and my granddaughter Demia.

Ptosphes's breath came more easily now, and he badly wanted that pipe. He rose and was turning toward the stairs when he saw a horseman riding uphill toward the castle. He wore armor but no helmet, and a sash with Prince Phrames' colors. Probably one of Phrames' loyal Beshtans.

"Ahoooo! Prince Ptosphes! Prince Phrames has sent me back to warn you. The Styphoni are on the march once more. Their scouts are barely a candle from Hostigos Town!"

"Thank you, and carry my thanks to Prince Phrames." *So the siege begins even sooner than we expected.*

The trooper made no move to turn his mount. Ptosphes glared down at him. "No, you can't come into the castle. Your Prince and your Great King need you more than I do."

"Prince—"

"Now, Dralm-damn you, turn that horse around and get it moving! If you're not gone before I count to ten you'll be the first casualty of the siege of Tarr-Hostigos."

Ptosphes drew his pistol but his roar had already startled the horse into movement. It wheeled, nearly losing its footing on the steep slope, then broke into a canter. By the time Ptosphes had counted to five, it was out of pistol range. The Beshtan was still looking back at the castle. Ptosphes hoped he would turn around and look where he was going before he rode into a ditch.

Once his pipe was drawing well, Ptosphes walked around the walls to where he had a good view to the southeast. That was the likely direction for the Grand Host, or at least where he hoped most to see them. Anyplace else would mean they had a too-godless- good chance of cutting off at least Kalvan's rearguard.

The southeast was empty of smoke clouds, and so were all the other directions. Were the Styphoni advancing along roads where there was nothing left that even a fanatical believer would consider worth burning? Or was the vanguard mercenaries, who would be thinking of having roofs over their heads and food in their bellies during the siege?

Tarr-Hostigos should have a bit of time before its walls *had* to be manned and kept manned until the Styphoni stormed them. Plenty of time, for what Ptosphes intended.

He pointed the stem of his pipe at the nearest sentry. "Take a message to Captain-General Harmakros. Summon everyone in the castle except the sentries to the outer courtyard."

"Every—?" the man began, then broke off at Ptosphes' look. "Everyone. Captain-General Harmakros. Yes, my Prince."

The soldier hurried off, as if he wanted to open the distance between himself and his Prince before Ptosphes showed any more signs of madness.

Ptosphes followed at a more leisurely pace.

III

By the time the garrison was gathered in the outer courtyard, the sun was high overhead. Even the twenty-foot walls cast short shadows. Ptosphes sweated in his armor, wishing the laggards would hurry and resting his hand on the hilt of his sword.

It was a newly forged Kalvan-style rapier, balanced for fighting on foot but quite long enough for his purposes now. The Great Sword of Hostigos, which he'd belted on the day he was proclaimed Prince, was on its way westward with Kalvan and Rylla. His grandson would need that Sword some day, when he ruled a realm so huge that Old Hostigos would barely rank as a respectable Princedom.

If the gods are merciful.

Ptosphes saw no more men joining the crowd. He drew the sword and raised it overhead in both hands. Sunlight blazed from the steel.

"Men of Hostigos. You all know why you are here. You all were told, when you offered to hold Tarr-Hostigos until our Great King and his family might reach safety. Every one of you has already earned honor in the eyes of Dralm Allfather, Galzar Wolfhead, and the other true gods, the gratitude of your Prince and Great King, and the goodwill of your comrades.

"Styphon's Grand Host is approaching faster than we thought. Within a candle, two at most, this castle will be surrounded by the mightiest army in the history of the Great Kingdoms. For every one of us, there will be a hundred of the enemy. When they camp, a mouse won't be getting out of this castle.

"Any man who wants to leave can still do so. I'll say nothing against him nor let anyone else say a word. He'll have to hurry, to catch up with our rearguard before nightfall, but there's an open road for any who want to take it. " He pointed toward the castle gate with his sword.

"For those who stay—you all know what kind of quarter Styphon's dogs gave us at Ardros. The lucky ones will have a quick death. The rest will have an appointment with Roxthar's Unholy Investigation."

A few hollow laughs sounded from the ranks; most faces were set and pale. All knew what had happened to the Hostigi prisoners after Ardros Field; few had not lost kin or friends in that butchery. Most of the prisoners not slaughtered outright were in the hands of the Investigation, doubtless envying their dead comrades.

Ptosphes lowered his sword and strode to the door of the woodshed on one side of the courtyard. Then he drew a line with the sword's point, through the dirt and straw covering the flagstones of the courtyard, from the woodshed to the blacksmith's forge on the other side. He then took a deep breath, sheathed his sword, and turned to face his men.

"All who want to stay—cross over this line and join me. Those who want to die somewhere else—stay where you are!"

Silence. Ptosphes could hear the stamping of horses from the stables on the far side of the courtyard. An unnaturally complete silence to be hanging over five hundred men. No one coughed, no one shuffled his feet. Ptosphes could have sworn some had ceased to breathe.

A thickset man in battered armor pushed his way from the rear into the open. Ptosphes tried not to stare too hard. It was Vurth.

Vurth, the peasant who'd been Kalvan's first host in this land, who owed his life and his family's to Kalvan's fighting skill. Who'd sent word of the Nostori raiders to Tarr-Hostigos, so that Rylla could lead out the cavalry who had cut off the raiders and found Kalvan.

Vurth, a peasant who might really be called Dralm's first chosen tool for bringing about everything which had happened since that spring night almost four years ago. Ptosphes wondered briefly what Patriarch Xentos would have to say about the theological propriety of that notion—if presiding over the squabbles of the League of Dralm in far-off Agrys City left him any time for such matters.

Much good may that do Xentos in the eyes of the gods, when the League sends only words of condolence instead of soldiers and muskets to those who fight its battles against Styphon.

Ptosphes examined the gray-haired peasant. His clothes and face were caked with mud and powder smoke, one shoulder was bandaged, and he limped. He wore the breastplate of some Harphaxi nobleman, once etched and gilded, now hacked and tarnished, over his homespun smock. On his head was a battered morion helmet, on his feet cavalry boots from two different corpses. He still carried the cavalryman's musketoon he'd acquired the night of Kalvan's coming, and both it and the powder flask at his belt were clean.

"First Prince, Captain-General Harmakros, people," Vurth began. "This isn't really a Council, so maybe I don't have the right to start off, as if I was Speaker for the Peasants like Phosg, Dralm keep him. I think I've a right to be heard, though."

Ptosphes would have cut down anyone who disagreed. The men saw this, and Vurth went on.

"Prince, most of us here either can't run, don't want to run, or don't have anywhere to run to. My farm has burned, my wife is dead and one son too. The other son's off with King Kalvan, in the Royal Dragoons, and my son-in-law Xykos is Captain of Queen Rylla's Lifeguards. Dralm keep all the daughters who ran off with mercenaries.

"Styphon's taken or chased off everything I had except my life. All I want to do with what's left of it is kill Styphon's dogs until they kill me. I'm too old to go climbing trees or hide in caves like a thief, even for that. I'd rather sit here and kill the bastards in comfort!"

Vurth shouldered his musketoon and stepped forward across the line before anyone could cheer.

Ptosphes felt his eyes burn and quickly blinked back the threatening tears. He stepped up beside Vurth and put his arm around the peasant's shoulders. Any land that bore men like this would be barren ground indeed for Styphon's House. Such men could be killed; they could not be frightened.

Harmakros' voice cut through the new silence.

"Lift that litter, you fools! You don't have to stay yourselves!"

The bearers' reply was nearly inaudible and totally disrespectful. They had the Captain-General across the line before Ptosphes stopped grinning.

Another man stepped out, then two more, then five, then a band of ten, then a band too numerous to count, and after that it was a steady stream. Ptosphes saw one gray-haired man telling a club footed boy no more than ten to stand where he was, then step out. The boy looked sullenly after his grandfather until he was sure the man couldn't see him, then slipped across the line.

Ptosphes turned his back on the men. He didn't want them to see his face until he could command it as a captain and a Prince ought to.

By the time he turned around, the space on the other side of the line was empty.

Ptosphes ran his eyes over the garrison, with the care of a man trained at the quick counting of large masses of men. There'd been just over five hundred before. No doubt a few had slipped off, perhaps as many as a man could count on his fingers and toes. Call it four hundred and eighty left behind, quite enough to do all the work Styphon's Grand Host would allow.

Ptosphes was fumbling for words of thanks when a sentry on the keep shouted. "Prince Ptosphes! Enemy scouts in Hostigos Town! On the east side, cavalry with two guns."

Guns up with the scouts meant they had orders to fight instead of hit and run. Who would have such orders? Perhaps the Zarthani Knights.

Ptosphes swallowed; the lump in his throat twitched but remained where it was. "What colors?" he managed to shout.

"King Demistophon's and a mercenary company's. Looks like a rearing white horse on a blue field."

The lump shrank. Mercenaries wouldn't burn a town they expected to provide them with dry beds and hot food, unless they had other orders. Such orders might not be obeyed, either, unless the man who gave them was watching.

With Grandbutcher Soton not up yet and Phidestros himself a mercenary, there might be no such man here. If Soton arrived after the Grand Host's advance guard had settled in—well, making mercenaries in another king's pay burn their own shelter and food was a task Ptosphes wouldn't wish even on Soton.

IV

Grand Captain-General Phidestros of Hos-Harphax felt his guts twist as the vanguard of his Iron Band rode by a burning farmhouse. A child lay on the steps, skull split.

In the farmyard itself, three of Roxthar's Holy Investigators were "questioning" a Hostigi woman, no doubt the child's mother. The Investigators wore hooded white robes with a red sun-wheel over the breast. The robes were well stained with mud and blood—some of the blood long dry.

"They can fight women and children well enough!" growled Grand Captain Kyblannos, commander of the Iron Band. "Where were Styphon's swine when we charged Kalvan's artillery at Ardros Field!"

Phidestros leaned out of his saddle to grip his friend's hand before he could draw a pistol and do something foolish. Not that half the Iron Band and Phidestros himself didn't feel the same.

Phidestros shut his ears against the woman's screams. Why in the name of every god couldn't the Styphoni at least find more private places to torture and maim? It was Roxthar, of course—Roxthar, with the fanatic's blindness to the opinions of others and total sense of his own rightness. He'd still better learn discretion, before half the Royal Army of Harphax and more than half the mercenaries started hunting Investigators instead of Hostigi.

Phidestros led veterans, men accustomed to danger, wounds, and death, for themselves and for others. He didn't lead butchers who reveled in killing like weasels set loose among turkey chicks!

Curse and blast the Holy Investigation and all its works! They were dragging honorable soldiers down into the same kind of sty they enjoyed, without doing Styphon's House on Earth all that much good. These priests seemed to forget too easily what soldiers learned young if they wished to grow old: men made desperate by fear will fight to the last.

Phidestros twisted his head and flexed his shoulders as much as his armor would allow, to ease the tautness. He should be the happiest man in the Great Kingdoms, yet he felt more fear of the future than he had ever felt of Kalvan.

Kalvan was not invincible. Ardros Field proved that. The greatest victory since Erasthames the Great defeated the Ruthani Confederation at Sestra more than four centuries ago, and won by a man who three years ago was lucky to count two hundred soldiers following his banner! A victory so great that the Grand Host had already released some of its mercenaries and set others to garrisoning captured castles. Five thousand of the best were hard on the heels of the fleeing Royal Army of Hos-Hostigos.

Phidestros knew he should be riding with those men, instead of playing steward to Archpriest Roxthar and his Investigators. Let Grand Master Soton invest Tarr-Hostigos while Phidestros pressed the pursuit until Kalvan was no more! As long as Kalvan was alive, he might rise again. A man who could conjure a Great Kingdom out of not much more than the gods' own air was no ordinary foe.

But try telling that to anyone else, including Grand Master Soton, who ought to know better! Phidestros could not understand why Soton deferred so much to Roxthar. The Grand Master was not only the highest-ranking soldier of Styphon's House, he was an Archpriest in his own right, the Investigator's equal in priestly rank.

A mystery, and one that demanded an answer soon. Otherwise they'd never run that wily fox Kalvan to earth before he found another burrow.

It would not be an answer easily come by, either. Undue curiosity about the affairs of the Investigation was a short road to a charge of "heresy."

The Iron Band started down the last slope into Hostigos Town, laid out on its alternating hills and dales. In the distance, Phidestros saw the

Kettlepot Mountains and Hostigos Gap, with Tarr-Hostigos perched atop two formidable mountains to the right of the Gap.

The first mountain held the main castle with its great keep surrounded by walls and gun towers. The second and higher peak held a tower with its own walls.

Removing Tarr-Hostigos from the path of the Grand Host was not going to be as simple as taking a splinter from a child's foot, regardless of what Roxthar thought. If Phidestros had his choice, he would leave a detachment to blockade the castle and let starvation do the rest.

But he was merely a Grand Captain-General, in a war run by priests. Also a Captain-General who answered to a Great King who'd mortgaged everything but his concubines' shifts (if they had any) to Styphon's House!

It was time to send the priests back to their temples and the counselors back to their castles so the soldiers could go on with finishing off Kalvan.

As they rode down toward Hostigos Town, Phidestros was pleased to see only two columns of smoke rising from it. There'd be dry beds at least for the next quarter-moon.

A rider galloped up, shouting for Phidestros. From his silvered armor and black-caparisoned horse with a silver sun-wheel on each quarter, he was a Knight of the Holy Lance.

"Hail, Grand Captain-General Phidestros! I am Commander Rythar of the Holy Lance, with a message from Grand Master Soton."

"Greetings, Commander Rythar. What is your master's pleasure?"

"The Grand Master requests your presence upon yonder hill."

The Commander raised his visor and pointed to a nearby hill. A Blade of sixty Knights stood in attendance on the diminutive figure of the Grand Master, whose blackened armor made a stark contrast to their polished finery.

Phidestros nodded to Kyblannos. The Grand Captain told off sixty of the Iron Band and placed them around his Captain-General until Phidestros felt like a babe in its nurse's arms. He held his peace; Kyblannos would be like a she-wolf with one cub toward his old captain until the day he died.

It took a few moments for the horses of Phidestros' party to get used to rough ground again, after several candles on the smooth paving of Kalvan's Great King's Highway. *Kalvan is a hard man not to respect, even in defeat,* was Phidestros' thought. *Many saw the wisdom of such roads. None were built, until Kalvan came.*

A quarter-candle took Phidestros up the hill to Soton's outpost. Phidestros dismounted and advanced to greet Soton, as Banner- Captain Geblon arrayed the Iron Band facing the Knights.

The two commanders clasped hands. Soton pointed to Tarr-Hostigos.

"A hard nut to crack, aye, Captain-General?"

"One to give any squirrel a bit of work. It's big enough to hold two thousand men and supplies for a year, if they don't mind horseflesh. We may see snow before we see a breach in those walls!"

"Rest easy, Captain-General. We've interrogated some prisoners—*not* as the Investigation does it, by the way. Kalvan's left only a skeleton garrison, five hundred men and some of those wrinkled like crab apples. We should have the castle invested in a few days. Then we can see about tracking Kalvan all the way to the Great Mountains if we must!"

Phidestros wanted to sing, dance, and embrace Soton, but dignity and caution shaped his tongue to a question. "Will His Bloodiness let us show such wisdom?"

"Guard your tongue, Phidestros. You are not so high that you cannot be made to lie down on the rack!" Soton's look would have stopped a charging bull.

This time frustration and disgust kept Phidestros altogether silent. Just how far into Roxthar's pocket *was* Soton? Before this year he would not have believed a man lived who could bind Soton to his will. Surely the mystery of Soton and Roxthar demanded a solution, before it threatened the victory so dearly bought with the blood of men Phidestros had led to battle!

When Phidestros found his tongue again, his voice was cold. "Yes, Grand Master. I have seen the fate of women and children who defy the Holy Investigator."

Soton's face paled and he looked away. "It is our duty to obey the

Temple's will," he muttered. "This war against women and babes is not my choice, either, Phidestros. But when the Hostigi heresy is scourged from the land, the Investigation will be ended."

If you believe that, Phidestros thought, you aren't half the man I'd thought you are.

"The commanders are to be billeted at Ptosphes's new palace in Hostigos Town," Soton continued. "I'll be going there myself, as soon as we finish this drawing of Tarr-Hostigos."

He pointed at a Knight sitting on a stump with a slate and charcoal in hand. Phidestros peered over the man's shoulder, to see a fine rendering of the castle, with every tower and gate clearly shown.

Best round up Kalvan's mapmakers as soon as we're settled in, he decided. *Some may have fled, and doubtless Soton will want his share. But this, please Galzar, is something soldiers can settle between them without listening to priests' babbling!*

V

A hundred petty matters kept Phidestros and his Iron Band out of Hostigos Town for much of the morning. By the time they'd covered the last furlongs of Old Tigo Road, the few fires were out. The streets were deserted, except for soldiers and chain gangs of prisoners, led by Roxthar's Investigators and Styphon's Own Guard, resplendent in their silvered armor and red capes.

Phidestros was hardly surprised to see the Guard acting as the Investigators' allies. The Temple Bands had a reputation as stout fighters, who neither asked nor gave quarter. That last habit had given them the nickname of "Styphon's Red Hand."

The chain gangs all seemed bound for Hostigos Square, which Phidestros found already half-filled with slave pens of Hostigi prisoners. The palace itself was garrisoned by Guardsmen standing practically shoulder-to-shoulder, and Investigators darted in and out like rats from a half-eaten corpse. Phidestros led the Iron Band toward the palace, ignoring the curses and threats of Styphoni brusquely pushed aside.

The Iron Band replied only with silence, and occasionally with a hand rested lightly on a pistol butt. Before it reached the palace, the Styphoni were giving way without protest.

As Phidestros dismounted, he knew one thing. He'd be cursed if he billeted any of his men in this nest of temple-rats! He'd say that the siege demanded all his attention and find quarters elsewhere! Otherwise the Iron Band would start the war against the Investigators here and now, and he'd be lucky to end up back commanding a company of every other captain's leavings!

VI

Danar Sirna's first thought on waking up was to wish that she hadn't. Being dead or at least asleep seemed the best solution to quite a number of her problems, starting with her crashing headache. The last thing she remembered was trying to escape from the Royal Foundry.... The screams and cries of her dying colleagues still ran through her head.

The first thing Sirna saw clearly was a dead man. Beyond him lay two more dead men, one with half of his face blown away. Was she in what passed for field hospitals here-and-now?

She was lying on a straw pallet, with a wood-beamed roof over her, whitewashed plaster walls around her, and a window in one of those walls. The warped wooden shutter was ajar; through the gap she could see what looked like a cobblestone street in Hostigos Town.

She must have been picked up and brought in by one side or another, and put in here because she looked dead or dying. The whole left side of her head not only throbbed horribly but felt caked and stiff with dried blood. A scalp wound like that could make you look dead to people in a hurry.

Sirna had just decided that sitting up was a bad idea when a board creaked behind her. She decided to face her visitor sitting.

She struggled up, groaned, and turned to see a woman well past middle age, made up in a fashion that would have announced her profession on many other time-lines besides this one.

"So you're alive," the painted lady said. "They call me Menandra. What's your name, sweetheart?" The voice was gruff and coarsened by alcohol, but not unfriendly.

Better say something. Sirna didn't dare nod, but her mouth was so dry that only a croak came out.

Menandra bawled something in a voice that would have rallied a cavalry regiment. Sirna winced. One of the house women appeared with a jug and a cup.

"Drink this."

Sirna rinsed her mouth out, then swallowed. It went down, heavily watered wine with some herbs in it. When she thought it was going to stay down, she asked, "What's been happening since—Ardros Field?" She realized she didn't know how long she'd been unconscious.

Menandra looked at the ceiling as she spoke. "Well, King Kalvan is on his way west with what's left of the—his men. Prince Ptosphes is holding the castle, to let him get away. We're playing host to Captain-General Phidestros' Iron Band. Does that answer you, girl?"

"What's Phidestros doing here?" Sirna asked.

Menandra's reply was a hoarse whisper. "I hear that the Captain-General's not too pleased with how Roxthar's Investigators are tearing up this town. He's supposed to be staying over there at the big headquarters, in what used to be Ptosphes' palace. But he spends most of his nights here or over by the siege works." She grinned. "Once he sets eyes on you, he won't be staying anywhere else."

Sirna strangled another groan. Menandra shrugged. "War's like that. Now, the next question is, what do we do with you now? Some peasants picked you up, thought you fit for ransoming. They had you in a cart when the Iron Band passed by. They ran you on into town in the cart, facedown on top of a load of squash with your skirt up to your arse."

"With my skirt—?"

The picture made Sirna giggle, then laugh. Once she started laughing she couldn't stop, although it made her head hurt worse. It also shook her stomach, which finally rebelled.

When Sirna stopped retching, Menandra was still standing over her, trying to look stem but not entirely succeeding. "As I said, what about you, girl? You're a long way from home and your friends at the Foundry are either dead or run off, the true gods alone know where."

"Run off?"

Menandra couldn't give many details, but what she said told Sirna very clearly that the survivors of the University Study Team had left her for dead. It took all her self-control not to cry. She not only felt sick, she was frightened.

"Not good for you, the more so since the Styphoni will be looking for people from the Foundry. Outlanders especially. I can probably protect you here at the Gull's Nest, if you're willing to work."

This was more than Sirna could digest in one gulp. Clearly Menandra was the owner and madam of the Gull's Nest (and why that name, this far from the sea?) and was quite willing to let her earn her keep, sick or not.

"No!"

"It's how I started out in Agrys City, girl. More years ago than either of us wants to think about. There's worse things than making a living on your back. Gives you a new view of the world, you might say."

There probably were worse things here-and-now than making a living as one of Menandra's whores. Right now Sirna couldn't think of them. She shook her head slowly.

"Well, you're handsome enough for it, and to spare."

Sirna shook her head again.

"I'll leave it be, then. Just remember, though—anything you make in the house, half goes to me. Or you go to the soldiers!"

Sirna closed her eyes and wished it all away. The smoke-blackened timbers were still there when she opened her eyes. She really was in a situation where she could be turned over to a band of mercenaries and passed from man to man until she died or they got tired of her. It was a long way from reading or even writing about "the inferior position of women" to experiencing it.

Deliberately, she closed and locked a door in her mind, on First Level and all the pleasures and privileges she had there, even on her chances of ever seeing it again. (Which were slim enough at best, with Kalvan defeated and her left for dead.) She would look forward, look this Styphon-cursed time-line squarely in the eye, and dare it to do its worst.

Not that it hasn't already given me its best shot—

She came back from this mental exercise to see Menandra looking positively concerned. "That crack on the head didn't addle your wits, did it?"

"I—don't think so. I must have slept off the worst of it. I was just thinking—what I'm going to do to those fatherless sons of the gods who ran off and left me."

That was no lie, either. She now understood emotionally as well as intellectually the concept of the blood feud. If she ever caught Outtime Studies Director Talgan Dreth alone in a dark place—

"By Yirtta's dugs, girl, I can't give charity! Phidestros' men may pay me if Styphon's House ever pays them. Then again they may not. If they don't want to and I ask, they may burn the place down!"

And pass the women around among themselves, Sirna added mentally. Somehow the idea was no longer so paralyzingly frightful, now that she'd closed that door to First Level.

"If you know anything about healing, even the smallest bit, you might make yourself useful. Phidestros is going to be sending his sick and hurt here. The Iron Band's Uncle Wolf was killed in the battle, and there aren't so many priests of Galzar that even a Captain-General can conjure them up. You help patch and purge Phidestros' men, and there won't be any trouble keeping you."

"Help those damned filthy Styphon's sons of—?" Sirna began.

Gently but emphatically, Menandra slapped her. At least it was probably intended as a gentle slap. Sirna had to shake her head a couple of times, to make sure her neck wasn't broken. Through the ringing in her ears, she heard Menandra warning her against saying anything less than complimentary about Styphon.

"Archpriest Roxthar's here with his Investigators. Anyone who blasphemes Styphon within a day's ride of him will wish she *had* been turned over to the soldiers. Yes, and the stallions and the draft oxen too!"

From what she'd heard of Roxthar, Sirna saw no reason to argue the point. "I'm sorry, Menandra. I'm still a little confused."

"Well, unconfuse yourself, girl. You might start with that head wound. Clean it up, and I'll think you're good enough to turn loose on Phidestros' men."

Menandra bawled for scissors, a mirror, hot water, and bandages, while Sirna took off her mud and blood-smeared clothes and examined her body for other injuries. A prize collection of black-and-blue marks was all she turned up. Her anger toward the people who'd abandoned her grew. If they hadn't been too panic-stricken to spend ten seconds examining her, they'd have learned she was alive and fit to be moved.

The head wound was a long shallow gash, probably a sword cut. She must have picked up the concussion when she fell. No signs of infection, but she made a thorough job of cleaning the wound, starting with cutting off the hair all around it. It was bleeding again by the time she was finished, and so was her lower lip where she'd bitten it. She finished by trimming her hair all around.

"You're cutting off one of your best parts, you know that, girl?" Menandra said.

Persistent, aren't you? "I'll be hard to recognize with my hair short. Maybe they'll even think I'm too ugly to bother."

"With a figure like yours? You've got a lot to learn about men, girl. Somebody's going to want what you've got if you shaved yourself bald! Best arrange to give it to a man big enough to fight off the rest. Or else you'll wish you'd taken my first offer."

What am I, a mare to go with the strongest and fiercest stallion in the herd?

Exactly.

Sirna sighed and stood up, swaying slightly but not really wanting to lie down again. That was one good sign. Another was that she was hungry.

"Is there anything to eat around here?"

Menandra chuckled. "You'll do, girl. Come on down to the kitchen and I'll see if the bread and tea are ready."

VII

Tiny clouds of white smoke rose three times from the Styphoni siege battery. Ptosphes started counting. At "five" the three shots crashed into Tarr-Hostigos. One struck the face of the outer wall, the others hit the left side of the breach. Rock dust as white as the powder smoke whirled up, carried down toward Ptosphes on the morning breeze. He tasted the grit on his tongue and teeth. It was a familiar taste by now, with the siege into its tenth day.

The men working on the barricade rising inside the breach barely looked up from their work. The barricade was made of heavy timbers from the buildings of the outer courtyard, flagstones from the courtyard itself, and stones from the breach itself. The men at work were lacing the timbers together with ropes and strips of leather, while others stood by, ready to haul a cannon on to the top of the barricade.

"Pretty old-fashioned way they have of doing things," said Master Gunner Thalmoth, who was standing beside Ptosphes. "Without those captured guns and the slaves to haul 'em up, they'd be sitting down on the level making faces at us."

Thalmoth was old enough to remember standing in the crowd with his father to see the newborn Ptosphes presented to the people of Hostigos as their future Prince. Too old to take the field, he'd taught at the University as well as lending a lifetime of artillery experience to testing the new Hostigi guns.

Ptosphes wondered if Thalmoth had volunteered to remain behind entirely because of his age. He'd been seen to lift powder barrels and wield handspikes on balky guns. Or did he perhaps hold himself responsible for the proof-testing explosion that killed four men and took off Captain-General Harmakros' leg on the eve of the campaign that led to Ardros Field?

Thalmoth owed an answer to that question only to Dralm or Galzar, not to an overcurious Prince.

"It's the Host's first big siege," Ptosphes said tolerantly. "No doubt they'll do better next time."

This morning he felt almost benign even toward the besieging Styphoni. It was a beautiful day, and not too hot. He'd eaten a good breakfast. The garrison's wounded were doing as well as could be expected. Best of all, the men of Tarr-Hostigos now knew they'd won the victory they *had* to win.

Last night a party of picked men had slipped into the besiegers' forward positions. Their score was twenty-eight taken prisoner, more than fifty killed, a magazine blown up, and three bombards spiked, all for the price of one man dead and four wounded.

All the prisoners claimed that Kalvan hadn't been overtaken. Some added that the men chasing him had been ordered back to join the siege. One said he'd heard a whole band was wiped out in an ambush by Kalvan's rearguard. Ptosphes suspected that the last man was trying to please his captors, who had nothing to lose by shooting him from a cannon.

The last stand at Tarr-Hostigos was *not* going to be a waste of lives. If that wasn't worth celebrating, then nothing was.

Of course, the odds against the besieger would rise still higher now that the Grand Host was bringing back their vanguard. Since those odds were already close to a hundred to one, who cared? Ptosphes rather liked Harmakros' way of putting it:

"Aren't we lucky? We'll *never* run out of targets now!"

That might have been Harmakros' fever speaking. In spite of his stump having been cleaned to drive out the fester-demons, Harmakros had been working far too hard for a man so badly hurt. However, most of the rest of the garrison seemed to feel the same way.

Prince Ptosphes continued his walk around the castle walls, Thalmoth following ten paces behind. The riflemen in the towers encouraged enemy musketeers to stay beyond accurate range, and the besiegers didn't waste cannon shot on single men. Ptosphes suspected that they were short of fireseed and saving what they had for the storming. No trouble of that kind for his people, even without the reserve of twelve tons of Styphon's Best in the cellar of the keep.

He inspected the gunners at the main gate and the siege battery at the bottom of the draw leading up to the gate. The battery had been laid out by someone who knew his business, which was also why it had no guns in it as yet. They would be needed for the storming, to keep the Hostigi on the gates from having target practice on the men coming up the draw. Until then, they would simply be on the wrong end of plunging fire from the gate towers.

Another hundred paces along the walls, and some of Ptosphes' good mood evaporated. On this side Archpriest Roxthar had his prison—really more of a stock pen—for the people he was Investigating. Like most of the besiegers' works, it was walled in timber and stone carted by slave gangs from Hostigos Town, but lacked their roof of old tents. At the rate the besiegers' works were swallowing the town, it soon wouldn't matter if they burned it or not.

A long line of gallows rose by the gate of the prison pen, most of them dangling bodies, and continued on down the road halfway to Hostigos Town. Ptosphes could smell the bodies that had been dangling more than a couple of days, even over the stable-and- powder-smoke reek of the siege.

The gallows seemed to be more burdened now than even a few days ago. No doubt the Styphoni had finished with their Hostigi slaves after they'd sweated and bled to haul the captured sixteen-pounders up the slope to the siege battery.

That whole affair had been as bloody in itself as some of the battles of the days before Kalvan. The Styphoni had killed a fair number of their own men, mining the places where Ptosphes' grandfather had carved the slopes into vertical faces. The Hostigi had also had to kill some of their own folk, weeping and cursing as they flailed at the gun teams with case shot and rifles.

The end of it was what had to be, when one side could spend men like water. The guns were in place and hammering at the walls of Tarr-Hostigos in a way even those ancient stones could not endure forever. Hostigi guns, Alkides' prize sixteen-pounders. No surprise that, considering that all of them except "Galzar's Teeth" had been lost at Ardros Field.

No surprise, and therefore something Ptosphes *should* have been able to do more about. He'd forgotten Kalvan's advice, given late one night when they'd all been emptying a jug of Ermut's brandy.

"Always plan against the worst thing your enemy can do. That way you'll be safe, no matter what he does. If he doesn't do his worst you'll win more easily."

Wise words. Clearly the army of Great King Truman had taught its captains well.

Ptosphes shook his head and lit his pipe. There was no call to feel sorry for himself. He had done too much of that. Besides, while he might not be fit for service in the hosts of Great King Truman, he was no bad captain for Tarr-Hostigos when every day it held was another victory over the Styphoni.

VIII

The man on what had been Menandra's best table writhed and twisted, and almost but not quite screamed. The four mercenaries holding him strained to keep him still.

"Lie quiet," Sirna muttered. "You lie quiet, or I'll have to use a sandbag on you. I don't want to do that. You may have already hurt your head, when the tunnel fell on you."

The soldier on the table sank his teeth into his lower lip. Blood came, but he lay still as Sirna cut open the flesh of his cheek over the finger-length splinter there and drew out the bloody wood. More blood flowed freely. Sirna let it flow while she picked out the last bits of wood, then bound up the wound in a dressing of boiled rags. By the time she'd finished the bandaging, the soldier had fainted, but he came awake as his comrades lifted him off the table.

"Sorry to be so much trouble, girl," the soldier said between clenched teeth. "But I wanted to look at something pretty."

Sirna grinned. "With the gods' favor and no fester-demons, you'll have two eyes to look at pretty girls. And a fine scar to attract the ones you want."

The scar would be a lifelong disfigurement—no reconstructive surgery here-and-now. Still, if the soldier was able to contemplate life with it....

She'd thought she'd been used to what people on Fourth Level could face, after almost three years with the University Team. Still it made a big difference, to live alone among such people, with the nearest person who would have ever heard of First Level at least a hundred miles away—farther if they'd kept on running. Not to mention the possibility of spending the rest of her life here-and-now.

On top of everything else, Styphon's soldiers! It wasn't easy to accept that men who fought for something as silly, irrational, even barbaric, as Styphon's House could be like other men. But they fought just as bravely, cried out just as loudly for their mothers when they hurt, and made just as many bawdy jokes that could still turn her face brighter than her cropped hair.

Or rather, it hadn't been easy to accept this, ten days ago. Now it sometimes seemed that she'd never believed anything else.

No more sick or wounded seemed to be coming, so Sirna sent one of the women with the knife and the salvaged bandages off to the kitchen to boil them clean. She also made at least her twentieth mental memo: *Borrow some better instruments from a priest of Galzar, or have the Iron Band's armorers make them.*

Another woman, face streaked with makeup, wiped down the table with a bucket of boiling water. Menandra herself brought Sirna a cup of hot turkey broth.

"You'd better eat something solid, you know," the madam said. "Even if it's only an omelet. Won't do, having you faint on top of men too hurt to enjoy it!"

"Oh, I'll eat something tonight." At the moment, the mere thought of solid food made her gag.

"Tonight—" Menandra began, then lowered her voice to a whisper so that none of the wounded on pallets along the other side of the room could hear.

"The talk in town is that it's tomorrow they go for the castle. So you'd *better* eat and sleep tonight, or by Yirtta I'll turn you over my knee and spank you!" She ran her fingers through Sirna's hair with one large greasy hand.

Sirna gulped her broth with both hands clasped tightly around the cup so Menandra wouldn't see that they were shaking. Seventeen wounded men in one day was bad enough. If they stormed the castle, it could be more like seventy—or seven hundred! Although she might have more help from the priests of Galzar if the promised reinforcements came up. Had they? She was trying to think of a tactful way to ask when the door to the street opened and a suit of armor wearing dusty leather breeches and boots strode in.

The suit of armor also had a brown beard and wide gray eyes, but it wasn't until the high-crested helmet came off that Sirna realized there was a man inside. When she saw that the man had a high forehead and a long scar across his right cheek, she knew who'd come to visit his wounded.

Grand Captain-General Phidestros waved the men trying to rise back on to their pallets with his free hand, set his helmet on the table, and took off his mud-caked gloves. Then he grinned at Sirna.

"You randy bastards! You've been keeping secret the best thing this wreck of a town has to offer. Where's your loyalty to your commander, you—?" The term would have been insulting as well as obscene in any other tone. The men replied in kind, except for Banner-Captain Geblon, on light duty today because of an attack of dysentery.

"She is Menandra's healer, Captain-General," Geblon said, trying to both look and sound innocent. "She has been marvelously chaste."

"I'm sure she has," Phidestros replied. "But has she been caught? If she hasn't, you aren't the men I thought you were!"

Sirna stopped blushing and started giggling. Phidestros bent down and gripped her by one arm, pulling her to her feet as easily as if she'd been a child. Seen close up, his long face showed deep lines, apparently gouged with a blunt chisel, then filled with dust.

By the time he'd led her into the hall where no one could see her, she was trying to stop giggling. Somehow she wanted to impress him favorably, and not only because he had the power of life and death over her.

"To speak plainly—what is your name, by the way?"

"Sirna."

"Speaking plainly, Sirna, I owe you for a good thirty of my men helped and at least two saved outright. Where did you learn to treat burns like Aygoll's?"

"My father had some skill in healing, and was always quick to learn anything someone else would teach. One year we lived not far from a smithy. They knew how to heal burns from molten metal."

"Curious. What you did for Aygoll is very much like what Kalvan is said to have taught, about driving out the fester-demons."

"Is it not possible that the gods can send wisdom to both good and evil men, and leave it to them how it shall be used?" She looked up to meet his eyes as she spoke, and she thought she kept her voice steady.

"It's not only possible, it happens all the time," Phidestros said. "Only don't try arguing the point with Holy Investigator Roxthar. He's threatening to purge the hosts of Styphon once he's finished with Hostigos."

"Aren't you speaking a little freely, if he's running—if he's that suspicious?"

Like most of the surviving population of Hostigos Town, Sirna had stayed indoors. Those whom urgent business or the search for food drove outside too often found themselves confronted by white-robed Investigators or squads of Styphon's Red Hand. Few of those returned. Now only rats and fools strayed outside: rumor had it that the Investigators were turning to house-to-house searches in East Hostigos Town.

"Afraid you won't be paid, Sirna?"

"That's not it at all! I just—I'm not like Menandra, you know. I'd feel sorry for a thrice-convicted rapist facing the Investigation."

"So would I, believe me." He grinned, displaying a mouthful of almost intact white teeth, which meant not only good health but good luck in battle.

"Menandra is no worse than the gods made her, but they were drunk that day and perhaps a little careless. No, Sirna. I'm in no danger. Not unless the Archpriests decide they don't need good soldiers anymore. That won't be until Kalvan's dead, and somehow 1 think that man is going to take a lot of killing."

Sirna would have kissed Phidestros if she hadn't known he would misinterpret the gesture. "I wouldn't be at all surprised if it did," she said.

"Which means that Roxthar is going to be dealing lightly with soldiers for a while. Healers who may be tainted with heresy aren't quite as indispensable. Remember that, and you may live to be paid for your work with the Iron Band.

"Oh, and by the way; I'll pay it right into your hands. If Menandra asks for a single brass piece, tell me. We'll roast our victory ox over her furniture."

The way Phidestros' voice and face changed in those last words made Sirna want to flinch away from his touch. She forced herself to stand still as he put a hand behind her back and urged her back toward the main room.

"Let's join the men, before they gamble away all their money wagering which one of us was on top!"

IX

Phidestros woke up the instant a hand pressed over his lips. Instinctively his right hand snaked underneath the bedroll his head rested on, to grip the poniard there.

Now another hand gripped his right wrist. Phidestros used his left hand to reach for the single-shot widow-maker he kept in a pouch next to his heart.

"For Galzar's sake, sir! It's me, Kyblannos!"

Phidestros stopped struggling when he recognized the voice, but didn't let go of the still-undrawn widow-maker.

"What in Regwarm's Hidey-hole is up now?"

"A parlay, sir. Some of the mercenary captains would like a private word with you, out of Archtorturer Roxthar's hearing."

"By the Wargod's Mace, couldn't they pick a more civilized hour?" Phidestros groaned.

At least the captains had picked the right place. The tent Phidestros used when he spent the night at the siege lines was a thousand paces from the nearest other tent. Men like Kyblannos guarded it, men who had been with Phidestros in the early days of the Iron Company, men who had no fear of priests or torturers. Men who had guarded him with their lives and would go on doing so.

Phidestros cursed again and sat up.

"Who wants to talk with me?"

"Grand Captains Brakkos, Demmos, and Thymestros, Captain Phidammes, Uncle Wolf Eurocles, and three other captains I could not recognize."

That was five of the best freelances in the Grand Host, leading about a sixth of its strength. Now that he was awake enough to think clearly, Phidestros found himself not altogether surprised.

The first attempt to storm Tarr-Hostigos had been a disaster. The attack up the mountainside at the breach and up the draw toward the gate had been bloodily repulsed. The Hostigi had thrown everything from barrels of fireseed to ordinary rocks at the storming parties, reducing them to bloody rags fifty paces from the walls.

In the northern work, a handful of Hostigi had slaughtered twenty besiegers for every man they lost before the scaling ladders finally reached the walls. They might have held as firmly as they had in the main castle, if it hadn't been for the newly arrived siege rifles.

Converted from the heavy boat swivels used by the Zarthani Knights against the Ruthani of the southern swamps, they could go anywhere three men could climb. Once in action, they outranged even a Hostigi rifleman perched on a tower. Ten of them had given the Grand Host the northern work of Tarr-Hostigos. Fifty might have given them the main castle.

At least they now had a place where heavy guns might play against the keep, once they were hauled up there. Given time, those guns would finish the work with no need for another attack.

Time, though, is just exactly what I won't have, he thought. *If the freelance captains don't take it away, Roxthar will. He knows only one way of solving this problem, and that's the bloodiest. Does he plan to bleed the Grand Host to a shell, so it cannot turn against him after Kalvan is overthrown?*

Phidestros began pulling on his clothes. "By the way, Kyblannos. What do they want? More gold?"

"I don't know, sir. Truly."

"Help me get my breastplate on, then let them in."

The captains slunk into the tent like foxes into a turkey yard. Uncle Wolf Eurocles was in the lead, chief among the Host's Uncle Wolfs and formerly a freelance Captain-General of some note in his own right. His hair was almost white and his beard iron gray, but his face was still ruddy and his back straight as a musket barrel.

When everyone was inside, Phidestros rose. "I won't apologize for poor hospitality. It's too late for that. What can I do for you gentlemen?"

Eurocles spoke first. "In the name of Galzar, can you bring this mad siege to an end?"

"Not without putting my jewels between the blades of Roxthar's clipping shears."

Nervous laughter skittered around the tent.

Grand Captain Brakkos spoke up next. "I thought you led this army, *Grand* Captain-General, not Roxthar's regiment of bedgowns."

"I command, but only so long as I do nothing to offend Archpriest Roxthar or Great King Lysandros. Where do you think I would have been if we had lost at Ardros Field? Even now, I have Grand Master Soton, Roxthar, and would-be successors all tugging at my swordarm.

"The real commander of this Host is the one who fills your pay chests with gold—and you all know it."

"Then not even you can stop this senseless assault on Tarr-Hostigos?" Eurocles asked.

"No, Uncle Wolf. Were it up to me I'd leave a blockading force with a few heavy guns, to starve the Hostigi out of their fortress or knock it down on their thick heads. I would take the rest of the Host after Kalvan until I caught him, then pickle his head as a gift for Lysandros.

"But our Holy Investigator decrees otherwise. As I would like to survive this siege, I am not going to disobey."

"May Galzar strike that blasphemer of Galzar dead!" Brakkos shouted.

"Hush, man! Even the walls have ears," a captain urged.

"Curse and blast Styphon and all his Archpriests!" Brakkos raved on. "This isn't the only gap in the mountains, for Galzar's sake! None of the others are half so stoutly defended. Let us push through one of them and fight Kalvan's fugitives, not sit here like owls in a thunderstorm!"

"Silence, Brakkos," Eurocles replied. "Your flapping tongue is a danger to us all." His steely gaze finally reduced Brakkos to stuttering.

"Captain-General Phidestros, *you* are the leader of this Host, and that is a sacred trust given by Galzar. You must stop this madness."

"If I had Galzar's hand to guide mine, I would. I do not. Only Styphon's branding iron and the headsman's ax rule here. I say again, and I hope for the last time—if I order the Host to do anything whatsoever that displeases Roxthar, my life will be forfeit and leave the Host under the command of Soton."

"Then stay and be Roxthar's slave if you will," Grand Captain Demnos snapped. "We shall do otherwise."

"Do anything else and your life won't be worth a bent pfennig," Phidestros replied. "Roxthar has a memory like Galzar's Muster Book."

"Styphon's tentacles do not cover the earth," Brakkos replied. "King Theovacar is always ready to hire freelances, and I've heard there's a revolt in Wulfula and a king taking oaths. Too, there are no Investigators in Hos-Zygros or Hos-Agrys."

"Not yet, my friends," Phidestros said, wearier than even the hour and a moon of work could explain. "Leave at your own risk. The day is Styphon's and his sun burns hot and reaches everywhere.

"If you must leave, do so at night, without a word to anyone. If Roxthar hears of your plans, the Red Hand will drown you in your own blood.

"Let it also be said that this is oathbreaking and I speak against it. Uncle Wolf, what say you?"

Eurocles shook his head. "The Captain-General speaks the truth. Any of you who desert this siege without his permission will be under Galzar's ban. I have no choice."

Brakkos spat on to the ground. "Priest, you are as weak-spined as our *Grand* Captain-General! Don't you see, when Roxthar and his butchers are through with Kalvan they will next turn on Dralm, then Lytris, then Yirtta Allmother, finally on Galzar himself! Fight before it is too late! We betray Phidestros, but we do not betray our god!"

In a thunderous silence, Brakkos left the tent.

It was Eurocles who broke the silence. “He and his men will be gone before dawn,” the priest said in a hushed voice. “By Galzar’s Mace, they are doomed. Yet I fear he may well be right.”

X

Prince Ptosphes looked around him at the battle-strained faces on the keep’s roof. At dawn they would face the twenty-first day of the siege; almost certainly they would face the second storming attempt.

The first one ten days ago had cost the garrison a hundred men, the Styphoni three thousand. It had gained the enemy the north tower, but shellfire from the keep had kept them from mounting guns there.

The second storming would be more dangerous. The enemy would certainly have some tactics devised to meet their shells. Those heavy rifles would come into play against the Hostigi marksmen who had butchered the mercenary captains.

Worst of all, this time Styphon’s Red Hand would be clutching at Tarr-Hostigos. Their massed columns had been gathering in Hostigos Town all day. Would they lead the assault, or bring up the rear to remind the vanguard that there was something more to be feared than Hostigi shells?

Two men carrying Captain-General Harmakros’ chair set it down with a thump. The two men carrying Harmakros himself gently lowered him into the chair, arranged the cushions behind him, and stepped back.

Even in the twilight, Ptosphes could see that Harmakros’ cheeks were too flushed for a man who was supposed to be healing well.

“Did you have wine at dinner?”

“Why not, Prince? It will take more wine than we have in Tarr-Hostigos to kill me before Styphon’s House does.”

Ptosphes sighed. With variations, he’d heard this at least twenty times today, since it had become obvious that the Styphoni were gathering again. No one expected to see tomorrow’s sunset. Nobody seemed to care, either, so long as they could take a proper escort with them. To be sure of doing that, everybody had worked all day as if demons would pounce on them the moment they dropped their tools or even stopped to take a deep breath.

Ptosphes looked the length of what was, for another night at least, *his* castle. The work done to protect the mortars showed most clearly. The four small ones now had stones banked around them, so that the shells bursting outside wouldn't do so much damage. The three larger mortars were back on their field carriages. They could move to prepared positions all over the courtyard as fast as the men on the ropes could pull them, then be firing again almost as soon as they stopped.

The four biggest "mortars" were still in the pit in the outer courtyard. They were really just an old twelve-pounder and three eight-pounders, with their breeches sunk into the earth and their muzzles raised. They were too heavy to move or mount anywhere else, and in any case they could reach everywhere around Tarr-Hostigos from the courtyard. Their crews were finishing a magazine of timbers covered with stones, to protect their shells and fireseed.

"Prince Ptosphes!" One of the riflemen on sentry duty was pointing toward the siege lines on the west side of the castle. "They're starting to move around before the light goes. Think they'll come tonight?" He sounded almost eager.

Ptosphes stared into the dusk, wishing for the hundredth time in the last four years that he had one of the far-seeing glasses of Great King Truman's army. But they were like Kalvan's old pistol—the Great King couldn't even teach his friends how to make the tools to make the tools to make the glasses!

Yet those skills *would* be learned. What the gods had taught once, they could teach again—and more easily, because they would be teaching men who were trying to learn and knew what power the new knowledge might give them.

If Kalvan's luck continued to hold, his children might live to look at a battlefield through far-seers, or even ride into battle aboard one of those armored wagons that moved without horses and carried guns that fired many times while a man was drawing a deep breath.

Ptosphes put aside thoughts of the future he wouldn't see and looked to where the rifleman was pointing. The man was right. Guns—heavy ones from the number of horses drawing them—were rolling slowly along behind the lines. It was too dark to make out more, but Ptosphes suspected that the missing Hostigi sixteen-pounders had just been found.

"Should we try a few shots, just to remind them that we're awake?" Harmakros asked.

"Not with the mortars. We want to save their shells. That little rifled bronze three-pounder on the inner gate, though—it might have the range."

"Kalvan said we shouldn't use case shot with rifled guns," Ptosphes said. "It damages the rifling. With solid shot, that three-pounder will do more good up here."

Harmakros' face asked what he was too tactful to put into words: how likely is it that any gun in Tarr-Hostigos will last long enough to damage itself, once the Grand Host advances? Perhaps he was also chafing at waiting like a bear tethered in a pit, for the dogs to come down within reach.

The hoisting tackle on the keep easily hauled the three-pounder up on to the roof, but not before darkness fell. Half a dozen shots produced a satisfactory outburst of shouts and curses from the Styphoni, but otherwise they seemed to have fallen off the edge of the world. After the half dozen failed to start a fire, Ptosphes ordered the gun to cease fire.

He made a final inspection, counting with special care the torches and tarpots laid ready, in case the Styphoni came at night. It wasn't likely; the chance of hitting friends in a night attack would not please the mercenary captains. It wasn't impossible, either, and Ptosphes was determined to follow Kalvan's teachings to the end (not far away now): prepare for *everything* that isn't impossible.

At last Ptosphes returned to the Great Hall, to find Harmakros asleep in the chair of state and snoring like volley fire from a company of musketeers. Ptosphes rolled himself in his cloak without taking off his armor, on a pallet as far from Harmakros as he could find.

He'd thought he might be too tired or uneasy to sleep, but instead he was drifting off into oblivion almost as soon as he'd stretched out his legs and lowered his head on to the dirt-stiffened cloth.

XI

Phidestros brushed the sleep out of his eyes and stared through the valley's early-morning shadows at the Grand Host's encampment. A splendid sight with its thousands of campfires—until one remembered that all these tens of thousands of men were chained to this desolate valley by a castle held by some five hundred old men and walking wounded. Meanwhile, the Usurper fled into the wilderness.

Phidestros realized now that it was in some measure his own fault that he was not free to ride on Kalvan's trail. He had not questioned Lysandros' orders that he should not go against the will of Grand Master Soton. Apart from the folly of divided command, he respected the man too much.

He had not realized how completely Soton would be in Roxthar's pocket. Nor had he considered the possibility with as much attention as he would have given to the effect of rain on the roads he needed to bring up fireseed! Had he done so, a few discreet questions at least might have already been asked, and the mystery closer to solution. Certainly he would have been able to do more than he had, against the Grand Master's seeming need for Roxthar's permission to break wind!

As it was, he was chief over the Grand Host only in name. In truth, he was first among equals—all of them hamstrung by Roxthar. The Investigator was utterly convinced that the root of Kalvan's heresy was to be found in Hostigos and equally determined to extirpate it if he had to Investigate every person in the Princedom! He would not allow any stone to be left unturned, including Tarr-Hostigos. Against that particular stone the Grand Host had bruised its foot for the best part of a moon, but with Galzar's favor that was about to end!

Phidestros also asked for Galzar's favor, to keep Investigators out of his promised lands of Beshta and Sashta. A small forest of poles already held the bodies of more than a quarter of Hostigos Town's people, those who had failed the Investigation. Add to that those who fled with Kalvan, and by spring there would hardly be enough Hostigi left to bury their dead!

If the Investigation came to his lands, Phidestros resolved it would not be *his* subjects who decorated gallows. He somehow doubted that Investigators with iron pincers would do as well against soldiers as they did against women and children. It might cost his own head to take Roxthar's, but he would have the pleasure of harvesting the Investigator's first!

The shadows began to fade. From his high vantage point, Phidestros saw the camps coming to life, like kicked anthills. He'd wanted to lead the Iron Band in the first assault himself, but Soton insisted on his staying safely in the rear. Captain-Generals, Soton stated emphatically, were *not* meant to be fired off like barrels of fireseed!

Soton was right, of course. Had Phidestros been in the vanguard during the first storming attempt, he might be dead along with so many others from Ptosphes's exploding cannonballs.

He might also have kept more influence over the mercenary captains. It would have been worth risking Soton's wrath to forestall the hornet's nest Brakkos' departure had unleashed. Or would unleash, as soon as the Red Hand could be spared from the siege to go and hunt the captain down. Roxthar had somehow realized that sending away his picked troops at this moment would end the siege and might end his own existence.

It still rankled, to be leading from behind. One more thing he would have to get used to, he supposed, along with asking who had married whom *before* he swore unquestioning obedience....

Phidestros cupped his hands around his pipe bowl and used the tinderbox to get a spark. When the pipe was drawing, he blew out a long plume of smoke, watching the rising morning breeze chase it away.

"Please, Captain-General," Banner-Captain Geblon said. "Would you get down? Otherwise the Hostigi will aim at your smoke."

Phidestros doubted that in this breeze even a Hostigi rifleman could hit a man at this distance, but obeyed. He could see as well, and make Geblon happy to boot.

The guns newly emplaced in the battery at the foot of the draw thumped. Their shots tore masonry from a gate tower. Another salvo followed, and white smoke rose in place of the morning mist.

Phidestros puffed on his pipe and prayed to all the true gods that today's butcher's bill would be a light one.

XII

Ptosphes was leading a cavalry charge at the climax of a great battle. The guns thundered and something else was growling like a whole forest full of hungry bears.

He looked down. He wasn't riding a horse, but standing on top of one of Great King Truman's iron wagons with its strange gun. Except that the wagon wasn't quite as Kalvan had described it—it had the head and tail of a horse, the mane flying into his face. As they rode downhill toward the lines of an enemy in the colors of Styphon's Red Hand, the wagon-horse turned its head to look at Ptosphes. Its eyes glowed a sinister green, and he knew that he was riding a creature possessed by demons.

He clawed for reins he couldn't find, trying to turn the creature so he wouldn't have to look into those eyes. No matter how desperately he groped, he couldn't find the reins. At last his fingers closed on something that felt like woolen cloth, which was a strange thing to make reins out of—

"Prince Ptosphes! Prince Ptosphes! Wake up!"

Nobody should be telling him to wake up in a dream and this was still a dream. He could still hear the thunder of guns, even if he couldn't hear the bearlike growling of the iron wagon.

"Prince Ptosphes! The Grand Host is coming!"

"Hu-rmipppp!" Ptosphes lurched into a sitting position before he realized that he was awake and clutching his blanket.

He also heard guns thundering and someone shouting in his ear that the Styphoni were attacking. The window showed gray instead of black. Two men ran toward it, carrying a heavy rifled musket and nearly tripping over Ptosphes as they came.

Ptosphes threw off the blanket and stood. The air of the keep already held a sodden heat. He felt obscurely resentful that so many men should have to fight their last battle on a miserably hot day.

Someone was pushing a cup of tea into his hands. He emptied it in three gulps and held it out again for more. The second cupful was half Ermut's brandy. He set the cup down on the nearest chest, retrieved his sword, and buckled it on.

Harmakros was sitting in the chair of state, wide awake and barking orders. His stump was propped up on a pillow-padded stool and two pistols hung from the arm of the chair.

"Good luck, Prince."

"The same to you, old friend."

That was all the speech Ptosphes allowed himself, even if it was probably the last time he would see Harmakros. If the riflemen were taking position before the arrow slits, there was hardly time to talk.

Chroniclers a hundred years from now will probably make up fine farewell speeches for both of us. Tutors will torment children by forcing them to learn those speeches.

As Ptosphes passed through the keep door on to the outer stairs, the gun-roar doubled, then doubled again. The mortars had opened fire. Whatever was coming at Tarr-Hostigos was now within their range.

Ptosphes hurried down the stairs as fast as he could without appearing uneasy. At the bottom he saw that the guards who saluted him were also busily piling tar-soaked brushwood under the timbers of the stairs. One torch and the easy way into the keep would go up in flames, making another line of defense for the last of the garrison.

From the tower over the gate between the courtyards, Ptosphes could see everywhere except directly behind the keep. Three large storming parties were advancing, one toward the breach made by the siege guns, one by the main gate, and one holding well back on the northeastern side. At a single glance, Ptosphes knew that nearly half the Grand Host must be hurling itself at the castle.

Heavy guns were now firing from the battery at the foot of the draw, over the heads of the column climbing. Big guns, too, even if maybe not the Hostigi sixteen-pounders. Ptosphes saw half the main gate flung backward off its hinges into the portcullis, which bent ominously.

A less well-aimed shot ploughed through the infantry of the storming column. They halted, giving the guns and musketeers on the gate towers an even better target. Their firing sounded like a single volley, and they fired three more times before the column moved again. It moved more slowly now, leaving behind it a trail of writhing, bloody bodies, like a dying bear dragging its guts behind as it sought to close with the hunter.

The column coming at the breach was taking most of its punishment from the mortars, whose crews were firing too fast to be much concerned with safety. Ptosphes saw one man knocked down and crushed as a mortar shifted on its base, and a shell with a fuse cut too short blew up just above the walls. A dozen defenders went down. The ones who rose again shook their fists at the mortar crews.

Now the guns beside Ptosphes were shooting. Another regiment was coming into sight behind the first one—armored men, marching under a black banner with a silver sun-wheel. Soton's Knights were fighting on foot today.

The Zarthani Knights lumbered through the gaps in the first line to take the lead. Ptosphes shouted, "Change to case shot!" It wasn't going to make any difference to the fate of Tarr-Hostigos now, but the more dead Knights, the better for Kalvan.

The guns aimed at the main gate were firing higher now, trying to silence the guns in the gate tower. One of them was disabled, but the other was still hurling case shot straight into the column, inflicting hideous losses. Guns from the other towers were now hammering at the column as well, scything down entire companies like farmers scything wheat.

Smoke gushed up from the enemy battery, more than one could expect from the discharge of even the largest gun. Ptosphes saw men flying into the air and others running with their clothing on fire. He heard the double-thump of an explosion—someone careless with fireseed—as the rate of fire increased.

More Hostigi case shot tore the main column—then suddenly it was breaking up and the men were running back down the draw in a futile effort to escape, some of their officers beating at them with halberds and swords, others joining the rout. From the walls of Tarr-Hostigos, cheers joined the gunfire.

Ptosphes had a moment of thinking that perhaps their doom wasn't so certain after all. One column broken, and its men looking as if they would be hard to rally for another attack. Do the same with the other two columns, and at least the mercenary captains might have the same second thoughts they'd had during the first storming attempt. If they had second thoughts and let Styphon's House know them, the False God himself couldn't keep the Archpriests from having to listen. And if the Archpriests chose to turn the Red Hand loose on the mercenaries, the Grand Host's war against Hostigos would become a civil war within its own ranks—

Ptosphes's moment of hope ended as he saw the column approaching the breach suddenly sprout scaling ladders. They were going to get in or at least close; the heavy mortars had fired off all their shells and round shot wouldn't do so well even against packed men—

The twelve-pounder on top of the barricade let fly with a triple charge of musket balls. Like a volley from a massed regiment it smashed into the column. Already ragged from climbing the slope, the column now barely deserved the name.

Hard on their heels came point-blank musketry that melted away more of the column. Every musketeer within range had six or seven loaded weapons ready to hand for just this moment. For a brief space, they could fire as fast as the rifles of Great King Truman's host, with their "magazines" of eight rounds.

These foes had their blood up, though, or maybe better captains. Then Ptosphes saw the blue and orange colors and recognized the Sacred Squares of Hos-Ktemnos, the best infantry in the Seven Kingdoms. They rose across the rubble before the breach like a blue wave, with clumps of musketeers on the flanks firing over the heads of the storming parties to keep down Hostigi fire. The crews of the useless heavy mortars drew swords and pistols and joined the mass of men struggling in the breach. Ptosphes drew his own sword, ready to join them if they showed signs of flagging.

One of the overheated four-pounders beside Ptosphes recoiled so violently that it snapped its breechings and knocked down Thalmoth. He lay with his thigh a mass of blood, white bone shining through the tom flesh, cursing the gun crew for not remembering what he'd taught them and asking for a pistol. Ptosphes gave him one of his own, as scaling ladders suddenly sprouted to either side of the breach.

The first ladder rose, then flew to pieces as a shot from nowhere split it from top to bottom. At least it came from what seemed like nowhere to Ptosphes, although he knew that what he could see and hear must be rapidly shrinking. This storming of Tarr-Hostigos was already making every other battle he'd seen sound like a mother's lullaby.

The rifled boat swivels were coming into action now. Dead men around them showed that the Hostigi riflemen weren't out of the fight yet. New gunners moved up to replace the dead, though, obviously eager to claim their share of glory. Ptosphes wondered what share of glory they would have if they hit more of their own men than the enemy's. Share of broken bones and heads, more likely.

More ladders rising now. The men on them must be some of the southern swampmen Soton had brought north—no armor, no clothing except leather leggings, and no weapons but hand axes and long wicked knives.

The mortar emplacement spewed flame, smoke, slabs of stone, and flying timbers. An enemy shot or a stray spark had touched off the remaining fireseed in the magazine. Most of the men in or around the pit went down where they stood.

Flying debris scythed into the rear of the Hostigi infantry holding the barricade at the breach. Their line wavered. Some charged forward, grappling with Styphoni and rolling down the rubble to die in the moat with them. Others gave way, and a volley of musketry cleared a path through the ones who stood. Across the dying and the dead of both sides, the Sacred Squares poured over the barricade and down into the outer courtyard.

It seemed to Ptosphes that the Styphoni reached the gatehouse where he stood in the time between one breath and the next. Bullets whistled around him; the men atop the keep were now firing on the inner wall without caring much who was there. His reluctance to turn his back on the enemy gave way to an indignant refusal to be shot in the back by his own men. He ran to the edge of the gun platform, sheathed his sword, dangled from the battlements with both hands until he was sure his arms would pull out of their sockets, then dropped to the inner courtyard.

It was a long drop for an armored man no longer young. Ptosphes went to his knees and was quite sure all his bones were jarred loose from one another. Thankfully, all of them seemed intact when he stood. Smoke was rising from the base of the stairs to the keep. He sprinted for them without stopping to take a breath.

Bullets tore through his jack and glanced off his breastplate, clipped his beard, and seared one hand. At first they came from both sides, then he heard a shout from above, "That's Prince Ptosphes, you wolf's bastard!" and the bullets from the keep stopped. A moment later a crash like the end of the world sounded from behind, followed by screams and curses that penetrated even the ringing in Ptosphes's ears and a choking wave of fireseed smoke. Some Styphoni with more zeal than sense must have used a petard on the inner gate, no doubt blowing it open but also demolishing a good many comrades as well!

Two of the swamp warriors reached the foot of the stairs before Ptosphes. He cut one down with his sword, knocked the ax out of the other's hand, leaped on to the stairs, and dashed up them with flames rising behind him almost as fast as he climbed. By the time he reached the top, the blood pounding in Ptosphes's ears drowned out every other sound. He leaned against the wall beyond the doorway, feeling the cool stone against his forehead and not hearing the outer door being shut and bolted behind him.

By the time he'd been led to a chair and had a cup of wine thrust into his hands, Ptosphes had enough of his wits back to think about what to do next. This was no normal siege, where the garrison of the keep was always given one last chance to surrender. This one would end with the Styphoni trying to bury the Hostigi under a pile of their own dead flesh if they couldn't finish the battle any other way.

If Phidestros and Soton and their captains had the wits the gods gave to fleas, they would launch the last attack as soon as they could, before their men had time to lose their battle-rage. Otherwise those men might start thinking of the kind of fight waiting for them behind the walls of the keep.

When Ptosphes had drunk the wine and could stand, he walked over to Harmakros in the chair of state. He had to walk carefully, to avoid stepping on exhausted men catching their breaths, cleaning their weapons, or just lying staring at the ceiling. The lightly wounded were taking care of each other; the badly wounded hadn't reached the keep.

"I lost sight of the column on the ridge. What of them?" he asked.

"They started to close when the column at the main gate ran," Harmakros replied. "Then the breach fell, and the ridgerunners drew back. Not without leaving a good many men behind, to be sure."

"What do we have left?"

Harmakros shrugged. "A hundred, maybe a few more."

"They'll come soon, wherever they do it." Ptosphes leaned against a stone archway and propped himself up with his sword. By the Twelve True Gods, he was getting old!

"I have men watching on the roof, and more men on the stairs relaying messages, my Prince. They won't catch us napping."

"Unless they kill the men on the roof."

"Not without shells, and maybe not even with them. Anyway, I'll wager a cask of Ermut's best brandy that they don't have any shells."

"Done," Ptosphes said. "But just in case they do...?"

"I've had the men on the roof build themselves a shelter with chests and rolled-up tapestries."

Some of those tapestries, Ptosphes realized, were probably part of his wife's dowry. Not that anybody except Rylla would be left to care before long, of course, and this was a better end for the tapestries than being looted or burned, eaten by vermin, or left to rot in the crumbling shell of the keep....

Ptosphes forced his mind away from such thoughts and climbed the stairs to the roof of the keep.

XIII

Seeing the Styphoni swarming over the shambles that had been his seat and home didn't improve Ptosphes's mood. It helped to see the men on the rifled three-pounder actually smiling as they carved notches in the smoke-stained oak of the gun carriage.

"The big one's for smashing the wheel of one siege gun. Didn't hit any of our people, either," the gunner added. "The four little ones are banners we knocked down. The circle is one of the swivels. We'd have got ourselves a second, but the Styphoni were too cowardly to man it again."

Never mind that the gunners probably hadn't done half the damage they thought they had. If they spent the last candle of their lives grinning and the last moments killing more Styphoni, what did anything else matter to them now?

Ptosphes had just descended to the Great Hall when a messenger followed him down the stairs. "They're moving a heavy field gun into the inner courtyard. One of theirs, though, from the number of men they've put to hauling it."

"Everyone to your places, men," Ptosphes said. He hesitated, then added, "It's been an honor to be your Prince and captain."

A ragged cheer rose, then outside the musketry began again, heavy, rapid fire. The expected message came down from the roof—bullets were mostly coming up, to keep the gun there out of action. Even a three-pound ball could wreck a gun carriage.

"Wait until they attack," Ptosphes ordered. "Then they'll have to cease fire or have spent bullets falling back on their friends." He doubted that the mercenaries or even the Knights would care to risk much of that. It had been a bad day for self-inflicted casualties on both sides; for the Styphoni it was about to get worse.

Galzar's muster-clerks are going to be working long hours today, Ptosphes thought both irreverently and irrelevantly.

Chrunngggg!

Something struck the outside of the wall—a solid shot, the report of its firing lost in the roar of musketry. "Not bad," Ptosphes said. "Sounds as if they hit just to the left of the door."

It took three more shots before the smashing of wood and the ringing of iron signaled a direct hit on the outer door. Two more shots completed the work. A rifleman crept into the doorway and peered over the wreckage.

"They're reloading, but they've lined up a storming party too. They can't be going to fire right over—here it comes— ayyyyhhhh!"

The pieces of the door flew into the Great Hall. So did the pieces of the rifleman. A cannonball rolled in after them, making the Hostigi do spritely dances to avoid it.

Harmakros unhooked his pistols from the arm of the chair of state, cocked them, and laid them in his lap, then raised an empty wine cup in salute to Ptosphes. "I'll claim that brandy, Prince. If they had shells, they'd have used one then."

"So it would seem."

Then from all the firing slits the sentries shouted that the storming party was on the way. The gun on the roof let fly, although no one bothered to tell Ptosphes if it hit anything. It fired a second time, a third.

As the fourth shot went off, the Styphoni burst into the Great Hall.

A ragged volley of pistols and muskets half-deafened Ptosphes. He saw the leading rank of the enemy stagger and go down, but realized that the men behind them now had shields of once-living flesh. He drew his own pistol and fired it over the heads of the six men who'd appointed themselves his last bodyguard. Then the Styphoni were everywhere.

Ptosphes decided that if demons ever really came into the world, they might look like Styphon's soldiers. The attackers wore every sort of armor and clothing except for those who wore little of either. They were black-faced, red-eyed, stinking, shrieking cries in no language intended for human ears, and waving strange weapons in more arms than the gods gave men.

The massed Styphoni gave Vurth a fine target for his musketoon. He shot one man, smashed in a second's face, then got a third in a wrestler's headlock and broke his neck before someone else ran him through. Vurth's diversion let Ptosphes break away from his bodyguards toward the fireplace and the concealed ladder leading down to the cellar. He had to be down there to do his last duty as Prince of Hostigos—not last Prince, the gods grant it!—and knew he might have already waited too long.

Four of the bodyguards stayed alive to reload their weapons and see that their Prince no longer needed them. They fired into the Styphoni, then closed with steel.

The first man to make a way past them, Harmakros shot in the head. The second man ran Harmakros through the stomach; the Duke returned the compliment with his second pistol. A third man wanted to either help his comrades or see if Harmakros was dead. Harmakros snatched the pistol from the man's belt, rammed the muzzle up under its owner's jaw, and pulled the trigger. The chair of state fell over, spilling out Harmakros' body as Ptosphes swung himself into the chimney.

He forced himself to go down the iron rungs of the ladder one at a time. It would help nobody except Styphon's House if he failed in his last duty by falling down the chimney and dashing out what the siege had left of his brains.

By the time he reached the bottom, he knew that if he had to climb back up again his heart would burst before he finished the climb. He'd been right; he would not have lived to see his grandchildren grow up even without this Dralm-damned war! However, this way he was at least spared years of listening to old Tharses and Rylla fussing at him, making him eat and sleep and rest as they thought proper, and generally trying to turn him into a corpse while he was still alive.

The blessed coolness of the cellar revived him a little. He found that he'd brought, his pipe, tobacco, and tinderbox with him, started to light up, stopped as he remembered the ironclad rules about smoking near fireseed, then laughed. It made precious little difference *what* anybody did down here now.

Ptosphes found the fireseed intact, all twelve tons of it minus a barrel or few. He also found the last of the magazine-keepers sitting at the foot of the stairs, along with his clubfooted grandson. The keeper was an old soldier past campaigning, with the grandson to support and no other kin. Ptosphes had given him the magazine by way of a pension.

"What can we do for you, my Prince?"

"If you have pistols—?"

The keeper showed an old cavalryman's matchlock. The boy produced a heavy-barreled boar-hunter's pistol.

"Good. Keep watch on the stairs."

With his pipe in his mouth, Ptosphes walked over to a row of small barrels, chose one, cracked it open, then laid a trail of fireseed a thumb wide and a finger deep to the main pile of larger barrels. Just to be safe, he borrowed one of the keeper's handspikes and knocked in the head of one of the larger barrels. Fireseed poured out, until a helmetful lay waiting at the end of the train, with the twelve tons waiting beyond.

By the time Ptosphes was finished, fists were hammering on the outside of the cellar door. Then he heard the more solid sounds of a chest or bench being swung against it. Wood cracked and metal pulling out of stone screeched, as a hinge gave way. The door half-swung, half-fell inward.

All three Hostigi fired together at the first silhouettes to appear. The answering volley sent bullets spanging around the cellar. One hit the boy in the thigh. The Styphoni drew back, except for the one who fell forward and rolled down the stairs to land at Ptosphes's feet.

He was as filthy as all the others and no more than eighteen. He was crying for his mother as he clasped his hands over a belly wound that under other circumstances would have killed him slowly over the next few days. Well, he'd be spared that, and he'd already lived longer than the keeper's grandson would, or Harmakros' son if the Grand Host overtook Kalvan.

Except that they wouldn't. Ptosphes knew this, although he couldn't have explained how he knew it. He was sure it was true knowledge, not a dead man's dreaming to make his death easier.

Since he was dead, why wait any longer, in case one of those Styphoni cursing so loudly at the top of the stairs wanted to come down and argue the point?

Ptosphes finished tamping the ball and wadding of his new load, checked the pan, then rested the pistol on one knee as he knocked the live coal from his pipe into the train of fireseed.

XIV

"Damn you, Sirna! What are you using in the wound? Galzar's Mace?"

Sirna ignored Phidestros' blustering. She knew she must be causing him agony, probing his wounded thigh with her limited skills and instruments improvised by the Iron Band's armorers from Menandra's kitchen utensils. He'd refused a sandbag, though, and she had to go on and extract that last piece she felt in the wound. Otherwise he would certainly lose his leg and probably his life. Then what would happen to her? Sirna told herself that her concern was thoroughly practical and continued digging.

Finally the probe clicked on the fragment again, this time loosening it until she could grip it between two blood-slimed fingers. It was a piece of stoneware, sharp-edged but solid. It wouldn't leave any more fragments in the wound (or so she told herself, because she knew that her hands would start shaking uncontrollably if she had to burrow back into that mangled flesh).

She held up the stoneware. Phidestros managed a grin. "So that's why they didn't run out of bullets. They saved up their last moon's trash and shot it at us!" Phidestros made a face and groaned. "That's not all the trash I'm going to get shot at me when Soton learns I got this kiss from Galzar rallying his swivel gunners not a hundred paces from the breach! My ears will hurt worse than this leg!"

Petty-Captain Phyllos lifted Phidestros' leg so that Sirna could bind it in the boiled remains of a shift. Phyllos' wrenched knee made him slow, but as long as he could stand he felt that he had to be on duty. Certainly he'd had more experience dealing with battle wounds than any of Menandra's girls, didn't mind taking orders from a woman who knew her business, and whipped into line any soldier who did.

At last Phidestros was bandaged. Sirna came as close as she could to offering a prayer for his recovery. She could no longer tell herself that her wish was entirely practical, either. Phidestros was too good a man to die, even if he was serving a particularly murderous brand of superstition

"Sorry to give you such a bad time," she said as four of the hastily recruited orderlies lifted Phidestros off the table. Half the Captain-General's bodyguard had escorted him to the Gull's Nest after he fell. She'd drafted most of them into helping with the wounded who'd been streaming in since dawn. And this was only one of the besiegers' hospitals! Galzar's Great Hall was going to be crammed to the rafters tonight.

"Menandra runs a fine whorehouse, but it's not much of a hospital," Sirna went on. "If I had some proper tools, or the help of a priest of Galzar—"

Phidestros sighed. "My lovely Sirna, if I knew where to find an Uncle Wolf who didn't already need two heads and six hands, I'd have him dragged to you. You're going to be all we have for today. When they carted me off I heard we already had two thousand men down."

"Two thousand!" Sirna shuddered at the implications. Phidestros had been hit early enough to reach the Gull's Nest before the storming of the keep. Two thousand men down in the time it took the Styphoni to close the walls. How many more in the fighting since—?

Thunder battered at her ears and the floor quivered. The door and all the window shutters banged wildly and dust rose until the room looked as if someone had fired a small cannon. Sirna looked frantically out the window, saw nothing but people gaping idiotically, knew she must be doing the same, and dashed out the door.

A vast cloud of gray smoke towered over Tarr-Hostigos, blotting out the whole castle and slowly swallowing the hillside below it. The top of the cloud was already several thousand feet high, spreading into something dreadfully like a fission bomb's mushroom. Sirna lived a moment with the nightmare that Kalvan had done the impossible, taking his time-line from a poor grade of gunpowder to fission bombs in four years.

The mushroom shape started to blur, and Sirna breathed more easily. The top of the cloud was simply spreading in a breeze not felt here in the lee of the hills. She watched the cloud start to trail off toward the southeast, bits and pieces of smoking debris dropping from it as it went.

Prince Ptosphes had given himself and the last of his men over to a quick death, destroying Tarr-Hostigos and more of his enemies than anyone would ever know.

Sirna wanted to weep, scream, pound her fists against something. For a moment she even wanted to die herself. There had to be something wrong with her, if she was still alive with so much death around her. The battle, the flight, her surgery at Menandra's, Roxthar's Investigation, and now the storming of Tarr-Hostigos—dead men and women, and children were everywhere.

Sirna didn't die. She didn't even have hysterics. Instead she gripped the porch railing until she knew she could stand without help. Around her Hostigos Town awoke from a stunned silence into a hideous din of bawled orders, howling dogs, shrieking women and children, horses neighing or galloping wildly about in panic, and an occasional pistol shot.

Menandra was standing in the doorway when Sirna turned. "Better come in quick, girl," she said. "The soldiers who lost comrades up there—they'll be wanting someone's blood for it. Can't keep it from being yours if you stand out there."

Sirna followed the older woman inside. She wasn't afraid of death itself. After today she never would be again. Ptosphes had shown her that death could sometimes be your best friend.

He'd also shown her that there were good and bad ways to die. No, not good and bad. That implied a simple moral distinction. If there was anything simple about death, Sirna hadn't seen it.

Wise and foolish ways? Better, but still an oversimplification.

Useful and useless? Yes. That wasn't a universally sound way of distinguishing kinds of death, but there probably wasn't any such thing. It certainly made sense here.

Staying outside to be shot or raped by soldiers mad with rage or wine would be a *useless* death. She wouldn't risk it. What she would do another time, she would decide when that time came.

A phrase from one of Scholar Danthor Dras' seminar lectures came back to her: "*The only universal rule of outtime work is that there are no universal rules.*"

XV

Soton cursed the Hostigi and their stubbornness that was costing the Grand Host so many lives. Half the storming party was inside Tarr-Hostigos, swarming over it like bees. Both courtyards were littered with bodies, most of them Styphoni. Clouds of smoke wreathed the keep, but before they rose Soton had seen even from his distant post the savage struggle to enter it.

Why in the name of all the gods hadn't Phidestros kept back, instead of closing the breach? Then there would have been someone to go down and put matters in order.

Instead Phidestros was wounded—badly, the tales ran. Small loss, with the last defenders of Hostigos dying even now and Kalvan fleeing toward the Trygath. If Phidestros was going to make a habit of such follies, perhaps it would be best if he stormed Hadron's Caverns the next time. If he didn't, Soton would make him wish he had!

The smoke around the keep eddied. Soton turned, to summon a messenger.

He never completed the turn. Instead something as invisible as the air but as hard as stone flung him to his knees. Thunder swelled until it seemed that someone was beating on his helmet with his own warhammer. Three Knights flew off the ledge, along with a shower of rocks. Soton knew he cried out at that sight, but couldn't hear his own voice.

He lay, gripping the ground as closely as he ever gripped a woman, until it stopped shaking. Then he rose to his knees, and when they did not betray him, to his feet.

The air was filled with acrid smoke and fine ash. Looking toward Tarr-Hostigos, he saw only a vast swirling cloud of smoke. Somewhere in that smoke was the entire storming party—one man in three of the Grand Host's strength.

One of the Knights was shrieking. "It's the Demon Kalvan! He's come to save his people! Great Styphon, save us!"

Soton smashed his gauntleted fist into the Knight's face. The man fell as if poleaxed. Soton didn't know what he was really smiting, the Knight or his own fear.

Slowly the air around what had been Tarr-Hostigos cleared. The slopes around it were alive with men, thousands of them all streaming away from the castle. Soton let out a deep breath he hadn't even known he was holding.

Another quarter-candle showed him what was left of Tarr-Hostigos. The keep was only a pile of smoking rubble, the towers had mostly lost their tops, and the walls looked to have been chewed by monsters. How many of the Grand Host lay there under the fallen stone or in fragments strewn across the hillside? The Grand Host would be far less grand by the time they were all counted, Soton was sure.

Yet—this should not have been a surprise. Desperate men will take desperate measures. Who had more experience fighting the desperate than Soton, Grand Master of the Zarthani Knights?

Soton smashed his fist against his armored thigh, insensible to the pain.

"Kalvan!" he shrieked. "Kalvan, you will pay for this! By Styphon's Wheel, I swear it!"

XVI

Verkan Vall finished lighting his pipe with an Aryan-Transpacific silver and ivory inlaid tinderbox, then turned back to the data screen and its display of information on one Khalid ib'n Hussein. The second cousin of a minor Palestinian prince assassinated five years earlier—on his subsector branch—Khalid was putting together a Mideastem superstate that included just about every Moslem nation except Turkey and Libya.

As this new Islamic Caliphate emerged, on most of its time-lines its pro-Western leanings seemed to be toppling the balance between Communism, that strange atheistic religion, and the so-called Free World. Another case of the inherent instability of the entire Europo-American, Hispano-Columbian Subsector!

Verkan made a note to send out some investigator to see if the Mideast had acquired some transtemporal hitchhiker like his friend Kalvan. One of the problems with transtemporal history was that it was always easier to spot the important historical turning points after the damage was done! There was that Paracop chief two thousand years ago, who hadn't paid any attention to an anonymous carpenter's son until the religion his death launched was already shaking whole subsectors to the foundations—

The red light on Verkan's desk lit up, announcing an important visitor. Verkan looked up to see Kostran Garth enter. The man's face was red from exertion, his breath came short as if he'd been running, and he was holding out a data-storage wafer in one hand.

"What is it?"

"This just arrived from the surveillance satellite on Kalvan's Time Line. I scanned it briefly—Dalla had it red-flagged—and I knew you'd want to see it right away."

From the look on Kostran's face, Verkan knew the wafer wasn't good news; only bad news ever traveled that fast. Verkan slipped the wafer into his viewer and watched the screen light up.

The views began with a satellite's-eye scan of Hostigos and the surrounding Princedoms, from an altitude that made them all look deceptively peaceful. The next shots were close-ups of Tarr-Hostigos. Verkan sighed with relief; at least he wasn't going to see Kalvan and his remaining soldiers caught like fish in a net.

The camera panned in closer, suggesting manned control of the cameras *(remember to commend Dalla for that precaution)*. A human wave was approaching the beleaguered castle; almost the whole Styphoni host seemed to be on the move. Closer still, and Verkan saw whole units going down under Hostigi shells and musketry.

Verkan sped up the fast-forward. Whatever was coming, he wanted to get it over with.

The attackers poured into the castle like ants over leftover dog food. Muzzle flashes showed that the keep still had some live defenders. Were Ptosphes and Harmakros among them—Ptosphes, who'd refused to leave his home, and Captain-General Harmakros, still worth any three men with two legs?

Suddenly everything vanished in a cloud of smoke. Verkan held his breath until the smoke began to clear. Slowly Tarr-Hostigos reappeared—or what had been Tarr-Hostigos.

Half the walls still stood, battered and leaning. Otherwise Ptosphes's seat was a pile of smoking rubble. Verkan saw where one aircar-sized chunk of stone had crushed an entire company of Styphoni. The slopes around the castle were covered with more Styphoni—lying still, crawling, stumbling, a few lucky enough to be able to run.

Verkan's fist slammed down on his desk. "By Dralm, Ptosphes did it!"

"What?"

"He did what even Kalvan couldn't do. He stopped the Grand Host in its tracks! Look at that mess! The bastards must have taken five, ten thousand casualties. That, my friend, is no longer a Grand Host. It's hardly even an army! By the time Soton and Phidestros sort things out, Kalvan will be safe in Grefftscharr."

Verkan rummaged a flask of Ermut's Best and two cups out of a drawer. "A toast, Kostran. A toast to the memory of a valiant Prince and his last and greatest victory!"

Kostran gagged at the taste of the brandy, but he was smiling as he said, "To Prince Ptosphes!"

XVII

Considering the Hostigi resistance, the four to five thousand casualties taken in entering Tarr-Hostigos surprised no one. From the stories brought in during the day with the wounded, Sirna concluded that another eight thousand at least must have been casualties of the great explosion. Including the earlier sortie that made roughly fifteen thousand casualties. Over half were dead, and half the wounded wouldn't fight again this year if at all. Sirna would have liked more accurate figures, but she was relieved to know that she could go on doing a University outtime observer's work even in the middle of a battle.

It would be embarrassing if she ever returned home and had to confess that she hadn't taken advantage of her "unique" opportunity to observe historically significant Fourth Level events. It would probably cost her that doctorate!

Sirna told herself this over and over again, to keep some grip on her sanity, as the wounded poured into the Gull's Nest. It was the first time she'd allowed herself to think of First Level since the day she woke up in Menandra's back bedroom. Somewhat to her surprise it helped.

Having some extra hands helped even more. More of the lightly wounded men turned to changing bandages or helping comrades to the privies. Menandra rolled up her sleeves and went to work setting bones, a skill she'd acquired in her younger days from cleaning up after tavern brawls in Agrys City. She also turned out all of her girls who could be trusted to know a clean bandage from a dirty one, which was more than Sirna had expected.

Another of Scholar Dras' bits of wisdom kept running through Sirna's mind: "The danger of paratemporal contamination doesn't come from the stupidity of lower-level people. It comes from the fact that they're inherently just about as smart as we are. Once they've been shown that something is possible, you would be surprised how fast they can pick it up and even start filling in gaps on their own."

Sirna knew that would never surprise her again.

By the time the western sky turned an appropriately bloody color, the flow of fresh wounded had stopped. Sirna trudged through the house on feet that felt shod in lead boots, checking splints and dressings she hadn't put on herself.

In the twilight outside she heard shouts and screams. Men, drunk or avenging dead comrades or simply celebrating being alive when they'd expected to be dead, were sacking Hostigos Town. The hard-eyed mercenary guards from the Iron Band kept the noise and the noisemakers safely outside.

At least she didn't hear the sinister crackling of flames, as she had during Rylla's campaign in Phaxos. The Styphoni weren't going to burn the town as long as they needed its roofs over their heads.

Sirna felt like a deer who'd somehow managed to be adopted by a pack of wolves. The Captain-General's men would protect her against all the other packs as long as she did what they expected. But that didn't make her a wolf. Somehow it was no longer hard to take for granted a situation she would have found unbelievably degrading two years ago. Not hard at all, when she listened to the screams outside.

She was changing the bandages on the stump of a man's arm when someone banged on the door to the street, loud enough to be heard over the din outside and the cries of the wounded inside. One of the house women looked through the peephole. Then she unbarred the door and jumped aside, with a look on her face that brought every fit man in the room to his feet.

Two of Styphon's Guardsmen strode in, their red cloaks flapping dramatically. Two more followed their white-robed charge inside, then stood flanking the door. Sirna saw hostile glances flicking over the Red Hands' clean clothing and silvered armor.

At least Holy Investigator Roxthar looked as if he'd worked today, and worked hard. His long hollow-cheeked face was coated with dust and soot and his robes were bloodstained and frayed. He reminded Sirna of a Fourth Level Judeo-Christian representation of the Devil.

For a moment she wondered if Kalvan was the only cross-time hitchhiker around. Then she remembered the file on the control time-line equivalents to the major Archpriests. On one other time-line Roxthar was purging Styphon's House almost as spectacularly as he was here. On several others he'd died mysteriously, doubtless courtesy of one of Archpriest Anaxthenes' handy little vials.

Phidestros smuggled to a sitting position and raised a hand in greeting. "Welcome, Your Sanctity. Today Hadron's Hall is filled to the bursting, but the first and vilest of the demons' nests has at last been burned out."

Roxthar nodded, as though acknowledging a remark about the weather, then looked around the room. His nostrils flared.

"So this den of flesh-selling has served as the Captain-General's nest. I wondered why we had so often lacked your esteemed company at the Palace."

From the Captain-General's face, Sirna knew his patience was strained nearly to the breaking point.

"I must admit, Your Sanctity, that I much prefer the cries of honest passion in this house to the constant uproar at the Palace. No offense meant, of course. Let Styphon's Will Be Done!"

Roxthar's face paled. "Do not presume, Captain-General, or you may yet find yourself enjoying the hospitality of my Investigators."

"They might find a soldier too much work, after so many women and children."

Roxthar's gray eyes turned into steel ball bearings. "Enough of this babble. We have the God of Gods to serve today. The Daemon Kalvan has fled, with the remnants of his host. The land he left behind is tainted with the evil he wrought, and the servants of his demons lurk everywhere. Let the Investigation of Styphon finish its work, *then* we can attend to lesser duties."

It was just as well Roxthar didn't smile. If he had, Sirna knew she would have laughed out loud, hoping to wake up on the other side of the abyss between her and the sane reality of Home Time Line, where people didn't blow up castles in wars over non-existent gods. Instead she bit her lip and unwound the last strip of bandage, then stood up to take the sterilized fresh dressing from the soldier holding the basin.

The movement drew Roxthar's eyes. Sirna felt their hard, unclean gaze on her all the time she was binding on the dressing, emptying the water into the slop bucket, and putting the old bandages into the empty basin to be returned to the cauldrons boiling in the kitchen. She was proud that her hands didn't tremble once.

At last there was nothing more to do except stand up and face the Investigator. He was now smiling, an expression to which his gaunt features hardly lent themselves. Sirna decided that she much preferred him expressionless.

"Those bandages have been boiled to drive out the fester-demons, have they not?"

"That is so, Your Sanctity." Sirna was relieved that she'd kept all traces of a tremor out of her voice.

"That is knowledge given by the servant of demons, Kalvan, you know."

You're not afraid of death anymore, Sirna reminded herself. Besides, Roxthar won't spare a heretic even if she goes down on the floor and kisses his feet. Do as you please and at least you can hope to go out with dignity, like Ptosphes.

"That is so, Your Sanctity. Yet the new compounding of fireseed was also brought by Kalvan. With the blessing of Styphon's holy priests, the new fireseed has been used in the guns of Styphon's Grand Host, to smite Styphon's enemies. Is it not possible that the knowledge of smiting the fester-demons may also be used to aid Styphon's cause?"

Roxthar's vices did not include being at a loss for words. "This may be so. Yet I see no priests of Styphon's House here, to bless your work so that it may drive out demons instead of letting them in. Also, it is too soon to tell what may come of this day's work. Not all demons leap forth at the wave of their servants' hands. Some bide their time."

If it weren't that her life was at stake, Sirna would have believed this conversation about demons and their servants totally absurd. "In your own words, Your Sanctity—that may be so. Yet I have been healing the men of the Iron Band since the siege began. In all of them, the wounds are cleaner than they would have been without my work. Ask the Captain-General or the men themselves!

"As for there being no priests here—today there were many wounded and few hands to heal them. Should I have let men who shed their blood for Styphon die, their wounds stinking and festering, because there is no priest to bless work that I *know* is wholesome and good? If I did that, then you *would* have good cause to bring me before the Investigation. I think what I have done is good service to the God of Gods, and I will pray for his blessing, and also for his mercy on you if you falsely accuse me."

She knew that the last sentences must have been audible on the streets outside, from the way the door guards were looking behind them. Roxthar's smile froze, then he shrugged.

"As Styphon wills it. I only know what I must do in his service, and also pray for his mercy if I misjudge what that is. You must come with us before the Investigation, and hope that witnesses may be found in your behalf."

Sirna knew that her last moment was close at hand, and also that she was going to spend it as a woman of this time-line rather than as a scholar of First Level. Her right hand was at waist level, closing around the hilt of a non-existent dagger, and she'd shifted her footing to open the distance between her and Roxthar. One of the Red Hands stepped forward—

—and stopped a yard from Sirna, as a dozen mercenaries drew entirely real swords and daggers. Two more armed with half-pikes appeared on the stairway and a third in the door to the hall, with a pistol.

"Archpriest Roxthar," Phidestros said, in a tone that reminded Sirna of a baron she'd once heard sentencing a poacher. "There is nothing but the truth in what this woman says. This I swear, by Styphon God of Gods and Galzar Wolfhead, by Yirtta Allmother and by Tranth who blesses the hands of the craftsman. My men will swear the same."

"How many of them?"

"As many as needed to make it unlawful for this woman to go before the Investigation, and ten more besides. The Iron Band knows good healing when it sees it."

One of the Red Hands started to draw his pistol at Phidestros' tone. An imperative and slightly frantic gesture from Roxthar stopped him. The Archpriest's good sense clearly extended to recognizing when he saw it a situation where one false move would leave him and his guards dead on the floor and the Investigation of Styphon's enemies in chaos.

"We value your judgment and honor you for your good work in the Holy Investigation," Phidestros went on, as big a lie as Sirna had ever heard anyone deliver with a straight face. "Therefore we will also swear to watch this woman day and night, and bring word to the Investigation of any evil effects from her healing."

Phidestros paused, then fired his final shot. "And is not one of Styphon's own signs of his presence among us his gift of healing?"

Roxthar's head jerked, but to Sirna's relief he stopped short of smiling. "As you wish, Captain-General. Clearly Styphon's favor is with you today, but this may not always be so. I shall return tomorrow, to see those wounded who have been healed in days past and to take the oaths you have promised."

The Investigator whirled and strode out so fast that his Guardsmen had to scurry to catch up with him. A chorus of harsh laughter and obscene remarks about why the Guardsmen had unbattered armor after a battle like this hurried their departure. Sirna also heard a few bawdy remarks, about who would have the job of watching her by night.

Sirna was told afterward that she didn't faint. She certainly remembered nothing until she found herself in a chair, her head pushed down between her knees and Menandra and Banner-Captain Geblon chafing her wrists so vigorously that they felt ready to catch fire. She kept her head down and let the chafing go on until the giddiness and the urge to vomit on an empty stomach passed.

"Sirna—"

"Get back down on that pallet, Captain-General!"

"I need to talk—"

"When you're down on the pallet. Not a word until then!" she demanded. Sitting cross-legged by Phidestros' pallet, Sirna could hear him without anyone else being able to eavesdrop. Geblon made sure of that, with help from Menandra.

"I'm sorry if I put you in danger," she began. "But I couldn't—"

"And you didn't, and there's no need to apologize," Phidestros interrupted, with a grin. "We are the Iron Band, and we can do nicely without temple-rats chittering in our ears in our own quarters. You, on the other hand—"

Phidestros reached over and put a hand on her knee. "You've got a petty-captain's share of pay for this past campaign coming, and more if Styphon's House pays any of the victory gift they've promised. That's enough to be a good dowry for you, or buy you a horse and cart with traveling rations and servants to take you home—if you have any home left."

"Or you could stay here and buy into a partnership with me," Menandra put in. "I'm not as young as I once was. Somebody I could leave the place to would be a comfort to me now."

Phidestros gave Sirna a smile that showed what he thought of the Gull's Nest's prospects after the Grand Host departed.

"A partnership—" Sirna began, then pressed her palms into her eyes until the pain and the swimming red fire killed the desire to laugh. She owed Menandra too much to ridicule the idea of staying in Hostigos Town and becoming assistant madam of a bordello!

"I don't advise any of those," Phidestros went on. "Roxthar can't try anything with us—or at least anything the rest of the Inner Circle or Grand Master Soton won't stop, as long as I'm Captain-General of the Grand Host of Styphon. Soton and Anaxthenes know good mercenaries are valuable, as long as Kalvan's still on the loose.

"You, on the other hand, he'll snap up like a weasel grabbing a new-hatched chick the moment you're out of our protection. You've humiliated him before men he distrusts. He'll forgive that the day Queen Rylla begs on her knees for a pardon from Styphon's House."

Phidestros was making sense—too much sense—but not telling her what to do. Or perhaps he assumed she already knew, and was waiting for her to offer it freely.

"I...1 suppose I could ride with the Iron Band, that is, if you've a place for a healer. I'd like to train some of your men to help me, if that could be arranged, because I really can't do it all myself—"

Phidestros was kissing her eyelids and cheeks as well as her lips. Sirna wasn't quite ready to kiss him back, but she didn't stop him, either. She managed to be deaf to the new chorus of cheers and bawdy remarks around her.

"Some of my girls may want to come with you," Menandra added. "Hostigos Town may not be the most comfortable place for a while. I've three or four who've earned out their time and may want to travel on. If you could train them too—"

It's insane! Here she was, planning to live as the healer to a band of Fourth Level mercenaries and madam to their field brothel. Not to mention, probably, mistress to their Captain-General—an idea that now left her feeling curious rather than degraded. *Although please, let the contraceptive implants not run out before I find a way home!*

It was insane—and it would keep her alive. If Roxthar's Investigators had to fight the Iron Band to reach her, they probably would give her up as not worth the trouble. If she had to sleep with Phidestros to keep his favor, she would at least be sleeping with an interesting man—and not interesting in a purely academic sense, either….

She would go with Phidestros and his men. She would do what they wanted her to do, and they would keep her alive until Great King Kalvan returned and took vengeance for this day and all the other crimes of Styphon's House.

Sirna was sure that day would come. It would be worth enduring much to be there to see it, and maybe, Dralm willing, help bring it about.

XVIII

Tortha Karf, former Paratime Police Chief and now a Paratime Commissioner, ploughed his way through the guards and secretaries into Chief Verkan's office. He found his successor sitting behind his horseshoe desk, face buried in his hands. Verkan's face reminded Tortha of his field-hands' wives back on his Fifth Level Sicily retreat. When he'd announced that he was forsaking his retirement, the women acted as if half the tribe's men had just died in battle!

"What's the matter, Vall? Has Dalla decided on another divorce?"

Verkan looked up, startled as if he hadn't known he had a visitor. "Oh, Tortha. It's just wool-gathering. My friend Kalvan's lost damned near everything. I just finished reviewing the tape on the fall of Tarr-Hostigos.

"Instead of leaving anything for the Styphoni, Ptosphes blew up the castle, the whole Styphoni storming party, and himself. Roxthar has turned his Investigators loose, and they're busy murdering, torturing, or harassing any Hostigi who didn't flee with Kalvan."

"Sounds as if Ptosphes made the best of a bad job. Nothing sad about taking that big an escort with you. As for the other Hostigi—they're just getting now what they've already had on all the other Styphon's House time-lines where they didn't have a Lord Kalvan to save them."

The Commissioner leaned over the desk and quietly continued. "Vall, you're a realist and a historian as well as a Paracop. You know all this. What's really bothering you?"

Verkan winced as if he'd been slapped, then laughed. "You really know how to go to the heart of things. Maybe I will too, if I sit at this desk another century or so."

Not much chance of that if he keeps taking every friend's bad luck so personally, thought Tortha. A shame, really, because apart from his Kalvan problem Verkan showed every sign of being an above-average Chief for the Paracops.

"Now, once again. What's eating you this way?"

"I let a good friend down, a friend who was counting on me. Here I've got all this power and I can't do a Dralm-damned thing to help without upsetting some bureaucrat or breaking some Paratime regulation."

"You're not making sense. You're falling into outtime guilt and loyalty patterns. If you weren't Chief I'd suggest you make a short visit to our Bureau of Psych Hygiene clinic."

"I'd rather be in the hands of Roxthar's Investigation!"

"That's where you might be right now, if you'd been captured at Ardros Field. There, or just one more corpse in a mass grave. You came close enough with that sucking chest wound you took. What good would either have done Kalvan? He's alive and so are you, and I think you can do him a lot more good that way. Where is he now, by the way?"

"The Hostigi survivors are gathering in Ulthor Town."

"Why haven't they crossed into the Trygath or Hos-Rathon, as it's called now?" Tortha asked.

"Because the traitor Nestros has been suborned by the Styphoni. If Kalvan leads his people into the Hos-Rathon, they'll have to face another army. One without tens of thousands of refugees tagging along."

"That doesn't sound too good," Tortha observed. "So, where will Kalvan go from there?"

Verkan shook his head. "He'll either gather all his forces and fight Nestros, or hire enough boats to take him across the Aesklos Sea."

"What will King Theovacar have to say about that?"

"He's not going to be happy, but he's in no position to stop Kalvan. He doesn't have a fleet near enough to make a difference, even if he knew what was going on. Remember, communications on Kalvan's Time Line are at best slow."

"What about the Grand Host? Archpriest Roxthar's not going to give up just because Kalvan's evaded his host. He'll be marching west as soon as the dust settles."

"He probably will be, but it's going to be a while." Verkan seemed more at ease now; his analysis of the situation began to flow with his usual fluency. "Ptosphes inflicted heavy casualties on the Grand Host and gave their morale a nasty jar. They're probably not fit for a long pursuit into hostile country now.

"Besides, the victors will be dividing the spoils. Probably falling out over them, sooner or later. This much land hasn't changed hands since the Zarthani Knights broke the Great River Confederation. Then there was only one real claimant, too. Now there are about six arguing over the pie."

"Then Kalvan should have a while to figure out what to do next," Tortha added. "In his place, I'd build a power base so that I could be a valuable ally to anyone who felt he didn't get his share of the pie."

"He could do that, selling his services in the Middle Kingdoms as a mercenary leader. Everybody's going to need soldiers, until the barbarians are beaten back. The only thing holding the Middle Kingdoms to Styphon's House was the fireseed secret, and that's blown away. King Theovacar might even find Kalvan useful against his own barons, if there aren't enough barbarians to fight."

"Vall, I think you've just described your own next opportunity," Tortha said. "King Theovacar knows Verkan the Trader. He also knows that you're a Baron of Hos-Hostigos. Who knows, you might lead him to make you one of his negotiators with his new royal guest, King Kalvan."

"Of course! It's going to take some planning and all the supplies I can beg, borrow, or steal on a few next-door time-lines, but—" Verkan frowned, then laughed out loud, a sound that made Tortha Karf want to do the same.

Tortha held his tongue, as Verkan tried to glare at him, then laughed again.

"You sly old dog! You planned this all along. Well, the penalty is going to be taking me and Dalla out to dinner at the Constellation House.

We can finish roughing out the plans there."

Verkan started to swivel his chair, then stopped. "Just as a suggestion, why don't we sit on the fact that I've recovered. The rumors that I'm sitting staring at the wall and still recovering from my wounds have already brought out into the open a few mice who think the cat's out to lunch. If we keep the rumors going a few more days, we may find a few more mice."

"You're not thinking of hiding it from Dalla, I hope?"

"If I did that, I *would* belong in the clinic!" Verkan said with a laugh. He swiveled his chair, and the rest of the world might have vanished in mist as Verkan started punching requests for data into his computer keyboard. Tortha Karf found a comfortable chair and leaned back with a contented sigh. The Verkan Vall he'd known for fifty years was back—and on the hunt again.

THE WIZARD TRADER WAR

JOHN F. CARR

I

1971 A.D.

Ex-Paratime Police Chief Tortha Karf entered the Chief's office and looked around in surprise. Hadron Dalla, the new Paratime Police Chief, had redecorated Verkan Vall's former office to the point where he hardly recognized the place. Gone was the chief's horseshoe desk—a signature piece of furniture that had survived the reign of four chiefs—along with Verkan's curio cabinets and all his assorted weaponry and framed paintings. Dalla had replaced the old desk with some modern monstrosity that was all glass and mirrors. The walls were covered with living pictures, wall screens and shimmering metallic hangings from Second Level Interplanetary while the old couch had been replaced with a divan from Imperial Macedonia, fit for an Empress.

The biggest surprise, however, was Dalla herself; she looked harried and her usual impeccable coif was in disarray, strands of hair shooting out of her upswept hairdo. Her Paratime Police greens looked as if she'd slept in them. She was crouched around her reading-screen as if it was a precious tablet someone was about to hijack.

"Chief Hadron, I got your message ball. What's going on?"

Dalla shook her head as if waking from a deep sleep. "Sorry, Tortha. I've been swamped for last five ten-days. You just can't believe…well, I guess, maybe you can."

Tortha laughed. "I've been through my share of crises."

"I'm sure you have," she said with a tone of reproach. "But not like this! We've got riots going on in Old Town Dhergabar and two tower bombings in the last ten-day. The Dhergabar Metropolitan Police Chief wants to borrow ten thousand of our field agents to help patrol the City and find the miscreants. The Prole Liberation Movement is demanding representation on the Executive Council, or else—"

"Back when I was Chief, we used to get the same kind of ultimatums from the Prole Protection League. The PPL was making those kind of demands even before ex-Chief Tharg was on the job. Nothing new there."

"You're wrong, Tortha. Things have changed. The Prole Liberation Movement is the militant arm of the Prole Protection League. They weren't kidnapping citizens and bombing towers when you were in office."

Tortha shook his head, sputtering like a big walrus surfacing for air. "I apologize. Things do sound as if they've gone to Nifflheim in a hand basket! What's Metro doing about it?"

"Metropolitan Police Chief Vothan Raldor believes that someone the proles call The Leader is behind all this."

"Are you telling me this is a religious issue?" Tortha asked. "Because if it is, we're all in trouble." The worst wars in Home Time Line history had occurred during the Mystic Rebellions.

"No, The Leader's just the 'man' who's supposed to lead the proles into citizenship and give them all longevity treatments. I haven't heard of any religious rites connected to his demands. No one knows who he is or what he represents. He's got the proles all lathered up and rioting in Old Town."

It would be hard to riot elsewhere, thought Tortha, *since the rest of Dhergabar consisted of anti-gravity spires and towers stretching toward the sky. Still, the proles far outnumbered citizens, many of whom were working or vacationing outtime. If they continued to attack the towers things could get messy in a hurry.*

"Have you thought of calling in the Army Strike Teams?"

"That's why I asked for your advice, Commissioner. Things are in a real precarious place in the Executive Council ever since Vall resigned and left office. The last Crisis of Confidence vote almost brought down Management. It wouldn't take much for the Opposition Party to wrest control of the Council."

Then calling in the army, Tortha decided, *would be a complete disaster. The Opposition Party would use it to show that Management has lost control over the capital. I know they're somehow behind this fracas, but proving it is almost impossible. The Opposition Party included almost as many scoundrels and scalawags as that Styphon's House racket on Aryan-Transpacific. He couldn't remember the last time things on Home Time Line had been so out of whack. What's going on in Dhergabar, other than politics as usual?*

It hadn't been that long since he'd retired, only a decade or so, and things had been going fine when he'd resigned. Verkan hadn't caused this mess, he hadn't been Chief long enough. Although, spending most of his time on Kalvan's Time Line hadn't helped the situation. He'd spent enough time there that he'd resigned his office—before he'd been forced to—and left it in Dalla's capable hands. No, this was a large scale operation put together behind the scenes over decades. Someone had to be behind it, but who? Dralm-damned if he could come up with anyone or a group that powerful and sinister. Opposition Party contained too many hacks and has-beens; they certainly weren't pulling the strings…dancing to them maybe, but not yanking them.

"Chief Vothan's a good man. Give the Metro Police whatever manpower he asks for and put some of our top Investigators to work and find out who or what's behind all this PLF nonsense. This mess stinks all the way up to Mars."

"I'll do that," Dalla replied. "Any other ideas?"

Tortha took a long drag on his pipe, drawing the smoke deep into his lungs. Fortunately, lung cancer and emphysema had been conquered eons ago by First Level medicine, so smoking was a harmless pastime. And one he could enjoy without any unproductive emotional and physical consequences.

"I think it's time to call an emergency meeting of the Paratime Commission. I'll give Dalgroth Sorn a call and have him set it up. It's time we did something about this prole problem for once and for all."

"Thanks, Tortha. I really miss Vall; he'd know what to do."

Tortha shrugged. "Maybe." He was still disappointed in Verkan Vall, even though he was the one who pushed him into becoming Paratime Police Chief. *Admit it, old man, he fought you all the way. It's time you shouldered some of the blame.* The boy had talent and good instincts, but he wasn't willing to wear the harness. Too bad. It looked like Home Time Line needed all the help it could get.

"How's Vall doing?" she asked.

Tortha took out his pipe and began to recharge it. "Well enough," he said, nodding. "He's busy now that Kalvan's crowned him King of Greffa. Verkan was forced into the position by Kalvan, almost the same way I got him to take my chair. Regardless of whose fault it is, once word hits First Level, the newsies will say he's gone native."

"I don't care about any of that. Is Vall in any danger from King Theovacar? I know Theovacar won't rest until he's back in Greffa and on the Iron Throne."

Tortha shrugged. "Kalvan left Verkan a couple thousand Hostigi regulars and he's been busy building his own little army. He's smart enough not to commit any obvious Paratime Contamination, but he's forgotten more military strategy and tactics than all of Theovacar's commanders combined. Plus, he's got Kalvan to back him up. If anyone's way in over his head, it's King Theovacar. He just doesn't know it yet."

II

Tortha and Vothan Raldor, Dhergabar Metropolitan Police Chief, took an air-taxi to Dalgroth Sorn's private residence in Dhergabar City to avoid any premature public notice of the special session of the Paratime Commission. They flew to the Trapezoid Tower and exited the taxi on the launch pad on the eightieth floor. They were met at the door by one of Dalgroth's household robots who took their coats and led them to the Commissioner for Security's study. Inside the other eight members of the Paratime Commission were seated at a U-shaped table.

Dalgroth, who had the face of an elderly lion with a toothache, offered drinks and *hors d' oeuvres*. Vothan ordered a Manhattan, while Tortha settled for a Scotch and water from the auto-bar. The other eight Paratime Commissioners already had their cigarettes lit and drinks in their hands.

"I'll assume this is important, or we all wouldn't have been called here to meet in private," Dalgroth stated. "What's on your mind, Tortha?"

Tortha stood up and said, "I'm going to let Police Chief Vothan Raldor get you up to speed before I make my recommendations."

He sat down and Vothan rose to his feet. The Metro Police Chief quickly sketched out the problems he was facing from the prole riots and the difficulties he was running into from influential Home Time Liners trying to protect their prole charges. "It's gotten so bad that we've got over two thousand men on permanent guard duty protecting the shops and townhouses in Old Town. It doesn't seem to matter to the proles; there's another riot almost every night. I'm at my wits end. I've had to stop dealing with non-violent crimes just to keep enough active men on riot duty. I need help and I need it now."

Vothan Raldor sat down.

Commissioner Armtar Rana, the only woman Commissioner, asked, "What do you expect us to do? Maybe it's time to call in the Army Strike Force to restore peace. This sounds like something you need to bring up before the Executive Council, not the Paratime Commission."

Tortha rose. "Good point, Commissioner Armtar. However, there's a good reason we're not bringing this before the Executive Council; it's too explosive. Plus, we need to act quickly and decisively without endless debate and backbiting. The Paratime Commission has the power to act on this issue. Quote: 'whenever Outtime conditions threaten the stability or safety of Home Time Line, the Paratime Commission has the authority to declare Martial Law.'"

"That maybe so, Commissioner Tortha," Commissioner Dalgroth noted. "But how do these riots, surely a matter of internal security, have anything to do with Outtime events or actions?"

Tortha took his pipe out of his mouth, pointing the stem at Dalgroth. "Because, this problem is caused by outtimers. These rioters are proles, not Citizens, workers and drones from Fifth Level Servsec and Industrial Sector."

Commissioner Lagrath Sart interjected, "Some of these so-called proles have been living on Home Time Line for four and five generations. You can't call these people outtimers, not in the usual sense. Many of them are Citizens in all but name."

Tortha took his time responding. Commissioner Lagrath Sart, a tall man with a short well-trimmed beard, was one of the few political appointees on the Paratime Commissioner and the only one who hadn't served with the Paratime Police. His loyalty, as far as Tortha was concerned, was suspect. Another reason he hadn't informed the Commission beforehand about why he had called the meeting. He'd have to convince the Commissioner for Security to isolate Lagrath after the meeting until the proposed actions were completed; otherwise all of Dhergabar would know about their deliberations by the following day.

"I don't care if these proles have families going back fifty generations, by law they're still outtimers. As I've said in the past, we've allowed far too many proles to immigrate to Home Time Line. They now outnumber Citizens four to one. When you consider that at any one time more than eighty percent of all Citizens are outtime, this means that the proles could easily take the upper hand on Home Time Line by sheer numbers alone."

"I've been having nightmares about that since the Prole Insurrection some two hundred years ago," interjected the Paratime Commissioner for Security. "That one made the Industrial Sector Rebellion look like a backyard picnic. Back then the Home Time Line didn't have a quarter of the proles we have today and there were over a million casualties. Some two hundred million proles were evacuated to Fifth Level during that fracas."

"Things are different now. People are attached to their servants," Commissioner Lagrath Sart rebutted. "The Citizens won't put up with the Paratime Police taking away their friends, lovers and servants."

"I believe they'd prefer it to having their throats slit in the middle of the night," offered Commissioner Valtan Ryk.

Lagrath shook his head in dismay, as though dealing with a person of limited intelligence. "Removing the proles won't wash no matter how you do it. The Proletariat Protective League will never allow it."

"Since when does the PPL dictate Home Time Line policy?" Tortha asked, his voice reverberating loudly through the room.

"Since they threw their units and support behind Opposition Party," Lagrath continued. "The people of First Level, Citizens and proles alike, have grown tired of Management arrogance and complacency. Management's run Home Time Line, and by extension Paratime, for several thousand years. And they've done it badly! The Party's out of touch with both the people and with the times."

"Are you running for office now, Commissioner Lagrath?" Dalgroth Sorn asked.

"No," he answered, no longer bothering to keep the snugness out of his tone. "I've been promised your office when Opposition Party takes control of the Executive Council. Once they hear of this cockamamie plan, that won't be long!"

Tortha looked around at the other seven Commissioners, as if to say "I told you so." He nodded to the Commissioner of Security. Dalgroth keyed in a code on his wrist com. Moments later three field agents of the Paratime Police entered the room, needlers drawn.

The Security Commissioner pointed out Lagrath Sart. "Take him to Fifth Level Police Terminal for questioning. I'll forward further instructions later."

They nodded and moved forward. Lagrath rose up spitting, "Don't you dare lay a finger upon my person!"

Tortha shook his head. *These youngsters sure have a lot to learn.*

Meanwhile, one of the Paratime Policemen jerked the Commissioner up out of his seat and took hold of his thumbs, pulled them behind Lagrath's back, forcing him to frog march his way out of the room.

"Do you think there's anything to his threats?" asked the woman Commissioner.

Tortha shrugged his shoulders. "We've put off this day of reckoning for far too long. It's possible we may no longer have the political muscle to do what we have to do. But that shouldn't stop us from trying."

Dalgroth Sorn nodded. "Tortha's right. We've sat on the prole problem, let the PPL organize and infiltrate Left Moderate and Opposition Parties. We only have ourselves to blame. When Verkan suggested dealing with the prole problem two years ago, we almost had the Chief investigated at that traitor Lagrath's instigation. He's been our leak all along. I should have had him hypno-meched years ago…."

"Why didn't you?" Tortha asked.

"You know why, Karf. He's my son-in-law. As it is, my daughter will read me out of the family, and my wife will go right along with her."

"Then you no longer have anything to lose, Sorn. It's time to bring in the strike teams and start a mass evacuation. I'll talk with Dalla about setting-up an evacuation conveyer-head to Fifth Level. We don't want them on Pol Term. Or even more than a few a few hundred thousand on any one time-line. Commissioner Galvath I want you to oversee a study on the best distribution sites. Commissioner Sorn and I will discuss the best way to present our conclusions to Management. The rest of you leave and work out some plans for the evacuation. And, remember, don't say a word about this meeting to anyone, not even your families—especially your wives!"

Dalgroth Sorn shook his head wearily. "Let's just hope this doesn't start the rebellion we're trying to fight. If word of this gets out, we're all finished!"

Tortha could only nod in agreement.

III

"How dare you go over my head like that!" Dalla demanded. "You old fools, you'll pull Management Party right down with you if you try to enforce any such draconian decree. What the Paratime Commission is committing is political suicide! I don't think any of you appreciate just how much the average Citizen values his proles, whether they be servants or friends—or in some cases, lovers."

Tortha recoiled. "It's the only reasonable and efficient way to deal with the prole problem, Chief—"

"Not on my watch!" Dalla interjected. "You think we've got riots now, wait until the Citizens learn that the Paratime Police are about to eject all their proles from Home Time Line. That's if the proles roll-over and accept being deported by the tens of millions. And where are we going to get the staff to herd them all, to say nothing of all the additional transtemporal conveyers we'll be needing for an operation this size? Even if everything went smoothly, which it won't, it could take years, and that's only if we stopped using most of our conveyers for Outtime work!"

"We thought we'd start with the most rebellious proles first—"

"Oh, like the Prole Liberation Movement members. And what do you think they're going to do while you attempt to arrest them? They'll either go into hiding or break into open rebellion. Now, wouldn't that make a pretty picture for the newsies!"

"No, of course not, Chief Hadron," said Paratime Security Commissioner Dalgroth Sorn. "We were just trying to come up with a permanent solution to a problem that's only going to get worse over time."

"Well, your solution is too late and too drastic," Dalla replied. Management will never go along with it, nor will the Paratime Police as long as I'm in charge. If the Paratime Commission tries to enforce such a decree, it will be the beginning of the end of First Level civilization as we know it."

In the cold light of day and faced with such determined opposition from someone he had counted on as an ally, Tortha could only agree. “You’re right, Dalla, we really didn’t think this through.”

Dalgroth Sorn looked at him as if the whole thing were his fault.

“Maybe we have become a bunch of ‘old fools,’ like you say,” Tortha added. “But that doesn’t solve the prole problem, either.”

“I don’t know if it can be solved at this late date,” Dalla said, shaking her head. My adopted sister Zinganna’s a former prole; or maybe you forgot?”

Tortha shrugged. Yes, he had forgotten.

“What we need to worry about first,” she said, “is how many people outside of the Paratime Commission know about this cockamamie idea of yours. Any answers, Commissioners?”

The Paratime Commissioner of security answered. “Only the members of the Paratime Commission were informed. Tortha and I were to inform you of our decision. We thought you’d help us work out the details before we announced the decree.”

“First thing you do, is forget there ever was such a decree. Destroy all recordings and records of your proceedings.”

They both nodded.

Tortha winced, “We do have another little problem.”

“By the Fangs of Fasif, what now?”

“I had to use my authority to arrest Commissioner Lagrath Sart, who appears to be a spy for Opposition Party, and had him sent to Fifth Level Pol-Term.”

“You did what?”

“He threatened to expose our Decree.”

“So you arrested him. Did you think of contacting me before you sent him to Police Terminal?”

“We didn’t have time. Temporary arrest and deportation are within the sphere of the Paratime Commission’s authority,” Tortha said

“Lucky for us,” Dalla replied sarcastically. “Now, how are you going to explain his disappearance? He’s very popular, being the youngest Paratime Commissioner, and has a number of important friends, including a lot of newsies. Now, Opposition’s going to know something is up.”

"But as long as they can't prove anything—"

"There'll be a big investigation over his disappearance, you have my personal guarantee! We need a cover story, Tortha. And it better be a good one."

"I have an idea," Tortha said. "Since Lagrath's been a critic of the Force, we can say he requested a trip to Police Terminal to see in person if there were any abuses going on. While there he had a fatal accident."

"Oh, great. This is your 'idea.' That must have taken all of ten seconds of thought."

"Cut the sarcasm," Tortha bellowed. He wasn't used to being talked to as if he were an idiot! Vall might have to put up with Dalla's sharp tongue, but he didn't have to. "We only did this at your instigation. You're the one who asked me for help!"

"I asked for help, not another disaster," she bounced back.

"That's enough out of both of you," the Commissioner of Paratime Security snapped. "We need to do something about Commissioner Lagrath. He's a loose cannon and there's no telling how much damage he could do to all of us if he ever got interviewed by the media."

"He has to disappear for a while," Dalla said. "Otherwise, we'll lose control of everything. It'll be the end for Management, the Paratime Police Department, all of us."

Tortha nodded. That was the first comment she'd made that he could agree with. "What if we say that Lagrath, as part of a Commission Inquest into the treatment of proles by the Paratime Police, was sent to Fifth Level Police Terminal? While he was interviewing one of the proles, he was snatched by the PLM."

The Commissioner of Security said, "I like it. It not only takes care of a big problem and potential leak, but it casts the proles in a dangerous light."

"I don't like it, but it does the job," Dalla said. "I'll have Gathon Dard, one of my special detectives, handle the operation. I'll get him on it right away. You two need to lay a paper trail and cue the other Commissioners onto what's going on. I'd suggest a hypno-mech block for the other Commissioners after you fill them in. This story is too hot for anything else!"

IV

Two ten-days later, Karoth Barg barged into Chief Dalla Hadron's office without a by-your-leave. "Chief, here's an update on the Shimmer Spire disaster."

Dalla winced. The Shimmer Spire, one of the largest apartment towers in Dhergabar and home to half a million citizens, had been A-bombed earlier that morning. There was a recorded message on Tri-V from the PLF, Prole Liberation Front, claiming responsibility. Half of Dhergabar City had to be evacuated due to high radiation and the other half was on standby. Paratime Police HQ had been so bombarded with calls and messages that she'd ordered the entire system shut down except for Code Red transmissions.

"What's the latest, Karoth?"

"Twenty-five thousand casualties and less than a dozen survivors. Those being residents leaving via one of the landing ports or the main landing stage. Everyone else is presumed dead, including over a hundred thousand Proles. They don't even care about their own kind, the bastards. The good news is that two-thirds of the citizens living there were outtime when the blast occurred."

The small atomic bomb had gone off in the early morning hours. It had been detonated on the bottom floor of the Shimmer Spire; the spire's collapsed-nickel exterior walls had acted like a chimney, sending the sun-hot blast of plasma upward through three thousand floors vaporizing everything and everyone in its path until it blew through the ventilation shafts at the top. No living being inside that inferno could have survived.

The explosion had reverberated throughout Dhergabar, as residents fled the City to escape the fallout and the possibility that other buildings had been sabotaged. Shelters across Home Time Line were filled to the bursting with evacuees from the capital city. Hospitals were overflowing from those with radiation sickness, heart-attacks and other aliments related to the bombing. While there had been previous terror attacks by the PRL, this was the first nuclear one.

There were political reverberations as well; many of the cities and towns refused to accept any Proles from Dhergabar and there was a growing call to ship all prole dissidents to Fifth Level Industrial or Service Sector. The Executive Council was in an Emergency Session attempting to come up with a solution to the growing prole unrest. Dalla was scheduled to give a report in less than an hour to the Executive Council, which meant she had lots to prepare.

"Plus, the PLF has released their demand," Karoth said, pausing dramatically.

"What is it?" Karoth was a hold-over from Verkan's administration and, if she ever got any time, Dalla planned to have him replaced with someone less in love with their own voice.

"The PLF demands Citizenship and longevity treatments for all proles on Home Time Line and provisional Citizenship for all those on Fifth Level."

"Ludicrous and unacceptable!" Dalla blurted.

Dalla was considered a liberal on the Prole Question, since she'd gone so far as to adopt one, Zinganna, as a sister. However, even she realized that was no way that Home Time Line could make all the Proles citizens, especially since proles outnumbered First Level Citizens several times over on Home Time Line alone. The result would be political chaos as the former servants paid back real and imagined slights and feuds; to say nothing of the actual costs of giving billions of new citizens the dole, housing, medical and longevity treatments. It would bankrupt the entire system, and that was just for starters….

Only an Opposition Party member would welcome such chaos. Not for the first time, Dalla wondered if they were actively behind the PFL.

Maybe next time it'll be the Paratime Building. "Karoth, I want radiation detectors as well as metal detectors placed on all entrances and landing ports of the Paratime Building. No one is to be admitted to the Building who isn't in the Department or with the Dhergabar Metropolitan Police."

"Yes, Chief."

"I'm expecting Metropolitan Police Chief Vothan Raldor; let me know when he arrives."

Secretary Karoth nodded, then handed her an info wafer and quickly exited her office. Dalla put the wafer into the slot and watched the explosion on her viewscreen. The five mile-high tower on the screen rocked from the force of the atomic fire inside, even as most of the force and radiation was contained by the building's collapsed-nickel walls until it reached the air vents on top. From a distance, it looked like a fireworks display as the vents at top of the Shimmer Spire blew off and a huge flare lanced into the sky. The flame was so bright that it briefly turned the screen completely white despite all the camera's special filters.

As visibility returned it was possible to see the other nearby towers and spires rocking back and forth as if caught in the throes of a major earthquake. *This is where most of the injuries occurred outside the stricken spire*, she thought. *People, furniture, robots and appliances were tossed around like toys as the great towers rocked back and forth.* The physical injuries were in the millions, filling every hospital and medical facility on Home Time Line to the bursting.

The political repercussions would be just as bad. Dalla wondered how deeply this attack would unsettle First Level firmament. She suspected the repercussions would shake the foundations of Home Time Line for the next thousand years.

She herself had been awakened as her apartment, in the Silver Spire, thrown off her bed at 0244 in the morning. Her first thought had been earthquake, even though they were rare in this section of the Major Landmass, or what was called Europe on Fourth Level Europo-American. She had, however, experienced quakes while outtime.

Karoth came bursting into her office again.

"What is it now?" she asked, biting her tongue.

"It's Yadd's *The Day in Dhergabar* show; you need to watch this!"

She hit the button that turned on the wallscreen at the front of her office. Yandar Yadd's supercilious face filled the screen. "What we should be asking ourselves is: How were the PLF able to smuggle an atomic weapon onto First Level? As we all know, it's the Paratime Police who are responsible for protecting us from smuggling and outtime contraband, especially weapons. Obviously, the Paracops haven't been doing their job.

"This has been true for a number of years, ever since Verkan Vall took over from former Chief Tortha Karf. Things have gotten even worse under Verkan's wife and replacement, Chief Tharn. I think it's time the citizens of Dhergabar demanded some answers." He paused to point his finger straight into Dalla's face. "Chief Tharn, you owe the people the truth about what's really going on."

Then he turned back to his audience. "Send those messages and electronic letters to the Executive Council and maybe we will get some answers!"

V

Hadron Tharn watched with great pleasure as the first airborne transports arrived from the Fifth Level Industrial Serv Sec world he'd named Revenge. Finally, he was getting his just desserts. The Wizard Traders would shortly be in charge of Home Time Line. It was in his power to make life on First Level a living nightmare for all of his enemies and detractors. He was going to enjoy every bit of their suffering. *The fools never realized my greatness! They will learn, and soon.*

He watched with glee from his penthouse high atop the Vothran Spire as the fighters began to drop their bombs on the Dhergabar Spaceport.

The first tower bombing had gone off this morning without a hitch. The sky was filled with fleeing aircars that buzzed across the city like mosquitos run amuck! They would all soon learn there was no refuge, no place on Home Time Line he could not reach out and destroy.

He heard a buzz from his personal communicator. Only one person alive had that number, Warntha Sarn, his Number One.

"Yes," he said into his lapel mic. "What is it?"

"Leader, the proles are exceeding their warrant. They're butchering every Citizen they come across."

"All of them?"

"No, some fools are actually trying to protect their masters. But many of the proles, especially those from the Serv-Sec Level, are running amuck killing any and all Citizens. They're using the weapons we provided to break into the towers and butcher the inhabitants, even the tame proles. I thought you'd want to know since it wasn't part of the *plan*."

"See if you can bring them to heel, Warnatha. There's no sense in all of this if all of Home Time Line is brought down!"

"I'll do what I can, but our own force is hugely outnumbered. We gravely underestimated the hatred they have for us!"

Having used that hatred and resentment to further his ambition to rule the world, Tharn understood that he may have unleashed a whirlwind. One not even The Leader could harness. For the first time in ages, he began to feel a sense of dread that he could not shake off....

VI

Karoth Barg brought in a platter full of coffee cups for the members of the Paratime Commission who were crowded into Dalla's office, then closed the door.

"As you all heard in my initial briefing, the proles are making an all-out assault on Home Time Line," Dalla announced. "They're attacking their owners in their own homes, in many cases murdering whole families! Others are ransacking entire buildings, going from apartment to apartment, looting them and murdering any Citizens they come across."

"This is unfathomable!" the Commissioner of Security yelled. "We must bring this to an end, even if it means the extermination of every prole on First Level!"

"I don't think we need to go that far, Commissioner," Dalla replied. "I've already sent orders to Pol Term for five Army Strike Teams to arrive in Dhergabar. They'll be arriving within thirty minutes. That should take care of this revolt—if that's what this whole thing is all about."

Commissioner Tortha Karf nodded. "They should have matters in hand in a few hours. Where are they arriving?"

"The big transposition depot outside Dhergabar city."

Tortha said, "Good. That's near enough the rocket field that they can go wherever they're needed."

Karoth Barg barged into the room. "Chief, the prole attacks are spreading. There are now reports of major prole uprisings in the following cities: Ravartol, Jarnabar, Sohram, Tergostar, Bongaran, Thalna-Jaarvizar, Synalyan and Vathardt. With lesser action in another thirty to forty locales."

Chief Dalla ordered, "Inspector Karoth, assemble as much information as you can on the worst of these hot spots. Have them ready before the strike teams arrive. I will pass the information on to Commander Verdar Zoln. I'll let him sort out what needs to be done."

Dalgroth Sorn, the Paratime Commissioner of Security, nodded his approval.

"What'll we do until then?" one of the Commissioners asked.

"I've already issued a red alert for all Paratime Police officers on Home Time Line ordering them to come to the Paratime Building immediately and sent a red warning boomerang ball to all those who are outtime. We'll assemble our forces here and give whatever help Commander Verdar determines he needs."

All the commissioners nodded. Dalla was glad to see they were accepting her leadership, since she hadn't been Chief long enough to give them much confidence in her ability to run the Department. Nor had her reputation before taking over as chief had much to recommend itself. She needed their full support if they were to survive this rebellion.

Suddenly Dalla's viewscreen turned red with black shooting arrows. An alarm filled the room with shrill screeching.

Everyone turned to stare. "What is it, now?" Tortha Karf asked.

Bad news, very bad news, she thought, but kept her thoughts to herself. "Let me find out, Commissioner."

First she turned off the klaxon and cleared her screen. Suddenly it was filled with a shot from the spaceport. A harried-looking traffic control officer with his blue cap pushed halfway off his head, cried: "Chief, some fifty to sixty unknown warships showed up on the field without authorization. Nor or they responding to my requests for information!"

"Give me a screen shot," she ordered. "Maybe an Army Strike Team arrived early?!"

A score of bat-winged fighters suddenly filled the screen. They lacked their normal insignia and were painted a matt black.

The commissioners crowded around.

Dalgroth Sorn cried. "What are they doing here?"

"What do you mean?" Dalla asked.

"Those ships are part of the mothballed fleet stationed on Fifth Level Industrial Level. Why are they here? Did you call them up by mistake?"

"How could I!" Dalla shouted. "I didn't even know they existed."

"By all the gods!" one of the commissioners cried out. "They're attacking all the ships at the spaceport. They're not supposed to be doing that!"

The screen was filled with the resulting carnage. Passenger ships and space yachts were disappearing in balls of red fire and back smoke. Tiny panic-stricken figures were running helter-skelter across the landing field. Suddenly the screen went black as the transmitter or station itself was destroyed.

The room was filled with questions and exclamations.

"Shut up!" Dalla shouted. "I need to think." If they no longer controlled the spaceport itself that meant the attached transposition terminal was broached. The strike team ships would be vaporized the minute they appeared at the depot!

Then some outside force took over her viewscreen and it went blank for about ten seconds, then a familiar figure dressed all in black, adorned with the usual military accoutrements typically worn by Fourth Level dictators or overlords, began to talk. "Fellow Home Timeliners this is The Leader speaking. The Prole Liberation Front, acting under my orders, has taken control of Dhergabar."

She knew that voice: it was her crazy little brother's! Was Tharn completely out of his mind? Of course he was! And it was partially her fault, too. As his surrogate mother, once her parents had abandoned them, she had covered-up for Tharn, even going so far as to use Verkan's influence with the Paracops to keep him out of the hands of the Bureau of Psychological Hygiene numerous times. What a terrible mistake!

"I want everyone to lay down their weapons and stop all resistance. And that includes the Paratime Police."

"What is this madman doing?" Dalgroth Sorn shouted. The rest of the commissioners broke out in a babble of questions, orders and exclamations.

"Shut up!" ordered Tortha Karf. "Let's find out what he wants."

"I want to tell the Paratime Police specifically to lay down their arms and cease all resistance."

"He's completely insane!" someone shouted.

Tortha Karf slapped a huge hand across the speaker's mouth. "Quiet!"

"Isn't that your brother, Chief? Can't you stop him?"

Dalla shook her head. No one controlled Tharn, not even he was in control of his unpredictable whims and rages.

"I want you to know that my followers are—at this moment—destroying every transposition conveyer depot in Dhergabar and every other city and rallying place on the planet."

Dalla's hand flew over her mouth. This was bad, really bad—actually terrible. By destroying all the First Level depots, Tharn was stranding every poor bastard from Home Time Line who was working or visiting outtime—billions of innocent people! Well, maybe innocent was the wrong word....

Tharn made a nasty smile, like an evil little boy who'd just torn the wings off a fly. "And as far as you parapolice creeps are concerned, if there's any more resistance I'll blow the entire Paratime Building sky-high. There's a thermo-nuclear device in your basement with a dead-man's switch so don't even think of trying to find it. You've got fifteen minutes to evacuate! After that, it's all GONE!"

The screen sent completely blank.

"My wife! My family!" someone shouted. "Let me out of here!"

Everyone was speaking at once.

Dalla made a loud piercing whistle. "Quiet down and listen! We don't have much time. It's obvious this operation is not only well planned, but completely out of our control. We must get everyone in this building down to the Main Depot Terminal and its affiliates, then get everyone transposed out of this building before it blows!"

"But where?" Dalgroth Sorn shouted.

"Who cares?" Tortha shouted. "To your outtime villas or whatever.

That's where I'm headed. Maybe later we can figure something out. But as far as I can determine, we've lost the battle, if not the war for First Level."

"Right," seconded Dalla. She fiddled with the screen until it went back on. "All Paratime officers evacuate the building immediately! There's a bomb set to go off in fourteen minutes. Evacuate to a safe place outtime. We will attempt to contact you later." She knew that was probably a lie, but it would help the exodus. Maybe Verkan would have a solution—if only she could get to Kalvan's Time Line in time.

Commissioner Dalgroth was already out the door on his way to the descent shaft. The others commissioners were milling around like lost sheep.

"Move!" she shouted as she headed for the door. She followed Tortha, grabbing his arm as he quickly exited the office.

"Where are you headed?" she asked.

"To my retreat on Sicily. This time I may be retired for good. What about you, Dalla? Are you going to Kalvan's Time Line to get Verkan?"

She shook her head. "It might attract my brother's attention, which is the last thing we need. In an emergency, we agreed to meet at our hideaway on Nerros. After that, I don't know. Now, let's get a move on!"

VII

Verkan felt the vibration of his kit-phone disguised as an idol of Wotan. Talking to one's personal idol was considered normal behavior in the Middle Kingdoms, as long as one wasn't too loud or obnoxious about it.

He quickly excused himself from the King's Presence Room and went to his private chamber. There were a number of advantages to being king, one of them being able to clear your schedule on a moment's notice.

"Verkan, here," he said, pressing the transmit button.

"Chief, it's Kostran. We've got problems."

"What?" he asked.

"You know the conveyer problem we've been having?"

"Of course, we haven't seen one in almost two ten-days."

"Well, one just materialized."

"Good!" he exclaimed. "It's about time."

There was a pause before Kostran continued. "It was a Paratime Police conveyer and it was badly damaged."

Verkan didn't like the sound of that. *By Blaxthakka's Beard, what's going on?* "Any survivors?"

"Yes, just one," Kostran said. "He's coming around now. You'd better get down here and interrogate him yourself."

"I will as soon as I can get Maldar and Kiro Soran to join me."

He sent out a red field alert and within a few minutes Maldar Dard and Kiro Soran showed up.

"What's going on, boss?" Maldar asked.

"Trouble with the conveyers."

Maldar nodded. "I was wondering if there was something going on. Traffic's been nonexistent the last week or so."

Shortly after taking over as king of Greffa, Verkan had done some remodeling on Theovacar's former summer palace. One major improvement was a conveyer-head built into a large section of what had been the original dungeon. He'd also had a lift put in from his private audience chamber to the collapsed-nickel lined conveyer-head station.

Verkan pressed the idol's ear and twisted, and a door slid open. They all entered and Verkan hit the keypad combination to the conveyer-head and the lift began its descent to the former dungeon. After landing and opening the door, he stepped out into a room large enough to hold a hundred-and-fifty foot conveyer with plenty of room for supplies and holding parties. There were about fifty cases of flintlock smoothbores resting against one wall and another couple of boxes containing high-density armor for his operatives to wear during hostilities.

He saw the ripped and scorched silver mesh dome of a fifty-foot conveyer sitting at the staging ground. Smoke was still coming off the mesh and he could smell the astringent odors of burnt permaplastic and metal. Someone had used a cutting tool to remove a large section of the dome and inside were five figures, in Paratime Police issue greens, lying on the floor. One Medico was bent over one of the figures, while the other two were examining the other bodies.

Chancellor Kostran Galth, still in his robes of office, was running towards him. "Chief, we've got four dead and one badly-wounded officer."

"Are they from here?" Verkan asked. There hadn't been any recent arrivals, nor any that were scheduled, either.

Kostran, his face pale, shook his head. "No one I know." His wife, Zinganna, had left over three ten-days ago to visit Dalla on Home Time Line.

Verkan ordered, "Everyone step back except the Medico."

After about a brief wait, that would have been interminable except for Verkan's First Level mental control, the Greffan team Medico got up and called Verkan to his side. The wounded officer had a gash in his forehead that had bled out into a large pool, but his worst injuries were from a series of bullet wounds to his torso that opened him up from his belly button to his breast bone. The Medico had stabilized the bleeding and had hooked him up a blood pump. It would keep him alive until they got to a robo-doc; although he needed a major trauma center rather than a field robo-doc.

The cloying smell of death filled the conveyor. The Medico looked at Verkan, saying, "I gave him something to ease the pain, but he won't remain conscious long. He can talk a little so you'd better make it quick."

Verkan got down on his knees, leaning over. "Officer, can I have your name and rank?"

"Sardrath Darn, Field Agent Second Class, sir," he mumbled.

"What happened, Darn?"

"We were returning to Home Time Line from Fourth Level, Viking-Vinland Subsector. When we arrived at the subterminal head at Synalyan, we were fired upon by troops dressed in bluish-gray uniforms." He paused, while a series of coughs wracked his body. "I was hit bad...."

"Fired upon at Home Time Line?" Verkan asked. "What's going on?"

"I don't know, sir. We bugged out as soon as we could set the controls, but some soldiers in blue uniforms started shooting...then something hit our conveyer."

He started coughing again. Verkan wasn't sure he'd survive this bout.

"Where are we, sir?"

"Fourth Level, Aryan-Transpacific, Styphon's House Subsector, Kalvan's Time Line."

"Oh…we were trying to make our way to Pol Term."

Police Terminal, Verkan thought. *The Synalyan Equivalent? That was Greffa here-and-now, but on Fourth Level Europo-American it would be Chicago. They were fortunate that the conveyer hadn't ended up there. All hell would have broken loose…if it hasn't already!*

VIII

"Where are you going, Chief?" the Commissioner in charge of Security asked, as Dalla made her way to the antigrav shaft with Tortha Karf.

She thought for a moment. "I'm going to meet up with Vall. We need him to take over. This is way too much for me to handle!"

"But…but you can't—" he blustered.

"You need to get moving yourself, Commissioner Dalgroth. Don't you have a wife and family?"

"Yes, but I'll need an aircar to get to our apartment. It's not safe to fly anymore!"

The Commissioner's eyes were bugged out and darting around as if he were looking for a bolthole for himself. She knew that it was already too late for anyone in Dhergabar outside of the Paratime Building—and they only had minutes.

There was the sound of another blast, strong enough to rock the Paratime Building as if it were made of straw. "There's no time. Either leave now and look for them, or join me at the antigrav shaft."

She left with Tortha before he could make up his mind and ran to the shaft, where they quickly made their way—although the descent seemed to take forever—down to the Paratime Building Main Depot Terminal. The place was crowded with Paratime Police officers, some in their official greens, others in outtime costumes. Cops were moving around as if in Brownian Motion, as though most of them had no idea of what to do.

Tortha bussed her on the cheek and said, "Give my best to Vall, will you?"

"Good luck," she said, as the ex-chief tore off on his way to his personal conveyer.

One of the Paracops ran up: "Chief, thank the heavens you're here! What are we supposed to do now?"

It was Dalzar Holk, her old bodyguard on Kalvan's Time Line and one of Verkan's key men.

"This building's set to go in minutes. We need to leave now—there's my personal conveyer." One of the privileges of being chief was she had her own conveyer parked in an easily assessable parking spot.

"Come with me! Before this place is blown sky high!"

She spotted a group of her personal bodyguards. She whistled loudly and they came running, ignoring the chaos all around them.

"We've been waiting for you," Dalon Sath, her head bodyguard said.

Dalla felt a wave of gratitude, but shook it off; she didn't have time to make nice. "Good." She pointed to Sath and the man next to him. "You two come with me and Dalzar. There's no room for any more. The rest of you find a conveyer and get the hell out of Dodge!"

These were veterans familiar with Europo-American slang and aphorisms. They took off at full speed to the nearest unoccupied conveyer.

IX

Hadron Tharn sat in his underground bunker and imagined the chaos happening all around him. He would have preferred to watch it in person, but even he was not immune to radiation exposure, explosions—or even a stray bullet. All local and satellite transmission lines were down so there were no longer any newscasts to watch. Every once in a while the ground would rumble or shake, indicating that chaos and destruction were nearby.

"Tharn," his private com announced. "Warntha, here."

"What's going on?" Tharn asked.

"The prole bastards have shafted us!"

"What do you mean?" Tharn barked.

"General Rammos is no longer working for us. He and the other proles are liberating Home Time Line for themselves."

Tharn ground his teeth together so hard he saw stars.

"What should I do, boss?" Warntha asked.

"Nothing! What about our team—can they do anything to stop them?"

"No. The proles hit us hard when we least expected it—most of the team has been discorporated. Me and a few others were busy setting the bombs at the University, so they missed us."

"Blaztha be damned! What do they think they're going to do, take over and run things? Not likely." Being the Leader in charge of First Level had long been his dream—no ungrateful band of ragamuffin proles were going to usurp his vision. Not if he had anything to say about it.

"Is there any chance we can still execute our plan?"

"No. Not with all our loyal commanders and most of our troops dead. The treacherous swine—"

"Enough! Then let's go to our scorched earth plan."

"Really?"

"Yes. You have more than enough bombs."

"I do."

"I want you to destroy Valdar Engineering and Manufacturing's plant." That was the facility that made all the Transtemporal conveyers. They'd already taken out the Central Administration Tower which had housed the Executive Council as well as the main library. "Next you need to destroy the Rhogom Institute and the Hydrax Scientific Center. Let the damn proles see if they could reinvent Transtemporal transportation all by themselves."

Warntha laughed. "Good luck with that!"

"I know."

"Were do we go, boss?"

"Not to any of the Fifth Level bases. When you're done, join me at my villa on Roman-Imperial." It was one of his secret hideaways that no one but Warntha knew about. Besides, if he had to live outtime, he might as well do it in style and in a place where he could indulge all his appetites without censure.

X

"What do we do now, Verkan?" Kostran Galth asked.

Verkan paused to light a cigarette. "That's a very good question. I can't stay here while Dalla might be stranded on First Level, or who knows where. It doesn't sound as if it's safe to transpose to Home Time Line, but that's where I'm needed. I wonder if this disaster could have been prevented if I stayed on First Level and done my job?"

Kostran shook his head. "Dalla is a damn good Chief, boss. You wouldn't have let her take the job, if you hadn't thought she could do it. If she and Commissioner Tortha didn't pick up on anything unusual, what makes you think you might have?"

Verkan let out a string of curses, then finished with, "You're probably right. Home Time Line has been riding on its merits for a long time; too busy robbing other time-lines to take care of itself. No innovations, no new scientific research, no new art, we've gotten fat and lazy—and maybe stupid as well. Look as this Wizard Trader mess. We've been picking at it for almost fifteen years and we're no closer to getting to the bottom of the Organization than we were when we started."

"But what about the people stranded on Home Time Line," Kostran said, as he ran his fingers through his hair.

Verkan suddenly realized that Kostran was very likely worried about his wife, Zinganna. She'd left some time ago to visit Dalla and was staying at their apartment in the Space Spire. Kostran was more worried about her than he was about his own wife. However, Dalla was very resourceful and if anyone could come out of this mess alive, it would be her.

The big problem they faced was while Paratime Police conveyers, which could theoretically travel to every and any time-line—or at least those that had been surveyed and entered into the time-line data base—could only travel spatially to wherever they were physically located. That was to Synalyan City on Home Time Line, which was a major terminal hub. Since they'd wanted to keep their presence out of the public eye, the Greffan base in the summer palace was located more than a mile outside the city of Synalyan itself, which like most First Level cities was comprised of tall anti-gravity towers and spires.

It might be possible for them to pull off a small reconnaissance mission. In fact, it was damn well necessary, if he was ever going to get to the bottom of what was going on.

"All right, here's what we're going to do," Verkan said. "It's too dangerous, since we don't have a clue as to what we are facing, to travel during day. So, instead we'll visit Synalyan in the middle of the night."

"What if the area's monitored?" Maldar Dard asked.

"The Greffan/Synalyan conveyer-head is underground. I had it put in and camouflaged the area around it so no one could stumble upon it. Otherwise, I was worried that some of the First Level newsies might find out about it and put it under surveillance in order to keep an eye on my comings and goings."

"It's a good thing you did, boss," Maldar said.

"If we detect any surveillance at all, we'll bug out immediately."

Kostran nodded in agreement. "Should I come along?"

Verkan shook his head. "I'll take the Medico, Zalthar Valn, as well as Soran and Maldar with me and leave you the rest of the Greffan team. You need to stay here in Greffa and run things as Chancellor while I'm gone."

"What'll I tell Kalvan when he asks where you are?" he asked.

"Tell him, Dalla's in trouble. He already knows she left Greffa to visit relatives in Xiphlon. Tell him she got kidnapped on her way there and that I've gone to rescue her."

"Do you think he'll buy that?" Kostran asked.

"Sure. It's exactly just what Kalvan would do if someone waylaid Rylla."

XI

Dalla sent her personal conveyer to a Fourth Level, Europo-American time-line where she and Verkan owned a villa outside the city in the Dhergabar Equivalent—Nice, France. The half-hour journey seemed to take forever as they passed a near infinity of time-lines on the way to their destination. For some reason, brief scenes of battle and violence seemed to predominate; she wasn't sure if it was the outside itself or the turmoil inside that was causing her to see so much violence all around her. Everyone else in the conveyer was strangely quiet, as if there was little left to say. She wondered how many of them had abandoned family and friends to join her in her feeble crusade to save some part of Home Time Line.

They reached the villa and left the conveyer at the hidden basement. Dalla checked the motion sensors, hidden camera footage and the other detectors to make sure that no one had been there since their last visit some three years before. Everything was clean and the small group made their way upstairs into the house itself.

They all took seats in the dining room while one of the men heated some of the hidden rations and prepared a meal for the team. Everything tasted like ashes in Dalla's mouth, but she knew it wasn't the reconstituted food, but her own emotions that were tainting everything. Her home, her family and friends—everything on Home Time Line was gone!

Dalzar finally broke the silence. "Chief, where do we go from here?"

"Nerros."

"What's that?"

"It's Verkan's and my hideaway. It's located on a small group of islands called the Bahamas on Fourth Level Europo-American, Hispania Subsector. It's a primitive subsector where the Office of the Holy Inquisition is still in operation in both the Old World and New World and the mechanical arts have not evolved much above the windmill and horse-drawn transportation, which is why we're not traveling there directly."

Dalzar grimaced. He knew all about the Inquisition, having been stranded on one of those time-lines a decade or so ago.

"Not only would we have to have the right papers and documents to travel to the New World, as they still call it, but we'd be subject to the Inquisition if somebody didn't like our looks or thought we spoke funny. Plus, it would take weeks, if not months, to travel from this equivalent to the Bahamas."

Dalla went on to fill them in on the particulars: There had been little development on most of the Caribbean Islands on that subsector. Verkan had possession of the island called Cayman Brac on most Hispano-Columbian subsectors and used it as their vacation home. He had named it Nerros after his hereditary home on Venus.

"But why live on a dangerous time-line in the Hispania Subsector? Why not have an outtime villa on one of the uninhabited Fifth Level time-lines?"

"Yes, that's the popular remedy. But you know Verkan; he follows his own path. He doesn't want to be surrounded by robo-servers or Fourth Level outtimers dragged away from their homes to be his servants, even if it might save their lives."

"So how did Verkan find this place?" one of them asked.

"Early in his career in the Department," Dalla answered, "Verkan rescued a party of Paratime tourists on the Hispano Subsector, who had run afoul of the local Inquisition. While he was there, he made the acquaintance of a Grandee, Luis Fernández, who was in charge of the expedition. In thanks for saving his clients and himself from the *Tribunal del Santo Oficio de la Inquisición*, Duke Ferandez granted Verkan Vall the small island almost forty years ago. Under Verkan's stewardship, Nerros has done well; at least, compared to the neighboring islands. The local villagers consider Verkan their patron and they grow tobacco and sugar cane. That's where we go when we want privacy and to spend time together."

Dalzar smiled. "I've had some of Verkan's hand-rolled cigarettes before. They're an excellent smoking experience."

"How long since you've been there?" Dalon inquired.

She sighed. "It's been almost five years since our last visit. We picked this time-line as our link to Nerros, because we could travel incognito—which we couldn't do on First Level—and because it is possible to travel from France to New York in six or seven days."

"Why don't we use an aircar?" Dalon asked. "That way we could get there by tomorrow morning."

Dalzar smiled. "You haven't spent much time on Europo-America, have you?"

He shook his head.

"Our aircars look a little too much like the 'flying saucers' the locals are always seeing in the skies. We don't use them on this sector anymore because they bring too much attention. The locals are dotty about aliens and unidentified objects. Plus, they have pretty advanced radar and other visual sensors on the sector. So it's safer to use the local transportation methods whenever possible."

"How long will it take us to get this show on the road?" Dalon asked.

"Not long," Dalla answered. "Let me plug in what the locals call a 'telephone' and I'll contact our usual travel agent. I expect we can find comfortable ocean transportation within a few days."

XII

Verkan's conveyer reached the Synalyan conveyer-head just after midnight. The small bunker was equipped with the usual surveillance devices so that Verkan could exit and enter without attracting attention.

The first thing he noticed was that the airwaves were dead, both local and transcontinental. *What in Great Blaxthakka's Beard is going on?*

He quickly used the big nightscope to check out Synalyan proper. The city was pretty much blacked out. Usually, the air space over the city would be surrounded by thousands of aircar running lights, darting and hovering around the city like fireflies. Some of the towers were at weird angles and none of the usual warning lights showed. He noted a few stuttering ground fires and wondered just what had happened to the city?

Maldar cried, "By all the gods, the rad meter is picking up all kinds of radiation! What just went down?"

"Let's see if we can find somebody and find out. "Maldar, what's the meter reading just outside the bunker?"

"A much lower radiation count locally. Nothing we can't tolerate for a short time. But it's hot as hell closer to those towers."

"How long can we stay here before our conveyer is detected?"

"That's a good question, Kiro. From the looks of things upstairs, I don't think there's anyone capable of doing a proper search. However, it's best to assume the worst. So we don't want to stay here much longer than an hour."

"Okay," Kiro replied.

"Take out your needlers and let's see what we can find upstairs," Verkan ordered

It was only a short way to the top of the bunker; no need for any lifts. Instead they walked up a short stairway leading to the bunker outer exit. The permasteel portal was bolted and only responded to Verkan's code which he keyed in.

The portal pressed upward through the camouflage and they walked into the still night air. Occasionally, the air was rent by a distant scream or the sounds of gunfire. Verkan felt as if he were walking in a graveyard.

Their personal nightscopes gave them almost perfect vision despite the dark of night.

"I see something, or someone!" Kiro Soran announced. He pointed to the left where there was a huddled form hidden in the bushes. They would have never seen it without the scopes.

"Are they alive?" Maldar asked.

"Let's find out," Verkan replied.

They approached and found a man who was shaking with fear as he heard their approach.

"We mean you no harm," Verkan said.

"Who are you?"

"Paratime Police."

"Pa...Police. I thought you were all dead or gone. That's what the newsies claimed after the Paratime Building went up."

"What happened to the Paratime Building?"

"It was hit with an atomic bomb The Leader had placed in the basement. They say it went off like a hundred-megaton firecracker—a total loss!"

Verkan shuddered. He hoped Dalla made it out in time but, regardless, thousands of his coworkers and friends must have died in that blast.

"Who is this 'Leader'?" he asked.

"I don't know. No one does. He claimed responsibility to the attack. Maybe he's a prole; there are enough of them running around. They're blood crazed—killed almost all the Citizens in my spire. The Serv Sec Proles are the worst!"

Verkan turned to the others. "This is what we've been warning the Executive Council about for years. Let's get back down to the bunker."

"What about him?" Maldar asked, pointing at the shivering man.

"Take him with us. I've got more questions to ask."

Back in the bunker, the Medico left to check out their captive while Verkan and the others discussed what to do.

"There's no use hanging around here," Maldar said.

"Right," Verkan answered. "First Level's done. Let's head back to Greffa. I want to brief Kostran on what we've learned."

"He deserves that, at least," Kiro said.

Verkan nodded, wondering what to tell someone when everything and everybody they had known outside the Department were gone. And that even the force was done. What any of them would do?

They waited for the Medico.

When he returned it was with a sour look on his face, shaking his head, he reported, "The poor bastard, he's done for. I don't know how many rads he took in, but he won't last until daybreak."

"Can I talk to him?" Verkan asked.

The Medico shrugged. "It won't hurt. He's in and out of consciousness, so make it quick."

Verkan returned a few minutes later. "He doesn't know any more than what he already told us. I fed him a few lies about getting better so he'd die in peace."

"It's time we leave and go back to Greffa City."

"Right, we might have searchers coming soon," Maldar said.

They all went back into the conveyer and Verkan keyed in their destination.

"Where do we go from here?" Kiro asked, as the near-infinity of time-line flashed by.

"Yeah, can't we fight back?" Maldar added.

Verkan sighed. "With what and whom? From what our wounded friend from Police Terminal told us, things aren't any better back on the Fourth Level than they are here on First Level. It's not like we have any special meeting places for outtime police to gather. We're on our own and I don't believe there's much we can do here. Does anyone disagree?"

They all nodded in agreement.

"Here's what I suggest. I'm going to find a way to get to Nerros, my hideaway on Fourth Level. It's a nice little island in the Bahamas with friendly islanders. Anyone who wants, can come with me. Or I'll help them get to wherever they want to go."

"That sounds more than fair," the Medico said. "I don't have a personal retreat; I was always too busy to set one up. So, if you don't mind, I'll go with you."

"That's fine," Verkan replied. "You can help take care of our island friends."

Maldar was the next to speak. "I'm like Valn; I don't have a place to go to, either. I'll go wherever you want, boss."

"Good."

"What about you, Kiro?"

"Sad to say it, but I've been married to my job for so long I don't have a personal life. I'm good to go."

Verkan smiled. "Maybe once we get to Nerros you'll have time to make one. It's not exactly a hot spot! Although, once in a while, we may have to fend off some of the local cannibals—"

"You're kidding, boss. Right?"

"No. Some of the local Caribs have been known to partake in the unspeakable. I've got a deal with the local Viceroy of Cuba so they don't bother us much. Although, every once in a while a few go off reservation."

"Sounds like fun," Maldar joked.

"So how are we going to get there?" Kiro asked.

"Well, for starters, we're on the right landmass. We'll take the conveyer to a spot on Fourth Level, Europo-American I've setup. From there, we'll take a plane ride to Miami. It won't be hard to get a boat to take us to Nerros."

"When are we leaving?" Maldar asked.

"Not for a ten-day or two. Remember, I'm king here and I've got a lot of responsibilities. I owe it to Kalvan to get the army ready just in case King Theovacar wants to take his former home back. Plus, I've got a lot to talk over with Kostran."

"Will he stay or go with us, boss?" Maldar asked.

"I really don't know. I'd prefer that he stay since I don't have any other replacement and I'd hate to leave Kalvan in the lurch."

Maldar winced. "Yeah, with his wife stranded or….dead on First Level, the poor bastard has got nowhere else to go. The rest of us are married to the job and don't have any close family to worry about."

Verkan nodded. "Normally that wouldn't be something to be happy about, but in this case it is. I just hope that Dalla made it out of the Paratime Building safely. I'm not going to get any sleep until I find out."

"You think she'll be at Nerros?" Maldar asked.

"I hope so. I've told her more than once it's our bolthole; the one place no one—other than Tortha—knows about. A place where we can be safe. I just hope she can get there."

XIII

Dalla sat inside the solar at their Nerros villa smoking and drinking a cocktail. She had actually enjoyed the trip over on the *Queen Mary 2*. It had been a welcome relief; for days she hadn't had to worry over what she needed to do—or could or couldn't do. Then a quick trip to the Nerros Equivalent on Fourth Level, from where they had transposed to Verkan's hideaway.

The natives had welcomed her and her guests with great glee. She got the idea that they were bored when nobody was around. Here on the island they lived a carefree life of fishing and hunting. Verkan, early on, had made a deal with the Viceroy of Cuba and he had ordered a series of punitive raids on the nearby Carib and Arawak Indians, letting them know that Nerros was off-limits for their raiding parties.

Since the villa's conveyer-head was in a sealed-off basement, she wondered what the natives thought when visitors magically appeared at the villa. From the special way she was treated, she suspected the tribespeople thought she and Verkan were minor deities who could appear and reappear at will, like some sort of island guardians. Their cohorts, like Dalzar and Salon Dath, were probably viewed as their agents.

She heard the door open as Dalzar and the others entered the solar, taking seats around the big table. They had brought their own drinks, and several of them were smoking pipes. Something most of them had taken up after spending time on Aryan-Transpacific.

Dalzar was the first to speak. "Any ideas on what to do, Chief?"

"I've been giving our situation a great deal of thought. With the Paratime Building destroyed and Pol Term on Fifth Level a wasteland, we don't have many options. Most of the Paracops who've survived the initial attack are stranded outtime—somewhere. Unfortunately, there was a major leak in the Department, so we can safely assume that all our usual hideouts and gathering places are either destroyed or are being watched. Since the Department conveyers are the only ones without governors tying them to the usual commercial and passenger routes, we can pretty much land on Home Time Line wherever we wish.

"Although, I can almost guarantee that wherever we land we'll find a reception party since our tracking devices will give our location away."

"Can't we disengage them somehow?" Salon asked.

Dalzar shook his head. "No. They are integral to the Transtemporal guidance devices. They were designed that way to guard the Paratime Secret and keep us from going wherever we wanted. That way the Survey Bureau knows just where we are and if we need help, they know where to send it."

"Or if someone wants to set up their own racket, they can find him."

Dalla nodded. "It was part of the original pact the Department made with the Executive Council. The Council wanted some tethers on the Department since we have the only conveyers that can go to any level or sector in Paratime."

"Can't Hadron and his minions use them to track us here?" Salon wanted to know.

Dalla made hand washing motions. "Not now. Since the Paratime Building was destroyed, all the tracking device registers and information on outtime conveyers is gone. Of course, we can't track them, either."

"So what are we doing here, other than surviving?" Dalzar asked.

"We're waiting for Vall. We have a pact: if there was ever a major emergency where we were cut off from First Level, we would meet here and figure out what to do. Or…?"

"Any idea when Verkan will arrive?" Salon wanted to know.

Dalla shrugged. "They don't get a lot of conveyers coming and going from Kalvan's Time Line. We'll just have to wait and see. I expect that there'll be some indication within the next ten-day. Until then, boys, try and relax."

She knew after what she'd witnessed on Home Time Line that was an impossible request. She was still in mourning for all the lives lost, friends gone forever—either discorporated or lost in Paratime. She hadn't even had time to warn her adopted sister Zinna. However, as a former prole, Zinna might have escaped the pogrom that would take the lives of most the remaining Citizens on First Level. Life as she knew it, as all the

Paratimers knew it, was over. Ten thousand years of civilization—gone!

And, most likely, never to return.

All due to the efforts of one man, a madman—her brother! She wanted to scream at the top of her lungs, but didn't want to upset the others. *How could he?! And how much of this is my fault?*

XIV

Several ten-days later, Dalla and her friends were sitting at the dining room table discussing what to do when a "ping" sounded.

"Someone's just arrived," she said, leading the way to the basement conveyer-head. They made their way cautiously down the stairs, needlers drawn.

Below they saw a thirty-foot conveyer with Verkan Vall standing beside it. "Darling," he cried, opening his arms.

Dalla rushed downstairs losing herself in Verkan's arms. "You made it!"

Verkan, still dressed in his Aryan-Transpacific royal robes, said, "Yes, just barely."

"They haven't attacked Kalvan's Time Line?"

He shook his head. "It was still clear when I left Greffa City. We made a quick stop at First Level. It's mostly inhabitable. What happened?"

Dalla shook her head and shouted: "It's all due to my sick little brother, blast and curse him! I always knew he was disturbed, but this!!! Tharn's behind some kind of prole-takeover of Home Time Line. If he was here, I'd wring his bloody neck!"

"Is he completely insane?" Verkan cried out.

"I fear so. He calls himself The Leader and he brought prole strike teams from Fifth Level to make attacks on Home Time Line. They went so far as to use atomic and nuclear weapons on Dhergabar, as well as the Paratime Building."

Verkan turned white and looked sick. "Is there anything we can do?"

"No, I don't think so. He launched an attack on Fifth Level Police Terminal, too! Now, with the Survey Division gone there's no way to track the Department conveyers and coordinate with the surviving police. He's also fixed it so none of the First Level people outtime can get back home since his agents have destroyed all the conveyer depots and rotundas on Home Time Line."

"This is an unmitigated disaster! But it doesn't look like there's a damn thing we can do...." Verkan trailed off. "From what we saw, First Level is in as bad a shape as some of the Second Level time-lines we used to quarantine."

"I don't believe there's anything we can do, either, Vall. And, I've had a lot more time to think about it. Now, it's time for us to figure out what *we're* going to do."

"We could leave for Aryan-Transpacific and join up with Kalvan and Rylla. What do you think of that idea?"

Dalla shook her head sadly. "It wouldn't work for long, dear. Kalvan's already in his forties.... And we're supposed to be his age. How long before we have to start dying our hair, use makeup and create phony wrinkles? Besides, do we really want to stay in Hostigos and watch all our friends grow old and discorporate, while we remain young?"

"No, you're right. I don't want to see Kalvan and Rylla in their dotage...with us unable to do anything to help. I see you brought some friends with you. We'll just have to stay here for now and make the best of a bad situation."

"What about Home Time Line?"

Verkan shook his head. "As a society, we bought and paid for this. It's a wonder it all lasted ten thousand years...."

Dalla nodded. "In a way, we're the fortunate ones. Just think about all those poor Paratimers who are permanently stuck outtime and don't know how or why."

Verkan summed it up. "They'll have to come to terms with it and make adjustments. It could be a lot worse."

"Yes, they could be dead. But what about the Paratime Secret?"

Verkan shrugged. "At this point, who cares? Let somebody else worry about it. Now, what's for dinner?"

The End

www.ingramcontent.com/pod-product-compliance
Lightning Source LLC
Chambersburg PA
CBHW060556310726
48982CB00008B/1138/J

* 9 7 8 0 9 3 7 9 1 2 7 6 8 *